The Cryptic Prophecy

Etherya's Earth, Book 6

By

REBECCA HEFNER

Contents

Cover Design: Starlight Cover Design, starlightcovers.com
Editor: Megan McKeever, NY Book Editors
Proofreader: Bryony Leah, www.bryonyleah.com

To Megan, my editor, therapist and voice of reason, depending on the day. This book would never have seen the light of day without your help, and I am truly grateful. Thank you for your friendship (and patience!) from the bottom of my heart.

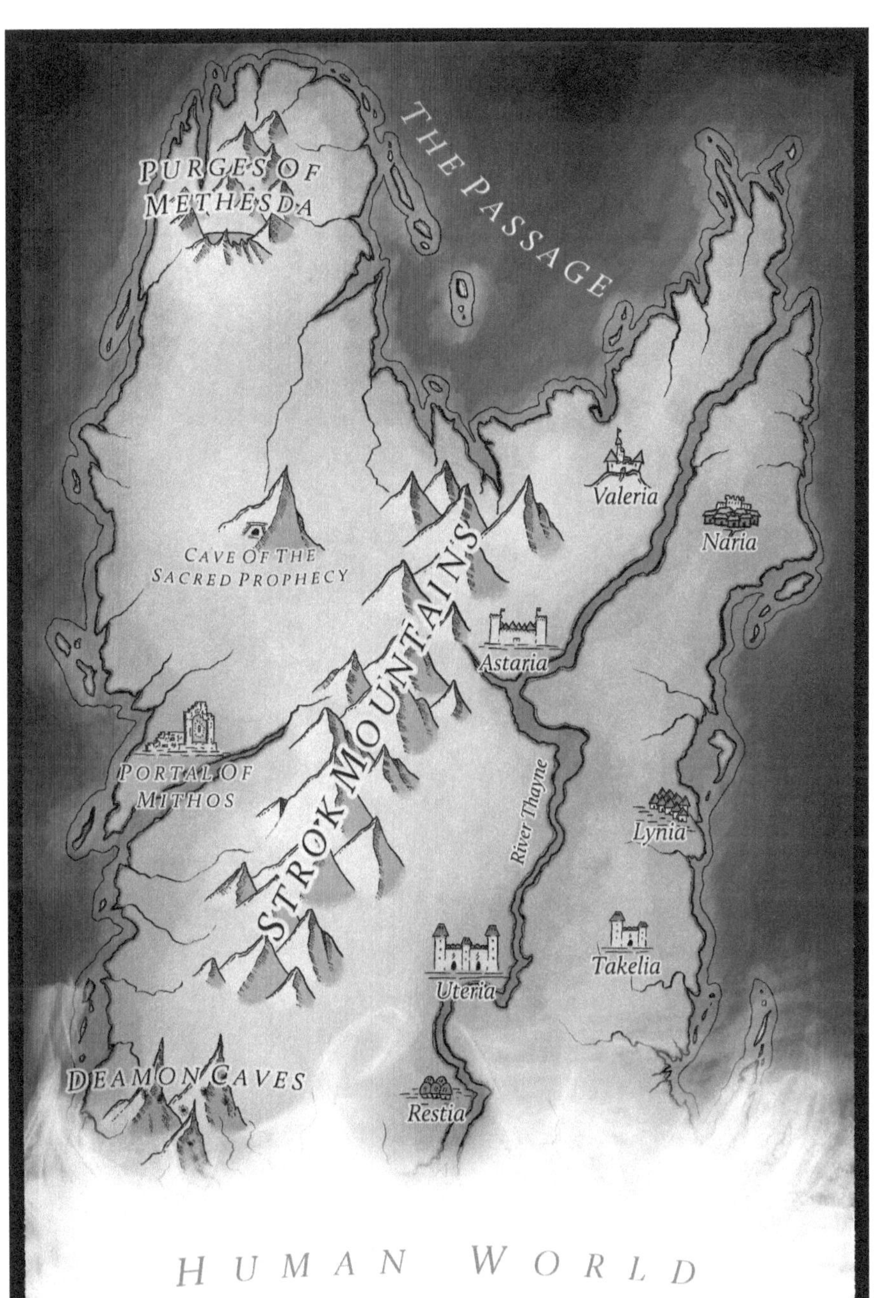

PURGES OF METHESDA
THE PASSAGE
Valeria
Naria
CAVE OF THE SACRED PROPHECY
STROK MOUNTAINS
Astaria
PORTAL OF MITHOS
River Thayne
Lynia
Uteria
Takelia
DEAMON CAVES
Restia
HUMAN WORLD

A Note from the Author

Hello, awesome readers of Etherya's Earth. I am so happy to begin this new phase of the series. If you're anything like me, you enjoy series where several couples fall in love and their children grow up to get their own love stories as the series progresses. The Cryptic Prophecy is the first book in the second generation of Etherya's Earth where we'll see the children of Miranda, Latimus, Darkrip and Evie fall in love, and I can't wait to bring them to you.

For now, enjoy Callie and Brecken's story as our beloved immortals chart a new path that will change their world forever. These two had some explosive chemistry, and Brecken ended up being really hot *and* romantic, which was perfect for our kind, sassy Callie. Also, Darkrip turned out to be slightly overprotective, which was so fun to write and had me snickering along the way. Happy reading, and thank you for taking the journey with me and the people who live in my head!

An excerpt from the diary of Calinda, daughter of Darkrip and Arderin

D ear Diary,

I'm writing to you from L.A. for one of the last times ever. Today, Mommy and Daddy told me we were moving back to the immortal world so we could be close to our family. Now that Mommy is a doctor, she wants to help people in our kingdom when they're sick. I'm proud of her, but it makes me sad because I really like it here.

Mommy says I'll make friends in no time, but I'm not so sure. In the human world, I have to hide my powers, but she says everyone will know about them in the immortal world. She and Daddy say I'm special, but I'm worried having powers will make the other kids think I'm weird.

Tomorrow is my seventh birthday, so I'll be enrolling in second grade at Takelia when we move. Daddy has been named Ambassador by Uncle Sathan and Aunt Miranda, so he's going to help make sure the compounds keep getting along. Mommy said it was the perfect job for him before she giggled, and then Daddy gave her a weird look where his face scrunched up. They're funny when they look at each other that way, and then Daddy always whispers he'll get her back once they go to bed. I don't understand how you can do anything when you're sleeping, but whatever.

Anyway, I'll keep you updated on how school goes. Hope it isn't awful. Wish me luck!

Love, Callie

Chapter 1

The Vampyre compound of Valeria, seventeen years after Heden married Sofia

Brecken, son of Maddox, would never forget the day his life changed forever. His boss—well, technically his boss's son, Zadicus—called him over with an absent hooking of his fingers as he stood by the window in the sitting room of his expansive mansion at Valeria.

"Come, Brecken," he said, eyes narrowing as he gazed out at the manicured lawn. "I have a question for you."

Brecken approached, only slightly gritting his teeth at the command. He wasn't a fan of Raoul's son, but he needed the income his job as bodyguard provided, so he put up with Zadicus's arrogance and dismissive attitude. Many aristocrats still treated laborers and soldiers as "beneath" them, although King Sathan and Queen Miranda discouraged it.

"Yes?" Brecken said, placing his crossed hands on the buckle of his belt as he stood in a wide-legged stance, waiting. He was a few inches taller than Zadicus, which brought him great pleasure for some reason. Perhaps it was because he knew he could kick the haughty prick's ass. Not only because of his size, but because he thought Zadicus rather soft. Of course, if ever accused of it, his ward would scoff and assert his dominance over all the other aristocrats he defeated in his weekly boxing matches.

It might be a good defense to some, but Brecken understood the matches were carefully planned in plushy-floored boxing rings with felt-covered ropes. Much different than the dirty fields where he'd scraped and clawed his way to becoming a formidable soldier. Brecken had worked hard to tone his body and his mind, and his commanding officers took notice.

When Raoul decided to hire a personal bodyguard for his son, Brecken's good friend Jack, adopted son of Latimus, suggested he apply. There had been scattered attacks from Bakari's Deamon army at Valeria and Uteria over the years, and many wealthy aristocrats felt safer having private security at their homes. They could afford it, and it created jobs, so Brecken kept his opinion on the matter to himself. It seemed a bit much since all the compounds were protected by immortal soldiers, but if a rich Vampyre or Slayer wanted a bodyguard in their personal space, who was he to argue? Although Brecken hadn't wanted to leave the army, the pay was substantially higher and allowed him to help support his mother and five sisters at Lynia. After some contemplation, he applied for the job and was hired within a week.

Several years in, he was used to his eccentric ward and could tell Zadicus disliked having a watchdog as much as Brecken disliked watching. But they both were products of their station in the realm, and they'd formed a bond of sorts. One based on necessity and mutual understanding rather than friendship, but sometimes, those were the ones that worked best.

Recently, Zadicus had approached Brecken, asking how much his silence would cost if he were to escape a few hours each week unaccompanied. Brecken had initially balked, knowing that letting Zadicus go anywhere in the realm without his protection was a violation of his contract with Raoul.

"We are both men who crave solace, Brecken," Zadicus said, determination in his ice-blue eyes. "If you give me a few hours a week to myself, I will pay your sister's tuition to the school for gifted students at Takelia."

Brecken had been floored by the offer. His youngest sister Rowena was the smartest of them all, and he hated she was relegated to the public school at Lynia. She had applied and been accepted to the school for the gifted and talented at Takelia, but their family couldn't afford it on the small stipend they received each month after their father was killed during an ambush on a Deamon-scouting mission over a decade ago. His mother worked as a seamstress, but that barely brought in enough for them to survive.

"If your father finds out, not only will I be fired, but I will be blacklisted as a bodyguard for eternity," Brecken replied. "I can't take the chance."

"We are not friends, but we both have a vested interest in keeping this from my father," Zadicus said, extending his hand. "Three hours per week in exchange for your sister's education."

Brecken stared at the man's hand for so long he thought he might retract it. Eventually, they shook, and the deal was made.

"Three hours per week. May the goddess keep you safe. I will set up comm devices with a secret channel for us to communicate and will be ready to answer your call at a moment's notice."

"I hope your sister takes this opportunity to lift herself out of poverty. An educated woman can go far in this realm thanks to Queen Miranda and Governor Evie."

"Yes," Brecken said, arching a brow. "Their decision to allow females to become combat soldiers has riled up some of the misogynists in our kingdom."

"Women should be protected by men," Zadicus said, dismissively waving his hand, "but it is their directive, so I'll choose to accept it."

Left unsaid between them was the blatant fact Zadicus himself needed the protection of a soldier, but Brecken decided to let it lie.

Now, several weeks into their deal, Rowena was thriving at her new school, and Zadicus seemed to be relishing his alone time. Brecken had no idea what he did during his excursions, but he always checked in over their secret channel and so far had returned home with Raoul none the wiser.

"For the goddess's sake, Brecken, are you listening?" Zadicus shouted, snapping his fingers as Brecken returned to the present moment. Straightening, his hands clenched on his belt from the man's irritable tone.

"Yes. What did you want to ask me?"

Eyes narrowing, Zadicus tilted his head, contemplating. "A while back, we were discussing our school days. I mentioned I hated schoolwork, and you said something about excelling at creative writing when you were a student. Do you remember?"

Brecken nodded, surprised the man recalled any of their prior conversations. "I loved school and honed my writing skills. I also figured it would help me pass the written army tests when I became a soldier."

Sighing, Zadicus ran a hand through his hair before trailing over to sit on the couch. "I always hated school. I paid one of our servants to do my homework for me. I found it exceedingly boring."

Brecken's lips twitched as he inwardly remarked he expected nothing less from the man who would inherit a fortune regardless of his performance in school.

"I'll pretend I don't see the smirk so we can continue our conversation," he said in a dry tone. "Since you excelled at creative writing, do you think you could possibly write love letters?'

Feeling his eyebrows draw together, he contemplated. "Love letters?"

"Yes," Zadicus said, slightly rolling his eyes. "As you know, I have set my sights on Callie. She is royalty and worthy of my hand and station. However, she is..."—he circled his hand, searching for the word—"high maintenance and requires extensive courting. I wrote her a poem, which she had the gall to snicker at several times before assuring me it was passable. I have a feeling she'd rather have love letters, but I have no idea where to start—which is where you come in."

Brecken studied the man who stared at him expectantly as disbelief coursed through his veins. "You want to hire me to write love letters to the woman you're courting?" he asked, slightly exasperated. "I understand you can afford anything you set your sights on, but isn't hiring another man to woo your girlfriend just a bit underhanded?"

"You don't have to make it seem nefarious," Zadicus said, standing. "Writing is something I'm terrible at, and apparently, it's a skill of yours. I'd actually be doing her a favor if you wrote to her instead of me."

Scoffing, Brecken shook his head. "No, thanks. I won't be any part of deceiving the woman you eventually plan to bond with."

"Goddess, you rural folk always see things with such rose-colored lenses."

Brecken's nostrils flared at the dismissive words, and he clenched his jaw to keep from telling the man to go to hell.

"I just want a bit of help. Like a wingman. You've told me you and Jack go out together and help each other flirt with women. I'm asking the same."

"Jack and I don't lie to the women we flirt with," Brecken said, holding up his hand when Zadicus opened his mouth to argue. "And even if I agreed, I'd be deceiving Jack since he's her adopted cousin. He's one of my best friends, and I have no desire to hurt him or Callie."

"How will she be hurt?" Zadicus asked, lifting his hands. "It will help move the process along, and she can finally bond with someone. It's common knowledge she isn't the most sought-after female in the realm. This will solidify her status as someone worthy so people don't focus on the prophecy."

Brecken took a moment to reflect on the Elven prophecy and the path the kingdom had followed since its discovery. When he was young, the realm had been embroiled in the vicious war with the Dark Lord Crimeous, Callie's grandfather, until Evie fulfilled the prophecy and saved them. The immortal world slipped into peaceful complacency, never realizing there were other threats on the horizon.

Bakari had appeared with a vengeance, determined to rule over the realm from which he felt ostracized when he was only a babe. Born between Latimus and Arderin, Bakari bore a mark on his inner thigh that the ancient soothsayers believed signified an evil hidden prophecy. Unbeknownst to his parents, Vampyre King Markdor and Queen Calla, the ancient soothsayers had transported him to the human world and left him to die. But Bakari survived and pieced together his past and was now determined to rule over the kingdom he believed was rightfully his.

Brecken thought it a sad tale, often wondering if the royal family would've welcomed and embraced Bakari if he'd returned to the kingdom with an open heart. Alas, it wasn't meant to be, and Bakari was intent upon destroying the Vampyre and Slayer royal families so he could rule in perpetuity. Another self-proclaimed demigod the immortals would have to vanquish before they could secure the peace they craved.

Added to the strife were the Elven scrolls Queen Miranda and Commander Kenden discovered several years ago in the long-forgotten soothsayer chamber at Restia. The scrolls held many prophecies, none more concerning than the one regarding Bakari and Callie:

Elven Prophecy #1

A lone Elf will survive our kingdom's destruction. He will evolve into a powerful being, castigated by the goddess Etherya. Embroiled in his hate, he will spawn children upon the Earth who will cause great devastation. The firstborn spawn of his firstborn spawn will align with the marked Vampyre prince to destroy Etherya's realm as we know it, and it will exist no more...

It was all a bit dramatic for Brecken, who favored practicality and succinctness, so he preferred the summarized version: Crimeous would spawn Darkrip, and Darkrip's firstborn child Callie would align with Bakari to pulverize the immortal realm. *Heavy.*

"If Callie is such an outcast, I'm surprised you decided to court her," Brecken said, resuming their conversation.

"Are you trying to piss me off?" Zadicus asked, scowling.

Brecken breathed a laugh. "No. It just seems as if your station is very important to you, and I'd think you'd want to solidify that with a bonded mate whose reputation is...unvarnished."

"Her reputation is fine," he muttered, beginning to pace. "She'll be a virgin on our wedding night thanks to a promise she made her mother, and I can work with the taint from the prophecy."

Brecken still thought it strange the man didn't care about his reputation since that was in direct opposition to everything he knew about Zadicus, but he remained silent.

"Regardless," Zadicus continued, "I would like your help. Agree to write some love letters to Callie, and I'll assure your mother gets the open seamstress position in the governor's mansion."

Feeling his eyes widen, Brecken pondered. The position paid five times what his mother made as a freelancer. "How soon could she start?"

"As soon as you write the first letter."

Inhaling a deep breath, Brecken let it churn in his gut, knowing what he was about to agree to was so very wrong. But he had his family to think about, and now that his father was gone, they were his responsibility.

"Okay," he said with a nod. "But I'll need to observe her to get an idea of what to write, and you'll need to give me feedback too."

"Yes, yes," Zadicus said dismissively. "She's planning on going to the street fair with Jack after she heals a horse at Restia tomorrow. Why don't you accompany them? You can take one of your sisters and act as if the meeting is a coincidence. As you know, we are having dinner with Aunt Melania and Uncle Cameron tomorrow night, and I will speak to them about hiring your mother."

Brecken had two days a week off from guarding Zadicus, and his ward always had dinner with his aunt and uncle on those occasions.

"All right. There's no need to manipulate the situation. I'll just call Jack and tell him I'd like to go with him. I'll take Rowena with me. She loves street fairs." Extending his hand, he enclosed it around Zadicus's and gave a resigned shake. Brecken knew Callie casually, having met her with Jack several times at Lynia and, more recently, when she began dating Zadicus. Frowning, he acknowledged his discontent at deceiving her.

She'd been nothing but gracious to him as he guarded them while Zadicus courted her. In fact, she treated him with a respect he wished his ward bestowed. Although Zadicus was cordial to him, he still treated him like a servant, often snapping his fingers or making underhanded remarks that would offend someone with a lesser temperament. Brecken was tough and usually brushed it off. After all, many aristocrats were raised to be dicks. It was just the way of the world.

Callie was different even though she was the daughter of royals. She had a generous heart and often spoke of the animals she healed throughout the kingdom. Feeling his lips twitch, Brecken recalled the last time she scolded Zadicus for his callous words. They'd been strolling in the garden, and Zadicus had summoned Brecken over from his spot several yards away where he'd been observing.

"Go inside and grab a wet cloth for us, will you, Brecken?" Zadicus asked. "I want to pick some flowers for Callie and wrap them in it so she can take them home."

"For the goddess's sake, Zadicus," Callie said, wrinkling her nose, "he's not your servant. If you want a cloth, go get it yourself. And honestly, you sent me a bouquet every day this week. I think I'm all flowered out."

"He doesn't mind—do you, Brecken?"

Brecken inwardly sighed, annoyed but used to the treatment. "It's fine—"

"No way," Callie interrupted, flashing him a brilliant smile. Goddess, but she was a looker, with a mass of black curls that fell down her back and stunning ocean-colored eyes. They were olive green in the center, like her father's, and sky blue on the rims like her mother's. "We're fine, Brecken. Feel free to go back to your corner in the shade. Thank you."

Her fingers encircled his wrist, and her soft skin grazed his, sending a jolt of arousal through his frame. Disengaging from her touch, he walked back to the house, standing in the shade as he observed them. Zadicus leaned down to kiss her forehead, and Brecken absently rubbed his wrist, still tingling from where she'd touched him. Closing his eyes for one brief second, he imagined pressing his lips to her forehead...to her full lips...to the curve of her neck...and then he promptly shut it down. Fantasizing about the girlfriend of his ward was a definite no-no.

And now, he'd signed up to deceive her. It certainly didn't sit well inside his core, but the income for his family was too valuable to deny. A governor's seamstress's salary could feed his entire family for decades, and their well-being was his priority. So, he would study Callie and write the letters for Zadicus.

"I think I'd like to head to the boxing club," Zadicus said, strolling toward the grand staircase. "Let me change, and I'll meet you back here."

With a brief nod, Brecken resumed his wide stance, hands clasped over his belt buckle, as he prayed to the goddess to forgive him for his future deception.

Dear Diary,

    I would like to officially report that being ten years old is the worst. We've been back in the realm for three years, and I still haven't made a lot of friends. It's hard when everyone looks at you like a freak and seems scared you're going to destroy the world. Daddy says they're dramatic and insignificant and they can go screw themselves (and then Mommy tells him not to use that word, although I'm obviously old enough to handle it. Sheesh!).

But the truth is: I think I **am** a freak. Yesterday, I discovered something really cool and really scary about myself at the same time. We were having dinner at Aunt Lila's, and I went to the creek behind the house afterward to catch lightning bugs. As I was trying to catch one in my jar, I heard something wail and looked over to find a tiny chipmunk lying in the grass. After rushing over, I could tell he was hurt and picked him up to examine him. He had blood on his fur and looked like he'd been half-eaten by something with really sharp teeth. I have no idea why, but for some reason, I felt like I could fix him. Closing my eyes, I held my hand over his wound and summoned my powers.

The little critter cried out, and I opened my eyes to see his wound healing. I was so excited—and so shocked—that I lost control of my power and felt it shoot through my arm into the chipmunk's body. He looked at me with his little beady eyes as his legs shook, and then he died in my hand.

"You ready for me to catch some lightning bugs with you?" Dad asked behind me.

Turning to him with tears streaming down my face, I lifted the animal. "I'm so sorry," I whispered. "I killed him. I didn't mean to. I was trying to heal him. It was working, and then...it wasn't."

He studied me before crouching down and examining the animal. Looking into my eyes, he stroked my hair. "It's okay, Callie." His voice was so soothing, and it made me feel a tiny bit better. "You tried your best."

"Does it mean I'm weird or...bad?"

"No," he said, shaking his head. "It makes sense you would inherit your mom's desire to heal and it would manifest through your powers. As long as you tried your best, that's all that matters."

"I think I can do it if I practice."

"Then we'll practice," he said, kissing my forehead.

After swiping my arm under my nose, I asked, "Can we bury him?"

"Absolutely. Let me get the shovel, and we'll have a proper funeral for him right here under the stars. Do you want your mom to help?"

I nodded before he went inside. I petted the chipmunk until he returned with Mom, and they helped me bury it. No one else came outside, and I knew Dad asked them to leave us alone. It was perfect because I decided I'm going to do my best to heal every animal I can in the future. Dad promised he'd help me learn to use my power, and I won't stop until I figure it out. Cross my heart.

Love, Callie

Chapter 2

Calinda, daughter of Darkrip and Arderin, kneeled beside the horse in the dim stable. Strained puffs of air exited the animal's wide nostrils, and its pain coursed through Callie as if it were her own.

"What do you think, Princess Calinda?" the horse's owner asked. "Will she be okay?"

"I told you to call me Callie, Shamus," she said, rising to look the man in the eye. "Tordor is the heir in this kingdom, and he can have all the fancy titles. I just want to be normal ol' me."

Shamus's lips twitched. "Sorry, princess, but I don't think you're like the rest of us. You're very special."

"Special," she muttered, striding to grab the bag she'd set by the barn door when she arrived. "People always call me that when they're afraid of me or want to avoid me."

"I assure you, ma'am, I don't want neither. I just want my horse to live. I need her for a whole heap of things at the farm and can't really afford another one right now."

"Yes," she said, crouching beside the horse and opening the bag. "The proclivity of Slayers and Vampyres to use horses on the rural compounds still baffles me. Aunt Miranda and Uncle Sathan built a magnificent railway connecting the compounds, which is a good start, but our people still haven't embraced driving cars—outside of battle, of course. The soldiers use four-wheelers quite frequently."

"They implemented a lot of fancy technology at Takelia since it's the newest compound, but I've never had much use for it, princess." He ran his fingers over the brown felt hat in his hands as she rummaged in the bag. "My wife, daughter and I do well here on the farm with what we have."

"Well, I guess that's all we can hope for," Callie said, pulling out the large plastic syringe and wiping it with an alcohol pad. "To be happy with what we've got."

"From your lips to the goddess's ears, ma'am."

"Callie," she corrected, resting her palm on the horse's side as the animal lay on the hay-covered ground. "All right, sweetie," she said, looking into the creature's dark eyes, "this will hurt for just a moment. We're going to withdraw some fluid so I can test it. And then I'm going to heal you. Okay?"

The horse nickered, and Callie smiled. Her abilities afforded her a connection with animals, and she could sense the creature's trust. Spreading her fingers wide, she inserted the needle, maintaining eye contact with the animal's deep brown orbs. The horse flinched slightly before Callie uttered a soft, "*Shhh...*" and she eventually relaxed on the ground.

Withdrawing the plunger, Callie extracted several milliliters of the dark red fluid from the abscess on the horse's stomach. Once finished, she placed the syringe in a plastic bag and deposited it in her medical bag.

Resting both palms on the horse's broad belly, she stared deeply into her eyes. "Okay, girl, you ready? This will be a bit uncomfortable for us both, but it will help. Close your eyes."

As if she understood the command, the creature closed her lids, the tiny black eyelashes stark against her brown mane.

Squeezing her eyes shut, Callie summoned the magic in her blood. It swam inside with dark and sticky remnants of her grandfather Crimeous's evil, alongside the reformed righteousness of her father, the regal valor of her grandmother Rina and great-grandfather Valktor and the feisty strength and self-healing properties inherited from her mother. The amalgamation of the powerful forces swirled and congealed in her veins, rushing toward the spot where her palms met the horse's skin. Letting it flow through, the energy enveloped the animal as it whimpered softly below.

Seconds later, Callie felt the horse release its pain. Sensing it was free from the sickness that had ailed it only moments earlier, Callie collapsed on the ground, pulling her hands from the animal and bringing her knees to her chest. Encircling them with her arms, she buried her face in her thighs and struggled to catch her breath.

"Princess?" Shamus asked, concern in his voice as her ears rang.

"Just need a minute," she said, holding up a hand, palm facing him. "It will pass. Just give me a sec..." Focusing on the yoga breathing techniques her mother taught her, Callie waited for the squeamish feeling inside her stomach to abate.

Moments later, the viscous energy left her body, and she lifted her head. Blinking rapidly, she stared up at Shamus. "Okay," she said, blowing out a breath. "I think we're both fine."

Proving her statement true, the horse whinnied before kicking its legs against the ground. After a few tries, she awkwardly rose, standing on strong legs, and elicited a joyful neigh before quickly trotting out the barn door to the attached fenced-in meadow.

"Wow, princess," Shamus said, bending and extending his hand to her. "That's something else. We Slayers always knew Vampyres had self-healing abilities, but you're the first person I know of who can heal others."

Grasping his hand, she let him pull her to her feet and swiped the hay off her jean-clad thighs. "Yes, it's a pretty cool party trick. All three of us—the grandkids of my woefully terrible Deamon King grandfather—inherited specific individualized traits, along with the ability to read others' thoughts and manipulate things with our minds. I got the ability to heal other living beings, my brother can walk through walls—which was super-creepy when I was a teenager, by the way—" she said, holding up a finger while Shamus chuckled, "and Rinada can render herself invisible. Much cooler in the whole 'things I inherited from creepy grandpa' scheme of things if you ask me," she teased, making quotation marks with her fingers.

"I think you all are amazing," he said, reverence in his tone. "You're hybrid children of some of the most powerful creatures on the planet. I told my wife she should come to the barn and meet you, but...well, she..."

"She's afraid," Callie said, giving a reassuring grin as she shrugged. "It's okay, Shamus. I'm used to it at this point."

"I don't mean no disrespect, ma'am—"

"It's totally fine," she said, waving a hand. "Call me if you need anything else for any of your animals."

Tilting his head, his eyes narrowed.

"What is it?"

Assessing her, he placed his hat on his head. "I just was wondering if it gets lonely sometimes. Being that different. There's comfort in blending in with the crowd sometimes."

"That there is," she said wistfully, lowering to close her bag. Grasping the handles, she straightened and extended her hand. "I'm happy I could help your horse, Shamus. I'll be handing over the sample to Nolan and Sadie to test. Bakari hasn't unleashed any new toxins that we know of in several months, but the threat is always there. Most likely, the abscess was caused by some bacteria she drank in the watering hole on the far side of the meadow. I would treat it before she drinks it again."

"Will do, princess," he said, shaking her hand. "Thank you so much for healing her."

"You're welcome." After a firm shake, she gave a salute and trailed out of the barn into the bright, sunny day.

Slinging her medical bag onto the passenger seat, she climbed into the four-wheeler and revved the engine. Putting the vehicle into gear, she pressed the pedal to the floor and began the drive to Takelia.

Shamus's farm at Restia was about a forty-five minute drive to Takelia, which would give her ample time to ponder the inner workings of her life as her hair blew in the wind and she soaked up the sun. She could've taken the train, since it connected all seven compounds of the immortal world, but she still would've had to find transportation from Restia's train station to the farm. No, it was better to drive through the open fields and enjoy the freedom she'd so deftly negotiated earlier.

Darkrip didn't like the idea of her driving to Restia alone. Bakari had amassed a powerful army, cloned from the Deamon inmates he'd sprung from Takelia's prison almost two decades ago. There was always a latent threat Bakari would launch a surprise attack or approach Callie and try to gain her alliance, especially since the prophecy declared they would align one day to destroy the world.

"Bakari hasn't ever approached me, Dad," she'd said to his reflection in the mirror of her vanity as she sat combing her hair earlier that morning. "I doubt he'll try today."

"If you recall, he did approach you," Darkrip said, crossing his arms over his chest as he loomed over her shoulder. "He took some of your hair from the playground swing when we lived in the human world."

"Yes, yes," she sighed, rolling her eyes as she dragged the brush through her long black curls. "And Tatiana used it to make the potion that allows Bakari to teleport like you and Aunt Evie. It's all my fault."

"It's not your fault," he said, cupping her shoulder. "I just don't want you to put yourself in harm's way."

Covering his hand, she smiled into his green eyes in the reflection. "What will you do if I bond with Zadicus and move in with him at Valeria? Will you come and check on me every day? Perhaps move into the room next door? Maybe you can listen while we—"

"Enough," he said, squeezing her shoulder. "I told you, if you ever mention having marital relations with anyone, I'll jump into the Purges of Methesda."

Snickering, she stood, shaking her head as she faced him. "Marital relations? Come on, Dad. You can say 'sex.'"

"Etherya help me," he muttered, glancing at the ceiling. Stepping back, he recrossed his arms and assessed her. "I won't let you go alone to heal the horse. Take a soldier with you."

"We both know I'm strong enough to overpower fifty soldiers," she said, lifting her hands in frustration. "I can read their thoughts, same as you, and although I can't transport, I did inherit the ability to crush things with my mind. I think I'll be fine."

"You're not a trained soldier—"

"I'm not a man," she said, thrusting up her chin. "Isn't that what you meant to say?"

"For god's sake," he said, rolling his eyes. "You and your mom play the sexism card anytime we have an argument. You know it's ridiculous considering I've never won an argument against either of you."

Callie smiled and squinted one eye. "You're right. I can't remember ever losing one…"

Chuckling, he stepped toward her and encircled her wrist. "You're my daughter, Callie. I love you. You and Creigen are proof I'm capable of doing good things in this wretched world. Let me keep you safe."

"Dad," she whispered, eyes welling as she cupped his cheeks. He'd always been such a strong, abiding constant in her life, and she loved him with every piece of her heart. "I'll be safe. Maybe you should say what you're really thinking. You're afraid Bakari is going to somehow contact me and manipulate me to his side. You're afraid I won't be able to deny the call of Grandfather's blood…of his evil."

Darkrip's eyes darted between hers. "You've never really had to fight the malevolence inside because your mother and I protected you." Palming her face, he ran his thumb over her cheek. "As you grow more independent, I worry I might have shielded you too much. I struggled with the darkness for centuries. I fear you haven't begun to comprehend how powerful it is."

Giving him a reassuring smile, she shook her head. "You and Mom did everything you could for us, but you can't keep me locked away forever. Hopefully, I'll be bonding soon, and there will be times you won't be there. You need to trust me. There's no way in hell I'd ever hurt anyone in our family. You know how important they are to me."

"You're telling that to the man who almost strangled me when I was pregnant with you," a sardonic voice chimed in from the doorway.

"Oh, brother," Darkrip muttered, glancing toward the door.

"Hey, Mom," Callie said, grinning as Arderin entered the room. "Dad was just worrying I'm going to turn into Grandfather and destroy the kingdom."

"Was he?" Arderin asked, standing on her toes and placing a peck on Darkrip's cheek. "How utterly fatalistic."

"Are you two really going to gang up on me when I was trying to protect our sweet, precious daughter?"

"The embellishment is a bit much," Arderin said, playfully rolling her eyes. "You heading out to Shamus's farm, sweetie?"

"Yes," Callie said, heading toward the bed and donning the light jacket that sat beside her medical bag. "Dad's worried."

"Fine—go on and get yourself abducted and murdered for all I care," he said, waving his hands in frustration as he turned to exit the room. "Goddess forbid I try to protect my own damn daughter—"

"Whoa, there," Arderin said, grabbing his wrist and drawing him to her side. "What your *sweet*, *loving* father meant to say is that we're going to settle on a compromise, right, darling?" She batted her eyelashes.

"I'm listening," he muttered.

"Callie, you'll carry the walkie on you at all times. If you see anything that's the least bit alarming, you'll radio Kenden and Latimus immediately and also send one of those weird telekinetic message thingies to your dad. Are we clear, young lady?"

"Mom, I'm almost twenty-five, for the goddess's sake—"

"Are we clear?" Arderin interrupted in the stern tone that implied she meant business.

"Yes, Mother," Callie said, contrite.

"Good. Darkrip, you'll have your spidey-sense all ready to go until she returns home, right?"

"Do I have a choice?"

"Stop it," she said, swatting his chest. "Agree with your wife, please."

"Yes, dear," he said, pecking her lips. "I'll be on alert. Callie, you have the walkie?"

"There's one in the four-wheeler. I'll radio Uncle Ken and Uncle Latimus before I head out."

"Fine," Darkrip said, rubbing the back of his neck. "I have a meeting with the compound governors today, but I can leave in a second if needed."

"My dad, the kingdom's ambassador. Who knew you'd be so great at instituting diplomacy between all the compounds?"

"Evie is a great governor, but that's too formal for me. I enjoy helping the seven governors run the realm. Ambassador was a good fit, and I need something to do while your mom floats around healing people at the clinics."

"Yes, it was world domination or ambassadorship. I'm so proud you chose the light," Arderin teased, sliding her arm around his waist. "Good luck with the horse, sweetheart. You're so wonderful to use your powers to help wounded animals. I'm so proud of you."

"Okay, no crying today, Mom," Callie said, noting the tears welling in her mother's eyes. "This is a happy day. We won another round against Dad."

Darkrip frowned as she stepped forward and gave them both a kiss.

"See you both when I get home. Love you!"

With that, she grabbed her bag and headed to Shamus's without so much as a blip from Bakari as she traversed the open fields between Takelia and Restia.

Now, on the way home, a slight melancholy settled in as she drove through the open air. She had no idea why—after all, she was *finally* being courted by a man who was well-respected and seemed determined to win her over. Zadicus romanced her with such zeal she sometimes marveled at how lucky she was to find him as her first love.

Callie had always been a romantic—a trait most likely inherited from her mother who was deeply in love with her father. Knowing her dad returned the sentiment gave Callie hope as she contemplated her own future. Zadicus was exceedingly handsome with his piercing blue eyes, austere features and jet-black hair. He embodied the regal appearance his aristocratic blood conveyed, and she enjoyed their passionate kisses when he visited Takelia to court her. Although she'd decided not to sleep with him until they bonded, it was nice to be desired by someone so handsome.

Arderin had always urged Callie to wait to make love until she bonded, and they had discussed it on several occasions as Callie grew into adulthood.

"Sweetie," Arderin had said during one of their discussions several years ago, "making love to someone is a big decision. I just want it to be as special as you deserve."

Callie had been moved by the words and the sentiment in her mother's voice. "I do like the idea of waiting until the time feels right. If it's the night of my bonding ceremony, so be it. It's not like anyone is beating my door down anyway."

"Someone will, and I can't wait for that day," Arderin said, running a soothing hand over Callie's curls.

She'd been right, as her mother often was. Two years later, she met Zadicus at a royal fundraiser at Valeria. The immortal royals were always holding fundraisers to encourage the wealthy aristocrats to fund the army, and this one had been particularly stuffy. Callie had exited onto the balcony of the castle at Valeria, and a smooth voice sounded in her ear.

"Are you as bored as I am?"

Glancing up at the handsome Vampyre, she grinned. "To death. These things suck. I attend because it makes my parents happy and shows my support of the cause, but, man, I hate them."

"They're not my cup of tea either." Warm breath caressed her ear as it blew the soft curls at her temple. "Want to take a walk by the river?"

She'd contemplated only a moment before giving a nod. "Sure. I can disappear for half an hour. Let's blow this joint."

They'd walked along the grassy riverbank, learning each other's stories as Callie's excitement grew at finally being pursued by a handsome, attentive suitor.

"So, you're Melania and Camron's nephew?" Callie asked. "I don't know them very well, but Lila is close with Camron."

"He's a great governor, and Melania is my father's sister."

Callie thoughtfully chewed her lip. "My dad mentioned a few times that Melania was once sympathetic to Bakari's cause. Aunt Lila always reminds him that she's chosen our side and that everyone deserves redemption."

"That's very kind of her. Melania has never spoken to me with anything other than support for the immortal royals."

"That's good. Perhaps she just made a mistake. None of us are perfect."

Zadicus halted, encircling her wrist and drawing her to his side. Blue eyes simmered in the moonlight as he stared down at her, desire swimming in the deep orbs.

"You seem pretty perfect to me, princess."

A laugh escaped her throat. "Then you really don't know me," she said, the words breathy and disjointed.

"That's something I would very much like to change."

"You would?" Her heart pounded as she stared up at his handsome features. No one had ever looked at her with such raw passion, and it was...exhilarating.

"Yes," he whispered, sliding a hand behind her neck and tilting her face. "Come here, princess. Let me taste you."

With that, Callie experienced the first truly passionate kiss of her life. She'd had a few others that were lackluster, but Zadicus embodied such zeal as he devoured her mouth. Afterward, she stared at him, attempting to catch her breath.

"I would like to court you, princess," he said, sliding his palm over her upper arm in warm, slow circles. "Should I ask your father? Forgive me, but growing up in an aristocratic family has made me quite formal."

Callie wrinkled her nose. "It's so different from the human world, but I think I quite like it. Yes, you can ask my dad to court me. If he doesn't disintegrate you on the spot, I'd very much like to be wooed."

Zadicus responded with a playful grimace but seemed undeterred. Days later, he embarked on a long discussion with Darkrip in their sitting room at Takelia. Darkrip had several reservations about Zadicus—the most glaring being that he was related to Melania. He also questioned why a high-ranking aristocrat would want to court someone as free-spirited as Callie. Although they were technically royals, their family unit was anything but traditional. But Zadicus had assured Darkrip his intentions were true, and Callie had all but begged him for his blessing. Finally, someone was eager to court her, and she was excited for the experience. Eventually, her father consented, and Zadicus began his courtship.

They'd now been dating for nine months, and Callie was all-consumed with zealous shows of affection from her handsome suitor. It was all quite overwhelming for Callie, who had struggled to find her place in the immortal world when they returned after Arderin completed her medical training. Being the focus of an evil prophecy wasn't the best way to fit in, and her teenage years had been tough. After going through her immortal change in her early twenties, she longed for affection and comradery with a partner. She and Zadicus certainly had mutual affection. Was she one hundred percent comfortable with him yet? Not really. But Callie figured those things took time, and she wasn't going to squander the chance to finally fall in love. They would eventually grow into a relationship similar to what her parents had, right? Gnawing her lip, Callie deliberated.

Zadicus had employed every tactic possible to win her love. Long walks by the river, moonlight picnics, flowers at every turn. Hell, he'd even written her poetry. Snickering as she drove the four-wheeler, she admitted his poetry was terrible. But the effort was sweet, and she hoped he didn't realize she thought it dreadful. There was no point in hurting his feelings after all.

Callie felt that within the next few months, Zadicus would ask her to bond. She would accept, although she would stick with her decision to wait until their wedding night to make love. The choice stemmed from a combination of several factors. Her promise to her mother she would wait until it felt right. Her desire to ensure Zadicus truly loved her with all his heart. And perhaps most important of all, the nagging feeling that her ardent suitor might be trying just a *bit* too hard.

The feeling swam in her gut, dark and heavy, and it created a secret doubt she hadn't expressed to anyone else. It was responsible for her slight melancholy and made her wonder if she was truly making the right decision. She considered herself a pretty chill person, and although the elaborate courting was nice, she didn't really need it. It was almost as if Zadicus had some strange ulterior motive to ensure she chose him.

Realizing she needed to express the feelings to someone she trusted, Callie slowed and parked in the open meadow. Pulling her phone from her bag, she called Jack.

"Hey," his deep voice said over the receiver. "You okay? I know you went to Shamus's farm today."

"Yeah," she said, picking at a frayed string hanging from one of the ripped holes in her jeans. "We're still on for the street fair tonight, right?"

"Yep. We'll be done at four. We're letting the soldiers go early so they can attend with their families. On that note, it's Brecken's night off, and he asked if he and Rowena can come with us. She's his youngest sister, if you remember."

"Oh, sure," she said as Brecken's face flashed through her mind. She was fond of Brecken and knew he was close with Jack. Now, she mostly saw him when he stood off in the distance protecting Zadicus. Callie always sensed his presence when he was near, which she attributed to her heightened senses from her Deamon blood.

Most wouldn't even sense the hulking bodyguard's presence—after all, it was his job to blend in and go unnoticed. But sometimes, she would catch him staring at her out of the corner of her eye and always felt a strange jolt of...*something*. Intensity? Awareness? She wasn't sure how to describe the feeling and usually wrote it off as a side effect of being observed. After all, it was a bit creepy to have another man watch you as you strolled with your suitor, even if he was a paid bodyguard.

The fact her suitor's protector was viscerally attractive was an entirely different rabbit hole Callie had no interest in chasing. Although, it was interesting to compare Brecken and Zadicus in those rare moments her mind went there. Zadicus was perfectly coiffed, attractive in a smooth, polished manner. Brecken was... *primal*. Sexy. Brooding. Sometimes, in those rare moments her eyes met his, golden flecks would flash in his deep brown eyes, and Callie would have to tamp down a shiver. Did they flash like that when he made love? Did the dark orbs simmer as he claimed his mate's body, marking her as *his*?

With a vicious shake of her head, Callie returned to reality. Why in the hell was she imagining Brecken having sex when she had a wonderful man expending excessive amounts of energy courting her? "Get it together, Callie," she muttered before resuming the call with Jack.

"Callie?"

"Sorry, I'm here. Should be fun. I like Brecken. I remember when we celebrated when you got him the bodyguard position. He paid for all my drinks, which wasn't necessary but was really nice. Obviously, I see him when I'm with Zadicus, but it's different. Anyway, it will be nice to hang with him outside of the whole bodyguard situation."

"I'm assuming Zadicus isn't coming?"

Callie chewed her lip. "No. I need a break from him. Please don't tell anyone else I said that. He's awesome, and I love hanging with him, but he's...*a lot* sometimes. I mean, sometimes, a girl just needs to Netflix and chill. He's kind of formal."

Jack's chuckle sounded in her ear. "He is, but I think you signed up for that. You *are* planning to bond with him, right?"

"Of course," she said, her tone cheerful, although the doubt lingered inside. "But I'm excited to hang with you guys. That's all."

"Sounds good. Want to meet me at my cabin at five? We can walk to town from there."

"Sure. I'll remind Dad I'll be home late so he won't have a heart attack. I'm in a four-wheeler, so I might get to you a bit early. Is that okay?"

"Yep. I'll leave the key in the lockbox hanging on the knob. Works out well since I don't have to reset the code considering you can unlock the thing with your powers."

"Perfect. I'll pick up some wine on the way. We can have a glass before we walk into town."

"Can't wait. See you in a bit."

The phone clicked, and Callie released a sigh. Spending time with Jack would clear her head, and she could always talk to him about Zadicus if she needed. Pressing her foot to the pedal, she told herself everything would be fine. Even people who loved each other needed a break sometimes. Zooming across the open field, she sped home to pick up the wine before driving to Lynia, excited for the evening ahead.

D ear Diary,

   I would like to report that I am **not** enjoying sixth grade. At this point, I'd love to stay home and have Glarys homeschool me, but Mom says it's important I learn to handle adversity and make friends. We're royals and have a duty to uphold, but it's hard when everyone thinks you're a freak who's going to destroy the kingdom.

   We started learning about the history of the immortal realm today, since that's part of the sixth-grade curriculum. After Miranda and Kenden discovered the hidden Elven scrolls, they wanted the contents to be taught across the realm. They're pretty vague, but they do give us glimpses of the extinct immortal species, and Miranda thinks it will help unite us. Now that Vampyres, Slayers and Deamons live on all the compounds, it's important we take lessons from the destruction of the Elves to help counteract and prevent our own mistakes.

   Well, that's great and all, but when you're the subject of one of those deadly prophecies, leaning about it in a classroom of your peers kind of sucks. Today, as the teacher was explaining Bakari's history and his mention in the Elven prophecy, she also referenced my role in the prophecy. Several of my classmates shot me mean looks from their desks, and others looked at me as if they were terrified.

   Afterward, when we went outside for lunch, no one would sit with me, so I sat alone like a super-dork. Some of the other kids snickered when I opened my soda and it sprayed all over my table. I shot them the bird, and my teacher sent me to the principal who said I had to go home for the day. You know what? That was just fine with me.

Mom picked me up, and we had a long talk when we got home. She says that one day, I'll find my people. People who accept me and love me just for me. I hope so because being an outcast really blows. At least I have Mom, Dad, Creigen, Jack and the rest of my family.
Love, Callie

Chapter 3

The day of the street fair, Brecken rose with the sun and went out for a run. He'd had a restless night tossing and turning as he envisioned Callie's reaction if she discovered his pact with Zadicus. Would those luminous eyes fill with tears? Or would she punch him in the nose and tell him to go to hell? Chuckling as he jogged, he realized he preferred the latter, if only so he could see her cheeks flush and observe the vibrant colors in her irises flare. For some reason, he imagined Callie angry would be fun. She was passionate and had a gregarious personality, which enthralled someone with his more stoic demeanor. What would she be like in bed? Would that passion translate between the sheets?

Swiping his damp forehead, Brecken told himself to shut it down and finish his jog. After a refreshing shower, he threw on jeans, a T-shirt and sneakers, happy to be free of his black tactical gear for the day. Raoul employed a floater security agent who observed Zadicus on his days off, and Brecken savored his free time. He did some chores around the cabin, prepared his Slayer blood weekly rations and washed the load of laundry that had been piling up for over a week. Eventually, the sun sat low in the afternoon sky, and he realized Rowena would be home from school. After running a comb through his thick, dark brown hair, he locked the door behind him and set off to his mother's house.

His cabin resided on a patch of land a few miles from the main square. His father had purchased the land centuries ago, and Brecken, being the oldest male, had inherited it. He thought the tradition antiquated and felt his mother should've inherited everything, but old Vampyre traditions took time to reform. Thankfully, Queen Miranda and Governor Evie were progressive and were slowly dragging the kingdom into modernity. Brecken had always believed in equality and supported the recent decision to allow females to become combat soldiers in the immortal army. Some of his friends and fellow soldiers he'd trained with were resistant, but Brecken felt they would come around, especially with the focus on defeating Bakari. Why not employ every willing and able soldier they could to vanquish the threat forever?

When Brecken had completed his military training, he used his meager savings to build his own cabin on the opposite side of his father's land. It afforded him privacy as he moved into adulthood and allowed his mother to retain the home she'd lived in for centuries. He sold it to her for one lira, and the property was now evenly divided—his mother owning her home and land, and he his. It felt much more equitable and allowed him to get a break from his five sisters. Although he loved them dearly, they were a lot to deal with for a man who craved his space.

After walking through the thicket of trees and brush that separated his cabin from his mother's home, he approached the front porch and climbed the stairs. Reaching for the doorknob, he didn't have the chance to touch it before Rowena swung the door open.

"*Ohmygod*, get me out of here!" she said, rolling her eyes. "Jordana's boyfriend broke up with her, and I can't take the drama."

Laughing at his twelve-year-old sister, who was quite dramatic herself, he stepped inside. "I thought this one was a keeper. Jordana really liked Axe."

"He told her they both needed to date other people since they were eighteen and graduating soon. She might never recover," Rowena said, resting the back of her hand on her forehead and imitating a swoon.

"I'm sure she'll be fine," he muttered, strolling through the hallway to the living room where his mother sat sewing a shirt. "Hi, Mom." Leaning down, he kissed her light brown hair, which was pulled into a bun.

"Hi, dear," she said, gesturing with her head for him to sit in the chair beside her. "You heard Jordana's life is over?"

His lips curved. "How tragic."

Breathing a laugh, she shook her head. "I keep reminding myself the goddess blessed me with five daughters for a reason. And with one wonderful son." Leaning over, she patted his cheek.

"I do my best. Where is everyone?"

"Jordana is in her room railing at the universe, I'm sure. Betsy and Ludika are at soccer practice. Nala is out back wielding her sword if I had to guess. She's intent on becoming a soldier like you. I hope to introduce her to Queen Miranda one day. What a boon that will be for our little teenage warrior."

Brecken lifted his brows, wondering if it would ever happen. Queen Miranda was lauded as a champion of the people who loved all citizens regardless of their wealth or status, but the opportunity for a poor, rural teenager to cross her path was limited at best. Not wanting to dampen his mother's spirits, he nodded. "Perhaps it will happen."

"You could ask Calinda to set up a meeting..."

"I'm not allowed to speak to my wards or their companions without being asked first, Mom. You know that. Although, I'll actually be hanging with Callie at the street fair tonight. If it comes up naturally, I'll try to remember to mention it, but I doubt that will happen."

"It would make your sister's year," she said, smiling. "Do try to remember."

"On another note, I have some fantastic news."

His mother's eyebrow arched. "Do tell. Did you finally meet the woman of your dreams and fall madly in love so you can give me some grandbabies?"

"Um, no," he said, lips flattening. "You'll be receiving a call tomorrow from the house manager at Valeria's governor's mansion. They're going to offer you the open seamstress position."

Her hands dropped to her lap as she stared at him with a stunned expression. "How? I'm sure there are other qualified candidates at Valeria who won't have to ride the train from Lynia."

"They want *you*, Mom." Encircling her wrist, he squeezed. "The girls are all old enough to take the train to school, and you don't need to be at home every day. I figured you wouldn't mind commuting for the extra income. It could be a game changer for our family."

"Oh, my," she said, resting her hand over her heart. "I could finally add an addition onto the house so Ludika can have her own room. And I can actually buy all the girls dresses to wear to their dances instead of recycling the old ones. And don't even get me started on how the hot water never works in the second bathroom. I could finally hire a plumber. Heck, I could build a third bathroom."

Overcome with the joy in her deep brown eyes, he nodded. "There are so many possibilities, and it will allow Rowena to go to university at one of the aristocratic compounds if she chooses. I hope you'll take the position, Mom. It's a great opportunity."

"Of course I'm taking it, boy!" She playfully swatted his arm. "How magnificent. What did you have to do to secure this for me?" Her eyebrow arched, and he swallowed thickly, understanding his mother could read him well.

"Nothing. I'm doing a good job for Zadicus. He mentioned the open position, and we had a discussion about it."

Her eyes darted between his. "If there's one thing you should've learned by now, it's that you shouldn't lie to your mother, Brecken."

Giving her a droll look, he stood. "I'm not lying."

Narrowing her eyes, she studied him. "You are, but you must have your reasons. Just remember your father is watching us from the Passage. We must live up to our moral code and make him proud."

Guilt swirled within before he pushed it away. Seeing things in black-and-white was a privilege people on the rural compounds sometimes didn't enjoy. He wouldn't feel bad for securing a position for his mother that would help his family. Wishing for different circumstances was a waste of time, so he leaned down and kissed his mother before pivoting to find Rowena and head to the street fair.

"Everything will be fine, Mom," he said from the doorway, hand resting on the frame. "I love you. We're off to the fair. I'll make sure Rowena gets some Slayer blood and we're home by ten."

"Have fun," she said, blowing him a kiss. "And thank you for the opportunity. I love you too, son."

Sparing her one last smile, Brecken located his sister and began the twenty-minute walk into town, telling himself the entire time to let go of his trepidation because it wouldn't change a damn thing.

Dear Diary,

    Well, I'm officially a teenager, and I can say without a doubt, it sucks. We had our first school dance yesterday, and Mom said I should go because we're all intent on living our lives even though Bakari is trying to destroy the realm. If that wasn't heavy enough, I realized two weeks ago that no one was going to ask me to the dance. Mom says I'm pretty, and Dad always mutters he can't believe there's two of us since I look just like her. I think she's beautiful, but I'm not sure I'm as pretty as she is. My body looks weird lately, and I just feel awkward.

Anyway, our family was over for dinner last week, and I overheard Mom and Dad telling everyone that no one had asked me to the dance. It was annoying, and I wish they would stay out of my business. I let it go because I didn't really want to talk about what a huge loser I was.

Mom bought me a really pretty dress and did my hair, so I looked okay, I guess. I spent the first hour of the dance drinking about a thousand cups of punch, hoping someone would ask me to dance, but no one did. So I made up a boyfriend in my mind.

His name is Henry (after Henry Cavill, of course. I might have left the human world, but that guy is hot no matter what realm you're in!), and he's everything I ever imagined. He smiles at me and tells me I'm pretty and thinks it's really cool I'm so smart and make straight As. He doesn't give a crap about the prophecy and wants to kiss me all the time. Yep, one day, I'll meet my Henry, and I can stop feeling like a freak.

Until then, I'll put up with the rejection and focus on the positives. I mean, life could be worse, right? I love my parents and my family, and my brother is okay too...most of the time. They've always accepted me, and that's what really matters. I can't wait for my Henry to meet them, whenever he shows up. I'll be waiting...

Love, Callie

Chapter 4

C allie arrived at Jack's cabin, teasing him when he opened the door with wet red hair spiked in a hundred different directions.

"Be careful going out in public like that, or Brienne won't ever take you back."

"Brienne and I are toast, I'm afraid," he said, stepping back and opening the door wider so she could step inside. "Apparently, I'm 'emotionally unavailable.'" He made quotation marks with his fingers. "Whatever that means."

"It just means you haven't met the right person yet. She's not your person, Jack."

His auburn eyebrows lifted. "And Zadicus is yours?"

"It seems so," she said, shrugging.

"I'm still not sure, but that's what courting is for, I guess." Closing the door, he gestured to the chairs in front of the fireplace. "Want to open the wine and have a glass before we walk to town?"

"Sure," she said, picking up one of the weapons that sat on the table by his front door.

"It's an improved TEC that Uncle Heden sent over. This is the prototype. I'm supposed to test it with Dad sometime over the next week."

She glanced up at him, concern in her eyes. "That means you'll have to encounter some Deamons."

"Yep," he said, smiling as if it were a normal occurrence to encounter vicious Deamon soldiers on a regular basis. Jack was extremely proud of his position as Chief Training Officer in the immortal army and his recent promotion to lieutenant. Callie knew he'd worked hard to attain it and didn't want anyone thinking he'd received special favors as the adopted son of Commander Latimus.

"General Garridan spotted a cluster of Deamons near the foothills of the Strok Mountains west of Uteria on their last scouting mission," he continued. "We'll probably launch a surprise attack and test the prototype. Not only does it kill a Deamon instantly like the old TECs, but it disintegrates them too, so there's nothing left behind to be cloned."

Her eyebrows lifted. "Go Uncle Heden...and Aunt Sofia. I'm sure she had just as much to do with it as he did."

"Most likely. They're both smart as hell."

Setting the weapon on the table, she turned and reached inside her bag. Lifting the bottle of wine, she shook it. "Cabernet. Your favorite."

"Sweet." Taking the bottle, Jack trailed to the kitchenette in the far corner and pulled two glasses from the cabinet. Callie walked over and opened the top drawer, locating the corkscrew. Setting the bottle on the counter, she screwed the cork free and poured them each a taste.

"It's good," Jack said after a hearty sip. "Fill me up."

"It's from Aunt Sofia's latest batch. I stopped home and grabbed it on the way here."

After filling their glasses, they clinked them together before drinking. "Man, it is good."

"Almost as good as the first time you had wine," he teased.

"Oh, goddess," she said, heading toward the two chairs that flanked the tiny fireplace on the far side of the cabin. "Don't remind me." She fell into the chair.

"I don't think I've ever seen that much puke," Jack said, sliding into the vacant seat. "You were ripped."

Rolling her eyes, she rested her palm on her forehead. "I was so pissed Dad wouldn't let me drink and declared I'd drink every bottle in the cellar when he wasn't looking."

"Well, you were only sixteen. I think he was right."

"*Pfft.* Sixteen going on a hundred. Having extraordinary powers and being the subject of a dreadful prophecy ages a person."

"Does it?" he mused, glancing at the ceiling.

"Yes," she said, extending her leg to gently kick him. "Anyway, I didn't even have to read your thoughts to know how pissed you were at me."

Holding up a finger, he said, "Let's also not discount the fact reading people's thoughts violates the oath you gave your father."

Sighing, she lifted the glass and sipped before nodding. "Yes, I promised him I wouldn't use my powers to read others' thoughts unless I was in danger. How utterly boring."

Chuckling, he lifted a shoulder. "I think it's just the right thing to do. Although, knowing you, you've probably cheated a few hundred times over the years."

Her eyes lit with excitement as she straightened in the chair. "Oh my god, I have! Want to hear some of the best things I've discovered? You can't tell anyone because they would *kill* me, but it's so fun. I swear, it only happened when I didn't realize I was doing it. I'm much better at controlling the power now that I'm older." She made an "X" over her heart.

"Sure. Hit me with the scandalous details."

"So, I'm pretty sure your parents are into some kinky costume role-play when they're alone—"

"Ew," he interrupted, holding up a hand. "My parents are off-limits. Move on to someone else, please."

"Oh, fine," she said with a harrumph. "You're no fun. Let me see..." Tapping her finger on her lips, she contemplated. "Oh! I accidentally read Aunt Miranda's thoughts when we had family dinner at Uteria at few years ago. Your dad was talking about his resistance to having women join the combat troops, and she was *pissed*. I mean, she had some really vivid images of strangling him and then kicking him in the nuts. It was so funny I almost spit out my drink!"

"Miranda's tough as nails, for sure," Jack said, chuckling at the image. "Thank the goddess Dad came around on the subject so she won't need to render him inept with her knee."

"Seriously. I know Evie and Miranda were both thrilled with that decision." She imbibed the wine as her expression grew pensive. "I also see sad things sometimes."

"Like what?"

"Tordor," she said, eyes narrowing as she contemplated the ceiling. "He isn't sure of his place in the world. He feels a bit lost considering he's supposed to be the heir but Miranda and Sathan are immortal. It doesn't really offer an open position for him in the realm. And Rinada and Creigen both have their doubts about their place here, as do I. Being the grandchild of Crimeous and possessing powers no one else has is isolating. I guess the kids of the royal family are all fucked up in their own ways. Except for you," she said, tilting her head. "You seem relatively normal."

"I'm pretty sure you're really saying I'm boring, but I'll let it slide."

"Nah," she said, waving her hand, "You're the life of the party."

"Man, you're a terrible liar." Standing, he extended his hand to her. "Drink up so we can head into town. And before you make fun of me again, I'll also comb my hair."

She swallowed the last of her wine and handed him the glass. Striding to the sink, he rinsed them and placed them in the basin.

"This cabin is hella cute and all, but you're the son of wealthy royals. Have you ever considered living in a home where the kitchen isn't in the same room as your bed?" She gestured around the tiny space.

"Not really," he said, wiping his hands on the dishtowel. "The cabin is all I need, and it's close to home. If I ever need a bigger place to stay, I can always spend the night at Mom and Dad's. But I like it here. Must seem strange to someone who's seen as much of the world as you."

"No judgement at all," she said, standing. "It's just tiny. But, hey, whatever makes you happy. Ready to go?"

Nodding, he slipped on his socks and sneakers and headed to the bathroom. Returning with freshly combed hair, he turned off the lights, and they headed outside.

They began the trek to Lynia's main square, which was about a ten-minute walk. Callie debated whether she should bring up her doubts about Zadicus, not wanting to make a big deal out something she wasn't sure even required a conversation.

"Might as well spit it out," he said, breaking the silence. "I've already realized you have something on your mind. Give it to me."

Grinning up at him, she squinted in the late-day sun. "Maybe I'm not the only one who can read minds in this twosome?"

"Maybe not." He tapped his finger on his temple. "Go on. I'll try to help if I can."

"I appreciate you always letting me vent to you. It's been tough making true friends here since half the people think I'm a freak."

"No, they don't," he said, shaking his head. "We talked about this dramatic streak, right?" Rubbing his chin, he glanced at the sky. "I'm sure we did..."

"Stop teasing me," she said, swatting his arm. "Being the granddaughter of Crimeous *and* the subject of a doomsday prophecy isn't a bed of roses, Jack." She studied the dirt walking path, eyes downcast, as she continued. "People recoil from me sometimes, especially on the more rural compounds. It's gotten better as we've settled into the kingdom and the people realized Dad and Evie aren't going to pulverize them, but Crimeous tortured them for centuries. That fear doesn't dissipate overnight. A portion of my blood is inherently evil, as is Rinada's, Creigen's, Dad's and Evie's."

"You've never shown a hint of evil, Callie."

She shot him an acerbic glance. "You're placating me."

"Look, I know you accidentally hurt some birds and a few chipmunks when you were younger. But you were trying to heal them when they died. You just had to grow into your power."

"I still feel bad for every animal I hurt. But only through those experiences did I figure out how to heal other living beings."

"Learning new things takes time. The fact you feel remorse they perished is what matters."

"I guess," she said with a sigh. "Or maybe I'm just destined to be a freak. I think that's why I was so taken by Zadicus. He really expended some serious energy courting me—like he'd be extremely lucky to be my bonded."

Jack halted, turning to face her. "He would be the luckiest man in the world. Is that what's bothering you?"

"Yes," she said, hating that she was emotional over something so trite. An attractive, kind man was going out of his way to court her. She should be thrilled. But intuition was also important, and hers was telling her something wasn't quite right.

"Why is he trying so hard, Jack? At first, I was consumed by the flattery, but now that we're close to becoming engaged, I..." She ran her hand through her dark curls. "I don't know, I'm having doubts. It's almost as if he has an agenda for courting me that I just can't see."

"I think his agenda is to make you his wife. That's how courting works, Callie."

"Yeah," she said, absently gnawing her lip. "But it's so *much*. I like feeling special, but I also just want to feel...*normal*. I've rarely felt normal except with our family."

"It makes sense to feel comfortable with your family. These things take time to develop."

"But will I ever feel comfortable in my own skin with him? I feel as if he doesn't get me sometimes."

"I don't know. Do you love him? If not, then maybe you should take a break so you can figure this out. Bonding with someone is a huge commitment, Callie. If you have doubts, you need to address them."

She worked her jaw as her gaze fell to his shoulder. "I think I love him. I mean, my god, Jack, how do I know? He's literally the first person who's ever shown romantic interest in me. I feel all the butterflies and enjoy making out with him. I'm certainly excited to have sex with him when we bond. I want to know what all the fuss is about."

"Okay, that's probably TMI," he muttered, rubbing his forehead, "but only you can decide if this is just normal relationship jitters or something more.".

"I just don't want to make a mistake." Slipping her arm into his, they resumed walking. "Maybe I'm overthinking it. Thanks for letting me vent. Perhaps I just needed to talk to someone."

"Life has a way of steering us where we need to go. You already know deep inside why you have doubts. Don't discount your intuition, Callie. It's usually a good barometer of things to come."

"Truth," she said with a nod. "Oh, is that Brecken?" she asked, spotting him and the girl by his side. Lifting her hand, she waved.

Brecken's full lips formed a smile before he leaned down, resting his hands on his knees. He smoothed a hand over his sister's hair, the sweet gesture sending a jolt of awareness down Callie's spine. She'd rarely observed emotion from the stoic man, and something about the gentle way he spoke to the girl called to her. His sister gave a wide grin before nodding up at him. Turning, she rushed toward them, stopping to stare up at Callie.

"My brother says I'm probably supposed to bow to you since you're a princess, but I don't know how," she said, lifting a shoulder.

"Oh, good heavens, no," Callie said, grimacing. Extending her hand, she asked, "How about a good ol'-fashioned handshake. I'm Callie."

"Rowena," she said, giving a firm shake. "I'm Brecken's youngest sister...and his favorite, but he'll never admit it."

"I don't have a favorite," he said, approaching and shooting her a playful glare. "But if I did, it *might* be you."

Biting her lip, Rowena smiled at Callie and held her hand to her face, mimicking telling a secret. "I'm totally his favorite," she whispered.

"Noted," Callie said, winking.

"Hey, man," Jack said, giving that weird high five thing men always did when they greeted. When they finished, Brecken faced her, his expression cordial as his eyes roved over her face. "Hey, Callie."

Callie suddenly wondered if she should've put on lip gloss after drinking wine. Did she have wine lips? Ew. Feeling a strange surge of heat on the back of her neck, she rubbed it as she smiled. "Hey, Brecken. Nice to see you outside of Zadicus's mansion. Glad you two could join us."

He gave a brief nod before directing his attention to his sister and asking her which booth she'd like to frequent first. Licking her lips, Callie rubbed her finger over them, hoping like hell she didn't look like a complete idiot. Reaching into her purse, she drew out her gloss and applied it before placing it back inside. Straightening her spine, she asked, "Where to first, guys?"

Brecken straightened, facing her and opening his mouth to answer. His gaze lowered to her lips, and Callie reflexively pressed them together.

"Rowena wants to start at the science booth," he finally said after an awkward silence. "She goes to Takelia's school for the gifted and talented, and they're studying physics right now."

"Oh, that's where I went," Callie said. "I loved the school even though I didn't have the greatest experience there."

"Why?" Rowena asked.

"Story for another time," she said, waving her hand and stepping forward. "Lead the way. I hear the Lynian museum curators who run the science booths have some awesome relics from our past. My grandmother, Queen Calla, used to collect meteorites that fell to Earth, and I think they have some pieces from her collection. Let's check them out." Extending her hand, she grasped Rowena's, and they began walking, Jack and Brecken falling into step behind them.

Callie could almost feel Brecken's gaze on her neck and told herself to get a grip. So what if he'd been looking at her lips before? He probably was just noticing her sparkly lip gloss. Pushing thoughts of the viscerally handsome man from her mind, she forged ahead with Rowena, excited to enjoy the street fair.

Well, Diary, today I turned eighteen. I'm pretty sure that means I'm too old to have a diary, so this will be my last entry (unless something really drastic happens and I need to vent. We all have our outlets!).

We had an awesome party at Takelia, and Mom even let me drink a beer. It tasted kind of gross and definitely wasn't as good as the wine I secretly drank with Jack a few years ago, but I didn't want to seem immature, so I sipped it until it was gone. Dad scolded her that she shouldn't give me any ideas about growing up too soon and muttered something about pulverizing any man who tried to touch me.

Well, he's in luck because no one's shown any interest. I swear, if a guy actually comes on to me one day, I'll probably say yes so fast his head will spin. Who doesn't want to be loved and desired? Now that I'm eighteen, I'd really like to see what all the fuss is about. Unfortunately, dating me seems to have about the same appeal as sticking a fork into a toaster. Good grief.

Of course, I'm still waiting for my Henry. Although I get discouraged sometimes, I'll never give up hope. I look at all the awesome women in my family and think about how long it took them to find love. I mean, it took Aunt Miranda a thousand years to find Uncle Sathan! Same for Mom, Lila and Evie, so I'm still a baby in this whole "find the love of your life" thing. I hope it doesn't take that long for me, but, hey, the journey only makes us stronger, right?

Anyway, it's been fun. Thanks for getting me through my awkward childhood. Hopefully, adulthood will be better. I'm going to try like hell not to destroy the world. We'll see how that goes. Wish me luck!

Love, Callie

Chapter 5

Brecken trailed behind Callie and Rowena, barely able to focus on his conversation with Jack since he'd sprung a massive erection the second he saw Callie's lips slathered in the glittery lip gloss. How in the hell was a man supposed to think rationally when someone as gorgeous as Callie enhanced those luscious lips? Glancing at Jack, he hoped his friend didn't notice his body's reaction. So far, his attraction to Callie had been passing—something he noted but didn't dwell on. Would it magnify now he'd agreed to observe her in order to write the letters? Hoping that wasn't the case, he stared at her mass of dark curls as they bobbed. He could almost feel the soft tresses clenched in his hand as he directed her head toward his straining shaft, begging her to spread that sparkly gloss all over his cock...

"Earth to Brecken," Jack said, waving his hand in front of his face.

"Sorry," he muttered. "What were you saying?"

"Just asking how your day off was going. We miss you at the training sessions, and everyone said to tell you hi."

"I miss them too," Brecken said, thinking of the soldiers in his old battalion. "We need to plan a night out, hopefully once Bakari is vanquished. It would be an awesome celebration."

"Definitely," Jack said with a nod. "Siora speaks highly of you. She says you're friends from school."

"Yes. She was thrilled to be one of the first female recruits. It's a boon for rural Lynians like us who grew up poor. The army pays well and allows us to support our families in ways we never would have."

"Dad and Kenden will ensure the soldiers are taken care of even after we defeat Bakari. I know they plan to maintain an army considering there are always unknown threats that can emerge."

"Glad to hear it. If Zadicus ever fires me, I'll come back in a heartbeat."

Chuckling, Jack patted him on the back. "Don't think it will happen, buddy, but you're always welcome."

Crossing the main square, they approached the first row of tents that lined the street.

"Bella!" a jubilant voice called before a man with salt-and-pepper hair rushed over from his booth to hug Callie. "You grow more beautiful every day. The spitting image of your mother." He kissed both cheeks before turning to Jack and extending his hand. "Hello, Lieutenant Jack. So lovely to see you on this fine evening."

"Hey, Antonio," Jack said, shaking his hand. "How's it going?"

"My heart is still broken that your beautiful mother married the brave commander instead of me," he said, dramatically resting his hand over his heart, "but otherwise, I'm surviving, my young friend."

Chuckling, Jack placed his hands on his hips. "I know you were a very close second to Dad, Antonio. If she didn't love him so much, she definitely would've chosen you."

"The words ease my old heart, boy," he said, bowing. "And who do we have here?"

"I'm Rowena," she said, extending her hand.

"Well, hello, Rowena. It's lovely to meet you."

"This is my brother, Brecken. He's surly. That's what my mom says when he comes over and doesn't want to talk to us. *'Your brother is a bit surly today, Rowena. Best to leave him alone,'*" she said, mimicking her mother's voice.

"There are four more just like her," Brecken said, his tone droll as he shook Antonio's hand. "You can understand my need for peace and quiet."

Chuckling, Antonio gave a nod. "Indeed." Beckoning them toward his tent, he stepped behind the table and gestured toward the gorgeous paintings. Landscapes, portraits and surreal masterpieces were all on display. "Would you like a painting for your mother, Callie? On the house for you, my dear."

"I'd never take one without paying you, Antonio," Callie said with a cheeky grin, "but I will be back to buy one sometime soon. Zadicus's parents love paintings, and I plan to buy them one of yours once I'm betrothed."

"Yes, I'm so happy to hear you have an ardent admirer, my dear," he said, clasping his hands in front of his chest. "I'm thrilled for you. Now, we have to find a nice young lady for our worthy lieutenant to bond with."

"The lieutenant is just fine flying solo right now, Antonio, but thanks," Jack said, his tone gently warning the man not to push it. "And I'll come back and check out the paintings one day soon. For now, we're heading into town to have a relaxing night off."

Antonio grinned as a woman approached his booth, appraising one of the paintings off to the side.

"Hello, ma'am," he said, pointing to the painting. "That one is on sale, and I've also reduced the price of this smaller print." He gestured toward the print that sat in a display holder on the table.

The woman craned her neck but didn't step closer. Tentatively, her gaze darted toward Callie before she shook her head. "I'll come back later. Thank you."

Callie's expression fell, and Brecken felt something well in his chest. As he observed the situation, he realized it was empathy. It was obvious the woman was wary of Callie, and Brecken felt the sudden need to protect her somehow.

"I'm Brecken," he said, extending his hand. "Son of Maddox and Wren. I live on the south side of the compound."

"I'm familiar with it," she said, unmoving as she assessed him. "I live on the north side near the cattle farms."

"I'm Jack, son of Latimus and Lila. I thought I'd met everyone who lived on Lynia at this point. Have we crossed paths before?"

"No," she said, not taking his hand either as her eyes darted to Callie. "I am thankful for your father and all he does to protect the kingdom. My husband was killed in the war against Crimeous. The Deamon Lord was an evil soul, and I fear there is more destruction to come."

"The future can be daunting," Callie said softly, taking a step forward. The woman recoiled and began to back away. Showing her palms, Callie shook her head. "I didn't mean to scare you."

"You are a vestige of Crimeous and a child of a terrible prophecy," the woman said, clutching her purse. "You should be locked away until Bakari is defeated."

"I have no desire to align with Bakari, ma'am—"

"Hateful creature!" the woman hissed before spitting on the ground. "Your existence denigrates my dear husband's soul." With an angry jerk of her head, she pivoted and walked away.

"My dear," Antonio said, his blue eyes filled with sympathy. "She doesn't know of what she speaks. Don't pay her any attention."

"It's okay," Callie said, her voice gravelly as her throat bobbed. "I'm used to it by now. Our people have been through a lot, and I'm a reminder of that pain. She has a right to her feelings."

"Fear leads to ignorance sometimes," Jack said, rubbing her shoulder. "Hopefully, once we defeat Bakari, this stuff won't happen."

"Yeah," she said, her lips forming a smile that didn't quite meet her eyes. "Well, let's see who else I can terrorize. As much as I hate scaring the living crap out of people, I'm starving, so we're heading into the street fair whether they like it or not."

"Go on, and have a good time, my friends," Antonio said, shooing them away. "And if anyone gives you trouble, you just let ol' Antonio know."

"Thank you," she whispered as her smile grew, and Brecken admired her strength. He'd always imagined Callie lived a charmed life since her parents were royals and hadn't considered what it must be like to live as the subject of a cataclysmic prophecy. Did people shun her often? She seemed resigned to the woman's treatment of her. Brecken admired her restraint. If anyone spoke to him like that, he'd certainly give them a piece of his mind. And if it were a man, he might subject his nose to a piece of his fist too.

"Oh, I see the science booth!" Rowena exclaimed before jogging ahead.

Jack smiled at Callie and jerked his head. "Come on. She's not worth it, Callie."

"I know. See you later, Antonio," she said, taking a step before staring at her shoe. "Go on. My sneaker is untied. I'll catch up."

Jack followed Rowena, but Brecken was frozen for some reason. Staring down at her as she tied her shoe, he had the sudden urge to stroke her hair. To soothe her and reassure her everything was going to be okay.

"All right," she said, rising and flashing him a brilliant smile. "Shoe is secured, and I'm ready to go."

Tilting his head, he studied her. "You handled that very well, princess."

"Ew. Don't call me that," she said, scrunching her nose. "I hate it, and also my dad calls my mom that, so it's really weird."

Breathing a laugh, he nodded. "Noted. I'm just impressed, that's all."

Shrugging, she turned and began walking while Brecken fell into step beside her. "It's happened all my life. Well, since we moved back here from L.A. People are scared of me, or think I'm a freak, or both. But my parents taught me that I can't control people's actions. I can only control my reaction, so that's what I do." She glanced up at him, and Brecken forced himself to focus on her sparkling eyes, which were almost as alluring as those sparkly lips. "Plus, we're royalty and have to set an example. So, I just deal with it."

"Like Jack said, hopefully, the burden will ease when we defeat Bakari. My father died in an ambush from one of his Deamon battalions when he was on a scouting mission over a decade ago. One of the slimy bastards shot him point-blank in the chest with an eight-shooter. He never stood a chance."

"Oh, Brecken, I'm so sorry," she said, her expression filled with such compassion he felt it wrap around his skin like a warm blanket. "And you have five sisters to look after. No wonder you put up with Zadicus. Now, I get it."

Lifting his eyebrows, he said, "I don't think you're supposed to speak about your future betrothed that way."

"Oh, I'm not saying it in a mean way," she said in a reassuring tone. "He knows he's stuffy and can be a bit dismissive sometimes. We've talked about it. He's working on it, but it takes time, especially when you're raised an aristocrat in the 'old world' mentality."

"I think your influence is good on him," Brecken said. "I'm happy you two found each other."

"Me too," she said wistfully. "I was sure I was going to die a washed-up spinster. Thank the goddess someone was willing to look past the prophecy and court me." Her tone was teasing, but Brecken understood the underlying context. Somewhere along the way, Callie had begun to believe she was unlovable. It nearly broke his usually impassive heart, considering she was kind and compassionate and one of the most gorgeous women he'd ever met.

Gazing down at her, Brecken felt a sudden sense of loss. What if they'd met under different circumstances? What if he'd been the first man to show interest in her? Would she have been open to dating a man far beneath her station who couldn't even fathom living the lavish lifestyle she was used to?

Deciding it never would've happened, Brecken pushed the thoughts away. Some things were just too far from reality. A royal princess didn't date blue-collar rural Vampyres from outlying compounds no matter how progressive their queen was. Brecken was a realist and understood his place in the world, and it was clear he and Callie didn't orbit the same circles.

Still, it was fun to imagine it for a moment. Holding her and being draped in all that long, silky hair while they were locked in a passionate embrace. Although he was pragmatic, he wouldn't lie to himself about wanting her. If he lived in a world where he had the chance to touch her, he'd latch on and never let go.

But he didn't live in that world, and neither did she, so he walked beside her, genuinely wishing she would find happiness with Zadicus. Perhaps writing the letters would help secure her happiness, and if they did, was it really such a terrible thing to do in the scheme of things?

Yes. The word floated through his brain, and his lips flattened. Yes, it was wrong. And Brecken had the strange feeling that the more he grew to know Callie, the worse he would feel about deceiving her. Feeling the aversion flow in his veins, he let it surge, understanding he deserved to feel like an ass because, well, he was one.

"Oh, she's so excited about the meteorites!" Callie called, pointing at Rowena as she stood in front of the science booth examining the rock. "Let me see." Approaching the booth, she smiled as Rowena held up the stone. Callie's excitement was as palpable as his sister's, and the weight of his deception sat on his shoulders, an unwanted but necessary burden.

"Well, they're excited about a bunch of rocks. Low bar, huh?" Jack teased, walking over.

"Yeah," Brecken said, rubbing his forehead.

"Come on. Let's check out the blacksmith's booth. He makes excellent swords and sparring weapons."

Nodding, Brecken followed his friend, pretending to examine the swords while watching Callie out of the corner of his eye the entire time.

Chapter 6

Bakari, son of Vampyre King Markdor and Queen Calla, sat at the desk in the cottage on the outskirts of the former Deamon caves. The cottage had been his home for years now and was protected by the invisibility shield Dr. Tyson concocted from a mix of chemicals and several hairs Bakari had collected from Evie's daughter, Rinada. The hybrid scientist was an expert at manipulating molecules to make various weapons and potions for Bakari, which added to his usefulness—for the time being anyway.

Bakari's ears pricked, and he straightened, head snapping toward the door. A moment later, he heard the crunch of leaves and branches outside. Rising, he stalked toward the door and pulled it open.

"Get in here before you're detected by one of Latimus's drones," Bakari ordered.

"Sorry," Zadicus said, frustration in his tone. "I can never find your house. The invisibility cloak is too good."

Closing the door, Bakari whirled around. "You're never to contact me unless I summon you. Showing up unannounced is dangerous and could ruin everything."

"I had no other way to contact you since we can't use phones or email as Heden and Sofia are so skilled at tracking devices. I'm sorry, but I felt the need to update you."

Worry began to spread in Bakari's chest. "Fine. We're shielded now that we're inside and the door is closed. Sit," he said, gesturing to the couch.

Once they were seated at each end, Zadicus cleared his throat.

"I am still on track to bond with Callie. I plan to propose to her on our eleven-month anniversary," he said, his tone devoid of passion. "I have devised a plan that will help move things along. She seemed enthralled by my gallant gestures when we began courting, but I fear the excitement is wearing off. Hopefully, this new tactic will help."

Bakari arched a brow. "You said wooing her would be easy."

Sighing, he rubbed his forehead. "I thought it would be, considering no one has ever courted her before. But we are very different people, and that is beginning to show."

"Well, then, I hope your new tactic works. I would ask you if you need help, but that wasn't part of our deal. You assured me you could win her over, Zadicus."

"Of course I can," Zadicus said, waving his hand. "I just felt you should know. I'll get her across the finish line. She's just so...*free-spirited*." His features contorted. "It's unbecoming and not what I anticipated from a daughter of royals."

Laughing, Bakari ran a hand over his black hair. "She is a stubborn young woman whose veins pulse with Crimeous's blood. What did you expect?"

"I expected a boring, biddable woman," Zadicus said, crossing his ankle over his thigh, waggling his foot as he scowled. "Aristocrats of my stature at Valeria envision bonding with respectful, supplicant females."

"You knew what you were signing up for when we devised this plan, Zadicus. If you want to back out, tell me now. I've had enough dissenters over the years. The one thing I admire about your Aunt Melania is that she was forthright enough to leave the cause and admit she didn't have the constitution to carry out my plan. I prefer that to someone who can't get the job done."

"I'll get it done," Zadicus snapped, "and I would urge you—"

The man gasped before clutching his throat as Bakari assessed him, cold and unyielding.

"I am the son of King Markdor and Queen Calla and future ruler of this realm. I would caution you not to speak to me in that tone again."

Zadicus nodded furiously before Bakari released his telekinetic hold on the man's throat. Watching the Vampyre sputter as he strove to catch his breath brought Bakari great pleasure. Once his struggles abated, Bakari sighed.

"We must be aligned," he said, lifting his chin in the austere manner he'd acquired over the centuries. "For our plan to work, you must bond with Callie, impregnate her and bring the child to me. I will barter her child's safety for her alliance with our cause. A mother's bond is the strongest I've ever seen. It is the only thing I can fathom that would make her dissent from her family. Once we have her acquiescence, we will complete the prophecy, and I can finally kill the royals, cementing my place as ruler of the immortal realm."

"Every mother but your own," Zadicus murmured.

Bristling, Bakari inched closer and spoke through clenched teeth. "What did you say?"

"Your mother cast you out to the human world and resumed her life as if you never existed. Let's hope Callie has more care for her own child—"

Lurching from the couch, Bakari stood, backhanding Zadicus before he rose and pressed his hand to his rapidly self-healing bleeding lip.

"If you touch me again, our agreement is off," Zadicus declared.

"Don't forget what you have to gain here, Zadicus. I have promised you governorship over all the compounds once I defeat the royal family. Your lust for approval by the aristocrats of the kingdom makes no sense to me, but I care not what motivates you as long as you accomplish your mission."

"My family has been overlooked for years by the royal family. They should've made me governor instead of Camron all those years ago, when Sathan named him to the position. Aunt Melania did her best to cement her place as a respected member of the council when she married Camron, but that will never be enough. I have been shunned by the royal family for too long. We both have."

"Yes," Bakari said, stepping back to create space between them. "Our goals are aligned. It is why I approached you in the first place. Callie often feels isolated and misunderstood in this world, and you have done an excellent job seducing her. We're extremely close to accomplishing our mission. Have you slept with her yet?"

He huffed and rubbed the back of his neck. "She made some asinine pact with her mother she would wait until the night of her bonding ceremony."

Bakari's lips twitched, and he realized it was in admiration.

"You have affection for her," Zadicus said, eyes narrowing. "Perhaps it is *you* who won't be able to complete the mission."

"Don't be ridiculous. I've observed her since she was born. I feel a certain...fondness for her," he said, circling his hand, "because I sense her restlessness and feelings of not belonging. They are familiar to what I felt in my youth. But when the time comes, I will do what I must."

"Kill her," he said, his voice low. "You'll kill them all."

"It must be done," Bakari said with a nod. "They are a pestilence on this kingdom. Their fondness for humans and desire to breed hybrids..." He grimaced, wiping a hand over his face. "It is appalling. I cannot let it go on. My parents' legacy deserves better. Immortals deserve a leader who will uphold eons of tradition and return the kingdom to greatness."

"And a governor like me who shares those views," Zadicus said before striding to the door. "I'll get her across the finish line and give you the child you seek." He pulled open the door before Bakari called his name.

"Yes?"

"You're still willing to give up the child you conceive?"

He scoffed. "I want no child with Crimeous's blood. I want a purebred Vampyre, with the royal, aristocratic blood of a Valerian. Once Callie and the child are dead, I will marry someone with a pristine bloodline who is biddable and respectable."

"Good," Bakari said, giving a dismissive nod. "Remember that we need her alive to align with me and fulfill the prophecy. She must not be harmed as we carry out our plan."

"Understood." With a final salute, Zadicus exited the cottage.

Bakari took a moment to digest the conversation before striding from the cottage and approaching the nearby cave. Latimus and Kenden had attempted to destroy all the Deamon caves after Crimeous's defeat, but thankfully, some were left unscathed. The entrance to the cave where Commander Vadik lived with the Deamon troops was also masked by the invisibility cloak. Waving his hand, the cave's entrance appeared, and Bakari entered.

He trailed through the darkened walkway until he arrived at the expansive dwelling where the soldiers resided. His cloned Deamon army was now exceedingly strong and formidable. Approaching Vadik, the soldier stood and saluted.

"Hello, King Bakari."

"Commander Vadik," he said with a nod. "I trust the soldiers are doing well in their training exercises."

"Yes," he replied with a curt tilt of his head.

"Excellent," Bakari said, glancing over the troops who mulled about in the cave. "Calinda will have a child in less than two years' time if all goes according to plan. That is when we will strike. One final battle to end this conflict once and for all."

"You have been patient, Bakari," a female voice said over his shoulder. "I am impressed. I sometimes wondered if you would rush the outcome."

"Time has different meaning when one is immortal, Ananda," he said, turning to face the woman, her skin marred and wrinkled under white hair since she'd gone through her immortal change later in life. "I would rather do things right than quickly."

"Very wise indeed, although the immortals have been valiant foes. I am humble enough to admit I underestimated them. Every toxin you've created to kill the Slayers has been remedied with an antidote from Sadie and Nolan almost immediately. You've had many skirmishes but haven't been able to beat them by brute force."

"I realized years ago the only way we would prevail was to gain Calinda's alliance—whether it be by choice or by force. The Elven prophecy discovered in the hidden scrolls carries much significance. I have been preparing the Deamon troops and injecting them with Dr. Tyson's potions to increase their muscle tone and strength. When we have the final battle, all pieces will be in place, and we will emerge victorious."

Closing the distance, she regarded both men who towered above her. "I will be happy once the conflict is over. I only want to live in peace in a realm restored to its former glory. One without hybrids and impure bloodlines. My niece's children are a disgrace, as is her entire family."

"On that, we are all agreed," Bakari said, cupping her shoulder. Ananda had become a mother figure of sorts in the years he'd known her, although she was too coldhearted to ever inspire true deep affection. "I will be king, Vadik will be Commander, Zadicus will govern the compounds and you will finally be able to move back into your ancestral home at Astaria and live out the rest of your days in peace."

"May the goddess make it so," she said softly.

Solemn in their united goal, the three members of Bakari's alliance basked in the hope that the prophecy would come true and Etherya's Earth would flourish once again.

Chapter 7

A few days after the street fair, Callie took the train to Valeria to see Zadicus. He'd asked her to dinner and promised the servants would set up a lovely table in the garden so they could eat under the stars. Wrinkling her nose, Callie admitted she would've preferred he set up the dinner himself, but she wouldn't hold it against him. It was the thought that counted, and she was happy he wanted to give her a special evening.

When she arrived, a servant took her light jacket, offering to bring it to her if she got cold later on. Thanking him, she went in search of Zadicus, finding him in the garden leaning over and smelling one of the beautiful red roses.

"Look at you enjoying nature," she teased, approaching and glancing at the roses. "They're beautiful."

He plucked one, causing her to emit a huff. "Oh, no, don't—"

"For you," he said, handing it to her. "From one beautiful flower to another."

Callie had to legitimately contain her laugh at the cheesy words and lifted the rose to her nose to hide her lips. Someone cleared their throat in the distance, and she glanced over, noticing Brecken pressing his lips together, trying like hell not to laugh. Goddess, he must've heard Zadicus's terrible line too. Crinkling her features, she shot him a playful glare before focusing back on Zadicus.

"I didn't want you to pluck it, but now that you have, I'll say thank you."

"Why?" he asked, perplexed.

"Because once you pluck it, it dies, Zadicus. I wanted it to live with the rest of its friends in the garden."

"Only you would accuse a flower of having friends, Callie," he said, extending his hand. She took it, and he led her to the table that was set up along the row of neatly trimmed hedges. "It's a plant, for the goddess's sake."

He pulled out her chair, and she sat, resting the rose on the table as she settled into the seat. When he sat down across from her, she smiled.

"That's one more difference between us, Zadicus. You see a plant where I see a living thing. Each tree and bush and flower has their own energy signature if you look close enough."

Spreading his napkin over his lap, his eyes narrowed. "Whatever you say, sweetheart. I had the cook prepare a nice dinner for us. I'm starting to enjoy food very much. I only ever drank Slayer blood before you, although my mother has always enjoyed food even though we don't need it."

Realizing he was done with the plant discussion, she rested her elbows on the table. "Yes, us hybrids need food and Slayer blood for sustenance. I guess we're mutts, in a sense."

"Your mother's Vampyre blood is so pure," he said, rubbing his chin. "My aristocratic blood will help enhance it when we have children."

Swallowing thickly, Callie let the seriousness of the statement wash over her. "That would mean you're planning to ask me to bond with you."

"Well, yes, sweetheart," he said, lifting his shoulders. "What do you think we were doing here? We've almost been together for a year. That's certainly enough time to be sure we're right for each other."

Callie wasn't so sure, but her desire to be with someone...to be *loved*...was intense, and she truly did appreciate Zadicus's efforts. She enjoyed spending time with him, and her heart always thrummed during their passionate kisses. Betrothal and bonding were the next natural steps. She'd always known this and expected it. In fact, she'd looked forward to it when they first began courting. Now? Well, her excitement had waned immensely, which worried her.

He asked her about her day, and they slipped into conversation, although Callie's thoughts lingered on her hesitations. After her discussion with Jack at the street fair, she wondered if she was moving too quickly with Zadicus. Was a year too soon to get engaged?

After dinner, they conversed as they finished their bottle of wine. Callie relaxed as the wine coursed through her veins, reminding herself to enjoy the moment. She shortened the stem of the rose and stuck it behind her ear, pleased when Zadicus's eyes flared with appreciation. Settling into the moment, she told herself to calm her fears. Things would work out if she let them progress naturally. She'd always believed that, so why stop now?

When they finished, Zadicus took her for a stroll around the garden and drew her into a fervent kiss. Callie kissed him back, annoyed when her thoughts drifted to Brecken. Was he watching them? Somehow, the idea rankled her, and when she drew back, she glanced around, relieved she couldn't see him. He must've wanted to give them a bit of privacy and was probably flanked along the side of the mansion.

Eventually, Zadicus walked her to the train. Brecken trailed several paces behind, far enough away to go unnoticed, but she felt his presence anyway. It was that strange energy she always felt between them, and it registered in every pore of her skin as they strolled. When she turned to walk down the train platform stairs, Zadicus grabbed her hand and stuck an envelope in her palm.

"What's this?" she asked, grinning.

"A letter. Read it when you're home in your bedroom and think of me. Good night, sweetheart." Leaning down, he kissed her cheek.

"Good night. Thank you for a lovely dinner."

She followed his directive, not opening the letter until she was at home with her face washed, teeth brushed and in her comfy PJs. Sitting on the edge of her bed, she opened the envelope and pulled out the letter.

My Dearest Callie,

Since my first attempt at poetry was dreadful, I thought I'd try my hand at writing you love letters. It's something I've never done before, but you deserve nothing less than sweet words of devotion.

For this first letter, I wanted to remark on your beauty. Yes, there will be other letters where I will go deeper, but for now, I'll focus on how gorgeous you are inside and out. Sometimes, when you look at me with those stunning ocean-colored eyes, I struggle to breathe. They're always filled with kindness and a slight bit of mischief, which makes me wonder where you got your sense of humor. It's quite attractive, and I enjoy your playful self-deprecation and teasing. As you know, I'm quite stoic and appreciate having someone like you around to remind me life doesn't always have to be so serious.

And your lips. Sometimes, they shine under the late-afternoon sunlight after you've covered them in gloss, and my mind can't focus on anything else but kissing you. Perhaps you've employed your powers against me, for you've put me under a spell I never want to break.

And finally, there is your generous spirit, which is most beautiful of all. You're able to look upon those who castigate you with compassion and scold anyone who speaks to servants or soldiers without respect. It is a magnificent quality that many might not even know you possess. But I know, and it solidifies how lucky I am to be your suitor. Hopefully, one day, I will be your bonded. I will continue to write you these letters to ensure it happens.

Love,
Zadicus

Callie finished the letter and then read it again, impressed with Zadicus's soulful words. It was much better than the poem he'd written her and called to the teenage girl deep within who'd never been asked to dance.

"He thinks you're beautiful," she said, folding the letter and gently rubbing it with her fingers. "It's very sweet."

Trailing to her desk, she placed the letter on top of the folded poem he'd also written, heart full from his romantic gesture. She would certainly tell him how lovely it was next time they were together. It appeared he planned to write her more, which warmed her heart.

Sliding into bed, Callie turned off the lamp and snuggled under the covers. Settling into her dreams, she was too tired to question why it was Brecken's handsome face she saw admiring her sparkly lip gloss instead of the man to which she would soon become betrothed.

Chapter 8

Zadicus continued his courtship of Callie, and she focused on being open to his lavish gifts and fervent devotion. As the weeks wore on, she knew they were moving toward inevitable betrothal, and her concerns lingered. She couldn't decide if they stemmed from true misgivings or if they were just commitment jitters considering Zadicus was her first ever suitor. A part of her felt guilty for having doubts. After all, Zadicus was known as one of the greatest catches in the kingdom, and he'd set his sights on her. Even with the prophecy that loomed large, he wanted her. It was evidence of his genuineness, and she reminded herself of this when the reservations surfaced.

Of course, it didn't help that Callie had begun having highly sexualized dreams about a certain bodyguard whose presence she always felt even when he couldn't be seen. She had no idea why her mind wandered to Brecken in the dark of night considering the man barely acknowledged her.

She tried to speak to him on occasion, when he accompanied them into Valeria's main square or during other functions she attended with Zadicus. He would always look at her with those deep bronze eyes and remain silent until Zadicus urged her along. On the scant occasions he did reply, it was with one-word mumbles and grunts. He certainly was a man of few words, and Callie figured remaining silent was a requirement of his job, so she let it lie.

Zadicus continued to write her beautiful letters that certainly helped alleviate her fears they were moving too fast. The letters gave her a glimpse into his head and confirmed he was indeed getting to know her on a deeper level.

He also made an effort to attend some functions with her, although she suspected he didn't have the same desire to help the citizens of the kingdom as she did—especially the ones on the rural compounds. But his family always donated generously to the army, and she accepted there were many ways people could help their fellow immortals.

Zadicus did attend one of Lila's library functions with her, which warmed her heart. Her aunt ran literacy programs throughout the kingdom and was determined to teach every member of the realm to read. She often held events on the outlying compounds, and during one such event, Callie offered to help. Zadicus tagged along, although he sat in the corner most of the day, explaining he needed to help solidify the invite list for a lavish party his mother was planning to throw.

"You go on and help Lila, sweetheart," he said, urging her toward the center of the large room. "I'll be here if you need me."

Callie joined her aunt and proceeded to spend hours helping the laborers who'd shown up. They represented all age ranges, and she was thrilled at the turnout. Brecken stood off to the side, hands crossed over his belt as he observed. The only moment he broke rank was when Rowena showed up and ran to him, giving him a hug before jogging over to Callie.

"I brought some books to donate," she said excitedly, pulling them from her bag. "They're fifth-grade science books, and since I'm the youngest, we don't need them anymore. Mom says she's popped out her last kid."

Chuckling, Callie took the books, recognizing some of them as the old textbooks she'd used in school. "This is fantastic, Rowena. Thank you for donating. Do you want to help us teach the others?"

Her brown eyes widened, so similar to Brecken's, and she nodded. "I'd love that. I want to be a professor one day."

"Awesome. Come on—I'll get you set up." After she was situated with several citizens, Callie approached Brecken, flashing a brilliant smile. "Your sister's awesome. Guess it's possible for *some* people in your family to have an outgoing personality."

He gave her a droll look, causing her to snicker. "Sorry, I'm sure you're really exciting when you're off duty."

"Excitement's overrated," he muttered, returning his gaze to the center of the room.

"No way." She scrunched her features. "I crave excitement. I can't wait to get back to the human world and see all the places I haven't been yet. Zadicus says he's going to take me there on our honeymoon once we bond and once we've hopefully defeated Bakari."

His expression remained impassive. "That's nice. Congratulations."

Breathing a laugh, she shook her head. "Don't you want to see other things? There's so much out there to explore."

Rust-colored eyes drifted to hers, locking on as her breath caught in her throat. "Some don't have the luxury of traveling the world. I have to work, and I enjoy working. That's enough for me."

"Anyone can make something happen if they wish," she said, lifting a finger. "I'm sure it wouldn't kill you to take a few days off."

He remained silent, causing her to emit a huff. "Oh, fine. Stand here against the wall and frown all day. Sounds exhilarating."

His lips twitched, and she grinned, elated she'd gotten the small reaction out of him. Lila called her over to help, and she sauntered away, determined to continue to try and crack the serious soldier.

That evening, Callie rode the train home, and Zadicus pressed another letter into her palm. She read it on the train, her heart full as she cherished the romantic words.

My Dearest Callie,

I must remark on how gorgeous you were the night we had dinner in the garden. When you placed the rose behind your ear and smiled, I realized I'd never seen anything more beautiful. Sometimes, my eyes linger on your cute half-fangs and I imagine how they would feel against my vein. As you may have guessed, I am enamored with your mouth, your lips and all facets of your stunning beauty.

I was taken by your idea that plants are living beings with unique energy signatures, just as we are. Forgive me for first dismissing it. After some thought, it makes perfect sense and only highlights your compassion. The way you use your powers to heal animals speaks volumes about your character. You've told me how physically taxing it is, but you continue to help animals in need even if it causes you temporary pain. It is selfless, and I am honored to be with someone with such a benevolent heart.

I realize I will never be worthy of you, but I will try my best to be the man you inspire me to be. I am thankful for your affection, but perhaps even more grateful for your friendship.

Love,

Zadicus

Callie folded the letter, pleased at the tender words. She was slowly coming to see Zadicus in a new light with the missives and was glad he took the time to write them. She craved a lover who was also her best friend, which required cultivation considering they were quite different, and was happy to receive confirmation he felt the same. It went a long way toward squelching her doubts, and she settled into the plushy train seat, excited for the future with her surprisingly eloquent suitor.

Brecken arrived at Zadicus's home shortly after sunrise, admitting he was in a terrible mood. He'd been writing letters to Callie for weeks and was slowly realizing something quite disconcerting: he was falling under the spell of the woman his ward was going to marry.

Of course, he'd never meant it to happen. Attraction was one thing, and Brecken had always accepted his attraction to Callie. She was a beautiful, charming woman, and being drawn to that was natural for any man. But over these past weeks, as he'd observed her and truly gotten to know her, he'd seen past the attraction to the woman within. And what he observed was, in a word, *magnificent*.

Never had he met someone with her combination of humor, charisma and compassion. She devoted her time to healing animals and helping others learn to read, all while charming his sister, who claimed to be her best friend.

"I'm pretty sure Callie already has a best friend," he'd muttered to Rowena one night as they sat on the porch at his mother's house.

"Who?" she asked, shrugging. "Jack, maybe. They're really close. Not Zadicus though. He barely spoke to her at the library. She's really nice, but sometimes, people are mean to her. It's annoying because she's super-cool, so I've decided I'm going to be her best friend."

"You're not worried about the prophecy? That she'll destroy the world?" Lifting his hands, he playfully shook them, mocking being scared.

"No way," Rowena said, waving her hand. "When we learned about the prophecy in school, the teacher insisted it was very vague. I'm not scared of some old scrolls."

"Well, that's very progressive of you, but not everyone shares your view."

Huffing, she crossed her arms and sat back in the chair. "I'll change this kingdom one day. You mark my words. Queen Miranda is going to love me, and I'll help her and Evie bring equality and practicality to the kingdom."

Brecken smiled at his sister, knowing she would accomplish anything she set her mind to. Her words about Callie rang true: many people in the kingdom shunned her because they were worried about the prophecy. Even with that knowledge, she forged ahead, helping her people. She seemed guided by genuine purpose to help others and to help animals, and he admired her ability to help people who castigated her. Others might have railed at the world, but not Callie. She somehow brushed it off and carried on with her life, which impressed the hell out of Brecken.

As the letters increased in frequency and he got to know her better, he understood they were no longer a ruse. Instead, they were his small way of telling her how special she was, even if she would never know they came from him. Entering Zadicus's large sitting room, Brecken strode to his place in the corner, waiting for his ward to appear. They were going to town to pick up some flowers for his mother's dinner party later that evening. Brecken had no idea why they didn't just cut them from the multitudes of flowers in the garden, but who was he to question aristocrats' actions?

Silently waiting, he recalled the last letter he'd written to Callie. Closing his eyes, the words scrolled through his mind:

My Dearest Callie,

I find it hard to articulate just how seamlessly you've drawn me under your spell. Never did I expect it, but I find myself barely able to think of anything but you. So often, my thoughts will drift to your sparkling cobalt eyes or your mellifluous laugh, and before I know it, I'm lost in you once again.

Observing you teach the citizens to read warmed my heart, and I was especially taken with your interactions with the teenagers. Some of them have already dropped out of school to help their parents at home, and your determination to ensure they have access to education is admirable. Sometimes, you speak of the unknowns of having your own children since they will inevitably inherit some of your powers, but you don't need to worry, Callie-lily. Your gracious heart and natural intuition will serve them well, and they will be lucky to call you Mom.

I am excited to see what the future will hold. You deserve nothing but happiness, and I will do everything in my power to ensure you receive it.

Love,

Zadicus

Lifting his lids, Brecken smirked at the nickname he'd fashioned. His mother's favorite flower was the calla lily, and it seemed fitting for Callie. Of course, she thought Zadicus had penned the name, which rankled him, but he left it in the letter anyway. Perhaps as a small indication of his affection for her, even if she would never know.

"Good morning," Zadicus said, breezing into the room. "I'll be ready to head to town in five minutes."

Brecken gave a nod. "We're going to the florist on Main Street?"

"Actually, no." Rummaging around on the desk, he filtered through some papers. "We're going to buy Callie a betrothal ring. I made up the bit about the flowers so I don't ruin the surprise."

The words caused Brecken's heart to slam in his chest, and he resisted the urge to rub the sting. This was bound to happen eventually, and he'd thought himself prepared for their betrothal. Apparently, his heart had other ideas. Inwardly commanding the pounding to cease, he tilted his head.

"I thought you would give her one of the rings from the family's collection."

"No," he said, absently shaking his head. "I've decided to buy her something new. Something more fitting for her remarkable bloodline."

Although the sentiment seemed genuine, Brecken thought he heard a twinge of distain in his ward's voice at the word "remarkable."

"Your letters have helped immensely," Zadicus continued, stacking papers as he organized. "And she's none the wiser, thank the goddess. I wasn't sure if I should rewrite them, but when I compared our handwriting, it was almost identical. Perhaps one thing we actually have in common." Glancing his way, Zadicus arched an eyebrow.

"Perhaps," Brecken muttered, inwardly remarking they were indeed as different as two men could be. For starters, he'd never deceive his girlfriend the way Zadicus deceived Callie.

But you are deceiving her...

The words filtered through his brain, causing him to clench his jaw. Goddess, he hated the fact he had any hand in the ruse. At first, he'd justified it because it had secured his mother's job, which she was happily settled into and thriving. As the weeks progressed and the guilt began to gnaw at him, he continued to justify his actions by acknowledging he was doing what was best for Callie. After all, he wanted her to be happy. She seemed to genuinely care for Zadicus and often spoke of how wonderful it was to be courted. She was ready to settle down and bond, and Zadicus fit perfectly into her world.

Nowhere in their reality did there exist a possibility where Brecken could court her instead. They might as well have come from two different planets. Callie, with her royal heritage and wanderlust, who dreamed of traveling the world. Brecken from a modest, rural family with no path toward ever being anything but a working class soldier. He just couldn't imagine a scenario where it could happen.

So he wrote the letters, hoping it would push her toward happiness. Zadicus was wealthy and could offer her everything her heart desired. Although he was eccentric, he was kind to her, except for the deception with the letters, which irked Brecken. But Zadicus admitted he was terrible at writing and only wanted to woo Callie in every way she deserved. The justification was enough for Brecken, although it had recently begun to wear thin. Realizing this was an opportunity to end the uncomfortable arrangement, Brecken cleared his throat.

"Once she accepts your betrothal, I assume you won't need me to write the letters anymore."

Zadicus looked up from his missive. "No. I'll relieve you of the duty. Your mother's position is secure, and you've earned it. Callie adores the letters, and they've accomplished the task. I appreciate your efforts."

Brecken nodded, feeling the melancholy wash over him at the knowledge he'd never have the opportunity to pen more letters to the woman who now consumed his thoughts. Perhaps he would write her one more—a secret letter in which he'd finally tell her everything he wished to say. Yes, that would bring him some closure and be quite cathartic.

Grinning, he realized how much he'd changed in the span of a few weeks. Brecken had never needed closure or felt desire to write secret letters to any of the women he'd casually courted in the past. But Callie was different, and he wasn't too proud to admit she'd had a profound effect on him. Somehow, she'd tunneled her way into his heart and cracked open a door that had been firmly sealed. It was humbling for someone with his unemotional nature, and he admired the headstrong woman who'd elicited the change. Although he was ashamed of his deception, he was grateful for the opportunity to get to know her.

"Come," Zadicus said, dragging him from the thoughts as he padded across the room. "Let's head to town. Time to get this over with."

Brecken thought it strange he saw the task as a chore considering picking out a bonding ring for Callie would bring him great pleasure. But they were different men, and Zadicus had probably seen more fancy jewelry in his lifetime than Brecken could imagine. What was one more ring to add to the pile? Perhaps it was commonplace to someone as wealthy as Zadicus.

Following his ward, they headed into the bright, warm day and began the trek to Valeria's main square.

Chapter 9

Two months later

Callie gazed into the mirror as Glarys tugged and maneuvered the mass of dark curls upon her head. After one particularly hard tug, she uttered an "*ouch*" before Glarys's eyes grew wide.

"Oh, I'm sorry, dear," she said, concern in her ice-blue eyes. "Too rough?"

"Yeah," Callie said, grinning into the reflection. "I'd like to keep half of it attached to my scalp."

"Of course, dear. I'll be more careful. Your hair is so gorgeous, and I want it to be perfect for your wedding day."

Callie ruminated on the upcoming ceremony, now only hours away, and gulped the water in her slightly shaking hand. Everything had happened so fast over the past few weeks, and she'd been swept up in the excitement. Zadicus had bought her a lovely diamond ring and given her a sweet proposal where he'd lowered to one knee and asked her to bond.

She'd stared at him with equal parts excitement and trepidation as she contemplated her answer. In that moment, the memories of their courtship flashed through her mind, and she realized he'd given her everything she'd ever craved. Most importantly, she cherished his heartfelt letters, which showcased a window into his soul she didn't see when they were together. It showed his vulnerability, being able to open himself that way, and Callie found it so thoughtful. Pushing her reservations aside, she'd agreed to become his bonded mate.

Now, sitting in front of the mirror as Glarys styled her hair, the doubts were surfacing once more, causing little pricks of anxiety to pulse in her stomach.

"It's okay to be nervous, sweetie," Glarys said, hands fussing with her curls. "I remember how anxious Latimus was on the day of his bonding ceremony to Lila, although he'd never admit it. These big events can be intimidating."

"Were you nervous on either of your bonding ceremony days?"

Glarys's lips pursed. "No," she said, shaking her head, "but I felt so comfortable with Victor and Sam. I never believed in soul mates until I met them, but I'm extremely lucky to have had two."

"Sam's such a sweetheart, and he's pretty hot, Glarys," Callie said with a wink. "I love that you're the older woman. I need pointers from you."

"Oh, hush with that nonsense," she said, cheeks growing red under her snow white hair. "I still sometimes wonder why he wants me when he could have any woman he set his sights on."

"Because you're amazing."

"Well, thank you, sweetie," she said, palming Callie's shoulder. "I think I'm all finished. Do you like it?"

"I do," Callie said, turning her head to look at the half-updo. "I think the style will compliment my dress."

Squeezing her shoulder, Glarys gave her a knowing look. "If you want to take a few minutes to walk along the river, I could cover for you. It might be good to take some time alone with your thoughts."

Rotating on the stool, Callie gazed up at the sage woman. "Really? That would be awesome."

"Sure thing," was her kind reply as she stroked Callie's cheek. "Go on through the back door, and I'll tell everyone you're touching up your makeup one last time."

"Thank you, Glarys," she said, standing and placing a kiss on her cheek. "I love you so much."

"I love you, dear," she whispered, and Callie noticed the glimmer of tears in her eyes. "Now, go on."

Thankful for the reprieve, Callie dashed down the staircase and out the back entrance on the ground floor of the east wing of Astaria's castle. She and Zadicus had decided to have their bonding ceremony in the grand garden at Astaria since it was the official royal Vampyre compound—and since Bakari hadn't been able to penetrate Etherya's protective wall—thus making it the most secure place for a formal ceremony.

Inhaling the fresh late-morning air, Callie strode to the river, thankful she was still in her sweatpants and tank top and not yet clad in her fancy dress. Several minutes later, she approached the riverbank, observing the tall, willowy grass, and was soothed by the gurgle of the water.

Sitting on the soft bank, she stretched out her legs, mesmerized by the white bubbles in the water as they ran over the rocks.

"You are foolish to ignore your intuition, Calinda, daughter of Darkrip."

Flinching, Callie scrambled to her feet and stared at the woman who'd materialized from thin air. "Hello, Tatiana," she said, taken with the woman's deep amber gaze. "You scared the crap out of me." Realizing she was holding her hand over her pounding heart, she lowered it, resting it on her hip as curiosity swelled.

"I'm sorry," Tatiana said with a slow tilt of her head. "I thought you would be used to teleportation thanks to your father and Aunt Evie."

"I'm jumpy, I guess," she said, wondering why the strange woman felt the need to approach her during her moment of solitude. "Big day and all."

"Yes," Tatiana said, glancing at the ground before reclaiming Callie's gaze. "For more reasons than you can fathom."

Callie's eyes narrowed. "What's that supposed to mean? Look, I know you and Uncle Heden are friends and he likes your whole dramatic, creepy proselytizer routine, but I'm not really a fan."

Leaning down, Tatiana plucked a wildflower from the ground before straightening and slowly plucking away the petals as she spoke. "I don't mean to be obtuse, but I felt it necessary to give you a slight push in the right direction."

"And what direction is that?"

Long lashes blinked over the woman's luminous eyes. "Toward the prophecy."

Callie clenched her jaw. "Look, I get that the prophecy says I'm going to destroy the world, but I'm pretty chill just living my life, healing animals and trying to fit into a world that doesn't really get me half the time. I don't care about some faded scrolls that were written a million years before I was born."

"Fate cares not whether it is acknowledged as long as it is realized."

Emitting a frustrated groan, Callie sliced her hand through the air. "I have no stake in something that was predicted eons before I was born. Not interested."

"Your resistance is palpable, and that is understandable," she said, pulling the last petal from the flower before dropping the stem to the ground. "I believe it originates from fear, and there is no shame in that."

"Really?" She crossed her arms. "And what is it that I'm so afraid of?"

Running a hand over her long brown curls, Tatiana sighed. "That you are making a mistake marrying Zadicus."

Callie huffed. "I love him."

Shrugging, she smiled. "It's a believable lie to most, but not to you. You know deep within the words are false."

"You think I'm dumb enough to agree to marry a man I don't love?"

Her nostrils flared as she inhaled, gazing over the gurgling river before returning her attention to Callie. "I think you feel alone, as most descendants of Crimeous do. I believe you were taken by Zadicus's sweet words and gallant efforts, and you wished to make a bold choice."

Considering her words, Callie realized they weren't exactly *wrong*. In fact, they rang quite true. "Searching for yourself becomes demoralizing after a while. Sometimes, you have to make a decision even if you have reservations."

"True," Tatiana said with a nod, "and I appreciate your ability to make a firm choice...but it is the wrong choice."

"Excuse me, but you have some nerve to show up here and assert you know anything about my choices—"

"Have you read his thoughts?"

Callie bristled. "Of course not."

Tatiana nodded slowly, considering. "It is noble to honor the promise you made your father, but know that your powers are a great gift bestowed upon you by the goddess. Although you should not use them for nefarious purposes, there are times when they must be employed."

"Absolutely not," Callie said, lifting her chin.

Sighing, Tatiana inched closer, gently cupping Callie's jaw. Her skin was warm, creating a connection Callie couldn't deny, and she was helpless to pull away.

"The prophecy states you will align with Bakari and '*destroy Etherya's realm as we know it, and it will exist no more.*'"

"I'm familiar with the prophecy, thanks," she muttered.

"Have you truly dissected the words?" Amber eyes darted between her own. "The immortal world has existed in its current state for eons. Would it be such a tragedy for it to be destroyed?"

Callie's eyes narrowed. "I don't know what you mean."

"Yes, you do. Stop denying your heritage and your calling, daughter of Darkrip. You shy away from your power and your duty as if it were evil. I assure you, it is not. There is great salvation in following our true destiny if we only have the courage to choose the hard path."

Callie's chin quivered as she struggled with the raging emotions that swirled inside from the cryptic conversation. "Sometimes, I hate the prophecy and my powers so much I want to scream. They've always made me feel weird and unaccepted...and then Zadicus came along and was so into me." She stared at the ground before returning her gaze to Tatiana. "I just want to be loved for who I am. Is that so much to ask?"

"There are many who love you just as you are, my dear," she said, leaning forward and placing a soft peck on her forehead. "Do not ever forget that." Stepping back, she lowered her hand as her full lips curved.

"You need me, Calinda, as much as I need you. You'll come to see that eventually. There is a connectedness we all share that cannot be denied."

"I have no idea what you're talking about," she said, exasperated at the woman's riddles.

"I know." Her lips twitched, and Callie would've been pissed, except the action seemed reverent instead of amused. "I will summon you again soon. Events have been set in motion that cannot be stopped. Follow your intuition until we meet again."

"Wait!" Callie called, the word floating across the river as the woman disappeared. Huffing in frustration, Callie collapsed on the grass, crossing her arms as she gazed upon the flowing water. "Well, *that* was confusing." she muttered, annoyed at the perplexing conversation. What events was she referring to? Whatever they were, it seemed the enigmatic woman was intent on contacting her again.

After replaying the disconcerting discussion in her mind no less than a zillion times—and tugging about a hundred blades of grass from the riverbank—Callie stood, wiping the dirt off her backside before trekking back to the castle. She was shaken by the encounter and realized she needed to speak to Zadicus before going forward with the ceremony. Heading inside, she set off in search of her betrothed, determined to have an open and honest conversation with him about her reservations. She owed him no less, and it would go a long way toward soothing the doubt that swirled deep within.

C allie traipsed through the large castle, eventually finding Zadicus in the foyer with his parents as they shrugged off their light jackets.

"Hi, sweetheart," he said when she breezed in the room.

"Hi. You're all right on time for the early prep. Raoul. Viessa," Callie said with a tilt of her head. With her own family, she would've probably greeted them with a peck on the cheek, but Zadicus's family was a bit more reserved. Still, she liked his parents and had always gotten along with them quite well. "It's great to see you both. If you don't mind, I'd like to steal Zadicus away for a private chat in the study. My parents are already in the garden, and I'm sure they'd love to share a glass of wine with you before the ceremony."

Surprise crossed Zadicus's face. "Sweetheart? Are you all right?"

"I'm fine. I just need to talk to you privately."

"Well, I think that's our cue, dear," Viessa said, waving Raoul toward the hallway. "We know the way. You two come meet us when you're done."

Sparing a glance at her husband, she gave a small jerk of her head, and they disappeared down the hallway.

"Callie? What's gotten into you? That was extremely rude. You didn't even bother to greet them properly."

"I mean, they're going to be my in-laws, right?" she said, lifting her hands. "Do we really need to be formal?"

"They are two of the most revered aristocrats at Valeria. Yes, it would be nice if you would treat them with the respect they deserve."

"And I'm the granddaughter of Markdor, Calla and Rina, but I don't need a red carpet every time I enter the room."

He glanced toward the ceiling in frustration before rubbing his forehead. "Fine. Let's talk in the study."

They headed toward the room off the main hallway, Zadicus gesturing her inside before he followed behind.

"Close the door, please."

He arched a brow before slowly closing the door. "This sounds serious"

"It is." Assessing him, she tilted her head. "Are we making a mistake, Zadicus?"

His ice-blue eyes grew wide. "You're asking me this two hours before our bonding ceremony?"

"It would seem so." Sighing, she struggled to articulate the doubt and hesitation that churned within. She didn't want to hurt his feelings but was shaken by her conversation with Tatiana. "I'm sorry to spring this on you, but I wonder if we moved too quickly."

"We've been courting for a year, Callie," he said, palms showing as he widened them at his waist. "We share affection and have much in common—"

"Do we? I'm not sure that's true."

He swallowed. "We both come from two of the purest bred Vampyre lineages."

"That has nothing to do with *us*," she said, lifting her hands. "We're just products of our parents knocking boots."

Grimacing, he ran a hand over his face. "It means something in our world, Callie, and unites us as aristocrats."

Her foot tapped on the floor as she studied him. "That's kind of a weird thing to have in common. Why do you never ask to come with me when I heal wounded animals across the kingdom?"

"You know that isn't my thing, sweetheart. You enjoy it, so I let you help the commoners."

Her eyebrow arched. "You *let* me?"

"You know what I mean," he said, rolling his eyes. "Are you trying to start a fight? That seems counterproductive two hours before we're set to bond."

"Counterproductive," she murmured, inching closer. "Such a strange word, and one someone would use for a mission rather than a mate." Narrowing her eyes, she studied him. "Am I some sort of mission for you, Zadicus?"

Expelling a breath, he ran his hands through his hair. "I really wish I'd known about these trust issues before I proposed. We'll definitely need to work on that."

Callie gnawed her lip, contemplating. Finally, she lifted her chin as emotion swirled inside. "This is hard for me to say, but I think we moved too fast. You were my first suitor, and I was extremely honored with your efforts, but we should've taken more time to get to know each other. Eternity is long freaking time, Zadicus. We have to call this off." She lifted her hands, giving a slight shrug. "I'm truly sorry and will publicly take full responsibility to mitigate any fallout."

"Sweetheart," he said, stepping forward, sliding his palms over her shoulders. "You're just having bonding jitters. It's completely normal."

Callie stared into his eyes, assessing the warmth from his hands, wondering why his touch didn't inspire passion. She'd always enjoyed their kisses but admitted they'd never set her body on fire. She'd always made the excuse that only happened in movies—and in the steamy romance novels Evie had supplied her with since she was a teenager. But perhaps she'd been wrong. Years ago, she'd imagined waiting for someone who inspired Henry Cavill-level passion. Why had she settled for less with Zadicus?

Narrowing her eyes, she struggled with the sudden urge to read his thoughts. Perhaps getting a glimpse into his mind would help her understand why she had such serious reservations. If she took a peek and found his motivations to be true, and his heart to be open, perhaps she could move forward with the ceremony. Knowing it was so very wrong but unable to stop herself after the disconcerting discussion with Tatiana, she focused her energy on crossing the barrier to his mind.

Something clanked in her brain as she attempted to extract his thoughts, preventing her from accessing what she sought. Realization entered his expression, and he drew back, dropping his hands as if she were on fire.

"What are you doing?" he hissed.

Craning her head, she studied him. "Why can't I read your thoughts?" she asked, the words slow and measured.

"Why are you *trying* to read my thoughts?" he demanded, frustration in his tone as he sliced a hand through the air. "Goddess, Callie! That's a huge violation of my privacy."

Frozen, ice circulated through her veins as comprehension washed over her. Clenching her fists, she said softly, "Someone has created a shield for you so I can't read your thoughts."

His throat bobbed as he swallowed, and silence spread thick and heavy between them.

"The only people capable of doing that are my father and Evie, neither of whom would, Tatiana whom you've never met and Bakari." Taking a measured step forward, she gazed up at his handsome, traitorous face, and whispered, "You bastard."

"Callie," he said, reaching for her before she recoiled, her stomach churning at his deception. "Sweetheart, I have no idea what you're talking about."

"Liar!" Holding up her hand, she used her powers to render him immobile. He stood before her, still as a stone except for his features, which were contorted into a mask of confusion, anger and fear.

"How dare you use your powers on me? I command you to let me go this instant—"

"Quiet!" she yelled, her outstretched hand shaking slightly as rage coursed through her body. "What did Bakari promise you? Good god, what did *you* promise him? What will he gain from your deception?"

"You're paranoid," he gritted. "Callie, this is absurd!"

"I wanted so badly to *loved*. Goddess, I was so stupid." Closing the distance between them, she gently placed the pad of her finger on his forehead, directly between his eyebrows. "If I want to rip away the barrier, I can, Zadicus. It will hurt—hell, it might kill you. Is that what you want? Is Bakari worth dying for?"

His eyes narrowed to angry slits, hatred whirling deep in the orbs, and Callie truly *saw* him for the first time: a vapid, petulant man consumed by his own demons and lust for power. "You make me sick," she spat.

A commotion sounded to her left, and she whirled, her finger still affixed to Zadicus's forehead. Bakari materialized into the room, causing her body to pulse with equal parts fear and apprehension.

"I'll kill him," she said, her tone ominous.

Sighing, he placed his hand on his hip, regarding her as if they were discussing where to have lunch rather than her betrothed's imminent death. "No, you won't, Calinda. You don't have it in you to hurt another living being. Not yet." His sky blue eyes roved over her. "Hopefully, one day, you will grow into your evil. If so, it will be truly magnificent."

Dropping her hand, she turned to face him. "I have no desire to embrace my grandfather's blood, nor do I care about the Elven prophecy."

"Your lie is easy to dismiss considering you approached Zadicus only minutes after Tatiana appeared to you. She is a nuisance I should've exterminated long ago."

"But you can't," Callie murmured, observing his reaction when he spoke her name. A reluctant reverence had flashed in his eyes. "You carry some sort of twisted affection for her."

"She was helpful in many ways when I realized who I truly am. I've always found the benefits of keeping her alive outweighed the consequences. Until now." Lifting his hand, he sliced it through the air, releasing Callie's spell. Zadicus sucked in a breath as he clutched his throat.

"Kill her," Zadicus demanded.

"So dramatic," Bakari said, rolling his eyes. "She's worth more than you can fathom." When the man opened his mouth to argue, Bakari shot him a look, causing Zadicus to cower. Slinking to the corner, he lowered into a chair to reclaim his breath.

"Calinda," Bakari said, holding up his hands. "You cannot fight the inevitable. I have powers that no other being on the planet possesses—thanks to Tatiana, Dr. Tyson and others. I've spent centuries plotting my revenge, and I *will* become ruler of this realm. I realize this can only be done after complete annihilation, followed by rebirth, and therefore, you must align with me to fulfill the prophecy."

"Never!" she vowed, spittle flying between her fangs as her body vibrated with emotion. "I love this kingdom and consider every person in this realm family. I would never harm them."

"But do they consider *you* family? An outcast raised in the human world who is a child of Crimeous and the subject of a deadly prophecy? Have you never questioned why you feel so alone here? Perhaps it is time to consider fulfilling the prophecy is the best course for the kingdom you profess to love."

The words were reminiscent of Tatiana's, causing her to bristle. A small tendril of acknowledgment blazed in her chest that the sentiment rang true. Was she supposed to bring about some sort of cataclysmic change for the immortal realm?

"Good," he said with a nod. "You're finally thinking like a child of Crimeous. Like a woman beginning to understand the gravity of the power she's been given. Embrace it, Calinda. It will bring your more happiness and more acceptance than you will ever find by denying your true heritage."

Suddenly, the door burst open, and Darkrip rushed inside. "Callie?" he asked, assessing the situation. His head snapped between her, Bakari and Zadicus. Lifting his hands, he spread his palms, attempting to freeze Bakari in place and telekinetically choke him.

"Oh, good, Daddy's here," Bakari mocked through clenched teeth, his fangs barely visible behind thinned lips. "If you want to do this now, I'm ready." Lifting his hands, he showed Darkrip his palms, which were visibly glowing.

Comprehension dawned as they slowly latched their gaze upon Bakari.

"How were you able to transport through Astaria's wall?" Darkrip almost whispered. "You haven't been able to get through for years."

"Dr. Tyson purchased some extremely powerful concoctions on his last visit to the human world. Years of experimentation finally paid off. As I informed Heden when we first met, I am a patient man. Every failure ultimately leads to success."

"How about this success, asshole?" a feminine voice asked behind Bakari before Evie materialized and punched him in the kidney. Sliding her arm around his neck, she choked him as he struggled to break free. Bakari landed a crushing blow to her side with his elbow, and she fell back, breathless. Rushing toward Zadicus, Bakari tugged him from the chair and began chanting unintelligible words in the cryptic language he used to render the dematerialization spell. In a flash, he disappeared, along with Zadicus.

"Fuck!" Evie yelled, rubbing her forehead. "I was so close to killing the bastard."

"I can't believe he figured out how to breach Astaria's protective wall," Darkrip said, approaching Callie and pulling her into his embrace. She shook in his arms as he soothed his hand over her hair. "Shh," he said, kissing her temple. "It's okay. I'm here."

"*Ohmygod*," she cried, burying her face in his neck and willing the tears away. "I'm so stupid, Dad."

"This is my fault," he said, his voice so comforting in her ear. "I had reservations about you bonding with Zadicus that I pushed away. This is the last time I listen to your mother."

"I won't even honor those words with a response," Arderin said, striding into the room and drawing them both into a firm hug. "Come here, baby." She rocked with them as Callie drew upon their strength. "You're okay now."

Lifting her head, she gazed back and forth between them. "I'm so sorry, guys," she whispered. Craning her neck, she glanced at Evie. "Really sorry."

"Listen, kid," Evie said, shrugging. "Shit happens, and people lie. Good thing you found out before you boned him because that would've been *really* awkward."

"Not helpful," Darkrip muttered.

"Well, it's true," she said, flipping her hair over her shoulder. "And you're welcome for saving your ass, dear brother." With a nod, she stalked from the room.

"How could I have been so stupid?" Callie asked, stepping from their embrace and rubbing her upper arms. "I thought he loved me. I should've known better."

"And what does that mean, young lady?" Arderin asked in her stern mom tone. "You're perfectly lovable."

"I'm a freak, Mom!" Callie said, all the swirling emotions twining into a mass of frustrated rage. "I've never fit in here. I've never fit in *anywhere*. All people see when they look at me is a vestige of Crimeous and someone who's the manifestation of a prophecy that will destroy them! It's awful." Lowering to the sofa, she buried her face in her hands, struggling to control the tears.

"Sweetie," Arderin said, sitting beside her and placing her arm over her shoulders. "We all have our crosses to bear. I know it's hard, but it makes us so much stronger in the end. You'll realize this one day."

"I just want to be a normal person who's not the subject of a cataclysmic prophecy," she said, lifting her face and swiping away the tears. "I'll never be normal, Mom."

"No, you won't," she said, soothing the hair at her temple. "And I, for one, am thankful for that. You and Creigen are special, and I love you just the way you are."

"Special," she sighed, blowing a breath over her bottom lip so it fanned her hair. "I'm so tired of hearing that." Lifting her gaze to Darkrip's, she noticed his crossed arms and furious expression. "I'm okay, Dad. You look like you're going to pulverize something."

"You're goddamned right I'm going to pulverize something," he muttered. "That bastard's face."

"Zadicus or Bakari?"

"Both."

Sighing, Arderin addressed Darkrip. "We need to inform everyone of what happened and call a council meeting. We'll need to piece everything together and try to figure out why Bakari was manipulating Zadicus into marrying Callie."

Silence blanketed the room as realization set in.

"He wanted leverage over me," Callie said softly. "It makes sense. If he controlled my bonded, he would have access to me...and to any children

I would have. He most likely wanted to create some sort of bargaining chip."

"And he could ultimately blackmail you for your alliance in fulfilling the prophecy," Darkrip said.

"Yes," she whispered, twining her fingers in her lap. "And I almost let him. So fucking stupid."

"Okay, we're not going to beat ourselves up," Arderin said, rubbing Callie's arm. "The crisis was averted, and you figured it out before it got out of hand. How did you figure it out, by the way?"

"I went on a walk by the river earlier and Tatiana appeared." She stared into her mother's piercing blue eyes. "She indicated that fulfilling the prophecy is my destiny. She and Bakari seem to agree on that."

"I thought she was on our side?" Arderin asked Darkrip.

"She's wily," he said, shaking his head. "My assessment is that Tatiana has one side: her own. Forces like good and evil aren't differentiated for her as they are for us. Instead, they are both sides of the same coin and flow in tandem with one another."

"Well, I'll take your word for it since you're the only one who's ever gotten a glimpse into her mind," Arderin said.

"Yes, she let her defenses down for a scant moment that evening we had dinner together when we visited Heden years ago. Sofia's wine might be the most magical concoction of all since it led to Tatiana dropping her shield. I saw inside her head only briefly, but it was...intense. She's not like any other creature I've ever encountered—human, immortal or otherwise."

"Heden swears she'd never hurt us," Arderin said, concern in her tone.

"I think he's right," Darkrip said, tilting his head. "She's...it's hard to explain. She's striving toward something none of us can see in our limited world view. That's the only way I know how to articulate what I saw," he finished, shrugging.

"Well, we need to cancel the ceremony and send the guests home. Raoul and Viessa will need to be notified," Arderin said. "I'm pretty sure they had no idea Zadicus was working with Bakari."

"I'll speak to them and confirm they were unaware," Darkrip said.

"After that, we should probably convene a short council meeting and discuss today's events with everyone. Are you up to that?" she asked, tucking a dark curl behind Callie's ear.

"Yes," Callie said, standing and straightening her shoulders. "I want to record today's events and then purge them from my memory. *Forever.*"

"Pushing away anger and hurt is only a temporary solution, sweetie," Arderin said, standing.

"I know, but I've been made a fool of, and I need some time to assess why I didn't listen to my gut. You both should understand that."

"Of course we do."

"Thank the goddess I figured it out before it was too late. Fuck that jerk."

Arderin shot Darkrip an acerbic glare. "Well, she sounds like your daughter."

He smiled, closing the distance between them until he cupped Callie's cheeks. "Fuck him is right, honey. And I *will* kill him one day. He hurt you, and that's unacceptable."

"Aw," Callie teased, tilting her head. "It's what every girl wants her father to say. I hope you'll threaten to kill every man I ever date."

"Every fucking one," Darkrip said, an amused glint in his eye.

"Man, we're a really weird family," Arderin said, glancing at the ceiling. "I know I should be concerned, but I just find it adorable." Shrugging, she extended her hand. "Come on, baby. Let's get to it so you can lick your wounds and start to put this all behind you."

Clutching her mother's hand, Callie inhaled a breath, fortifying herself, and followed her parents from the room.

Chapter 10

L ater that evening, Callie sat at the end of the large conference table in the council room at Astaria. The members of the council flanked her, all seated in the leather chairs that surrounded the table. Her father, Evie and Kenden sat to her left; Larkin, Aron, Lila and Latimus on her right. Miranda sat at the head of the table, Sathan planted in the foremost seat at the front corner, firm and attentive.

Miranda's face was a mask of frustrated anger as she gazed across the table at Callie. "Thank you for being so forthright, Callie," she said, resting her hands on the table as she leaned forward. "It takes a lot of strength to document what happened today with such candidness, especially since it was supposed to be a happy day of celebration. I'm so sorry."

Callie felt the sting of tears in her eyes and pushed them away, determined to embody the strength Miranda extolled. "I'm happy to help. What happened today signifies Bakari's determination to rule the kingdom, and we can't let that happen."

"We've given him ample chance to show a sliver of goodness," Latimus said. "I don't relish hurting my brother, but he must be vanquished. It's the only path forward for our people to live in peace." Sitting back in his chair, he laced his fingers atop the table. "I believe we've pieced together the story. After questioning Raoul and Viessa, I firmly believe they had no knowledge of Zadicus's alliance with Bakari. They seemed as sad and distraught as we all are before they left for Valeria. The good news is that Zadicus's failure ended up showing Bakari's hand. He's intent on aligning with Callie to fulfill the prophecy."

"Just a reminder that I am *not* on board with that plan," Callie said, raising a finger in the air as she tried to lift the heavy mood. The last thing she wanted was to be pitied. She might have made mistakes along the way, but she was no victim.

"We know you don't want to destroy the world, sweetie," Lila said in her gentle, supportive tone.

"Yes, I think we're all in agreement on that," Latimus said with a wink, instantly softening Callie. Gratefulness for her family and their unwavering support washed over her.

Gazing back at the group, he continued. "It is imperative we enter the final phase of our plan. We will draw Bakari, along with Commander Vadik and his troops, to a final battle on the field between Takelia and Uteria in one month's time. Bakari is dead set on fulfilling the Elven prophecy—which is never going to happen," he uttered, eying the council members, "but it makes Callie a target, and that's unacceptable."

"Agreed," Evie said with a nod. "And now that some of our more *hardheaded* members have agreed to let women become combat soldiers, I'm confident we can secure victory." She batted her eyelashes at Latimus as he frowned.

"It wasn't because I think women aren't capable, Evie—"

"Misogynist," she coughed loudly into her fist.

"That's incredibly unfair!"

"Okay, okay," Miranda said, standing and holding up her hands. "As much as I agree with Evie on this one, there's no need to rehash something that's been debated and decided. We're all happy women have joined the troops, and I think it will exponentially increase our chances of defeating Bakari."

"I only wanted to protect the women of our kingdom," Latimus murmured, dark eyebrows drawing together.

"Oh, I'm sorry," Evie said, reaching for her purse and pulling out her phone. Lifting it to her ear, she nodded. "Yes, he's right here." Extending it across the table to Latimus, she said, "It's the Middle Ages calling—"

"All right," Kenden interrupted, gently taking the phone from her hand. "My wife gets a kick out of torturing you, Latimus. You won, sweetheart. Let's move on."

"Fine," she said, rolling her eyes. "But if anyone in this room in possession of a penis ever utters the words *'women can't do,'* followed by literally anything, I have a mind to detach said penis from their body. Capisce?"

Callie observed several throats bob as the men remailed silent. Damn, her aunt was badass.

"Back to the business at hand," Miranda said, giving Evie a nod of solidarity. "I think we're all in agreement. The battle will commence one month from today, at sunrise. Ken and Latimus, are you confident you can draw Bakari's entire army to the field south of Takelia for the battle?"

"Yes," Kenden said with a nod. "Sadie has run extensive psychological profiles on Bakari. We believe he will respond to our call for an ultimate battle if we appeal to his ego and lust for power."

"And now, it seems he *wants* a battle in the hopes Callie will align with him," Latimus said. "We'll use his inflated sense of superiority against him and finally rid the planet of him and his supporters."

"Excellent," Miranda said. "I know we've tried many tactics over the years and were hesitant to enter into full-on war with Bakari after the War of the Species ended. Our people were tired, and we handled Bakari's attacks and poisons effectively but were never able to fully contain him. His Deamon army continues to grow, and it's time to put an end to this for good. Please let me know what you need to be fully prepared. I already approved the purchase order for the new TECs, but if we need more, just send a request my way."

"Will do," Kenden said. "Jack will continue training the new recruits, both *male* and *female*." He glanced at his wife before continuing. "Sadie and Nolan have also been testing antidote serums for every possible chemical combination of Dr. Tyson's we've discovered so far. If Bakari's army deploys chemicals on the battlefield, the docs will be stationed at infirmary tents nearby, ready to treat any Slayer soldiers affected. Thankfully, the Vampyre soldiers won't be affected due to their self-healing abilities."

"Arderin will be in the infirmary tents too," Darkrip said, resignation in his tone. "I tried to talk her out of it but stopped wasting my breath about five seconds in. Stubborn woman."

"I can volunteer too, Dad," Callie said. "I want to help."

"That's appreciated," Miranda said before Darkrip could speak, "but we want the kids as far away from the battle so you're safe. You're the future of our kingdom, and if something happens to the older generation, we'll need you to lead. Sathan and I will be with you, although I'd love to fight the bastards, but we trust the army to get the job done."

"Most of us aren't kids anymore, Aunt Miranda," she said, frustration lacing her tone, "and I think we all want to lead by helping with the battle."

"I know, and it means a lot." She smiled as she slid her hand over her husband's shoulder. "But Sathan and I have decided. Don't make us pull the 'king and queen' card. That would make us huge losers. Believe me, I want to kick Bakari's ass too, but we all have roles we need to play."

"Okay," Callie said softly, understanding the logic of remaining safe while the troops battled.

"Good." Straightening, Miranda assessed the room. "I think we're done then. Callie, thank you for helping us piece everything together. We love you very much, and that jerk will get what's coming to him."

"I called Camron and informed him Zadicus will be taken into custody if he's spotted on any of the compounds," Lila said. "Aligning with Bakari is unacceptable, and he will face consequences if he is apprehended."

"We should've known since Zadicus is related to Melania," Latimus muttered.

"Melania renounced Bakari years ago," Lila said, her tone firm. "If we don't embrace forgiveness and reformation, we're no better than our enemies."

"I'll let you do the embracing. I'm all set."

She glared at him before he scrunched his features, causing her to laugh. "My stern bonded. One day, I'll soften you up." She gave him a wink.

"Okay, get a room." Evie stood. "Come on," she said to Kenden. "I'm ready to hug our daughter, go home and put today behind us."

The meeting adjourned, everyone rushing to Callie to give her a warm hug. Overwhelmed by the love of her family, she accepted their embraces, reminding herself how lucky she was even if the day had royally sucked. Leaving the conference room, she trailed to the sitting room where her brother and cousins were waiting. They stood as she entered, their expressions lined with supportive concern.

"I'm okay, guys," she said, hugging Rinada, Adelyn and Symon before her brother pulled her into his side.

"Fuck that guy," Creigen said, rubbing her upper arm. "He wasn't good enough for you, sis."

"Thanks, Creig. Remember how awesome I am next time we argue about who's smarter."

"What's there to argue about? It's obviously me." He pointed his thumbs at his chest.

"As if," she responded, playfully shoving him.

"You ready, Rin?" Evie asked, craning her neck around the doorframe. "Dad and I want to head home."

"Ready," Rinada said, swiping her dark mahogany-colored hair over her shoulder before waving goodbye to everyone.

Her cousins and brother filtered out of the room until she was left alone with Jack, who slowly approached her.

"Callie," he said softly, his deep brown eyes laced with concern, "are you okay?"

"Yeah," she said, thankful for their close bond. "I mean, it sucks, but you knew my doubts about him. Guess I should've listened to my gut."

He smiled, the gesture filled with affection. "You deserve so much better. One day, you'll meet the person who's supposed to be your partner. I know it."

"Maybe we both will," she said, giving him a cheeky grin. "And we'll look back on today as a bad memory. Maybe we'll even laugh about it."

"I know we will." He cupped her arm, giving it a reassuring squeeze.

"In the meantime, I think I need a good cry alone while I inhale ice cream."

He breathed a laugh. "I'm sure Glarys can scrounge up ice cream in a snap."

"I'm sure she can." Grinning, she pulled him into a hug. "Thank you, Jack. I just need to process everything. I'm going to tell Mom and Dad I want to stay here tonight. I'll sleep in Heden's old room. It's still got the kick-ass flat-screen he set up years ago, along with his rom-com collection, which he always maintained was for 'research.'" Drawing back, she chuckled as she made quotation marks with her fingers. "I know he secretly loves *Pretty Woman*."

"I think he quotes *The Princess Bride* on an hourly basis," Jack affirmed.

"Exactly." Running her hand through her hair, she sighed. "I'll be fine,"—she held up a finger—"but I reserve the right to reach out if I need a shoulder to cry on."

"Always. You know you're my favorite cousin."

She squinted. "I'm pretty sure I heard you tell Rinada that last week."

"Me?" He pointed at his chest, his features a mask of mock innocence. "No way."

"Get out of here," she said, swatting his chest, already feeling better from his gentle teasing.

Glarys chose that moment to stride into the room. "There you are, dear. My goodness, what a crappy day. Would you like some ice cream? I have rocky road all ready to go in the freezer."

She and Jack shared a smile. "I'd love that, Glarys. Do you and Sam mind if I stay at Astaria? If I go home, Mom and Dad will hover. It's sweet but smothering."

"You're always welcome here, dear," she said, placing her arm over her shoulders. "Jack, do you want to stay too?"

"I've got an early training tomorrow," he said, leaning down to kiss the kind woman on the forehead, "but thanks. Take care of our girl."

"I will." Ice-blue eyes sparkled under Glarys's cap of white curls as she waved goodbye before he exited.

"Well, let's get you all set up. I have some of your mother's old clothes you can wear if you want to change out of those. She left them behind when she moved to the human world all those years ago. We'll get you all nice and comfy, sweetheart."

Enveloped in the caring mother figure's embrace, Callie followed her to the kitchen of the massive home, thankful for the support of every person in her extended family.

D arkrip was exhausted by the time the terrible day ended. After the council meeting, where Callie had informed everyone of the day's events and the subsequent ending of her betrothal, he'd longed to comfort her. She'd appeared both vulnerable and strong, reminding him how proud he was of his willful, headstrong daughter. As she recounted the details, he'd yearned to turn back time and prevent her pain.

Afterward, Darkrip had expected her to come home to Takelia but also understood her need for solitude.

"Glarys said I can stay in Heden's old room, Dad," she'd said, putting on a brave face even though hurt swam in her eyes. "I just want to be alone right now."

He'd studied her, tamping down the urge to pull her close and transport her home. Once she was there, she couldn't argue, and he'd be able to comfort her.

"I'm too powerful for you to transport," she said, giving a cheeky grin. "You won't be able to overpower me."

"Are you reading my thoughts?"

"No way. It's written all over your face that you want to whisk me home and comfort me. It's really sweet, but I need space."

Leaning down, he kissed her forehead. "I love you, Callie. Please call if you need me, no matter how late."

"Thanks, Dad," she whispered, the warble in her voice almost breaking his heart.

Now home, he slowly unbuttoned his starchy shirt as his mind wandered. He could disintegrate the damn thing off, but the slow, measured movements of his fingers offered a mundane task to occupy his thoughts. Once he'd shucked everything but his boxer briefs, he stared at his reflection in the mirror atop the dresser.

His ears had slight points, a vestige of his father's Deamon heritage. Of their *Elven* heritage. Miranda and Kenden had discovered the hidden Elven scrolls years ago, and they extolled some pretty outlandish stories. Some were prophecies, some were history, written down long ago and forgotten when the Elven world was destroyed. All were from a realm long assumed dead.

But Crimeous had survived, which meant others could have survived as well. Darkrip knew this to be true, and he'd stopped fighting the denial long ago. His father's blood gave him the ability to sense things others couldn't, and he would bet his life there were other Elven descendants that roamed Etherya's Earth. If not in the immortal world, then in the human world, where they could easily blend in with the oblivious species.

"Creigen is headphones-deep in his video game," Arderin said, entering the bedroom and trailing to his side. "I'd be worried that our eighteen-year-old son is so enamored with video games if I didn't know he used it to pick up girls. It's kind of geeky-sweet. Heden would be proud."

"How did they grow up so fast?" Darkrip asked, his gaze claiming hers in the reflection. "Yesterday, I was changing Callie's diaper, and now, they're both adults, falling in love and making adult mistakes."

"I don't know," she sighed, resting her chin on his shoulder. "I mean, we could have another one if you're missing the diaper phase."

Darkrip balked. "Uh, I'm all set, thanks. Two is enough, especially after the shit show we experienced today. I mean, I love them, but let's quit while we're ahead."

Chuckling, she nipped his shoulder. "Fine. But we'll keep practicing just in case."

His green eyes smoldered with desire in the reflection as his skin warmed. "Why are you wearing clothes?" he growled. Closing his eyes, he dematerialized her dress, leaving her in her bra and panties.

"I appreciate your desire, husband," she said in a sultry tone, touching her lips to his ear and setting his body on fire. "But we need to discuss something first."

Sliding against her smooth skin, he turned, drawing her close and aligning their bodies. "Dear wife, I can't think of anything to possibly talk about when you're pressed against me like this." Nudging her nose with his, he pushed his rapidly swelling erection between the juncture of her thighs.

"Darkrip," she whispered against his lips. "I need your word."

"I'll promise anything if you let me fuck you," he murmured, gliding his hand to her ass and squeezing the firm flesh.

"Obviously, I'm going to let you fuck me," she teased, rolling her eyes. "But I need your word you won't hunt him down. Latimus and Kenden have a plan for the final battle, and I don't want your vengeance getting in the way."

"As much as I want to murder that aristocratic bastard, I'll leave him be. Zadicus means nothing in the big scheme. I'm on board with the final battle. Evie and I are going to perfect a forcefield we can use against Bakari once he's drawn out on the battlefield. It will allow us to disintegrate every Deamon along with him so none can be cloned. We won't fuck it up this time. I'm over this fucking conflict."

"My husband, the noble warrior. I always knew you had it in you." She playfully bit his bottom lip.

"You saw the good in me before anyone else," he said, his tone reverent.

"Your mother saw it long before me. I just picked up where she left off."

Rina's face flashed in Darkrip's mind as he stroked Arderin's cheek with his thumb.

"Sweetheart?" she called softly.

"I wish she could meet Callie, Creigen and Rinada. Evie honored Mother when they named their daughter after her. I hope she'd be proud of the man I've become, even if I let Callie down today."

"You didn't let her down," Arderin said, sliding her arms around his neck. "You let her make her own mistakes. It's what we must do if she's going to learn to navigate the world. She has my wanderlust, and we can't keep her here forever. I'm surprised she's stayed with us this long and hasn't decided to get her own place."

"Today will always be a defining moment for her. I fear her innocence was shattered."

"Callie?" Arderin asked, scoffing. "She hasn't been innocent for a long time, dear. You choose to see her as your precocious little girl, but she's a woman who's slowly recognizing her own strength. I think today was exactly what she needed."

"But he hurt her," Darkrip said, feeling his heart rip open. "He hurt our little girl, Arderin."

"I know." The strokes of her fingers against the back of his neck were soothing. "It sucks. I'm hurting for her as much as you are."

Resting his forehead against hers, Darkrip held his wife, thankful for her stubborn strength and unwavering support. "I lived a solitary life for so long, swearing I didn't need anyone." He softly brushed her lips with his. "Now, I can't imagine surviving without the three of you. You're all I care about."

She stared into his eyes before cracking a smile. "Man, you've become really dramatic in your old age. Are you going for an Emmy there, old man?"

Growling, he crouched down, cupping her ass and lifting her. Squealing, she instinctively wrapped her legs around his waist, joyfully laughing as he carried her to the bed. Falling to the mattress, he cradled her, cushioning her fall before he loomed over her.

"You're going to pay for that smart mouth, princess."

Her tongue darted out, slow and deliberate, bathing her ruby red lips.

"Don't threaten me with a good time."

"You little bitch," he murmured, lowering to lick her wet lips. Extending his tongue, he ran it over the sensitive flesh, from corner to corner, as she shivered below him.

"I'd be pissed you call me that in bed, except it gets me really hot." Arousal flashed in her eyes.

"Good," he muttered, pecking her lips. "Now, open that smart mouth, sweetheart. We're going to put it to good use." Rising, he closed his eyes, dematerializing their remaining garments. Lifting his lids, he palmed his cock, beginning to stroke as he climbed over her and straddled her.

"You love my smart mouth."

Thrusting his fingers into her thick hair, he tugged, loving her arousal-laden gasp. Her eyes glazed with desire, and her lips hung open, wet and ready. Moving closer, he touched the tip of his aching shaft to her wet mouth. His wife smiled as he felt himself drowning in her piercing blue eyes. And then, she closed around him, and all he felt was pure, unadulterated bliss.

<h1 style="text-align:center">Chapter 11</h1>

Callie lay in bed watching the rom-com in Heden's old bedroom. She thought staying at Astaria would give her some much needed peace and quiet so she could digest her thoughts. Instead, she was restless. Throwing off the covers, she trailed to the dresser and rummaged in her bag. Locating the diary, she pulled it out, gently stroking the withered collection of musings from her younger self.

As she read the flowing scrawl, scattered with "i"s with heart-shaped dots, she tried like hell not to blame herself for being an idiot. The pages were filled with paragraphs upon paragraphs detailing her longing to be loved. Reading over the words, her loneliness was palpable on the slightly faded pages. No wonder she believed Zadicus when he'd courted her so zealously. She'd craved affection and had been ripe for a ruse. Her yearning to be loved had ultimately made her discount her gut feelings, and she vowed to never let that happen again. From this day forward, Callie would always trust her intuition and explore her doubts when something didn't feel right.

What baffled her most were the love letters Zadicus had written. They'd seemed so heartfelt and genuine, and she could barely believe he'd been able to pull it off. After all, he wasn't the most perceptive man, and she wondered how he'd noticed so many of the things he mentioned. Reaching into her bag, she pulled out the letters, which she'd packed along with her diary in a sentimental moment. The poem he'd originally written her was also in the pile, and she stacked the papers on the dresser. Reaching for one, she read it, and then another, noting the observant words.

Sometimes, your lips shine under the late-afternoon sunlight after you've covered them in gloss, and my mind can't focus on anything else but kissing you.

When you placed the rose behind your ear and smiled, I realized I'd never seen anything more beautiful.

Observing you teach the citizens to read warmed my heart, and I was especially taken with your interactions with the teenagers.

Sometimes, you speak of the unknowns of having your own children since they will inevitably inherit some of your powers, but you don't need to worry, Callie-lily.

Narrowing her eyes, Callie focused on the nickname. Now that she thought about it, Zadicus had never called her that except in his letters. How strange he would create a nickname for her and never use it.

It was also weird that he mentioned her volunteering at the literacy function since he'd sat in the corner the entire time working on the invite list for his mother's dinner party. In fact, she had no idea he'd even noticed she spent time with the teens who attended. The only person who'd seemed to notice was Brecken, considering Rowena had been in attendance. Callie remembered speaking to him as he stood against the wall, observing in his quiet, watchful manner.

Come to think of it, Brecken had been present during *all* of the moments mentioned in the letters. The literary function, the dinner where she stuck the rose in her hair...the street fair where she'd slathered on lip gloss. Searching her brain, Callie tried to remember if she'd worn lip gloss on her dates with Zadicus. She usually preferred to wear lipstick and only used lip gloss as a backup when she was in less formal situations. Like when she was worried she had wine lips and was accompanying a sexy bodyguard to a street fair...

Straightening in her seat, Callie's heart began to pound. As she pondered, she couldn't recall a time when she'd worn lip gloss instead of lipstick with Zadicus. Grasping the letters, she began to furiously read through them, quickly realizing every single occurrence happened under Brecken's watch. Glancing at the folded poem Zadicus originally penned for her when they first began courting, she reached for it with shaking fingers.

Lifting it, she opened it and read the prose. By the goddess, it was terrible, and so different from the flowing words that comprised the letters. Picking up the most recent letter, she held it beside the poem.

At first glance, the writing looked identical. But as Callie narrowed her eyes and looked closer, the differences began to show. Tiny things she never would've noticed unless something drastic happened, causing her to look.

Something like her betrothed outing himself as a traitor who'd aligned with her nefarious uncle...

Swallowing thickly, Callie compared the writing, noting the inconsistencies. The slashes across the "t"s were different—the ones in the poem slanting upward while the ones in the letter were perfectly level. The "C" in her name also had a slight curl at the bottom in the letter but didn't in the poem. And the "Z" in Zadicus was quite large in the signature of the poem and rather small in the letter.

Lowering the missives, Callie pondered as blood thrummed through her veins. Glancing at the handwriting, there was only one conclusion she could draw: They were written by different people. Zadicus had written her the poem. *Brecken had written her the letters.*

Somehow, she knew it was inexorably true. Considering she'd just declared not to ignore her intuition, she let the realization sink in. For some reason, Brecken had aligned with Zadicus to deceive her. There was no other explanation, considering it was Zadicus who gave her each letter. Brecken wrote them and then passed them along to Zadicus to give to her.

A soft cry leaped from her throat as her eyes welled. What possible motive could Brecken have for agreeing to such a thing? Did he only do it to help his ward, or was he secretly aligned with Bakari too? Stacking the papers, she stared into the reflection as hurt and confusion swirled in her eyes.

"That son of a bitch," she murmured, rubbing her hand over her collarbone. "Why would he do this?"

Callie had no idea, but as the acknowledgment of his deception washed over her, fury swelled deep within. Her features grew more resolved in the reflection, and she knew what she had to do. Rising, she rested her palms on the vanity and stared into her furious eyes.

"You're going to confront him and figure out if he was also working with Bakari."

It was the right thing to do considering she would need to tell the council if Brecken was indeed aligned with her uncle. Even though she was pissed, something inside her railed against the notion Brecken would align with Bakari. He was a soldier and a protector, and so loving with Rowena. The idea that Zadicus was vulnerable to Bakari's machinations wasn't impossible to imagine. The notion that Brecken would align with him? It just didn't make sense at all. Knowing there was only one way to find out, she stuffed the letters into her bag and texted Jack.

Callie: Brecken lives on the south side of Lynia near Antonio's neighborhood, right?

A text bubble appeared, and she anxiously gnawed her lip.

Jack: Yep. His cabin is about a mile from Antonio's. Why?

Callie: No reason. Just wondering.

She could almost see her cousin's sardonic look flash through her mind.

Jack: Callie? What are you up to?

Callie: Nothing. I promise. You know I'd tell you if anything was wrong. For now, I'm crashing. Long day of being betrayed and all. Love you.

There was a pause before she noticed him typing.

Jack: I'm always here for you. Don't forget that. Love you too. Night.

Expelling a breath through puffed cheeks, she thanked the goddess he'd let it go.

Tossing the bag over her shoulder, she quietly walked through the house, toward the barracks, until she stepped into the expansive garage. Locating the keys to the nearby four-wheeler on the key rack that hung by the door, she threw her bag on the passenger seat. After backing out, she ensured the garage door was locked and secure.

And then, she set out into the night, under the silver moonlight, toward Brecken's cabin at Lynia.

<h1 style="text-align:center">Chapter 12</h1>

B recken milled around his cabin, washing the cup from which he'd recently imbibed Slayer blood before depositing it in the rack. Drying his hands on the dish towel, he stared out the tiny window above the sink, his thoughts consumed with Callie as they had been since Jack called to tell him the news about Zadicus's alliance with Bakari and the canceled wedding. Raoul had also called to inform him they no longer needed his services. Brecken had heard Viessa crying in the background, and he clenched his teeth, frustrated at the pain Zadicus had caused everyone who loved him.

He hurt for everyone involved in the terrible situation and wished like hell he could smash Zadicus's nose about a zillion times with his fist. First on his list of grievances was the fact he'd hurt Callie. Guilt consumed him as he acknowledged he'd also had a hand in Zadicus's deception, even if only a small one. She deserved so much better, and he railed at himself for ever agreeing to Zadicus's stupid ruse. Gritting his teeth, he realized he was two seconds from ripping the dish towel in half and laid it over the counter to dry. Clad only in sweatpants, he strode over to the bed and sat on the edge, wondering what the hell to do.

He didn't think Callie would figure out he wrote the letters, but if she did, it would cause her yet another round of anguish. The woman who'd shown such kindness to him and his sister, and healed animals throughout the kingdom, would experience another crushing betrayal. Falling back on the bed, Brecken rubbed his hands over his face, furious at himself.

In truth, the guilt had already been too much to bear before he learned the wedding was called off. Brecken had already decided he was going to resign from his position as bodyguard and rejoin the army before

Raoul had contacted him. Along with the guilt was the knowledge that somewhere along the way, he'd fallen for Callie. Hook, line and sinker, Brecken—who had never caught feelings for any of the women he'd casually courted in the past—was a goner.

The letters had become all too real, and he worried his affection for her would turn to obsession if he continued to see her every day. Plus, he couldn't stand the thought of her pregnant with Zadicus's child. Goddess, it made his stomach churn, causing him to realize she was the first woman he'd ever imagined pregnant with *his* child. Before Callie, Brecken had been perfectly happy being a bachelor. Now, all he wanted was to hold her...and soothe her...and care for her in all the ways she deserved.

"You really fucked up, man," he muttered, harshly rubbing his eyes. "And you helped that asshole betray her. You are some kind of jerk."

A loud banging sounded at his front door, and he lurched to a sitting position, feeling his eyes widen. Behind the pounding, he heard Callie's furious voice.

"I know you're in there, asshole!" *Thunk. Thunk. Thunk.* "And I know you wrote the letters!"

"Shit!" Brecken hissed, rising and running his hand through his hair. Callie was smart—hell, she'd gone to the special school Rowena attended. Of course she'd figured out he wrote the letters. Steeling himself, he strode to the door, preparing himself for her wrath. She deserved to rail at him, and he'd let her—although he wasn't going to grovel.

The intentions behind his actions had been pure, even if they were ultimately wrong, and the ruse had gotten him closer to Callie. It had allowed him to get to know her in a way he never would have otherwise. Considering his feelings for her, he was grateful for the opportunity to write the letters, although he knew she wouldn't see it that way.

Inhaling a deep breath, he gripped the handle and yanked the door open.

C allie banged on the door, the letters clutched in her other hand as she fought the urge to scream. The excessive pounds echoed through the surrounding meadow before the door swung open. Brecken stared back at her, his expression impassive as his brown orbs simmered.

"I heard you the first time you knocked—"

Her palm crashed into his cheek so hard it stung. His nostrils flared as a muscle ticked in his jaw. Lifting her hand, she swung to strike him again. Brecken caught her wrist, quick as lightning, and squeezed.

"I'll give you one because you deserve it. But that's it, Callie."

Emitting a frustrated huff, she yanked her wrist from his grasp. "You bastard!"

His shoulders softened, and she swore she saw a flash of remorse in his eyes. Sighing, he stepped back and opened the door wider. "Come in. It looks like it's going to pour. And if we're going to have a screaming match, I'd rather do it inside."

Narrowing her eyes, she clenched her teeth so hard she wondered why they didn't disintegrate. "Why did you do it? I thought you hated Bakari. Why would you help Zadicus deceive me?"

Expelling a breath, he pinched the bridge of his nose and shook his head. "I didn't know he was working with Bakari, Callie." Reclaiming her gaze, he spoke with sincerity. "I know you have no reason to believe me, but it's the truth."

Her eyes fell to his bare chest as she pondered, and she told herself she didn't give a damn he had a perfect eight-pack under a smattering of tiny brown hairs. Nope. Not in the slightest.

"Please," he said, gesturing with his head. "Come in. I might even consider letting you slap me again if you come inside so we can argue in private." His lips curved, the tips of his fangs resting on his full lower lip. "Come on, Callie."

Lifting her chin, she breezed by him, striding into the center of the room before pivoting. The cabin was small, with one main room and what she guessed was a bathroom off to the side. The main room had a large bed against the far wall, a carpeted floor where she now stood, a fireplace to her left, a desk off to the side and a kitchenette to her right. It certainly wasn't fancy, but it was clean and well-kept.

"Not quite Zadicus's mansion," Brecken muttered, not meeting her eyes as he approached. Callie sensed resignation in his voice and realized he was embarrassed. As strange as it was, she wanted to comfort him. Before she could stop the words, they flew from her throat.

"It's nice," she said, shrugging. "Very organized and clean. It doesn't really matter how big your house is. The most important thing is that it feels like home."

His eyes latched onto hers, and she cleared her throat at the intense look.

"What?" she asked, exasperated.

"I just—" He broke off, rubbing the back of his neck. "I thought you'd prefer something fancy since you're a royal princess."

"Well, you thought wrong," she said, straightening her spine. "And since we're discussing things that are wrong, let's discuss the fact that you *wrote love letters for a man intent on deceiving me!*" Her voice rose with each word as she shook the papers in her hand.

"Do you want to sit—?"

"No, I don't want to sit down," she said, stomping her foot. "I want to know why you would do something so awful! What did I ever do to you?"

Heaving a sigh, he walked toward the desk and perched on the side, stretching his legs before him and crossing them at the ankles. He looked like a damn fitness model in his gray sweatpants and bare feet, and she crossed her arms as she waited.

"Zadicus asked me to write the letters to you the day before we went to the street fair. He said he was a terrible writer and remembered I'd mentioned excelling at creative writing in school."

"Impressive. Who knew you'd use your skills to make a fool out of me? Nice job."

He shot her a droll look. "I said no at first, but he offered to secure a seamstress position for my mother at the governor's mansion. It increased her salary exponentially, and I knew it would allow her to give my sisters things they could never have without it. So, I agreed. I knew it was wrong, but I agreed."

Callie thought of Rowena and the fantastic time they'd had at the street fair and the literacy function. She was a sweet, vivacious girl, and Callie wanted the best for her. Glancing at the carpet, she absently rubbed her arm, contemplating his motives. Although the action was terrible, at least the motive behind the action had been pure.

"I wish I could make it up to you, but I can't," he said, running his hand though his hair, resulting in wayward spiked tufts that looked so sexy Callie felt her skin flush. The scruff of his beard had grown in, and she quickly realized comfortable-at-home Brecken was just as hot as bodyguard-in-tactical-gear Brecken. Maybe even more so. Swiping a hand over her face, she pushed the thoughts away.

"I mean, you could say you're sorry. That might be one small step in trying to make it up to me." She held her thumb and index finger an inch apart.

Brecken just stared at her, arms crossed over his chest as he seemed to ponder.

"Um, hi," she said, waving her hand. "Did you hear me? You could apologize. It's really easy. You just move your lips and say the words '*I'm*' and then '*sorry*.'" Pointing to her mouth, she said it again slowly. "*I...am...sorry...Callie.* See? Piece of cake."

His lips twitched, causing fury to well in her gut. "Are you *laughing* at me?"

"Never," he said, pursing his lips to suppress an obvious laugh.

"You son of a bitch! I can't believe you. I want a fucking apology—"

"No," he interjected, rising and slowly stalking toward her. "I'll take responsibility for hurting you, but I won't apologize for writing the letters."

Feeling her throat bob, she tilted her head to stare at him, wondering why he was suddenly so close. The heat of his body seemed to meld with hers, and tiny flames of awareness flickered along her flushed skin. "You can't even bring yourself to apologize to me?" she asked softly, wondering why the sting of tears pulsed in tandem with her ragged heartbeat.

"No," he almost whispered, gently touching the skin of her upper arm, bare as she stood in her tank top and velour sweatpants. Gazing into her eyes, he slowly trailed his fingers down her arm, the caress so tender and arousing all at once. Reaching her hand, he grasped the letters and tugged them free.

"I won't apologize for doing something that brought me closer to you." Lifting the letters, he shook them. "Everything I wrote was true, Callie. Every. Single. Word."

She licked her suddenly parched lips, her body inflaming when desire sparked in his eyes. "But you called me your love," she said, noticing the rasp in her voice. "Your Callie-lily."

He grinned as his cheeks flushed. "Calla lilies are my mom's favorite flower. She talks about them all the time. How they're the most beautiful flower in every garden where they grow. It just sort of came to me and it seemed fitting for you."

"Because you think I'm beautiful?" she asked, feeling her brows draw together.

Amusement entered his expression. "Well, it seems we've gone from seeking an apology to fishing for compliments."

Scowling, she swatted his arm. "Screw you. For a second, I almost believed you. Damn it! Why am I so fucking gullible?" Uttering a frustrating groan, she pivoted, burying her face in her hand. "Screw the promise I made Dad. From now on, I'm reading everyone's fucking mind."

"Hey," he said, encircling her arm and gently turning her. "I'm joking with you, hon. Of course you're beautiful." He lifted the letters. "Maybe I'm a bit embarrassed because I poured my heart out to you. I know you're hurt, but this sucks for me too. I wrote sappy letters to someone who would never see me that way."

Callie's brow furrowed. "How do you know? You never gave me a choice. You just forged full steam ahead and deceived me. I'm having a really hard time seeing *you* as the victim here."

She sensed the wheels churning in his mind before he backed away and set the letters on the desk. Opening the top drawer, he reached inside and pulled out a folded piece of paper. Stepping toward her, he extended it.

"The damage is done, and you think I'm a huge jerk, so I might as well bare it all."

Callie stared at the paper, wondering if she should read it.

"Go on," he said, shaking it. "It will be highly embarrassing for me, but it will put us on more even ground. We can both feel like exposed idiots. It's the least I can do. Fair warning: It's a doozy. I have no idea how you'll react to it."

Curiosity swamped her as she reached for the letter. Unfolding it, she turned away and began to read, craving a small bit of privacy so she could truly digest whatever the missive held.

My Sweet Callie-lily,

Tomorrow, you'll bond with the man meant to be your mate. We live in a world where people choose who they love based on tradition and status, and I don't begrudge you for choosing Zadicus. It only makes sense based on your heritage, and I truly hope you find all the happiness you deserve.

There are so many things I want to tell you, but I understand it's better if I keep my secrets to ensure your happiness. So many times over these past few weeks, I wanted to tell you I wrote you the letters. That I was the one who longed for you from afar and was enthralled by your beauty, kindness and soulful laugh. But that would serve no purpose except to out me as a fool. Someone who decided to fall for a woman who could never be his.

Selfishly, a part of me kept the secret because I knew you'd be furious. It would create a rift between you and Zadicus and ruin the friendship we've started to build. I truly hope we can remain friends once you've bonded. I've decided that seeing you every day as you build your life with Zadicus would be too painful, so I will be resigning as his bodyguard and reapplying for the army. Still, I know I'll see you with Jack from time to time, and during those encounters, I hope our friendship will continue to grow. If you smile at me during those fleeting moments, that will be enough to fill my soul. It has to be, and I accept that.

Be happy, Callie-lily. Never stop grabbing the world by the horns and pushing through. I've never met someone as resilient as you, even though you've been faced with undeserved challenges. Others might crumble or curse the world, but you just forge ahead with grace and bravery. It is magnificent. **You** *are magnificent. Thank you for letting me know you, if only just a little. You've opened my eyes to possibilities I never considered. I always relished being alone, but you've shown me there can be beauty in caring for someone else deep in your heart.*

Love, Your Stoic Soldier, Brecken

Callie's chin trembled as she finished, and her hands shook as they held the letter. Struggling to catch her breath, she slowly rotated to gaze at Brecken. He stared back at her, resignation crossing his handsome features, along with something tender and...raw.

"Brecken," she whispered, slowly shaking her head. "I don't know what to say..."

He grinned and lifted his shoulder. "Not really sure there's much to say after that."

Folding the letter, she trailed over and gently placed it on the desk. Facing him, she tentatively stepped forward, heart lurching each time she took a step. When mere inches finally separated them, she lifted her hands, gently placing them over his pecs. He closed his eyes, appearing to cherish her touch, before slowly opening them and sliding his hands to cover hers.

"Callie," he whispered.

"I didn't know," she said, shaking her head, the movements almost imperceptible.

"I didn't know either." He squeezed her hands. "About Zadicus working with Bakari. I swear, if I'd known, I would've ripped the bastard's testicles off."

Breathing a laugh, she bit her lip. "You sound like my dad. He's first in line."

"Good. We'll murder both of them."

His thumbs smoothed the backs of her hands, caressing as she digested the letter.

"You still lied to me though. Why?"

"I'm a practical person, Callie. I saw an opportunity to help my family, and I took it. It was selfish and wrong, and I'm sorry for that. I never thought I'd develop feelings for you. It knocked me off my feet. You have a profound effect on people. I don't even think you realize it. You opened me up and made me feel all these uncomfortable emotions I had no idea how to handle. I should be pissed," he teased, his lips forming a tender smile.

Callie gazed at him, enthralled by the heat of his skin beneath her palms and the arousal that was rapidly increasing deep in her core. Letting it surge, she felt a twinge between her thighs and noticed his nostrils slightly flare.

"You smell so good," he murmured, his tone reverent as he stroked her cheek with the backs of his fingers.

"I think I'm aroused," she said, her voice gravelly.

"You're definitely aroused." Staring into her with desire-laden eyes, he inhaled a deep breath before slowly exhaling. "It smells amazing. I want to suck every fucking drop from between your pretty thighs."

The words slammed into her like a freight train, breaking the dam wide open. She shuddered and pressed her legs together as slickness coated the soft skin.

"I've never had sex. I was waiting for my bonding night."

"I know."

Rolling her tongue around her suddenly dry mouth, she pressed her fingernails into his chest, searching for a stronghold, elated when he uttered a soft hiss.

"I mean, it is still *technically* my bonding night."

His eyes darted between hers. "I don't want to be a replacement, Callie. I want it to mean something to you."

"Obviously, losing my virginity to you would mean something."

"You can lose your virginity to anyone. Maybe you should wait until you meet the man you'll actually bond with someday."

The statement elicited sadness and a bit of frustration. "Maybe I'll bond with you one day, Shakespeare. Have you considered that? Hmm?"

He bristled, causing her heart to fall to her knees.

"Wow. Okay, maybe I got the wrong impression here." Pulling away, she halted when he encircled her wrist.

"Wait," he said, drawing her close. "I just... This is a heavy discussion, Callie. You were engaged to another man hours ago. I think we just need to breathe a second."

"Breathe," she muttered, rolling her eyes. "I'm tired of breathing. Of always being altruistic and pragmatic. Where has that gotten me? To jilted bride status for the whole kingdom to see. Fuck that. I want to *live*. To throw caution to the wind and be selfish and needy for one damn night." Disengaging from him, she gripped the hem of her shirt and tugged it off, tossing it on the floor. His eyes widened as he stared at her breasts, encased in a lacy black bra.

"Callie," he whispered, hesitation marring his handsome features.

Sliding her arms around his neck, she rose to her toes. "I think it's time to stop talking, soldier."

"How the hell am I supposed to think when you're half-naked?" he asked, rubbing the tip of his nose against hers.

"You're not...and neither am I," she said, chucking her brows. Sliding her fingers into the thick hair at his nape, she squeezed, loving the slight growl he emitted as he tugged her tighter against his body. "Brecken?"

"Yes, honey," he whispered, barely grazing her lips with his.

"I want you to take my virginity."

His large frame shuddered in her arms, and she laughed with joy.

"Now, who's laughing at whom?" he teased.

Staring into his limitless eyes, Callie understood that every decision in her life thus far had been a step toward this very moment. She'd always held back with Zadicus, telling herself she would develop a burning passion for him. But deep in her heart, she acknowledged she'd never felt one ounce of the desire she now felt in Brecken's embrace. Never felt the thrumming arousal, or the wetness lining her inner thighs, or the tingle on every inch of her skin as she anticipated his touch.

Somehow, she'd waited for Brecken and ended up in his arms, exactly where she was supposed to be. Callie felt the sentiment deep in her bones and vowed to seize the moment. No more waiting for what felt right. It was time to just *feel*. To experience what she was destined to experience on her bonding night, with the man who'd written such beautiful words to her. Staring deep into his soul, she spoke with clarity and resolve.

"Make love to me, Brecken."

His eyes searched hers, hooded and filled with desire. "Are you sure? I don't want you to regret this—"

"I won't," she murmured, covering his lips with her fingers.

He placed a soft kiss against them before continuing. "Once I start loving you, I won't stop until I've kissed every inch of your body. Do you understand?"

"Yes, you daft man. That's what I'm asking you to do."

Chuckling, he rested his forehead against hers. He gazed into her eyes as his thumb caressed her heated cheek. "I'm terrified you'll regret this, hon. That you're angry and hurt, and that I don't deserve to touch you after the way I deceived you." Sliding his fingers into the hair at the nape of her neck, he almost growled. "And still, knowing all that, I'm not sure I can stop myself."

"Brecken?"

"Hmm?"

Nipping his bottom lip, she reveled in his soft moan. "Stop talking and fuck me—"

He all but sucked the words from her mouth, plunging his tongue deep inside as she mewled. Losing her grip on reality, she relaxed into his hard frame as he surged his straining erection into the juncture of her thighs.

Praying to the goddess she would be good at sex, she held on for dear life, determined not to let go until they were both sated and replete—and she was no longer a virgin.

Chapter 13

B recken swirled his tongue over Callie's, drawing her essence into his mouth as he struggled to breathe. She tasted like the honeysuckles he used to pluck and savor from the bushes that grew in his back yard, but so much sweeter since it was enhanced by the smell of her arousal. The aroma surrounded him, almost suffocating as he longed to tear off her clothes and plunge himself into the wet depths of her core. But this was her first time, and although he knew he didn't deserve to touch her, it was impossible to stop now. Knowing that, he was determined to focus on her pleasure and make her scream in ecstasy before he even thought of experiencing his own release.

Bending his knees, he palmed the luscious globes of her ass, lifting her as she yelped. Her legs instinctively wrapped around his waist, and he carried her to the desk, swiping the papers to the floor in one fell swoop.

"Hey!" she said, pouting as he set her atop the wooden surface. "I want to keep those. They're so romantic even if they were a bit underhanded."

Brecken glanced at the letters scattered on the floor. "I'm never going to live it down, am I?"

"Nope," she said, giving him an adorable grin. "I reserve the right to make you feel terrible about writing them forever."

Hooking his fingers in the waistband of her sweatpants, he began to tug. "I'm happy you want to keep them," he murmured against her lips, tugging her pants and underwear down her legs. "I think they're the only reason you're letting me touch you right now."

"Truth," she said, arching an eyebrow as he tossed her pants aside. "Thank the goddess I figured it out."

Reaching behind her, he unclasped her bra as he gazed into her eyes. "I was terrified you were going to." Pulling the lacy fabric from her body, he dropped it before sliding his palms over her abdomen, just below her breasts. Tenderly, he caressed as her skin trembled beneath. "And I thought you'd hate me forever."

Resting her hands on the desk, the little minx grinned and thrust her breasts high, making his mouth water as his erection strained inside his pants. "Well, then, make it up to me, soldier."

Sliding his hands behind her knees, he dragged her toward him, situating his straining cock between her thighs. He couldn't touch her there yet—one feel of that slick arousal, and he'd lose it. So he pressed against her and slid his hand into her hair, clenching her curls. After a soft tug, her head fell back, exposing the smooth skin of her neck. Lowering his lips, he pressed them to her pulsing vein.

She emitted a high-pitched moan that shot straight to his dick as he began to trail kisses over her neck, down to her collarbone and over the swell of her breast. Sighing his name, she locked her ankles behind his back and thrust her fingers into his thick hair.

Brecken trailed his tongue over her skin, wondering if he'd ever tasted anything so good. Circling her nipple and the darkened areola, he placed wet kisses as she whimpered beneath him.

"Look at me, Callie-lily," he rasped, needed to stare into her gorgeous eyes as he sucked that tight, puckered little nipple between his lips. Her eyes latched onto his, the ocean orbs swimming with desire, and his knees almost buckled at the sight of her swollen lips and flushed cheeks. Opening his lips, he gently placed them over her nipple, drawing the bud into his mouth and sucking it deep inside.

"*Ohmygod...*" she breathed, legs clenching his waist as she fisted his hair, sending jolts of pleasure through his frame. "Brecken..."

He moaned against her skin, sucking the taut bud as he gazed at her. Goddess, he could spend every moment for the rest of eternity right here, nestled against her body as she moaned above him. Popping her nipple from his mouth, he extended his tongue, flicking the nub in short strokes as her back arched.

"Do you like that, honey?"

"What do you think?" she rasped, her fingers so tight in his hair he wondered if she would rip it out. Hell, he didn't care as long as she stayed right here in his arms, squirming and pliant as he loved her. "Oh, *please*...do the other one."

Breathing a laugh against her warm skin, he trailed a row of kisses between her breasts until he reached the other nipple. Licking his lips, he formed a circle and blew a slow breath on the pebbled nub.

"Fuck!" she hissed, her heels digging into his buttocks as she clutched him. "Don't tease me."

"That's the best part, hon," he said, nudging her nipple with his nose. "I want to draw this out and make you feel good."

"I feel so good," she groaned, head falling back as he placed soft pecks on the underside of her breast. "Damn it. You're driving me crazy."

Deciding to end the delicious torture for them both, he closed his mouth over her breast, pulling her against his tongue. Her body trembled, mimicking his own tremors as he reveled in the pleasure of finally being in the arms of the woman he'd only dreamed of touching. It was humbling, the way she wrapped around him as if he were her guidepost, and he vowed to support her as he took her over the edge.

After sucking her nipple into a tight, straining point, he drew back, needing to gaze upon her naked beauty for one moment. Panting beneath him, she stared at him with hooded eyes as her pert nipples strained toward him, wet and glistening from his ministrations.

Placing his hand between her breasts, he slid his palm down her abdomen and across her navel. Tiny goose bumps sprang beneath his touch, her body quivering as he eventually reached her mound. Cupping her, he slid his finger between her drenched folds.

"I'm going to make you come over and over again, honey," he whispered, gliding his finger back and forth in a slow slide. "Let's make you come right here against my hand so we can take the edge off."

"Okay," she whispered, pushing against his hand. Chuckling, he searched, locating her opening and circling it with his finger.

"You're greedy," he teased, gathering her wetness as he prepared to plunge inside.

"I've only ever done this to myself," she whispered, the words breathy as she clung to him.

"Who do you think about when you play with yourself?"

Her half-fangs squished her lips as she grinned. "Henry Cavill."

"Superman?" He arched a brow. "Wow. That's a lot to live up to, hon."

"I have faith in you, soldier." Inching closer, her eyes narrowed as she seemed to contemplate. Finally, she said softly, "I thought about you too sometimes. I would dream about you and couldn't understand why. I mean, you're really hot, but I probably should've been dreaming about my betrothed."

"Fuck him," Brecken muttered.

"It seems I wanted to fuck you," was her sultry reply. "I'd wake up all sweaty after dreaming we were together, and I'd reach down and touch myself—"

Her words broke off with a gasp as he surged a finger inside her taut channel. "Like this?"

"Oh, yes…" she moaned, lips parted as she gazed at him while he slid his finger back and forth. "Like that. Just like that…"

"Fuck, you're so tight and wet," he rasped, adding another finger and pushing deep inside, trying to find the spot that would make her scream. Rubbing her silken walls, he hooked his fingers, thrilled when a ragged moan leaped from her throat.

"Right there," he said, lowering his lips to her neck and kissing a path to her ear. Resting his lips on the shell of her ear, he murmured, "Fuck my hand, Callie. I'm going to make you explode."

She undulated her hips, thrusting against his fingers as he rimmed her ear with his wet tongue. Placing the heel of his hand against her clit, he pressed against it, stimulating the tiny bundle of nerves as his fingers milked the spot deep within. Her sweet, wet honey flowed over his hand and fingers, drenching him with her arousal. Closing his teeth around her earlobe, he lightly bit the tender flesh before drawing it between his lips.

"Oh, god," she moaned, head thrown back as her hips pushed against his hand. "I think I'm going to come."

"Yes, honey," he crooned in her ear, his hand working at a furious pace as he strove to give her pleasure. "You're going to come all over me, aren't you?"

Her spine snapped, body jerking as she cried his name, and joy swelled in his chest. Thrilled he could give her such pleasure, he whispered words of love and desire in her ear as the orgasm tore through her frame. Unabandoned, she opened for him, like the calla lilies that inspired her nickname, and he was overwhelmed by her acquiescence and trust. Goddess knew, he probably didn't deserve it, but he would drink it in, imbibing like a parched vagabond as she gave him everything. Her body. Her forgiveness. Her innocence.

Expelling a deep breath, Callie lifted her head, eyes sparkling as she struggled to catch her breath. Gazing deep into those cobalt orbs, his lips curved.

"Well, well, it seems that someone has put Henry to shame," she teased.

Chuckling, he drew his hand from her core and lifted his fingers to his mouth. They were coated with her essence and he began to lick it away. "I had the fleeting thought I was taking your innocence, but I quickly realized that's ridiculous." Sticking his finger between his lips, he sucked her honey before moving to the next. "You're not innocent at all, are you? Look at those fucking eyes and swollen lips. You ready to go again?"

Giving a sated sigh, she nodded, adorable as she bit her lip. "But I want to make you feel good too."

"I feel so good right now," he said, sliding his hands to cup her ass and lifting her. She held tight as he walked them to the bed, lowering her and stretching out above her lithe body. "You're naked in my bed," he murmured, caressing her cheek. "I'm in fucking heaven, honey."

Grinning, she encircled his neck and shimmied against him. "Take off your pants."

"Not yet. I'm going to make you come again. And then, if you still want to make love, we'll do that too."

Her fingers sifted through his hair, causing him to shiver. "I'm not changing my mind, Brecken. I want this. I want *you*."

His eyes darted over her face as he brushed away the hair at her temple. "I'm sorry for deceiving you, Callie. I just need to say that one more time. I'm so humbled you can forgive me."

"I understand your motives." Lifting her hand, she cupped his jaw. "But please don't lie to me again, okay? I mean, I could read your thoughts if I wanted to, but then I'd be violating your trust. Let's just be honest with each other from here."

"I can do that." Lowering, he placed a peck on her lips. "Now, I remember promising to lick every drop of your arousal. Let's get you nice and wet again so I can taste you."

Giggling, she gently pushed his head lower. "If you insist. And keep up the dirty talk. It's so freaking sexy."

His deep chuckle rumbled against her skin as he kissed his way down her stomach. His lips moved between her breasts and down to her navel. Staring into her eyes, his tongue dipped into the tiny indention before moving lower. Encircling her thighs with his broad hands, he dragged her toward the edge of the bed. Resting on his knees, he grinned at her from between her legs as she gazed at him, eyes simmering with lust.

"Look at you," he whispered, palming her inner thighs and spreading her legs. Her wet folds called to him, and he leaned in, gently smoothing his lips over the tender flesh. "Callie," he whispered, the words reverberating off her soft skin, "you're so pretty."

Her nose scrunched. "Can you be pretty down there?"

Laughing, he pushed her thighs wider and nodded. "Oh, yeah. You're a fucking goddess down here, honey." Placing his fingers on her folds, he pulled her open, feeling his cock jerk as he stared at her deepest place. Unable to hold back any longer, he buried his face in her center and began to feast.

She moaned above him as he licked a long trail over her opening, up to her clit, and flicked it with his tongue. Aiming to take her even higher than before, he closed his lips over the sensitive bud, sucking it in rhythmic movements as he circled her opening with his finger. Delving one finger into her channel, he slid it back and forth as his mouth worked her clit.

Callie writhed on the bed, fists clenching the comforter before she eventually reached down and thrust her fingers in his hair. Blood surged to Brecken's shaft when she drew him closer, rubbing her core against his face as he loved her. Goddess, she was so sexy like this, unencumbered as she pushed into his face, straining for release. Inserting another finger, he plunged them back and forth as his tongue flicked the engorged nub at the hood of her mound.

Finally, she screamed, losing control and wrapping her legs around his head. Brecken chuckled against her wet folds, accepting that if he suffocated with his face buried in her sweet pussy, it would be a magnificent way to enter the Passage. Eventually, she relaxed, her legs falling to the bed as her frame turned limp atop the comforter.

Rising, he shrugged off his pants, tossing them to the floor before crawling over her. Aligning his body with hers, he cupped her cheek, resting his weight on his other arm so he didn't crush her.

"Earth to Callie," he teased, kissing the tip of her nose. "Are you okay?"

"Sensory overload," she murmured, curls sliding over the bed as she shook her head. "My muscles melted."

His low-toned laugh surrounded them. "We don't have to do anything else, hon. I can just hold you and let you enjoy the high."

Squinting with one eye, she ran her calf over his. "No way, soldier. It's time. Make love to me."

His practical brain railed at him that he should give her more time. That losing her virginity was a huge decision that shouldn't be made after discovering a terrible betrayal. Sliding between her thighs, his body—and his cock—overrode his objections, pulverizing them to dust in his mind. Gripping her leg, he hooked it around his waist, elated when she used it to tug him closer.

"Do you want me to grab a condom?"

Although Vampyres couldn't transmit diseases due to their self-healing abilities, there was still a chance of pregnancy.

"No. Sadie gave me an IUD years ago to help regulate my periods. Go for it, soldier."

Wondering if he'd ever gazed upon anyone so simultaneously cute and sexy, he reached for his throbbing cock. Encircling the base, he aligned the sensitive head with her opening, closing his eyes in ecstasy when it dragged through her wet folds. She emitted a tiny mewl beneath him, and his lids flew open as his eyes latched onto hers.

Staring deep into those fathomless blue-green orbs, he began to push inside.

"Ohhhhh..." she whimpered as her arms and leg drew him closer. "Oh, yes...that feels...*Brecken*..."

"I'm right here, Callie-lily," he said, pushing into her tight channel inch by slow, excruciating inch. The plushy walls of her core squeezed him, pushing back at the invasion, and he gritted his teeth at the extreme pleasure.

"Relax, hon," he whispered, his heart slamming in his chest when she melted beneath him. The gesture showed such openness, and it moved something in his stoic soul. Driving deeper, he eventually reached the hilt. "You okay?"

She nodded and dug her nails into his shoulders. "Don't hold back."

Eliciting a feral growl, he began to move his hips, dragging his engorged cock through her swollen folds as she arched to meet him. Their bodies moved in tandem, learning each other's rhythm as he tried to hold off his release. He'd dreamed of fucking her for so long he was half-afraid he'd lose it before pleasing her.

"I feel you everywhere," she whispered, face contorting with pleasure as he moved deep within. "Holy shit, you're huge."

He froze, looming above her as he assessed. "Am I hurting you?"

"No way." Furiously shaking her head, she speared her nails into his skin. "Don't stop. It was just getting good."

Breathing a laugh, he resumed thrusting inside her warm body, lowering his head to capture her lips. He'd never really laughed while having sex, and it freed something, causing him to open himself to her. Together, they both bloomed into something more—two people who might never have connected except for the extraordinary circumstances that led them to this very night. Although he hated that Callie had experienced pain, he was exceedingly thankful for the opportunity to make love to her.

Cradling her head, he kissed her, thorough and deep, as he claimed her body. Her taut channel drenched him, enclosing him in a fist of silken pleasure, as he felt his muscles tighten. Sliding a hand under her body, he palmed her ass, lifting her to him each time he thrust inside. Striving to hit the inner spot he'd found with his fingers, he jutted against her swollen walls with the head of his cock.

"Right there," she whimpered, head tossing on the bed. "*Oh, god*, right there...keep hitting it..."

Gritting his teeth, he surged inside, ramming his cock against the tiny spot. Her nails speared his skin, most likely drawing blood, sending a surge of pleasure-pain through his entire body. Feeling his balls tighten, he buried his face in her neck and reached for the pinnacle.

She bowed beneath him, launching into an orgasm seconds before his own crashed down his spine, causing him to jerk his hips in a frenzied rush against her quaking body. Releasing a guttural groan into the sweat-soaked skin of her neck, he began shooting his release deep inside her body, coating her core...marking her as his.

"*Mine*," he gritted into her nape as she shuddered beneath him.

"Oh, god..." she moaned, lost in the climax as their bodies released and convulsed. Encircling her with his arms, he melded their bodies, admiring how perfectly they fit together. The thought was terribly sappy and quite unlike him, but the woman had turned everything else upside down. It was probably inevitable she'd turn him into a romantic dope.

His hips jerked as the last jets of release shot into her slick center. Relaxing against her, he cuddled her close, admitting he was a goner. God, he'd never craved cuddling in his entire life. Now, all he wanted was to hold her tight and never let go.

Lifting a shaking hand, she sifted her fingers through his hair. "Are you laughing?"

He nodded against her neck. "You've turned me into a pansy."

Her joyful chuckle enveloped them, and she kissed his ear. "How so?"

Raising his head, which now seemed to weigh more than a four-wheeler, he stared into her sated eyes. "I've turned into a letter-writing dope. Let's leave it there."

Snickering, she scrunched her features. "It's sweet. I want you to write me more."

"Shit." Pecking her lips, he shook his head. "I've created a monster."

They exchanged lazy smiles, stroking each other's heated skin as their gazes mingled. Finally, he asked softly, "Are you okay?"

Nodding, she cupped his jaw. "That was amazing." His cock twitched inside her, causing her to gasp. "I still feel you."

"I wish I could stay here forever," he murmured.

A loud clap of thunder sounded outside, jolting them, and Brecken felt himself slipping. Hating to leave her gorgeous body, he kissed her cheek before slowly rising. "Stay here."

"I'm not going anywhere," she said, lifting her arms over her head as she stretched over the bed. "Best workout *ever*."

He strode to the bathroom and wet a cloth before returning to her. Lifting her leg, he placed her ankle on his shoulder, opening her so he could clean away the evidence of their loving. She gazed at him, curls strewn over the bed, looking like a sated queen.

When he was done, he wiped his cock, mourning the loss of her essence spread over the sensitive skin. Once he recovered, he'd take her again—slower this time—and treasure that wet warmth spread around him.

"Can I ask you something weird?"

"Sure." He walked to the bed, sitting on the edge.

Rising to her knees, she tilted her head. "Have you ever danced in the rain? It's one of my favorite things. I used to do it with my mom when I had a bad day at school. She said it cleansed everything away so we could start the next day fresh."

"That's pretty cool. I've never tried it."

"Well, I had a pretty shitty day—except for the past hour, of course." She winked, sending his heart right back into overdrive. "So I'd really like to wash it away. Any chance you'd want to do it with me? I'm pretty sure it's pouring from the sound of the thunder." She pointed to the ceiling.

"Sure, I'm game." Standing, he extended his hand.

Taking it, she leaped from the bed, throwing on her clothes while he tugged on his sweatpants. Grabbing his hand, she dragged him outside until they stood in the wet grass while large droplets fell from above. Extending her arms, she began to twirl, mouth open as she tried to drink the drops. Brecken thought she looked like a regal imp, intent on showing the world it wouldn't get the best of her. In a word, she was glorious.

"Isn't it fun?" she asked, halting mid-twirl. "Come on, you have to twirl!"

Feeling like an idiot, he extended his arms and began to turn, overjoyed by the sound of her effervescent laughter. "See?"

"It feels good!" he said, excited most of all by her gregarious smile.

"I'm not a virgin anymore!" she yelled, and he froze, his features drawing together.

"Jeez, Callie, my mom's cabin is just across that meadow." He pointed toward the deep thicket of trees and brush that sat at the far side of his lawn. "Keep it down."

"Not on your life, buster. I've waited too long to find my Henry."

He scowled. "Should I be worried about this Henry Cavill obsession you have?"

Tossing her head back, her neck glistened from the dewy rain. "No way. You're my new Henry, and you're so damn sexy, Brecken."

Approaching her, he decided he'd gone long enough without touching her. Tugging her close, he drew her into a passionate kiss as droplets coated their sated bodies. Pulling back, she laced her arms around his neck. "I know you don't want to be sappy, but I'd really like to cuddle with you...and then I want to bone again, obviously."

"I've never cuddled before, so I might be bad at it."

"Well, I'm no expert either, but we could figure it out together. I mean, if you want to. I think I'd like snuggling with you while it storms outside. Sounds pretty romantic." She waggled her eyebrows.

Crouching down, he lifted her as she squealed. Placing a firm kiss on her lips, he strode across the yard. "Dancing in the rain and cuddling. Damn, woman. At this rate, you're going to get another letter out of me before sunrise."

"*My hero*," she sighed, holding onto him as he walked up the porch steps.

Carrying her inside, he shut the door behind them and located some towels so they could dry off. And then, Brecken cuddled with a woman for the first time in his life, noting it was nothing short of magnificent since it was his gorgeous Callie in his arms.

Eventually, the cuddling turned to another round of hot sex, which almost blew his mind.

And then, at his woman's request, he wrote her another damn love letter, pretending he hated it but secretly enamored with her smile as he read it to her before sunrise in his deep, reverent tone.

Chapter 14

Bakari paced inside the cave, furious and fierce.

"You had one job, Zadicus," he said, jutting his finger in the man's face as he sat on the nearby rock. "Goddess, I never should've recruited you in the first place. I knew you didn't have the temerity to see this through. You're no better than your aunt."

"Callie is powerful," Zadicus said, standing and lifting his arms. "The shield you placed was imperceptible until she decided to look for it. You can't blame me for her discovery."

"Said like the victim you are," Bakari spat, turning to face Commander Vadik. "Has Dr. Tyson returned from the human world?"

"Yes," Vadik said with a nod. "He's in the lab working on various potions." Gesturing toward the tunnel, he asked, "Would you like me to summon him?"

"No need," Dr. Tyson answered, appearing from the mouth of the tunnel. "I'm here. What do you require of me, Bakari?"

Bakari studied the hybrid, who professed to be half-Slayer and half-Vampyre, although Bakari knew the truth. The slight points of his ears would be imperceptible to most, but Bakari had met other Elven-Vampyre hybrids over his long life, all of them in the human world, passing as the inferior species.

"You procured the elements needed to create the new potion, Quaygon?"

"Yes," he said, holding up a small vial. "And I've asked you to call me by my human name rather than my immortal one."

"Yes, yes," Bakari said, waving a dismissive hand. "The concoction is as potent as promised?"

"We will need to test it on a live subject, but I am confident in its potency."

"Good. I have just the subject we need." Extending his hand toward Zadicus, Bakari narrowed his eyes, summoning the powers that swirled in his blood as a result of all the concoctions Dr. Tyson had formulated thus far. After a moment, he froze Zadicus in place.

"What are you doing?" the man asked, eyes widening in fear. "Bakari...please. I'm sorry I failed with Callie. I can fix it, I swear."

"Stop groveling," Bakari gritted through clenched teeth. "Your life as you knew it is over. You've been outed as a traitor and can never return to immortal society. It is time for you to embrace your true purpose."

Glancing at the doctor, he urged him over by hooking the fingers of his free hand. "Come, Dr. Tyson. It is time to test the new potion."

"I can give him two CCs to start. Otherwise, it will be too much."

"How many CCs will turn him into the soldier we need?"

Dr. Tyson's eyebrows drew together as he studied the vial. "Five or six, but that's too much for a first dose."

"Give him six CCs," Bakari commanded.

"You don't understand. That dose will effectively kill him. All that will remain is brute strength and the ability to follow orders."

"Good. Perhaps I should've transformed him from the beginning. Inject the potion, Dr. Tyson."

"Please, no..." Zadicus pleaded, chin trembling as he stood frozen.

"I'm sorry, my friend. You'll have better use to me this way. Failure must be punished at all costs. I hope your soul finds its way to the Passage." Glaring at Dr. Tyson, he commanded in a low tone, "Inject the potion."

Dr. Tyson's throat bobbed before he stepped forward, pulling a syringe from the pocket of the white lab coat he wore. Inserting it in the vial, he withdrew six CCs and approached Zadicus. Lifting the man's sleeve, he thrust the needle into his arm.

Zadicus gasped, ice-blue eyes laced with fear as Dr. Tyson injected the potion into his body. For a moment, all was silent...and then, the vein in Zadicus's neck began to pulse wildly. The man screamed, his fangs glistening in the dim light of the torches that lined the cave walls as his skin began to bulge and transform. Bakari observed with labored breaths, power surging through his frame at the creation before him.

"He might not be able to withstand the transformation," Dr. Tyson murmured.

"He will," Bakari said, willing it to happen.

Zadicus's gaze locked with his, filled with terror and confusion, before the light inside suddenly dimmed. Any last vestige of the Vampyre's soul left his body, leaving a robotic warrior in its place. Releasing the freezing spell, Bakari spoke.

"Step forward, warrior."

The creature followed the command, stoic and steady. "I am at your command, Bakari." His voice was lower, less filled with nuance and life, and Bakari was pleased.

"Excellent job, Dr. Tyson. His self-healing abilities will be magnified?"

"Yes," the man said softly, seemingly overcome with the gravity of the transformation. "He's essentially been transformed into a super soldier. As long as you give him Slayer blood every few days, he will remain a powerful asset. He now possesses the strength of twenty Vampyre soldiers."

"Good. That will come in handy during our final skirmish. The immortals are intent on one ultimate battle to end this war, and I aim to give them one. Commander Vadik, you will instill Zadicus into your lineup immediately and train him to fight alongside the Deamon troops."

"Yes, sir."

Bakari thought he noticed a hint of annoyance in the man's expression. "Do you want to voice a concern?"

"No," Vadik said, shaking his head. "I'm just ready to end this conflict. It has raged for too long. I want to end the war and instill Deamon supremacy over the caves once again. We will create our utopia there in Crimeous's name while you rule the immortal world. It is time for the species to be separate once again, as the goddess intended. I don't relish the idea of having a genetically modified Vampyre on my squad, but I see the advantage."

"Good," Bakari said. "You will have your utopia soon enough, Vadik. We all will. For now, I require some rest."

The men gave a respectful bow before Bakari exited and returned to his cottage. Now that his plan to blackmail Callie through Zadicus had backfired, he was determined to find another way to secure her alliance.

Entering his cabin, he stripped down to his underwear, noting the slight throbbing on his inner thigh where his mark was branded. After pouring a decanter of Slayer blood, he sat in the broad-backed chair beside the fireplace, tracing his finger over the pentagram that had been embedded on his pale skin since birth. The symbol signified the hidden Elven prophecy that was discovered when Miranda and Kenden found the secret scrolls at Restia. It was the reason he had been exiled from the realm by the soothsayers, and he felt a deep calling to fulfill it. When he'd learned of Callie's role in the prophecy, he knew it was only a matter of time before he secured her alliance. Patience had always been his virtue, and reimagining the world took time and careful effort.

Sipping the thick liquid, he wondered if perhaps he'd approached the situation from the wrong perspective. Callie often felt ostracized due to her powers and lack of acceptance in the realm. Perhaps he could approach her himself. If anyone understood being cast out from the very people who were supposed to accept you, it was Bakari. Did they possess enough common ground for her to consider listening to him?

Thinking back on their conversation at Astaria, Bakari remembered the jolt that flashed in her eyes when he'd mentioned the prophecy. Was it possible she saw a miniscule advantage to destroying the immortal world as it existed now?

Understanding there was only one way to find out, Bakari mulled different scenarios in which he could approach her until he crawled into bed, still mindful of the pulsing black mark upon his thigh.

Callie's eyes fluttered open, and she assessed the darkened surroundings. A steady cadence sounded to her right, and she turned to find Brecken softly snoring as his head rested upon the pillow. Smiling, she reached for him, aching to swipe the tuft of hair from his forehead. Halting, she decided to study him a bit longer as he slept.

For the love of the goddess, she'd lost her virginity last night. Not to the man she'd promised herself to for the better part of a year, but to Brecken, the sexy bodyguard who'd been in the background the entire time. Callie had always enjoyed their playful banter and gentle ribbing. She thought him quite serious and loved teasing him, especially when those full lips quirked at her chiding. He would feign indifference, but she usually caught the amusement in his eyes. But somehow, she'd missed the affection lurking just beneath the mirth. Why hadn't she seen it?

For someone who could read minds, she was seriously daft. Settling on her back, she glared at the ceiling, trying like hell not to beat herself up for missing so many things. Zadicus's betrayal, the letters, and Brecken's affection for her. By the goddess, she'd missed them all. Callie considered herself a pretty intelligent person and wondered why she'd been so oblivious.

Pondering, she thought back to the way she was raised. Her parents were always so careful to support and encourage her since she'd been bestowed with her father's powers. They'd done an excellent job, and she loved them dearly, but their encouragement probably created a false sense of complacency for her. She trusted others because her world was safe. What would've happened if circumstances were different? If her grandfather's evil blood had been set free and allowed to dictate her actions without her parents' intervention?

Shivering, Callie realized she didn't relish that thought. She was determined to live a life of honor, worthy of her station. She looked up to her parents, Miranda, Evie and everyone in her family and wanted so badly to be a force for good in the kingdom. Lost in thought, she didn't hear Brecken rouse beside her until his finger gently grazed her arm.

"Hey," she said softly, turning to face him.

"Hey." His raspy voice rolled over her, sending a rush of arousal to her core. By the goddess, he was so fucking sexy. Now the door had been opened, Callie was pretty sure she wanted to bang him at every opportunity. "It was hard to sleep with the excessive teeth grinding."

Breathing a laugh, she bit her lip. "Sorry. I was just thinking about my childhood and what made me so fucking gullible. And I was also thinking we should probably just bang every day for eternity."

Lazy brown eyes assessed her as he rubbed her arm. "You're not gullible, hon. Zadicus worked hard to deceive you, and he fooled me too. I'm pissed I didn't discover his alliance with Bakari. He negotiated several hours a week away from my watch, and that's probably when he met with him. I'm furious I let him manipulate me too."

"I guess no one's perfect," she said, wrinkling her nose. "But we have to be smarter from now on."

"Definitely."

"Miranda's probably going to want to question you in front of the council too."

As if on cue, Callie's phone dinged. Reaching for it, she picked it up from the bedside table and scrolled through the texts.

"Everything okay?" he asked.

"Yeah," she said, her finger moving over the screen. "Miranda and Sathan have called an emergency council meeting and she wants the rest of my family to attend as well. Apparently, Tatiana contacted Uncle Heden last night, and I'm somehow involved. She also wants to question you afterward." Gazing at him, she smiled. "You'll get to meet my family. How sweet."

His expression was impassive, causing her to wonder if her playful teasing crossed a line. After all, they'd had sex, but what did that mean? Did they start courting now? The jilted bride and the out-of-work bodyguard. What a pair.

Callie had no idea, but one thing was certain: she liked Brecken. The sex had been amazing, but beyond that, she actually enjoyed his company. He was a good man who'd handled Zadicus's arrogant commands with grace and treated his sister like gold. Callie longed to dig deeper. To see him with his mother and other sisters and grow their connection. They already had explosive chemistry and affection. What if it could grow into love?

"Did I scare you away?" she asked, heart thrumming as she awaited his answer.

"No." Inching closer, he rested his head on his palm, elbow firm on the mattress as his other hand caressed her collarbone. "I just have no idea how to navigate this. You were betrothed to someone else yesterday, and we come from different worlds, Callie. You haven't even had time to process things."

"Well, I *did* give you my virginity. I think that counts for something."

A breathy laugh escaped his lips before he leaned down to give her a soft kiss. "It means so much, hon. Honestly, I'm overwhelmed. Part of me thinks I'm dreaming."

"Wait till you meet my dad. More like a nightmare. He's a bit overprotective." She held her finger and thumb an inch apart.

"How pissed is he at Zadicus?"

Shrugging, she considered. "Somewhere between crushing his balls and murder."

Pursing his lips, he nodded. "Same here."

"You two can align in your hatred of my ex-betrothed. It's what every girl dreams of."

Grinning, his eyes darted over her face, and she could see the wheels churning in his mind. "Let's not decide anything now. I want to make love to you one more time, to convince myself this is real."

Sliding her hand between their bodies, she encircled his cock, thick and turgid as it nudged against her thigh. "Oh, I think it's pretty real," she said in a sultry voice.

Uttering a soft moan, he jutted into her hand. "From virgin to sex goddess in one night."

"Sex goddess?" she asked, eyes widening. "Oh, I like that."

"I like it too, you little tease." Sliding over her, he wedged himself between her legs. "We'll talk after the council meeting today, okay, hon?"

Sliding her arms around his neck, she nodded. "Okay. Get to work, soldier."

Gazing into her eyes, he drew her close, aligning their bodies. Callie spread her legs wide, inviting him to ravish her. Gripping her shoulder, he anchored her and surged inside. No foreplay this time. Just raw, passionate connection with her lover. Clutching him, she rode the wave, allowing him to take her to the peak as she shuddered in his arms.

Chapter 15

After her passionate morning tryst with Brecken, Callie headed home in the four-wheeler. She felt a bit guilty lying to her parents—after all, they believed she'd spent the night at Astaria. But she was an adult, for the goddess's sake, and had every right to spend the night wherever she damn well pleased. Once home, she took a long, warm shower, touching herself between her thighs and remarking on the slight soreness. Her Vampyre blood had self-healing properties, but Brecken was *huge*. In her opinion, at least, which probably didn't amount to much since his was the only erect cock she'd ever seen. Still, she decided he was the most studly, prolific lover ever and snickered under the spray at her silly musings.

Refreshed, she threw on her sandals, jeans and tank top and headed to Uteria. Her parents had texted her to meet them there since they'd already headed over. Darkrip was meeting Evie to practice their combined forcefield, and Arderin had promised to help Lila prepare some lunch for the council members.

On the drive to Uteria, Callie's thoughts drifted to Brecken. She would certainly see him since he was slated to meet with the council directly after their meeting to discuss Tatiana's contact with Heden. Would he remain stoic and give her that sexy smirk when they saw each other? Or would he allow the lust in those deep bronze eyes to simmer?

She wasn't sure, but she realized she wanted their relationship to remain secret for a little while longer. Not because she was ashamed or embarrassed. Brecken was a kind, thoughtful man, and any woman would be lucky to have him as her partner. Instead, she was still angry and a bit embarrassed at her own predicament and the fact that by now, the entire kingdom must know of her canceled nuptials. It would be nice to develop a relationship with Brecken outside of the watchful eye of others. Although she loved her parents and her family with her whole heart, they were a *lot* sometimes, and she knew they would meddle if they found out.

Arriving at Uteria, Callie parked beside the barracks and headed into the castle. Entering the conference room, she noticed the council members floating about. Her father, Latimus and Jack were already seated, and others milled around, sliding into open seats. Callie slid in between Larkin and Aron, flashing them both a smile.

"How are you today, Callie?" Larkin asked with a gentle smile. He was a valiant Slayer soldier who'd fought to protect his people for centuries. Callie thought him so brave and liked him immensely. He was a bit of a loner, which called to her since she often found it easier to spend time alone rather than attempt to hang with people who didn't understand her.

"I'm fine," she said, reaching over to squeeze his hand. "Thank you for asking. I'm navigating through the embarrassment phase and will soon enter the '*thank the goddess I dodged a bullet*' phase, hopefully." She made quotation marks with her fingers.

Chuckling, he winked. "I'm sure you will. You're pretty amazing and quite beautiful. I know you'll find someone who fits you better than Zadicus. You deserve that."

"Maybe one day." Studying him, she asked, "Have you ever found anyone who fit? The idea seems so faraway at the moment, but maybe you can give me hope."

His expression turned wistful, and a hint of sadness entered his brown eyes. "I found someone once...but he..." Glancing down, he twirled his thumbs together atop the table. "He died."

Callie's eyebrows lifted, and she tamped down her surprise. She didn't realize Larkin was attracted to men and certainly didn't realize he'd once been in love and lost his lover. "I'm so sorry," she whispered, encircling his wrist. "I'd love to hear your story one day. I know our kingdom is super-stuffy and still somewhat antiquated, but I spent the first seven years of my life in L.A. It was a beautiful place filled with acceptance of who people were no matter who they loved."

"I'd like to tell you one day. It's not something I talk about very much—I'm a pretty private person. You know, stoic soldier and all." His lips curved into a sweet smile. "But I think talking to you about it would be nice. I haven't talked about him for a long time."

"Then we'll do that one day. My only request is that we have lots of wine present so you can relax and tell me every last detail."

"I'd like that, princess. Thank you." He squeezed her hand atop his wrist with his free one before Miranda strode into the room, effectively ending their conversation.

"Thank you all for showing up this morning for another meeting. As you know, Heden and Sofia received a transmission from Tatiana, and we wanted to address it expeditiously."

"I can take it from here, Miranda," Heden's voice boomed as his face appeared on the screen of the large TV mounted on the conference room wall. "Can you all hear me?"

"Loud and clear," Miranda said, sliding into her chair. "You've done a great job with the newest communication updates, Heden."

"Piece of cake. We needed to upgrade everything so we could video chat with you all yesterday since we couldn't attend the bonding ceremony. Sorry to hear about Zadicus, baby toad. Want me to smash his face in?"

Callie's heart swelled at the nickname, used only by Heden. "I'm okay, Uncle Heden. Thank you."

"Of course. I've always got your back. Once Sofia stopped flirting with me long enough to let me work, I really enjoyed upgrading the systems last week. Although the wedding didn't happen, the upgrade was timely and will only improve our communications between the human and immortal realms."

Sofia appeared, palming Heden's face and pushing him out of the way to face the camera. "What my husband is *trying* to say is that I did *all* the work and he now wants to take all the credit. I wrote the entire front end code of the most recent upgrade, and he figured out a teeny, tiny part of the back end."

"I like your back end a lot better," Heden teased, smacking her butt. "Guys, I think I might need to take five—"

"I'm leaving," Sofia said, rolling her eyes as she gave him a playful scowl. "As you know, the twins are leaving for their high-school field trip to Paris tomorrow, and I'm a nervous wreck, which is why we couldn't come to the bonding ceremony. We love you very much, Callie, and I'm making an extra special batch of wine to drink with you one day while we imagine punching that bastard right in his nose."

"Can't wait, Aunt Sofia. I appreciate your support, and you know I love your wine."

Sofia smoothed her fingers over Heden's thick hair. "I'll be helping the kids pack while Heden updates you. He's got all the info, but please text me if he carries on." She pulled her phone from her back pocket and wiggled it. "I'll be happy to save you."

"Thank you, Sofia," Miranda said, chuckling.

Sofia waved, smiling under her springy black hair, now with tiny white streaks that coursed through the strands, and smacked a kiss on Heden's lips before exiting the frame.

"She's obviously obsessed with me," Heden said, shrugging. "Can't say I blame her. Look at this handsome mug." He pointed to himself as everyone laughed around the table.

Callie noticed the hair at his temples had started to turn gray ever so slightly, but he still was as handsome as he'd been all those years ago when he chose to become human so he could be with Sofia. Emitting an inner sigh, Callie wondered if she'd ever find someone who would make such a valiant choice for her. Her thoughts drifted to Brecken, and she shut them down immediately. Plenty of time to digest that later.

"As you know, Tatiana hasn't appeared to us in years," Heden said, holding up a finger. "Until yesterday when she appeared to Callie. Now, she seems ready for another chat, but she's summoning us to her this time."

"How so?" Miranda asked.

"Last night, we received an email from an encrypted address. It simply read, '*Calinda can find me here.*'"

Heden's face disappeared from the screen, and a picture of a rock appeared, surrounded by dirt and a few sparse cacti.

"A rock?" Callie asked, squinting to see the images carved across it. "Are those Native American drawings?"

"That they are, baby toad," he said, zooming in on the stone. "This rock sits in the Arizona desert in a national forest called the Sierra Ancha Wilderness Area. It has a rich history from being colonized by American Indigenous People over a thousand years ago who are now called the Hohokam."

"And she wants *me* to find her there?" Callie asked, pointing at herself.

"Yes," Heden said with a nod. "I'm not quite sure what's going on, but she's suddenly all up in your grill, Callie. I'm certainly not psychic, but I have a feeling this is all tied into the prophecy."

"She did say yesterday that she has more she wants to discuss with me," Callie said, chewing her lip. "I thought she'd appear to me again, but if she wants me to come to her, there must be a reason."

"From my conversations with Tatiana over the years, she has the blood of many human ancestors flowing through her veins from several different cultures. Sofia and I believe one of those cultures are the Hokokam. They have long disbanded and descended into other tribes, but it's possible Tatiana has ties to the area. Perhaps she's staying in the ruins there or working on one of her weird concoctions that require ingredients only found in the desert. I'm not sure, but she's requesting your presence, Callie."

"Absolutely not," Darkrip said, shaking his head. "No way in hell is Callie going to the human world to rendezvous with some witch whose motives we can't fathom. End of discussion."

"Ahem," Callie said, clearing her throat. "While I appreciate your concern, Dad, I'll remind you that I'm a grown woman and can make my own decisions, thank you very much."

"Not in this instance. I can't protect you since I'm needed here to work with Evie to fortify and practice our skills for the final battle with Bakari."

"I wasn't asking you to go with me," Callie said, feeling her nostrils flare. "In case you've forgotten, I have powers of my own and am extremely capable of defending myself."

"No," Darkrip said, crossing his arms over his chest. "Not happening."

"Not that I want to argue with the man who can pulverize my head into a million pieces," Heden chimed in, "but having Callie approach Tatiana if she is in fact summoning her could actually increase our chances against Bakari. Although Tatiana has remained neutral up to this point, her appearance and interference yesterday opened a door. I think she might be ready to choose a side. To choose *our* side."

"She could supply us with information on every potion she's ever designed for Bakari and inform us of any plans he might have divulged," Callie murmured, eyes narrowing as she debated the advantage of following the lead.

"Absolutely. The thing is, I think Tatiana *wants* to talk. Call it some sort of weird intuition, but I think she's extremely invested in our conflict. For whatever reason, she's chosen Callie as the person to communicate with."

"I think she wants me to fulfill the prophecy," Callie said, leaning forward and resting her forearms on the table. "I don't think she sees the prophecy as something evil, but instead as something…"—she circled her hand, searching for the word—"necessary."

"I'm not letting my daughter travel to the human world alone. I don't care that she grew up there, that she has powers, nor how old she is. It's not fucking happening." Darkrip's tone was firm.

Callie clenched her jaw, ready to give him a piece of her mind, before Jack interjected.

"So, I have an idea," he said, leaning forward and resting his palms on the table. "Brecken is outside waiting to be deposed about Zadicus. He's trained in private security and is unemployed at the moment."

"He should've figured out that Zadicus was working with Bakari," Darkrip muttered. "I'm looking forward to debriefing him."

"So am I," Jack said with a nod. "Brecken is a good friend, and I trust him implicitly. After we question him, I'm sure you'll find he knew nothing of Zadicus's deception. I think he should accompany Callie to the human world. He's a trained soldier and will keep her safe."

Callie's heart slammed at the suggestion. It made perfect sense and would allow her to spend some time with the man who now consumed her thoughts. "I think it's a great idea. I consider Brecken a friend and would feel comfortable with him as my companion."

Darkrip's lips thinned as he considered. "Maybe I should just go with you. If you all are intent on Callie chasing this lead, I want to ensure her safety."

"We need to practice the forcefield, Darkrip," Evie said. "This is different than the shield we created to kill father thanks to all the dark potions running through Bakari's blood. I don't want to lose time practicing with you, especially since the final battle is only weeks away."

Sighing, Darkrip nodded. "Fine. Jack, you trust Brecken with Callie's safety?"

"I do," Jack said with a nod.

"All right. I'm open to agreeing to it once we question Brecken and confirm he had nothing to do with Zadicus's deception. I could always read his thoughts if I have concerns."

Callie's eyes widened, and she straightened in her chair. No way in hell did she want her father reading Brecken's thoughts. He'd discover she'd slept with him, and that would open a can of worms she wasn't ready to discuss with anyone.

"You made an oath not to read people's thoughts, Dad. It's a violation of his privacy."

Darkrip scowled. "I want to be sure his intentions are true."

"I think he'll alleviate any concerns during his questioning," Jack said. "We spoke this morning, and he informed me he intends to rejoin the army now that he's no longer employed as a bodyguard. He's a good man, Uncle Darkrip, and wants to protect our people."

"Fine," Darkrip said, running a hand over his face. "I won't read his thoughts unless I sense something dire. I look forward to the debriefing."

"Then it's settled," Callie said, thankful for one small crisis averted. "Uncle Heden, you'll prepare supplies for us for the mission?"

"Got you covered," Heden said. "You'll need fake IDs to rent a car, credit cards for lodging and supplies, an untraceable prepaid phone that works on their grid and everything else a trip to the human world requires. I'm going to overnight everything to a parcel delivery locker in Phoenix for you. Once you retrieve the package, you can rent a car and drive to the site. It's about a hundred miles east of Phoenix."

"Perfect. Thank you."

"Sure thing. You both stay safe, okay? I don't think Tatiana has any ill intentions, but keep your guard up."

They discussed for a while longer before Miranda ended the meeting. Afterward, Callie beelined toward the hallway, smiling at Brecken who stood as she approached.

"Hi," she said, feeling awkward since she wanted to hug him but also not wanting to incite any curiosity from her family. "So, a lot of stuff just happened in the meeting. They're going to question you in a few minutes. Heads-up: They want you to accompany me on a mission to the human world."

Surprise laced his expression. "What?"

"They'll explain it to you in the meeting. I'll be there too and will interject if needed. Whatever you do, look 'trustworthy,' okay?" She made quotation marks with her fingers. "The last thing I need is Dad reading your thoughts and knowing we boned our brains out last night."

Arderin chose that moment to appear at her side. "How are you doing today, baby? Can your ol' mom give you a hug?"

"Hey, Mom," she said, embracing her as she shot Brecken a gaze over her shoulder, silently telling him to remain cool. He just smirked at her, and she tamped down a laugh. Of course he would remain stoic and calm. It was Brecken after all. If anyone needed to remember to be chill in their twosome, it was Callie. Drawing back, she smiled at her mother.

"I'm doing okay. Thanks for checking on me."

"Of course, sweetie." Facing Brecken, she extended her hand. "I'm Arderin, and you must be Brecken. So nice to meet you."

Callie smiled at the sight of her mother shaking hands with the man who'd written her such beautiful letters. One day, she would tell Arderin about his sweet words, knowing she would adore them as much as Callie did.

"Nice to meet you, uh…"

"You don't have to address me formally," Arderin said, shaking her head. "Just Arderin is fine."

"I'm honored to meet you, Arderin," he said with a reverent tilt of his head. "I haven't met many royals in my life."

"Well, get ready, because you're about to meet them all." She gave a cheeky grin. "Oh, and don't mind my husband. He's a surly grump and will most likely interrogate the hell out of you."

"I'm ready, ma'am. Bring it on."

"Oh, I like him," Arderin said, smiling at Callie. "He'll be a good companion on your trip, sweetie."

"I think you're right," Callie said, giving him a tender smile. "Can't wait."

"Okay, let's get this show on the road. Come on. You can sit beside me, Brecken," Arderin said, gesturing with her hand. "I'll try to save you from my husband."

Brecken fell into step beside her, and Callie followed them to the conference room, grinning from ear to ear at the natural comradery between her mother and her secret lover.

T he meeting with Brecken went well, and the council members all recognized fairly quickly that he hadn't known about Zadicus's deception.

"I made an error in judgement, agreeing to Zadicus's request to have a few hours alone each week," Brecken admitted, lacing his fingers atop the table as he sat beside Arderin. "He bribed me by agreeing to pay my sister's tuition to Takelia's school for the gifted and talented. There was no way we could afford to send her without his help, but I should've declined."

"I think we can all understand that motivation," Arderin said, placing a supportive hand over his arm. "We're a close family and would move mountains to help those we love. Right, guys?"

"It should've occurred to you he was doing something nefarious if he sought to be free from your watch," Darkrip muttered, arms crossed as he assessed Brecken. "The lack of perception is completely unacceptable for a trained private security agent."

"That's a bit harsh, dear," Arderin said.

"He's right," Brecken said, shrugging. "It was a severe lapse in judgement and all I can do is learn from it. Unfortunately, I can't change the past. It led to him deceiving Callie, and I'm extremely remorseful and frustrated at that."

Darkrip studied him through slitted lids. Eventually, he sighed and ran a hand through his dark hair. "Fine. I don't sense any deception in your demeanor. It was an honest mistake, but we can't afford mistakes from this point forward. Especially if you're going to accompany my daughter to the human world."

"I will protect her with my life," Brecken said, straightening and lifting his chin. "You have my word."

The council members exchanged glances before Miranda cleared her throat at the head of the table. "Okay, I think we've gotten what we needed. Let's take a vote on moving forward with Callie approaching Tatiana in the human world and Brecken accompanying her."

After a unanimous vote, Miranda addressed Brecken. "I understand you wish to reapply for the army now that you no longer have a bodyguard post."

"Yes, ma'am."

"Good. We'll go ahead and recommission you so you will be paid for protecting Callie."

Lifting his hands, he shook his head. "I'm happy to accompany Callie without pay. It's the least I can do to atone for not discovering Zadicus's deception."

"It's a noble offer, but I insist," Miranda said. "We pay our soldiers around here. You all are appreciated and deserve every penny."

Brecken swallowed, causing Callie to wonder if he felt uncomfortable accepting pay since they were now sexually involved. Deciding she'd question him about it on their trip, she spoke up. "Please accept the commission, Brecken. I'm a *lot* to deal with. Jack says I'm exceptionally dramatic." She swiped her hair over her shoulder, causing several of the council members to chuckle.

"Okay," he said, giving her a smile that sent tingles to every cell in her skin. Did anyone else notice how sexy he was? Feeling flushed, she squelched the urge to fan herself. "Thank you, Queen Miranda. I look forward to protecting Callie and to a successful mission."

Murmurs of agreement and encouragement filtered through the room, and Callie prepared herself for task ahead. She had no idea why Tatiana was summoning her, but she was determined to find out and help her people.

Chapter 16

T ordor, son of King Sathan and Queen Miranda, wiped his hands together, displacing the dirt from the wooden stake he'd just shoved into the ground. Turning toward the woman who stood with arms crossed over her chest in an angry stance, he said, "I think you're all set, Luna."

"*Pfft*," she hissed, glaring at the man who stood on the other side of the fence. "I'm sure his vicious little spawns can still find a way to cross onto my property if they try."

"I'm sorry the kids came onto your property and that Scooter dug the hole in your yard," the man said, glancing down at the dog panting beside him. "I'll do a better job of keeping an eye on them."

"You do that," Luna said with a tilt of her head, "or next time, I'm filing trespassing charges."

"I think Kildor has learned his lesson, right?" Tordor asked the Deamon who'd recently purchased the property next to the aristocratic woman.

"I definitely have. I'm very sorry, Luna."

"The fact that your parents are now letting Deamons move to Astaria is appalling enough, but I won't let them on my property."

Tordor assessed her, feeling she was mere seconds away from spitting on Kildor's shoes. "There are many Deamons who were unwilling participants in Crimeous's plans, Luna. Those that renounced him and embraced the kingdom are free to live on any of the compounds. It's important to my parents—and to me—that we are united as one kingdom of immortals."

"A kingdom of criminals—"

"The goddess teaches repentance and forgiveness," Tordor interrupted, cupping her shoulder. "It's time you get on board. I wouldn't want to have to tell my parents you're unsupportive of their policies."

"Of course, I respect our king and queen," she said, appearing slightly chagrined. "As a Vampyre, I was supportive of aligning with the Slayers. I guess I have a harder time with the Deamons. I've never understood their purpose on Etherya's Earth."

"Crimeous created us to be an army for his vengeance against Etherya, but all I've ever wanted is to live in peace, Luna. My wife was tortured by him for centuries, and I was forced to fight in an army I never supported. Now, we just want to live a quiet life with our children...and Scooter," Kildor said, leaning down to pet the pooch on the head.

"Fine, but don't come on my property again. Prince Tordor, thank you for replacing the fence post. I wasn't strong enough to do it myself after the little critter dug around it."

"You're welcome, Luna. Anytime."

With a dismissive nod, she turned to walk back to her home, situated in the distance across the sprawling yard.

"Whew, that was close. I thought she was going to report me to your father." Kildor swiped his arm across his forehead, wiping away the sweat. "Thank you for intervening."

"Of course," Tordor said. "I know she says she wants to be left alone, but my dad has known Luna for centuries. He has it on good authority she loves the fancy teas the vendors sell in Astaria's main square. Maybe pick her up a box next time you're in town."

"I sure will. Thanks for the suggestion. You're quite exceptional at diplomacy, my prince." He gave a bow. "I wish I could find a way to properly thank you."

"Just keep Scooter off her lawn," Tordor said, craning his neck to look at the pup. He whimpered as if he knew he was in hot water. "He's a cute little thing, but I don't think Luna's a fan."

Laughing, Kildor shook his head. "Got that message loud and clear. Thank you. See you around Astaria."

"See you." With a salute, Tordor headed back to his four-wheeler and revved the engine, setting off toward his home. Uteria's castle had been his home for his twenty-six years on the planet, along with the castle at Astaria. His parents had split time between the two compounds as they worked to reunite the Slayer and Vampyre kingdoms. They both had their appeal, but he found the castle at Uteria more welcoming, whereas the castle at Astaria was more austere. Still, both housed some wonderful childhood memories, and he cherished them all.

When he finally pulled up to Uteria's wall and drove through, he noticed several of the council members exiting in their various vehicles. Thankful he'd missed yet another stuffy council meeting, he parked his four-wheeler behind the barracks and spoke to a few of the soldiers milling about before heading inside the castle. It seemed quiet, and he searched for signs of life, finally finding his mother in the sitting room, examining what looked to be knitting loops and yarn.

"Uh, Mom?" he asked, assessing her as she sat on the couch. "Are you...knitting?"

Miranda expelled a breath through her lips as they flapped together, making an exasperated sound. "Lila gave me this starter kit before she left. She says kitting is relaxing and reduces stress." Lifting the sticks, she shrugged. "All I see when I look at these things are weapons. Like, really cool knitting nunchucks." Rising, she swiped them through the air. "See? I feel like fighting with these bad boys would be much more relaxing than knitting."

Chuckling, Tordor held up his hands. "Don't shoot...or, uh, stab, I guess? I *do* need both my eyes if I'm going to inherit the kingdom one day."

Laughing, she tossed the loops toward the couch and approached him with open arms. "Come here, sweetie. I missed you at the meeting." They embraced, Tordor rubbing his chin on her silky black hair.

"I'm sure you and Dad had everything covered. You always do."

Drawing back, she cupped his cheeks. "Do you have a few minutes to sit and chat with your mom? I'd love to hear how it went with Luna. Man, she's a See You Next Tuesday if I ever met one."

Unable to control his laugh, Tordor nodded as they sat on the couch. "She's not so bad. All bluster and no bite if you ask me. But no one said uniting the species would be easy. You and Dad knew that from the beginning. There's still a lot of distrust and misconception out there, and these things take time."

Smiling, Miranda squeezed his hand. "My son, the peacemaker. You possess a diplomatic quality I've rarely seen in others. You're like the hate whisperer or something."

"Well, I'm the child of two people hell-bent on peace. It was probably embedded in my DNA from the start."

She studied him, smiling as love shone in her eyes. "Our baby who isn't a baby anymore. Man, I still remember when you were born. Your dad doted over you like nothing I'd ever seen. Our perfect little heir."

"I'm pretty sure I'm far from perfect, but okay," he said, leaning back and resting his arm over the back of the couch.

Sighing, she settled into the couch before speaking. "Your father wishes you would attend the council meetings—"

"Are we really going to have this discussion again, Mom?"

"Don't interrupt me, young man," she said, holding up a finger. "I don't care how old you are, I'm still your mother."

"Yes, ma'am," he said, feeling his lips form a pout.

"The frown is cute though. You look just like your father."

Grinning, he squeezed her hand. "Go on. Tell me what a disappointment I am. I'm ready for the lecture."

"You're not a disappointment," she said, scooting closer and palming his cheek. "I hate it when you say that."

"I'm the heir to a kingdom with two immortal rulers who were born for the roles. It's a job I don't want, nor one I deserve. I love having you two rule while I implement diplomacy for our people. It's what makes me happy."

"I was so proud when you set up the Office of Official Complaints for the realm. Not only did it save me a ton of paperwork, but it freed up so much time for me and your father when you began addressing the complaints."

"I enjoy it, Mom. As I've told you a thousand times, I don't enjoy the council meetings or strategizing for war. It's not my strength. My strength is figuring out how to bring people together on a personal basis. I think there's nobility in that, even if I'm not fulfilling the role I was born for."

"Look," she said, swiping her fingers through her hair, "I can give you a million speeches about how your grandfather lectured me on my duties as heir. They were all antiquated and went against everything I wanted for my life. All I ever wanted to was to instill peace for our people and maybe to kick a little ass along the way." She winked. "So if you've found something that makes you happy, I'm all for it. Your dad's a bit less progressive, so we'll have to push him along."

"I know how much he wanted a male heir, and I want to make him proud. I just need to do it in my own way."

"I know, sweetie. It does break my heart a tiny bit that you don't want to attend the council meetings,"—she held her thumb and index finger an inch apart—"but I'm not going to force you. I always promised I wouldn't make my father's mistakes when I had kids. Hopefully, I'm fulfilling that oath with you."

"Have you and Dad talked about having another baby? I know you've discussed it over the years, but it's never been the right time. It would give you someone else to fixate over." He gave a cheeky grin, indicating his teasing.

"I would like to have a little girl one day," she said wistfully, glancing toward the ceiling. "But then I remember being pregnant with you and how I literally emptied my guts into the toilet every day, and I always decide to push it off."

He took her hand, lacing their fingers. "I'm sorry your pregnancy with me was so rough, and I know the birth wasn't a bed of roses either. You're amazing, Mom. It's one of the reasons I don't want to let you down."

"You've never let me down and never will." Clutching his hand, she arched a brow. "And you can blame your blood-sucking father for the tough pregnancy. It's all his fault."

Tordor breathed a laugh. "Well, I can't really disparage his Vampyre lineage since it's half of my DNA too."

"I guess not." Sighing, she shook her head. "I don't know. I do want to have another baby one day. Maybe once we beat Bakari and the kingdom is at peace, I'll pop out another one."

"Well, you know I'd love to have a baby sister or brother, and I'd help in any way I can."

Eyes sparkling, she leaned closer. "Or you could have a baby of your own. You're certainly old enough to find a nice young lady to settle down with."

Sighing, he shook his head. "I'm not ready. It took you a thousand years to find Dad. Give me some time."

Deep green eyes darted between his. "I know it's hard to find someone who gets you when you're the heir, but you'll never meet anyone if you don't put yourself out there. I don't think it would kill you to go on a date here and there. I'm sure there are so many women who would love to spend time with you."

Tordor struggled with his response, not understanding how to explain his feelings to her. For whatever reason, he didn't feel a pressing need to date or to settle down. Although he loved helping the people of the kingdom and was very sociable, he also had a hard time connecting with people on an intimate level. The idea of baring himself to someone—of literally stripping bare and allowing them to see into his soul—was foreign to him. Instead, he actually preferred flying solo. It gave him independence and the freedom to chart his own path.

Tordor could only see himself experiencing sexual attraction for a woman after making a strong emotional connection with her. He had no interest in casual dating or hooking up. Many aristocratic women of the realm would love to snag the kingdom's prince, and he had no interest in being anyone's prize. No, he'd rather wait until it felt right—until he met someone he clicked with. For some reason, he felt as if he would just *know* when that person came along.

And it was why he was still, in his mid-twenties, a virgin.

Whereas other men might have felt shame or embarrassment at that fact, Tordor didn't at all. He was a confident man and intrinsically knew he wanted to share his first time with someone he cared deeply for. Hopefully, with someone he *loved*. There was no shame in that aspiration, and he refused to settle for less than what he truly wanted.

Of course, explaining this to his mom was difficult and slightly awkward, so he fidgeted on the couch, attempting to come up with some way to discuss it with her.

"It's okay," she said, her features filled with compassion. "You don't have to explain. Sorry for being a nosy mom. I just want you to be happy."

"I'm perfectly happy with my life, Mom. I promise."

"Then we'll leave it at that. If you ever want to talk to me, I'm always here."

"I don't want to take time away from your knitting," he teased, gazing at the discarded knitting kit.

"Um, yeah, don't tell Lila, but there's no way I'm taking up knitting. I'd rather spar with the troops. I appreciate her efforts, but we'll just put this one down as a loss."

Standing, he tugged her to her feet and encircled her in his arms. He towered over her, but her embrace was as comforting to him as it had been when he was small. "I love you, Mom."

"I love you so much, sweetheart. Keep up the good work. You're sowing peace in our little kingdom one conflict at a time."

"Happy to do it." Drawing back, he smoothed her hair. "I'm going to grab a workout before I head to Takelia later today. One of the street vendors filed a complaint against another who sells a similar product. I'm going to try and get them to work together. I think if they join forces, they could actually sell more than they sell individually. We'll see if it works."

"If anyone can make it happen, you can. Have a good day, sweetie."

Placing a kiss on her silken head, Tordor exited the room to change into his workout clothes. Reminiscing on the conversation, he was glad his mom understood him well enough to let him chart his own course. For now, he was happy, although he would like to experience love one day. Would it take centuries, as it had for his parents? Or would he meet someone in the near future while he was still relatively young in the scheme of immortals? Tordor wasn't sure, but he was excited to find out whenever his life turned in that direction. For now, he was content implementing diplomacy in the realm his parents ruled, and for their people, whom he cherished deep in his heart.

After the meeting, Callie was whisked away by her parents and returned to Takelia. It made sense to Brecken they would want to comfort her after yesterday's events, but he still felt the loss of her presence. After one night with her, he wanted more...everything she could give him, so he could see her cheeky grin and chide him with her playful teasing. The good news was that he would get to spend a lot of time with her on their mission. It was as if the goddess had answered his request to be near her, and he would take full advantage. Striding down the front stairs of Uteria's castle, he headed toward the train station so he could head back to Lynia.

"Hey, man," Jack called, pulling up in a four-wheeler. "You survived the meeting."

"Yeah," Brecken said, sliding his hands in his pockets. "Thank the goddess. Ambassador Darkrip is tough."

"That he is. I'm heading to a training at Lynia. Want a ride?"

"You don't mind?"

"Nope. Come to think of it, you should attend if you can. I know your mission with Callie starts tomorrow morning, but you're officially a soldier again, and I'm sure everyone would love to see you. Might as well get back on the horse."

Brecken pondered, admitting it was a good idea. Packing wouldn't take much time, since he could only carry a small bag through the ether, and he might as well use his spare time to entrench himself back in the battalion.

"Let's do it," he said, climbing in the passenger seat. "I just need to stop at home and change into my training gear. I wanted to look presentable for the council."

"No prob, man."

They set off through the open fields, chatting about the events of the past few days, their families and other topics. After changing in his cabin, Brecken climbed back into the vehicle, and Jack drove them to the sparring field.

Pulling up to the open meadow, Brecken realized how much he'd missed being a soldier. The smell of the dirt and grass that composed the training field called to him, and his fellow soldiers greeted him with firm handshakes and pats on the back.

"Well, well, look what the cat dragged in," a gruff female voice chimed. "The fancy bodyguard has decided to grace us with his presence yet again."

"Hey, Siora," he said, grinning at his lifelong friend. She'd grown up on a farm not too far from his home, and they'd attended school together. He'd always appreciated her frank nature and forthright attitude. In a nutshell, she was badass, and he felt she embodied the characteristics Miranda and Evie were intent on implementing in the kingdom.

"You're finally a soldier," he said, giving her a salute. "I'm proud of you. Have you kicked everyone's ass yet?"

Scoffing, she narrowed her eyes. "I'm close. Radomir and Cian are ranked higher in our training class, but I'm a close third. By the time the final battle with Bakari arrives, I'm determined to become co-leader of one of the battalions. And soon thereafter, I'll become the first female battalion leader in the immortal army. Mark my words."

"I have no doubt. If anyone can do it, you can."

Tilting her head, she studied him. "So, you're accompanying the fancy princess with the cryptic prophecy hanging over her head to the human world. Interesting."

"Wow," he muttered, rubbing his neck. "Word travels fast around here."

"She's beautiful like her mother. Careful you don't decide to do more than protect her, if you catch my drift. It's not a good idea to get googly eyes for someone who couldn't fathom falling for peasants like us."

"And how would you know?" he asked, arching a brow. "How many aristocrats have you fallen for?"

Emitting a "*pfft,*" she waved her hand. "As if. The only aristocrats I know are Jack, Commander Latimus and General Garridan. Jack and the commander are okay, but Garridan is another story."

"Do tell," he said, sensing there was more to the story considering her cheeks flushed ever so slightly at the mention of General Garridan.

"He's a misogynist pig," she said. "Doesn't think women should be in the army no matter what he says out loud. Thinks we all should be prissy and do as we're told." She bowed in a dramatic curtsy before batting her eyelashes. "Oh, my," she said, placing the back of her hand on her forehead, "I feel so faint. I hope a big, strong man will come along and save me."

Snickering, Brecken assessed her. Not only did she possess a wicked dry sense of humor, but she was a natural soldier. No one would ever describe her as demure or prissy. No—Siora was a warrior and an asset to the army. She had a muscular build and was physically stronger than half their male soldiers, although she would probably spit at that statement and pronounce she was stronger than *all* of them.

"I think asking you to do anyone's bidding is a ship that sailed long ago. You're a powerhouse, Siora. Whoever bonds with you is going to be a very lucky man."

"I have no desire to bond with anyone," she said, sparing him a droll glare. "Flying solo is where it's at. And you don't have to placate me. I know I'm not pretty like the fancy princess and all the other aristocratic women. Garridan's all but betrothed to Celine. Hope he has enough patience to find her lady parts under the formal gowns she still insists on wearing. Waste of good fabric if you ask me."

Brecken studied her short hair, sky blue eyes and tan skin, darker than most Vampyres since she'd been training outside. She was quite stunning, with long, thick eyelashes that surrounded her almond-shaped eyes and full red lips. Aristocrats might prefer smaller, willowy woman—hell, who was he to know?—but the right man would find Siora's tall, voluptuous build sexy. He hoped she would find a mate one day who could navigate through her tough exterior because she was extremely deserving of love.

"Why are you smiling at me weird?" she muttered.

"No reason. I just think you're pretty amazing, and I know there's someone out there who'll think you're as beautiful as I do."

A dash of red scarred her cheeks before her eyes narrowed. "Okay, this conversation took a turn. I'll say 'thank you' because my father taught me to accept compliments when given. And then I'll get back to training, because all I've ever wanted to be is a soldier and don't give a damn about anyone's opinion of my appearance."

Brecken smiled, understanding she was mostly bark with little bite.

"Don't get yourself killed in the human world, okay? I kind of like you. Now, leave me alone so I can get back to work." With a wink, she trailed over to join the troops at the obstacle course.

Jack appeared at his side, giving him orders to join the troops, and just like that, Brecken was one of the crew again. He threw himself into the training, excelling at the obstacle course before sparring with several of the soldiers. It felt amazing to work his muscles, and he knew he'd sleep like the dead when he finally made it home.

Sure enough, he wandered into his house long after the sun set, exhausted but elated from the day's events. After packing a small bag, he lifted his phone to text Callie.

Brecken: You didn't text me even though I gave you my number, so I hope you're not reconsidering your vow to sleep with me for eternity. I'm counting on limitless sex until my ultimate demise.

He smiled, hoping she would laugh at his teasing words.

Callie: OMG. I wanted to text you about a zillion times today but didn't want to be _that_ girl.

Brecken: What girl?

Callie: You know, needy, **you-took-my-virginity-so-now-I'm-obsessed-with-you girl. I'm sure you've met your fair share of those. Wait, don't tell me. Ew. I don't want to hear about you with any other girls. Okay, wait, now I'm being that girl again. Help.**

Chuckling, he reveled in how damn funny she was.

Brecken: Don't worry. You're cool. I won't mistake you for someone needy. I mean, you chose an aristocratic douche over me while I wrote you sappy love letters. Maybe I'm the needy one.

Callie: No way. Let's just agree we're both awesome and not needy at all.

Brecken: Done.

Chewing his inner lip, he debated telling her how much he missed her. Were they there yet? Everything had happened so fast. Maybe she was at home mourning the loss of her relationship with Zadicus.

Callie: I miss you. I'm so excited to spend some time with you on our mission. Hope that's not too much. Just tell me if it's too much and I'll chill.

Thrilled at the words, his thumbs moved across the keypad.

Brecken: I miss you too, hon. I promise I'll keep you safe. Can't wait to see you.

Callie: Safe is good, but you're going to bone me too, right? I can't stop thinking about being with you again.

Although her sentiments thrilled him, he also didn't relish being a rebound. He wanted to make sure they didn't move too fast so she could adequately process what happened with Zadicus.

Brecken: We'll see. It's hard for me to keep my hands off you, especially now that I've touched you, but I don't want to be a consolation prize, Callie.

Callie: YOU'RE NOT! But I understand your concerns. Let's get to the human world and have a nice, long talk at the hotel. I think we need to do that to set some expectations. I'm determined to be honest and clear about what I want moving forward. No more mistakes. Deal?

Brecken: Deal. Sleep tight, hon. I'll see you at 9:00 a.m. at the ether.

Callie: See you then.

She sent him a kiss emoji, and he grinned before setting his phone on the nightstand. After prepping for bed, he slipped between the covers and placed his hands under his head. Staring at the ceiling, he let her scent wash over him, still fresh upon the sheets from their lovemaking. Closing his eyes, he gave over to exhaustion and joined her in his dreams.

Chapter 17

B recken drove to the ether the next morning ready to tackle the mission head-on. He'd never been to the human world, and the excitement of the new experience thrummed in his veins, along with the anticipation of spending time with Callie. Last night's dreams of her had been vivid, and he'd woken up in a pool of sweat with a raging hard-on. Brecken couldn't remember ever being more viscerally attracted to a woman, and he couldn't wait to taste her again.

When he pulled up to the ether, he noticed Darkrip embrace Callie as he cut the engine. Squelching the lascivious thoughts, he grabbed his small backpack from the bed of the vehicle and slung it on. Although Callie's father had taken a vow not to read others' thoughts, Brecken didn't want them front of mind, just in case the Slayer-Deamon's resolve slipped.

"Hello, Ambassador Darkrip," he said, approaching. "It's nice to see you again."

He gave a curt nod, and Brecken was reminded of Arderin's assessment that he was a grump. "Callie has a phone that can communicate with me through the ether," Darkrip said, his tone crisp and businesslike. "If you need me, please don't hesitate to call."

"We will, sir. I promise to protect her with my life." He extended his hand, and Darkrip stared at it before he gave it a firm shake.

"Um, hi," Callie said, raising her hand. "I'm capable of strangling multiple attackers with my mind and all, but, hey, if you two want to commiserate about protecting me, go ahead and waste your breath."

"I just want you to be safe, sweetheart," Darkrip said, drawing her into a hug and kissing her temple. "Please stay in contact with us."

"I will, Dad, but Heden warned us there won't be cell service at Tatiana's location in the desert."

"Then call me as soon as you reach an area with service."

"I will." Facing Brecken, she smiled, jump-starting his pulse as her eyes sparkled in the morning sun. "Ready?"

"Ready."

Darkrip stood firm as they walked to the ether, and Brecken urged her to enter first. She stepped through the viscous, cloudy substance, and he followed close behind.

After wading through the dense barrier, they exited onto soft ground covered with dirt. Struggling to catch his breath, Brecken searched for Callie.

"Whew," she said from a few feet away, hands resting above her knees as she bent over. "I've waded through that stuff a hundred times, but I still feel like I'm going to pass out when I reach the other side. You okay? The first time is always a doozy."

"It's no picnic, but I'll survive." Approaching, he smoothed her hair away from her shoulder. "Are you okay?"

"Yeah." Straightening, she flashed him a dazzling smile that damn near buckled his knees. "Welcome to the human world. It's so exciting here—in my opinion at least. I can't wait for you to see it."

At the moment, all he cared to see was her gorgeous face as her palpable excitement at being in the human world surrounded them. Inching closer, he slid his palm over the back of her neck.

"Did you miss me?"

Chuckling, she nodded. "Yeah. Did you miss me?"

Sliding his arm around her waist, her drew her into his body. "I dreamed of you," he murmured, nudging her nose with his.

"Oh, how exciting. What were we doing—?"

Inhaling the words from her lips, he drew her into a sizzling kiss, unable to exist for one moment longer without tasting her. Her high-pitched mewl shot down his throat, causing his dick to jerk in his pants as he surged against her. Their tongues warred and mated, fighting in a battle where both ultimately won. Finally, he retreated, placing soft kisses on her swollen lips as her lids slowly lifted.

"Wow," she whispered, shaking her head. "You almost let me marry Zadicus when you kiss like that? I should be pissed."

"Don't remind me," he said, scowling.

She exhaled a soft breath. "Don't remind me either. I feel like such an idiot."

Smoothing his hand over her curls, he searched her ocean-colored eyes. "Are you okay, hon? You must be hurting from everything that's happened over the past few days."

Sighing, she lifted a shoulder. "I am. It's so hard for me to understand why one person would viciously deceive another. I know some in the kingdom think my dad and Evie are inherently evil, but they're just my family. I've never seen anything from them as remotely awful as what Zadicus did to me."

"He's a small-minded man who couldn't get out of his own way," Brecken soothed, stroking her hair. "He's not worth your tears."

Her features scrunched. "Tears? No fucking way. I want to interrogate him. Tie him to a chair and backhand his perfect aristocratic nose until he explains his motives and begs for my forgiveness."

Laughing, Brecken nodded. "It's a nice fantasy." His brows drew together before continuing. "Bakari will most likely kill him, Callie. Now that he's been banished from the realm, he'll be useless to him."

"I know." Swallowing thickly, her gaze fell to his chest. "That's why I'm not railing at the universe. Zadicus sealed his own fate, and I'm truly sad he chose the wrong path. Raoul and Viessa were always very nice to me. They were a bit cold and formal, as some aristocrats are, but they're good people. I hate what he did to all of us, but he'll get his comeuppance. Of course, I'm angry, but mostly, I'm just sad."

"That says a lot about you," he murmured, lowering his hand to squeeze hers. "Your compassion is one of the things I admire most about you."

"Thank you," she said, her soft smile inciting relief deep within. The last thing he wanted was to enter into a tense discussion, but he also wanted to check in and make sure she was okay. "I'm taking it day by day, and I think that's all I can do. It certainly helps that a sexy, kind soldier is helping me pick up the pieces. I didn't expect it, but I'm grateful."

Emotion overwhelmed him as he stared at her, longing to tell her *he* was the grateful one. For her forgiveness, her understanding, her affection and the amazing gift she'd given him when she'd opened herself during their lovemaking. Of course, that would make him sound like a bigger sap than he already was, so he gave his signature smirk before winking. "I'll try and stick around, since I've promised to protect you and all. You're okay."

Giggling, she swatted his chest. "Jerk."

Stealing a swift kiss, he straightened and searched the surroundings. "We're in the woods adjacent to the park with the ballfield as planned. According to the email your Uncle Heden sent us last night, the locker where he shipped our supplies is across the street."

Drawing back, she extended her hand. "Lead the way, soldier."

Lacing his fingers with hers, they trekked across the street and entered the facility with the lockers. After punching in the six-digit code Heden had sent them, Brecken swung open the locker door to find a cardboard box wrapped in cellophane.

"I'd bet anything this cellophane was specially fashioned by Heden and Sofia so the detectors couldn't pick up the weapons inside," Callie said, removing the box and closing the locker.

"Agreed. We should find a secure place to open it. I don't want to incite suspicion in any humans who might be nearby, and I'm sure this place has cameras."

"I saw a fast-food restaurant down the road. Let's go there. One of us can open it in a bathroom stall and hide the weapons so they're imperceptible."

They trailed to the restaurant and decided Brecken should assemble the contents in the men's bathroom. Once equipped, he returned to Callie, who was slurping a milkshake at one of the booths.

"How did you get a milkshake?" he asked, sliding into the seat across from her. "I have all the money."

"I kept a stash from my allowance when I was a kid. Brought ten whole dollars with me." Lifting some bills from her back pocket, she shrugged. "Well, eight dollars now." Taking another slurp of the milkshake, she grinned. "So worth it. This is awesome. I miss human comfort food. It's so good."

Glancing around, he took in the surroundings. "So, this is a human restaurant. It seems more...*plastic* than I imagined."

Chuckling, she circled her hand. "This is a fast-food restaurant, so it's not fancy. There are definitely other places that aren't as bright and sterile-looking."

His eyes darted over her face as the newness of his surroundings set in. "There's so much to see. It's daunting for a soldier's kid from Lynia who never expected to see anything beyond the borders of the compound. If we weren't on a mission, I'd ask you to show me your favorite places."

Her lips closed around the straw, sucking the milkshake as he imagined her performing the act on the now rapidly swelling flesh between his legs. Popping her lips from the straw, she said, "Maybe we can come back one day and I can show you around. I do have a canceled honeymoon trip I need to make up for."

Brecken gave her a soft smile, not wanting to ruin the moment by bringing up the obvious point that an excursion to the human world was a luxury he couldn't afford. Not only could he literally not afford it on his military salary, but soldiers didn't take time off from the army, apart from a predetermined day or two that was pre-negotiated with their commanding officer. It was a reminder they were worlds apart, and he could never give her the things Zadicus had promised her.

"Wow, did I lose you?" she asked, waving her hand. "Bueller?"

His eyebrows drew together. "What's Bueller?"

Breathing a laugh, she shook her head. "One of Uncle Heden's favorite movies. I'll show you sometime. Anyway, you zoned out for a moment there."

"I'm here," he said, tabling the morose thoughts. Reaching for the supplies, he slid an ID and a folded wad of cash toward her. "Here are your credentials."

Lifting the ID, she studied it. "Calinda Marie Jones. It was the surname we used all those years ago when we lived here. I always thought Mom and Dad could've come up with something a *bit* more creative, but whatever."

Brecken laughed as she picked up the prepaid phone Heden sent them. Once it was up and running, Callie used the credit card to purchase internet browsing and rented a car from the dealer a few blocks away. After finishing her milkshake, they walked to the rental car dealer and then drove to the hotel, where they rented two rooms side by side.

Entering the elevator, she grinned up at him when the doors closed. "So, I didn't want to make it weird, but I'm a bit put out you didn't want to share a room."

Sparing her a glance, he said, "I figured you'd like your own space. Didn't want to assume anything."

"Space is good, but don't be surprised if I come knocking on your door, soldier."

Arching a brow, he reveled in her sultry grin. "I won't mind at all." Lowering, he rested his lips on the shell of her ear. "I like what happens when you knock on my door unannounced."

She bit her lip, giving him an adorable smile as the elevator dinged. Exiting on the third floor, they located their rooms, and Callie called his name before heading inside.

"Yeah?" Brecken asked softly.

"I'm going to need to eat eventually. It's warm here, and I saw an Italian place a few blocks away. Want me to pick up pizza and we can eat by the pool?"

"That sounds nice."

"I'll pick up wine too," she said, giving a cheeky grin. "In the hopes of getting you tipsy and possibly taking advantage of you."

A laugh escaped his lips. "Okay, but not too much. We need to leave around sunrise in the morning. We'll stop at a store along the way to buy a tent and some supplies before heading to the desert. Your Uncle

Heden thinks Tatiana might be residing in the ruins, so we might need to camp there several days. He also indicated she does things on her own timeline and in her own way, and it's impractical for us to drive back to Phoenix every night."

"Ten-four," she said, giving a salute. "I'll be ready to rough it."

Chuckling, he inserted the plastic key in the door. "Call me when you're ready to go get the food so I can walk with you."

After entering the room, Brecken tossed his bag on the table and fell onto the bed, rubbing his face as he imagined Callie in a bikini by the pool. Judging by the size of her bag, it would be small, most likely only covering small swaths of her smooth skin. Eagerness for the night ahead curled in his gut, and he grinned like a lovesick teenager, anticipating their evening together.

Chapter 18

Callie spent the day catching up on all things human, realizing how much she'd missed the world she grew up in all those years ago. She also watched four *Saved by the Bell* reruns before the sun began to set, indicating it was time to order dinner. She'd loved the show as a kid, although Zack Morris was a bit more of a dick than she remembered. Still, it brought back memories, and she enjoyed the nostalgia.

After placing the dinner order, she searched through her bag to find something to wear to the pool. Figuring she might like to swim after they ate, she threw on her bikini under some cutoff shorts and a loose tank top. Tugging on her sandals, she headed to Brecken's room.

He opened the door after her swift knock, and she almost balked at how viscerally sexy her handsome soldier was. How in the hell had she ever even looked at Zadicus when Brecken was nearby? She'd always thought Zadicus quite handsome in a coiffed sort of way, but Brecken's raw sexuality was engrossing. In reality, she'd seen what she wanted to see. A man who was bestowing the love she craved, even if he was wrong for her. Determined to be wiser in the future, she straightened her shoulders.

"Ready?"

"Ready," Brecken said, stepping out and closing the door behind him. He was wearing shorts, a black T-shirt and athletic slip-ons perfectly situated for their pool excursion. Callie's eyes drifted over his biceps, muscled and tanned under his shirt sleeves, and her mouth turned dry as sandpaper. Arousal slammed through her as she tamped down the urge to climb him like a tree. A very tall, hard, sexy-as-hell tree.

"Callie?"

"Oh, sorry," she said, turning to follow him to the elevator. "Got lost in a daydream." A *super-hot, erotic daydream.*

Resisting the urge to fan herself, she entered the elevator and took her place at his side. His scent washed over her—picked up by her Vampyre senses—and she closed her eyes, inhaling the musky sandalwood aroma. She'd woken up covered in his scent after they made love and longed to have it envelop every inch of her body again.

The elevator chimed, indicating they'd reached the lobby, and Callie's eyes flew open. Exiting, they traveled through the whooshing automatic doors of the hotel and started down the sidewalk toward the Italian restaurant, making sure to pick up a bottle of wine along the way.

They chatted about the new female recruits and the pet guinea pig Callie had healed for a little boy at Naria a few days ago. The conversation flowed, and she was enamored by how comfortable she felt with him. She never felt the need to be anyone other than herself with Brecken, even when they'd had playful conversations when he was guarding Zadicus. It was refreshing to be in the presence of someone with whom she didn't have to hold pretenses, and she realized how precious it was. Zadicus had always been quite formal, and it had sometimes rankled her.

After picking up the pizza, they headed to the pool located behind the hotel. Sitting in two long plastic chairs, they munched on the food as they stared up at the star-filled sky.

"It looks the same as it does in the immortal world," Callie said, head resting on the tall chair as she ate the remaining crust. "That's one of the things I always liked about the nighttime sky."

"Although they're two different worlds, everyone sees the same sky when they look up," he remarked in his smooth baritone.

"Mm-hmm," she said, swallowing the last of her pizza before wiping off the crumbs. "It was comforting for someone like me who had trouble fitting in sometimes."

Brecken finished his slice and wiped his hands on a napkin before setting it aside. Tilting his head against the chair, he looked at her with compassion in his eyes. "I'd love to hear your stories, if you want to tell me."

It was such a sweet offer, said in his soothing voice, and Callie couldn't resist. Relaxing in her chair, she opened up to him, telling him about her awkward experiences and all the things she'd written in her diary. He listened intently, asking intermittent questions throughout, sometimes stroking her arm when she recalled a particularly painful moment.

"I'm sorry you felt lost, Callie-lily," he said, the nickname causing her to shiver. "You returned to a world you didn't know with a prophecy over your head, and you still managed to become a kind, caring person. Many people wouldn't be so strong. It's really admirable."

"Well, it also led me to latching onto the first guy who showed any interest in me, and look where that led me." She rolled her eyes. "So I didn't handle it *that* well."

"You did the best you could. We all want to be loved, Callie. That's just natural."

Blood thrummed through her veins as she assessed him. "Do you want to be loved?"

"Of course," he said, eyebrows drawing together. "And I want to make my father proud. My mom and sisters are my responsibility now, and I do my best to ensure their happiness."

"That's so sweet," she said, squeezing his hand as she held it between the chairs. "Rowena is awesome. I'd love to meet your mom and your other sisters."

"They're a handful," he said, giving her a sardonic glare. "Careful what you ask for."

Laughing, she swung his hand, thoroughly enjoying the conversation. "Well, I'm a handful, so we'll definitely get along."

"I love that about you," he said, waggling his brows. "Your personality is so vivacious, hon. It moves something in me since I'm a bit reserved."

"You?" she asked, feigning surprise. "I hadn't noticed."

"Imp," he muttered, lifting her hand and nipping her fingers. "You deserve someone who can give you everything you want. I hate that the prophecy made you feel like you weren't worthy of love or affection. That's not even close to true. You're amazing, Callie."

"You're pretty amazing too, you know?"

Exhaling a soft breath, he shrugged. "The thing is, I'm not, hon. I'm not rich or aristocratic or any of the things you deserve. I'm just a poor guy from Lynia who wants to protect our people."

"Brecken," she said, leaning closer to accentuate her point. "Protecting our people is extremely admirable. And there are so many qualities you're not giving yourself credit for. Look at the beautiful letters you wrote me. They're Shakespeare-level good."

"Uh, yeah, I briefly remember learning about him in school, although we didn't focus on him since he was human. I remember him being wordy." He gazed at the sky and rubbed his chin.

"Well, you're rather wordy in your letters,"—she lifted a finger when he shot her a glare—"but I really like it."

"If you say so," he muttered. "I'm terrified you're going to tell my army buddies I wrote them. I'll never live it down."

"I'll keep them secret if you like." She swung their hands between the chairs. "Something just for us."

Emotion laced his bronze orbs. "I like the sound of that."

"When I think of the letters, and the way you are with Rowena, and the steps you take to ensure your family is secure...Brecken, those are wonderful qualities that are so much more important than money."

His thumb traced the skin of her hand as he pondered. "You should be with someone who can take you places, Callie. Who can show you the world and take the time to enjoy it with you."

"And why can't you do those things?"

He scoffed. "Because I have to work, hon. Soldiers don't just traipse off to the human world and take vacations. That's a luxury we don't have. And my cabin is the only home I'll ever be able to afford. That, along with helping my family, takes up most of my salary, especially now that I'm not in private security."

"So, um, a few things," she said, releasing his hand and sitting up in her chair. Ticking her fingers, she said, "First, I'm a royal, which means I have money even though I didn't do anything to earn it."

"I wouldn't dream of touching your money, Callie—"

"Hey," she said, glowering. "I let you talk, and now it's my turn."

Grinning, he nodded. "Go on. Sorry."

Tilting her head, she continued. "I enjoy healing animals and am basically the kingdom's veterinarian. Self-proclaimed, of course." She rubbed her fingernails over her chest before blowing on them while Brecken chuckled. "I do it for free because I want to help our people and it's the right thing to do. I've always seen bonding with someone as a partnership. When I do marry one day, what's mine will be his, and vice versa."

"That was easy to say when you were bonding with Zadicus."

"It would be easy to say if I were bonding with *anyone*," she said, exasperated. "I don't care about material things. I never have. Now, do I want to travel the human world and see places I've never seen? Of course. But not all the time. I enjoy healing animals in the immortal world, and my family is there, which is very important to me. But I can certainly take a vacation here and there."

"That's great, but—"

"But nothing," she interjected, arching a brow. "I happen to know the commander of the immortal army." Lifting her hand to her mouth, she whispered, "He's my uncle."

Tossing back his head, Brecken gave a laugh as his Adam's apple shone in the moonlight. Drawn to him, she imagined leaning over and plunging her fangs into the vein that pulsed at his neck.

"I know he's your uncle," he finally said, mirth in his eyes. "But asking for special favors is not my style, hon."

"Oh, fine. I know for a fact Jack takes days off from training, and a few days off won't kill you. That's all I'm saying."

"You can be with anyone, Callie," he said, his expression reverent under the silver moonlight. "So much has happened over the past few days, and I want you to remember that."

Her teeth gnawed her lip as she pondered. "Maybe, but I also have peculiarities a partner would need to accept. First, there's the prophecy, which scares the crap out of most people."

"People are scared of things they don't understand. That has nothing to do with you."

Smiling, she let the sentiment sink in. "You're one of the few people who don't see it as weird. I don't know why, but it's pretty awesome." Sighing, she waved her hand. "Anyway, besides the prophecy, there's the fact that any kids I have will inevitably inherit some of my powers. I don't know which ones, and it's a lot to ask a partner to accept. Zadicus and I spoke about it, and he assured me it didn't matter, which I now know was just a line of crap to placate me and send me on my way."

"Asshole," Brecken muttered, swiping a hand over his face. "Anyone who truly loves you will embrace your children's powers, Callie."

"I hope so," she said wistfully.

"I mean, I'm no expert. There's nothing remarkable or special about my blood. I'm just a seamstress's kid from a rural compound who finished high school and joined the army the next day. It's why I bent over backward to send Rowena to her special school. I want more for her."

Emotion flooded her heart at the soulful words. His devotion to his family was so attractive to her, and she marveled at his dedication to their well-being. Clenching his hand, she felt the sting of tears as she gazed upon his handsome features.

"You're a good man," she whispered.

They gazed into each other for a long, solemn moment before Callie scrunched her nose. "Okay, soldier, I think we've completed the serious discussion portion of the evening. You're convinced you're unremarkable, and I'm a jilted bride with strange powers. Maybe we're, like, some weird superhero duo or something."

A hearty laugh bounded from his throat. "Maybe so."

"No matter what, you're smokin' hot, and I aim to take advantage of it." Scooching off the chair, she shrugged off her shorts and tank top, tossing them aside before extending her hand. "Since we seem to have this area to ourselves, I'd very much like to play with you in the pool."

His eyes raked over her frame clad in her skimpy white bikini, and Callie swore she saw a tenting in his shorts. "Define play," he said, his tone sexy and gravelly.

"I'd rather show you," was her sultry reply as she waggled her brows.

Chuckling, he grasped her hand and rose before tugging off his shirt and tossing it aside. "I play dirty sometimes, hon. Careful."

"Ohhhh..." Her eyes grew wide as anticipation hummed in her veins. "Should I be worried?"

Fast as lightning, his hand snaked around her wrist, drawing her into his body. Crouching down, he lifted her over his shoulder and carried her to the pool. Eliciting a squeal, she held on for dear life, hoping like hell he wouldn't drop her.

Brecken stopped at the edge of the deep end and swung her around, holding her above the pool as she giggled.

"You wouldn't," she said, noting the mischief in his eyes.

"You said you wanted to play, honey," he said, his tone both menacing and teasing as he held her above the pool.

"I take it back—"

Gasping, the words were cut off when he tossed her into the air. Closing her eyes, Callie inhaled a huge breath...before crashing into the warm water as Brecken's deep laugh echoed above her.

B recken observed Callie surface, gasping for air as her arms flailed.

"You son of a bitch!" Her tone was filled with laughter rather than anger, causing him to smile.

Wading in the deep water, she jerked her head. "Come on in. It feels great, actually."

Throwing caution to the wind, he sucked in a breath and cannonballed into the water. Bobbing above the surface, he swam toward her, scowling when she splashed him.

"Hey!"

"That's for throwing me in," she said, sliding her arms around his neck.

His arm snaked around her waist, and he guided them to the wall, swimming to a point where his feet touched the bottom. Callie wrapped around him, her legs slick in the wetness as his back rested against the wall.

"We probably shouldn't make out in the hotel pool," he said, gripping her butt to hold her in place. "I'm supposed to be protecting you. Hell, Bakari could be watching at this very moment."

"I can protect myself," she said, her tone regal and confident. "And besides, I think Bakari has a lot of other shit to deal with, including the fact he's training an army in the immortal world and dealing with my shithead ex-betrothed."

"True," he said, gently squeezing the globes of her ass as they settled in the water.

Ever so slowly, she trailed her hand over the curve of his neck, down the scratchy hairs of his chest and eventually, to the waistband of his shorts. "Ooohhh," she said, hooking a finger inside the elastic. "What do we have here?"

Brecken had been hard as a rock since she'd first bared all that smooth, luscious skin in the skimpy bikini. Now, with her hand inches from his cock, he thought he might combust into a pile of unsated lust at any second.

"Is it really a good idea to do this in a public hotel pool, Callie?"

Mischief flashed in her blue-green eyes as she slowly slid her hand under the fabric, gliding it to his massive erection. Her fingers encircled him, and he sucked in a sharp breath.

"Do what?" she asked seductively.

Unable to utter a response, Brecken heaved air into his lungs, praying to the goddess he wouldn't pass out and drown in the damn pool.

"Do you like it when I move my hand like this?" Gripping him in a firm vise, she began stroking him from base to tip, and he closed his eyes in ecstasy.

"Someone might see..." he gritted through clenched teeth.

"The hotel is a freaking ghost town, Brecken. I want to make you feel good."

Lifting his lids, he stared into her limitless eyes. They blazed with desire, her lips still swollen from their recent kiss. Lifting his hand, he smoothed his thumb over her lip. "You're so beautiful," he whispered, cupping her jaw.

She smiled, the gesture transforming her features into something so breathtaking Brecken knew he'd see the image in every future dream. Her hand worked along his cock, smooth and steady in the warm water, and he felt like a fool for already feeling his climax on the horizon.

"That feels so good, hon," he murmured, sliding his hand to clench the hair at her nape. "When you touch me, I want to fucking explode."

"Good," she replied, slowly licking her lips. "Don't forget, I'm the virgin here. Well, until recently."

"Now, you're a sex queen," he teased, nipping her lips.

"You're goddamned right I am." Gliding her other hand under his shorts, she cupped his balls, massaging them as she stroked his cock. He squeezed the flesh of her ass, holding her so she didn't fall.

"Do you like that?"

"Yes," he rasped. "I'm going to come in the fucking pool. Shit. I'm pretty sure that's going to get us an extra cleaning charge on the bill."

Throwing back her head, she laughed, the skin of her neck glistening in the moonlight. "I'll work it off," she said, reclaiming his gaze as she arched a brow. "I want you to come. I love touching you this way."

"Callie..." he groaned, gripping her ass and her hair, feeling his balls tighten as she maneuvered them in her hand.

"I can talk dirty too, you know?" Leaning forward, she touched her lips to his ear and spoke with a gravel-laden voice. "Come while I stroke your cock, soldier," she commanded, causing him to moan with pleasure. "And then take me inside and fuck me."

Giving into the pleasure, Brecken closed his eyes, pulling her close and burying his face in her neck. His hips pumped into her hand, mindless and jerking, as he scraped his fangs over her nape.

"*Oh, god,*" she moaned, pressing the flesh against his lips. "Bite me."

"Not yet, honey," he groaned, sucking the sweet skin of her neck between his lips. Drinking blood was considered sacred in Vampyre culture, and was usually only done between bonded mates. Brecken had never drunk from a woman during sex, and he felt it too intimate since their relationship was so new. Still, he longed to taste her that way, and now that the door had been opened, it would most likely become one more thing to dream about when he thought of Callie.

"One day," she whispered in his ear, her hands moving with ardent fervor. "One day, you'll taste me that way too."

"Oh, *fuck...*" he groaned, pressing his face into her neck before mumbling unintelligible words as his body shook with pleasure. Gasping her name, he embraced the orgasm, letting it claim his body as he clutched her.

"*Yesss,*" she hissed in his ear, sending him into overdrive as he jerked and sputtered in her hand. Jets of release shot from his cock as she continued to stroke him, driving him insane with lust.

"No more," he cried, lowering his hand to stop the maddening, pleasurable strokes. "Oh...*god...*"

His large frame shuddered and quaked in her arms as she lifted her hand to stroke his scalp, the points of her nails digging deep and adding to the bliss. Brecken encircled her with his arms, drawing her into every nook of his body as he emptied himself against her. Sighing as his muscles quivered, he nuzzled her nape with his nose.

"Damn, that was really hot," she said, chuckling. "You're so fucking sexy, Brecken."

"Right now, I think I'm just dead," he mumbled into her neck. "You decimated me."

Her fingers caressed his scalp as they lounged in the water, replete and sated. "I'm glad I made you feel good. I had weird hang-ups that I was going to be bad at sex."

Lifting his head, which felt like it weighed a hundred pounds, he stared into her eyes. "Why in the world would you think that?"

Shrugging, her gaze lowered to his chest. "I just told you what happened in middle and high school. I was a pariah who didn't get asked to one dance."

Placing his fingers under her chin, he tilted her face to reclaim her gaze. "If I could go back in time, I'd beat up all those middle school losers for you. And then I'd dance with you, even though I hate to dance."

Her brilliant smile buckled his knees. "My hero."

Running his hand over her wet curls, he longed to return the favor. "Let's go inside so I can taste you again."

"Ohhhhh, are we going to have a sleepover?"

"Fuck yes, we are."

Constricting his fingers on the swell of her ass, he straightened, reveling in her laugh as she wrapped her legs tighter around his waist. Wading through the pool, he lifted them both out, strong and secure, and walked them to the chairs.

After cleaning up the remnants of their dinner, they headed inside to his room, where Brecken took his time removing the scraps of her bikini before submerging himself in her gorgeous body.

Chapter 19

Callie slept more soundly than she had in ages. The hollow in Brecken's chest was perfectly tailored for her cheek, and his deep breaths soothed her as they lay entwined in the hotel bed. After making love, they'd showered and fallen asleep, exhausted by their travels and sexy trysts. When they awoke, he loved her once more, slow and thorough as he stared into her with those deep bronze eyes.

As he loomed above her, his strong hips undulating into hers, she felt a deep connection, as if their energies were entwined along with their bodies. Never had she felt so cherished as when he surged inside and whispered, "Take me deep, Callie-lily. Open for me, honey."

She pressed her legs against the bed, offering herself to him as they reached for ultimate pleasure. In those moments, her mind drifted to the future, and she began to allow herself to dream. What if he was her mate? The one she was meant to be with this whole time? Perhaps Zadicus was just a blip in the road that led her to her strong, thoughtful soldier.

After they recovered from their lovemaking, they prepared for the day and gathered their belongings before heading to the lobby and paying the bill. Once situated in the rental car, they drove to the recreational equipment store to purchase a tent, sleeping bags and the other essentials they would need to survive in the desert for several days.

After stocking up on nonperishable food and water at the grocery store, Brecken secured the stash in the trunk before closing it and wiping his hands.

"Well, I think we've got everything we need. Ready to head to the desert?"

"Ready," she said, sliding into the passenger seat as he sat behind the wheel. "I have a million questions buzzing in my brain."

They discussed her questions as they drove. What did Tatiana want to say to her? Was she ready to choose a side? Was she even in the desert, or was she screwing with them? She was known to be fickle and flighty at times, and Callie hoped she wasn't leading them on a wild-goose chase.

Two hours later, they drove past a sign labeled "Sierra Ancha Wilderness Area" and pulled into one of the open spaces in the sparsely populated parking lot. Glancing around, Callie noticed the rugged terrain swathed by cacti and brush. In the distance, she spotted red rocks and jagged mountains and thanked the goddess Brecken was with her. She was an adventurous person, but hanging out by herself in an arid desert didn't really hold much appeal.

"Well, we made it," he said, opening his door and heading to the trunk. "We'll take as much as we can carry in our packs with the assumption it might be several days until we get back to the car."

Nodding, Callie began packing her backpack, making sure to include a blanket, sleeping bag and as much of the packaged food as she could carry without collapsing. Being half-Vampyre made her strong, and being Crimeous's granddaughter gave her the ability to hover the pack above the ground, although that took energy. Wrinkling her nose, she decided she'd keep it as light as possible. Fainting in the desert wasn't really high on her agenda, thank you very much.

"Y'all heading out for a hike?" a genial deep voice asked behind them.

Whirling, Callie looked to see a gray-haired man approaching with a woman who looked to be similar in age beside him. Covering her heart with her hand, she nodded. "Yep. Sorry, you scared me."

"Sorry, ma'am," he said with a sheepish grin. "I'm Vernon, and this is my wife Katherine. We didn't mean to scare the bejesus out of you. We both retired last year and are traveling across the country in that RV over there." He pointed to a large vehicle, and his wife extended her hand.

"Katherine Grant," she said, shaking Callie's hand and then Brecken's. "Sorry we scared you. Vernon and I just spent two nights camping by the ruins. We figured we'd warn you about the drifters living out there."

"Drifters?" Callie asked.

"They seemed to be of Native American descent, but I can't be sure," Vernon replied. "We saw at least four of them and figure they're living in the ruins. Doesn't bother me since they're not bothering anyone, but they didn't seem too friendly. We tried to approach them and offer some food, and they declined. Probably just want to be left alone. Hell, I can understand that, I guess. Kat here hasn't left my side for a year, and I've forgotten what it's like to read the paper in silence." He slipped his arm across her shoulders, smiling as he teased her.

"Oh, he's just being mean," she said, swatting his chest, "and no one reads the paper anymore, dear." Facing Callie, she said, "He loves spending time with me and won't let me have a damn minute to myself. It's been that way ever since we got married over forty years ago. Perhaps you two can understand. You have the look of young lovers."

"Do we now?" Callie asked, smiling up at Brecken. "Did you hear that, darling?"

"Yes, dear, loud and clear," he teased, winking at Callie before facing Vernon and Kat. "I appreciate the warning. We'll stay alert. Are you going to stay another night here in the park?"

"We're on our way to Cabo San Lucas. Vernon promised me a week in paradise. We're getting on the road in a bit and will head to the next park along the way to camp for a few days. Eventually, we'll make it to the Baja Peninsula."

"How lovely," Callie said wistfully. "There's a species of jackrabbit found only on the island of Espiritu Santo near Cabo San Lucas. One of my bucket list goals is to see one of them someday."

"Well, we'll have to check out Espiritu Santo as well," Kat said, looking at Vernon. "Add it to the list, dear."

"Already added," he said, tapping his temple.

"We wish you luck on your camping excursion," Kat said with a nod. "The terrain isn't too rough, and you seem well-stocked. Good luck and stay well."

"Nice to meet you both," Callie called as she and Brecken waved goodbye. Strapping her pack on her back, she beamed up at Brecken. "Ready to eat my dust?"

Arching a brow, his expression turned droll. "Actually, I was already debating how much you'll slow me down."

With a "*pfft*," Callie pivoted and began walking to the trail, leaving him behind to lock up the car.

"Head starts don't count!" he called behind her.

"See you at the ruins." She held up her hand and gave a wave.

He eventually caught up to her, and they hiked under the blazing sun, stopping several times along the way to drink water and Slayer blood.

"How much longer, do you think?" she asked, sitting on one of the large stones beside the trail.

"An hour at most until we get to the ruins. Interesting about the people living there. It's possible they're armed, so I want you to stay alert. I've got the gun strapped to my belt and a knife in my boot, just in case."

Nodding, Callie screwed the top back on her canister and fell into step beside him, reaching over to grab his hand before lacing their fingers. He grinned down at her, squeezing her hand as they plodded along the trail.

Rewarding him with a blazing smile, they trekked deep into the desert, clutching each other's hand every step of the way.

A s the sun hung low in the afternoon sky, Brecken and Callie approached the rocky cliffs. They stood tall, surrounded by green and brown brush, creating a natural open cavern with a dry creek bed that ran down the middle. As they entered the cavern, hiking between two high cliff walls, Callie noticed the first opening in the red rock about fifty feet ahead.

"See that?" she asked softly, pointing. "It looks like a man-made doorway fashioned into the rock of the cliff. The edges are too precise to be natural."

"Yep," Brecken said, pulling up the images of the maps he'd stored on his phone. "This is where Heden said we'd find Tatiana."

They continued forward, rocks crunching beneath their sneakers on the dusty path, until they stopped before a stone that jutted in the middle of the trail. Crouching down, Callie ran her fingers over the drawings etched on the rock.

"The trail that leads to those ruins with the door has been recently used," Brecken said, eyes narrowed as he stared at them in the distance. "This is most likely where the drifters are staying."

Standing, Callie wiped her hands on the thighs of the thin cargo pants she'd packed for hiking in the desert. "I don't see anyone—"

A bristling sounded behind them, and they both whirled around, noticing the rock that fell from several feet above the grassy embankment. It clanked down the hill and landed with a soft thud on the dirt ground.

"Stay close," he said, encircling her wrist and drawing her behind his body. "Let's see if there are any other ruins built into the cliffs."

He led them forward, and they walked several yards, passing the man-made opening before easing around the side of the embankment to find an enclave of ancient ruins. Red and brown stones were stacked to form small shelters, each with openings set several feet apart. The dwellings were set into the cliffside, offering them natural protection and privacy.

"Whoa," Callie breathed, taking in the site as the gravity of the moment set in. An ancient culture of humans had lived here, each with their own family, history and story. Awed by the energy of the place, which seeped deep into her bones, she barely heard the soft giggle behind her.

Turning, her gaze fell on a little boy who crouched behind a nearby rock wall. It was part of the ruins, and several rocks at the top had seen better days, which allowed her to see the boy's full head of black hair.

"It seems like we have a hiking buddy, Brecken," she said, placing her finger over her lips as she stepped toward the rock.

His hand snaked out, grasping her arm to halt her. "It might not be safe," he murmured.

"It's fine," she said softly, her expression urging him to let her go. When he released her arm, she tentatively approached the rock. "I love meeting new hiking buddies, but I walk really fast. Do you think you can keep up with me?"

The boy's head raised above the rock, his gaze locking with hers. He whispered something, but it was carried away by the wind, and she stepped closer.

"I didn't catch that. I *think* you said you were too slow to keep up with my pace."

"I hike fast too," he said, slowly sliding out from behind the wall. His fingers twisted together as he studied her, looking both curious and anxious.

"Well, that's great to hear. We'll have to become friends then. My name is Callie. What's yours?"

Curious eyes observed her as he stood silent.

"No name?" she asked, grinning over her shoulder at Brecken. "Okay then, I'll just have to make one up for you."

He gnawed his lip, visibly debating if he should divulge the information. Finally, he tilted his head and whispered, "*Ho'ok.*"

Callie's eyes narrowed. "That's your name?"

Lifting his hand, he pointed at her. "*Ho'ok*," he repeated.

Callie looked at Brecken, who had slowly inched up beside her. "I don't understand."

"It's the name of a powerful witch in his people's folklore," a woman's voice called behind them. "He senses your powers and thinks you're a witch."

Turning to face her, Callie said, "No more a witch than you are, Tatiana."

Tatiana smiled and gave a gentle nod. "Agreed. Come here, Adriel." Extending her hand, she gestured to the boy. "Come now, Callie is not a witch, although she is very powerful. She is my friend, and I would like you to meet her."

Adriel tentatively approached, taking Tatiana's hand before gazing up at Callie. "Hello," he said softly.

"Hello, Adriel. Nice to meet you. This is my friend, Brecken."

Brecken bent down, resting his hands above his knees so he was on eye level with the boy. "Hello, Adriel. That's a super-cool name."

"It means 'symbol of skill,'" he said, lifting his arms and flexing his biceps.

Brecken and Callie laughed as Tatiana ruffled his hair. "As you can see, he wants to be a warrior one day like you, son of Maddox and Wren. With his tenacious nature, I have no doubt he will succeed." Leaning down, she kissed his head. "Go on inside and find your mother. I smell dinner, and you must be hungry."

Giving a short wave, he ran off toward one of the structures built into the cliffs and bounded inside.

"I'm a bit overwhelmed to finally get to meet the mysterious Tatiana in person," Brecken said, placing his hands on his hips. "I'm not sure whether to be terrified or elated."

"Perhaps you should just be," Tatiana said with a shrug.

"She likes to speak in riddles," Callie muttered.

"I sense your disapproval, Calinda, and I am sorry you experienced hurt after I approached you by the river. I haven't felt emotion in so long I sometimes forget how crushing it can be."

The words spurred sadness in Callie's heart. "That sounds lonely. We all crave emotion and affection, don't we?"

Her full lips formed a smile, although it held no joy. "I had affection once, and the loss of it almost killed me. But that is a story for another time." Glancing around the ruins, her expression was thoughtful. "A family lives here, as the human couple already informed you in the parking lot. They are descended from the tribes of people who thrived here centuries ago."

"Do they need something from me?" Callie asked, lifting her hands. "Is that why you summoned me here?"

"Yes," she said, gesturing to the nearby rocks. "Please, these are flat enough for us to sit on while we speak. The sun will set soon, and you will need to set up camp. There is a clearing just over there that will allow the early morning sun to heat your tent before you rise. You will be safe here, I assure you."

They sat on the rocks assessing each other as Tatiana gathered her thoughts. "Long ago, I traveled through this area when the people who are now known as the Hohokam lived here. I made many friends, one of whom became like a sister to me."

Callie remained silent, interested in the story Tatiana would surely weave.

"Eventually, the woman became sick, and the time of her death drew near. The moment before she passed, she asked me to keep watch over her children. *All* of her children, for however many generations they would roam the Earth."

"Okay," Callie said. "I'm pretty lost, but keep going."

Chuckling, Tatiana smoothed her hand over the rock. "You are quite funny, daughter of Darkrip. I appreciate your sense of humor."

"Uh, thanks, I guess. So, you were telling me about the deathbed promise to your friend," she said, circling her hand in a gesture to continue.

"Yes. Elu was her name. It means 'beautiful' in Zuni, which was spoken here at the time. For centuries, I have kept my promise to her. I was able to see—in the way I see things others cannot—that one of her descendants would become very important to the future of the planet."

"*Heavy*," Brecken murmured.

"I often deal in heavy," she said with a dismissive shrug. "Elu's descendants are members of the family that now inhabits these ruins. One of her lineage is a woman named Kasa, who has two boys of her own. One of them is Adriel, whom you just met." Rising, she stared up at the rapidly darkening sky, gray now that the sun had set behind the cliffs. "The other is named Nuka, which aptly means 'younger brother.'"

Urging them to stand, she began walking toward the dwellings. Callie and Brecken rose and followed her until they stopped at the door of one of the structures. "You may want to cover your nose. The smell can be quite pungent. I have been mixing various potions to no avail."

She stepped inside, and Callie looked at Brecken before following her, comforted by the fact he was behind her. After her eyes adjusted to the dimness, her gaze fell to the boy lying on the bed of furs in the corner. His skin was drenched with sweat, and his eyes were glassy. They approached, and Callie covered her nose and mouth with her hand. The odor of herbs and medicine was potent but not overwhelming. No, the scent she smelled was from the boy himself. Stopping beside the bed, she acknowledged the gut-churning aroma.

The little boy who lay in the furs was surrounded by the stench of death.

Training her gaze on Tatiana, she felt the urge to weep. The boy was suffering from intense pain, and she longed to free him from it.

"Yes, Calinda," Tatiana said, gently cupping her shoulder. "That is why I've brought you here. I need you to heal the child."

Staring down at the boy, Callie shook her head. "I don't use my healing powers on humans or Slayers. Dad was always clear they could only be used on animals. The energy transfer between evolved beings is too unstable. It could kill us both."

Tatiana's features remained impassive. "The risk is high, but you are both children of great importance in this world. Heal the boy, and I will align with your cause to defeat Bakari."

Sucking in a breath, Callie deliberated.

"The boy's life for my alliance," Tatiana said, piercing the silence. "He has only days left, so I will give you until morning to decide. Choose wisely, Calinda, as I am to play a role in the final battle that you cannot foresee. I am encouraged by the choice you made after we spoke by the River Thayne. Hopefully, you will continue to make choices worthy of your station. I will return when the sun has risen above the southwest cliff." She gestured toward the far-off cliffs. "Until then, take solace in Brecken's embrace and let him be a sounding board for your fears."

Glancing at Brecken, Callie muttered, "Well, I guess she knows we're together."

"He is a worthy match for you, Calinda," she said, backing toward the entrance of the dwelling. "Draw on his strength to help make your choice." Closing her eyes, the rocky walls rumbled slightly before she vanished into thin air.

Callie stared down at the boy, overcome by his short, labored breaths and the way his small fingers clutched the furs. Resigned, she looked at Brecken. Concern swam in his eyes as she opened her mouth to speak.

"If I can save his life, I have to do it," she whispered.

A muscle ticked in his jaw. "I know."

Swallowing thickly, Callie prepared herself for a night of deep deliberation, already acknowledging she was going to risk her life to save the child.

Chapter 20

U pon exiting the dwelling, Callie observed the woman who stood outside. She had long, silky black hair, spun into a braid that snaked down her side and almost reached her waist. She wore faded jeans, sneakers and a sweatshirt that read, "Arizona Diamondbacks." Glancing toward Nuka's dwelling, her features contorted in anguish.

"It is hard for me to visit him when he is in so much pain," she said, her throat bobbing as she swallowed. "Tatiana has been helping me, and we are eternally grateful. She has kept the promise she made to my ancestor for centuries."

"You must be Kasa," Callie said.

The woman nodded and gestured toward a nearby doorway built into the cliff. "You met my son, Adriel, and my husband, Lonan, is inside as well. We would like to offer you food and answer any questions about Nuka. Please." She gestured toward the dwelling.

"We met some people in the parking lot who warned us you weren't too friendly," Brecken said, his tone slightly hesitant.

"That is my husband's fault," she said, a look of annoyance crossing her face. "He's wary of strangers and was quite rude to them when they offered us some food."

"I can provide for our family," a man said, exiting the dwelling. "We don't need charity."

"They were just being nice, dear." Pointing at Brecken, she asked, "Is he stubborn as a mule too?"

Callie grinned. "Eh, he's okay. I think I'm probably the stubborn one between the two of us."

"Probably?" Brecken teased, and she punched his arm.

"I am on edge from our son's sickness," Lonan said, trailing toward his wife and placing his arm across her shoulders. "I'm sorry." He placed a firm kiss on her lips.

Sighing, she shrugged. "It's hard to stay mad when he apologizes with the sad face. Come on inside. We are about to sit down for dinner."

Callie and Brecken followed them inside, and she inwardly remarked how nice their home was for a dwelling built into a cliffside. Beautiful tapestries lined the rocky walls and the floor was covered in soft-woven carpets. A cauldron hung above a fire in the corner, and Callie noticed Adriel sitting beside it playing a handheld video game.

"Although we've decided to live separate from modern society for the time being, little boys still crave their video games," Kasa said. "We let him play an hour per day until the batteries die and Lonan can hike to the nearest town to buy more."

"Yes!" Adriel said, pumping his fist. "I beat level fifty-three."

"That's wonderful, but it's time to put it away and eat dinner, Adriel."

Sighing, he nodded and clicked off the game. Setting it aside, he beamed at Brecken and Callie. "We never get any visitors here except some random hikers and Tatiana. You can sit beside me if you like," he said, waving his hand over the carpet.

"I'd love to," Callie said, striding toward him and sitting down. "Thank you."

"You're welcome." He was adorable as he gave her a gap-toothed grin.

Eventually, they all sat near the cauldron, and Kasa began filling bowls with the stew that marinated inside. "It's coyote stew," she said, handing a bowl to Callie. "Lonan hunts them, and we eat what he brings home."

Lifting the bowl to her nose, Callie inhaled, noting it smelled delicious. She wasn't sure about the ingredients but figured it wouldn't kill her if everyone else was eating it. Taking the spoon Kasa handed her, she took a tentative taste.

"Wow, this is fantastic," she said, consuming another spoonful. "Thank you, Kasa."

"You're welcome. Brecken?" Kasa asked, handing him a bowl.

"I hope you don't think it's rude of me to decline," he said, holding up his hand. "I don't eat food all that much."

She nodded and handed the bowl to Adriel before preparing one for herself and Lonan. They sipped the stew, the wooden spoons clanking against the brown clay bowls, as Kasa studied Brecken.

"Is this because you drink blood to survive?"

"Yes," he said with a nod. "It's something humans wouldn't usually know, but I'm guessing Tatiana already told you I'm a Vampyre."

"She did." Kasa took another bite before continuing. "And she also told us of your unique heritage, Callie."

"Unique is one way to put it," she mumbled.

"Callie is magnificent, and some people in our realm aren't wise enough to realize it quite yet," Brecken said, placing his hand on her back and slowly rubbing.

Callie's heart melted at the beautiful words, and she gave him a wink. "It's been hard living between two worlds and not quite fitting in, but I'm not going to whine about it. I've had it a lot better than most, and I'm thankful for that."

"I appreciate your gratitude. It is an important quality to possess."

Nodding, Callie gave her a sympathetic smile. "I'm so sorry about Nuka. When did he become sick?"

"It's been two months now," she said, eyes welling with tears as she set down the bowl. "He complained of a stomach ache at first, and I thought it was something he ate. But then he began having chills and developed a fever. I sent a prayer to the universe, hoping Tatiana would hear the call, and she appeared. She takes her oath to my ancestor very seriously and has tried to help."

"It seemed she made a lot of potions from what I saw in Nuka's dwelling. I can't believe none of them helped. Her concoctions are extremely powerful and have given a Vampyre in our realm the ability to transport."

"She does not understand why they are ineffective," Kasa said, running her fingers over the rug. "Lonan took Nuka to see a doctor in Phoenix who performed a multitude of tests, and the results showed no disease. It is baffling. We cannot treat a problem we cannot diagnose."

"That's strange," Callie said, feeling her eyebrows draw together. "He's obviously very sick."

"Would it help if you put him in a hospital?" Brecken asked. "I don't want to pry about why you're living out here, but it might help."

"I lost my job over a year ago, and we couldn't afford rent anymore," Lonan said. "This was our ancestors' home, and Kasa and I felt a calling to live here for a while and try to connect with our heritage. It might seem strange to some, but we've been happy out here...until Nuka became sick."

"The doctors wouldn't admit him because he doesn't have a diagnosable condition for them to treat—"

"And because we don't have health insurance," Lonan mumbled.

"That too," Kasa sighed. "Regardless, Tatiana sees much more with her mind than we do with our eyes. She believes Nuka possesses special abilities and must be healed by someone who does as well. Although Tatiana is powerful, her spells and potions are external. You were born with the ability to heal, so she believes you can help him. She also believes there is a greater purpose connecting you to Nuka."

"What purpose?"

"She has latched onto the belief that you are meant to heal our son in exchange for her alliance in your cause to defeat Bakari."

Callie finished her stew, sipping from the bowl before placing it on the ground. Contemplating, she gnawed her lip as she debated the repercussions of healing the boy. "So far, I've only used my power to heal animals. There is an energy transfer that happens during the healing process that we've never been able to understand. My father and aunt Evie tried to study it, but we've never figured out how to collect any of the energy. I'm telling you this so you understand what you're asking. The outcome could be disastrous."

"I understand he could die, but he will die without your help, so I am willing to take the chance."

Callie rubbed her arm. "It's possible I could die too. It's a huge risk for both of us."

"I'm so sorry to ask you to put your life in danger," Kasa said, reaching over to grasp her husband's hand. "We are strangers, and you owe us nothing. If you decide not to heal our son, we will accept that choice. What we are asking of you is extremely unfair, and we would not ask if we had another option."

Blowing out a breath as her lips fluttered, Callie contemplated. "I'm pretty sure I've already decided to do it." She gave a slight shrug, feeling her lips curve into a compassionate smile. "But I need to spend some time contemplating the repercussions. We have no way to reach my family since there's no cell service or internet access here. A part of me wants to go home and discuss with them before I heal Nuka."

"We don't have time for you to travel home," Kasa pleaded. "Tatiana said Nuka only has a days to live. Oh, god," she cried, burying her face in her hands. "I can't lose him, Lonan."

Her husband slid closer, embracing her as she cried on his shoulder. "I know, sweetheart. It's okay."

"She cries a lot," Adriel said, staring up at Callie. "It makes my chest hurt right here." He rubbed his hand over his heart, the gesture calling to Callie as she sifted her fingers through his thick hair.

"I get that, kid. I bet your heart hurts for your brother too."

He nodded. "Really bad. I miss playing with him. He's my best friend."

Callie looked over at Brecken, and he gave her a sympathetic smile. "Hard to say no to that."

"It sure is."

Kasa's tears abated, and she lifted her head, wiping the wetness from her cheeks. "I'm sorry. The pain and sadness are overwhelming sometimes. Please take the night to contemplate. Do you want to sleep in the dwelling next door?"

"We'll set up our tent outside in the spot Tatiana suggested," Brecken said. "But thank you."

"Of course." Sliding toward the cauldron, she scooped some stew into a clean bowl. "I need to take this to Nuka and sit with him while Lonan gets Adriel to bed. If you need anything during the night, please let us know."

"We will," Callie said, rising as Brecken stood beside her. "Have a good visit with Nuka, and thanks for the stew. It was really good."

After saying good night, Brecken and Callie headed to the cliffside clearing about fifty feet away, and he set up the tent while Callie tried like hell to find a cell signal. Holding up the phone, she trailed around, frustrated, and eventually gave up.

"No service?" Brecken asked as he popped the last part of the tent in place.

"Nope, but we knew that. I really want to talk to my parents right now. The two of them always have such great perspectives on things. They're usually different perspectives, which helps me come to a logical conclusion based on their combined advice."

"Well," he said, holding out his hand, "I'm not as powerful as Darkrip, nor as educated as Arderin, but I have two good ears and would love to listen to you try to talk yourself out of healing a sick child."

Her cheeks puffed as she took his hand. "Yeah, you already know I'm going to do it. But I'd like to talk about it anyway."

Nodding, he led her into the tent, zipping it once they were inside. They changed into shorts, and Callie threw on a soft tank top before Brecken zipped their sleeping bags together. Callie lay down beside him, comforted by his soft caresses as he held her inside the plushy fabric. Resting her head on his chest, she began to relay her fears, thankful for her strong soldier who listened intently and offered her solace.

Brecken's fingers sifted through Callie's curls as she nuzzled into his body. She spoke about her fears of healing Nuka, the musings sometimes drifting to philosophical questions about suffering and death. Lifting her head, she cradled her face as her elbow rested on his chest.

"You must think about death since you're a soldier. What do you think happens when we die?"

"I believe in the Passage and hope I go there," he said, smoothing the hair at her temple.

"Not *after* we die," she said, holding up a finger, "but *when* we die. That moment it all begins to slip away."

"Well, hopefully, I'll never have to find out," he teased, "but if I do, I imagine it will be peaceful. You know, like whatever pain you're experiencing just melts away and your soul is free."

"That's beautiful," she said with a soft smile. "I should've expected it from all the poetic letters you wrote."

They stared into each other's eyes, silently communicating until he spoke. "I think you have to do it," he said, acceptance lacing his expression. "If you're looking for my opinion, there it is."

"I agree. Securing Tatiana's alliance is key. With her help, we can hopefully end this conflict once and for all."

"And you'll be free of the prophecy," he murmured.

"Unless I destroy the world," she muttered.

"Never gonna happen," he said, sifting his fingers through her hair. "You're too pretty to cause the apocalypse."

Breathing a laugh, she dramatically swiped a curl over her shoulder. "I guess I'm okay."

Their chuckles mingled as she slithered atop his body. Lowering her lips, she pressed them to Brecken's, drawing him into a slow, languid kiss as she reached between their bodies. Reaching into his boxer briefs, she pulled his aching shaft through the slit and pushed the fabric of her tiny shorts aside. Grasping him, she ran the head of his cock through her slick essence as he palmed her hips. As their lips consumed each other, she slowly slid over his straining shaft, enveloping him in her wetness.

"Goddess, you feel so good," he murmured, using his hands to guide her as she writhed atop his body. The slick inner walls of her channel gripped him, so snug he never wanted to let go.

Resting her palms flat on either side of his head, she anchored above, undulating back and forth in a rhythm that drove him wild. Every time her drenched folds ran along his sensitive flesh was more pleasurable than the last. Digging his fingers into the swells of her ass, he increased the pace, bucking his hips to push himself deep inside her quaking body.

"I feel so connected to you," she whispered, her dark curls tickling his chest as she loved him. "How is that possible?"

"Come here," he whispered, threading his fingers in her hair and drawing her into a blazing kiss. Their tongues mated, breath mingling as they slid over each other...into each other.

Lowering his hand, his finger delved between her folds as she rode him, locating the sensitive bud under the hood of her mound. Pressing the pad of his finger to the engorged nub, he stimulated it, groaning when she mewled and increased the gyration of her hips. Determined to let her remain in control, he surged inside, their bodies working in tandem to reach their peak.

"Let go, Callie," he rasped against her lips, his finger circling her clit in firm, rapid strokes as she trembled. "Let me see you come, honey."

Her spine snapped, head tossing back as she flew over the edge. The rapid movements drew him deeper into her body, and he thrust, surging as far as he could go as the base of his spine began to tingle. Gritting his teeth, he pummeled her quivering frame, feeling her pulse around his turgid cock. Unable to hold back the release, a growl escaped the back of his throat as he began to come, coating her core with the evidence of his desire.

She collapsed against him, squeezing him with her thighs as she straddled him, gripping him with her tight channel as he emptied everything inside her. Scrambling to catch his breath, he buried his face in her soft curls, drowning in the scent of his gorgeous Callie. His frame jerked as he expelled the last of his release, and she clung to him, arms and legs wrapped around him until he didn't know where he ended and where she began. Awash with contentment, he stroked her hair as their bodies cooled.

"Brecken?" she mumbled into his chest.

"Hmm?"

"I don't want to fight what's happening between us," she said, the words lazy and sated as her fingers softly caressed his neck.

Joy coursed through him even though he had reservations. The nagging notion that she would be wrapped in another man's arms if certain circumstances hadn't occurred lingered in his mind as well as the discussion they'd had at the pool. He loved being with her, but it didn't change the fact he would never be wealthy or revered.

"Neither do I. Let's focus on you healing Nuka and gaining Tatiana's alliance while we let what's between us breathe."

"Okay." She snuggled into him, sending sated jolts of bliss through his body. "I feel like healing Nuka and gaining Tatiana's alliance is part of something bigger. If it helps us defeat Bakari and leave the prophecy behind, I'm all in."

"That's really brave," he said, kissing her hair. "I'll be there the whole time while you heal him, honey. You're not alone."

"I know. Thank you, Brecken. Night."

Tucking the sleeping bag around them, he encircled her in his arms, content to have her sprawled against him for eternity. "Night."

Closing his eyes, he fell asleep as he so often dreamed, with Callie in his embrace.

Bakari stood under the night sky, observing the troops as they sparred. Zadicus in his new form was magnificent, and Bakari felt the warrior increased the probability of destroying the royal family. As he stood atop the hill, he heard a rustling to his side and turned to observe Tatiana appear.

"Hello," he said with a brisk nod. "I wondered when you would appear to me again. As you can see, the potion Dr. Tyson created has transformed Zadicus into a formidable weapon."

Tatiana's eyes narrowed as she watched Zadicus spar with the Deamon soldiers. He plowed through them one by one, as if they were feathers he was plucking from a down pillow. Sucking in a breath, she slowly shook her head. "You killed him."

"He is still alive."

"His soul is dead," she snapped, her gaze angry as she stared up at him. "Have you learned nothing in all your centuries on the planet? Death is not for you to wield like a god. You assign yourself too much importance."

"You're the one who aligned with me, Tatiana."

"I *helped* you," she said, lifting a finger, "but you've never had my allegiance."

"Semantics," he said, giving a frustrated wave. "Why are you here? Did you come to lecture me?"

Lifting her chin, she spoke into the gentle breeze. "I have come to inform you I have decided to align with the immortal royals."

Anger swelled deep in Bakari's gut, causing him to face her and lift his hands. "Why would you align with them? I thought you saw the purpose of my cause."

"I saw the purpose of pushing you toward the moment when you will fulfill the prophecy with Calinda. We are close to the conclusion of this woeful story, and I, for one, am glad." Lifting a shoulder, her lips formed a crooked smile. "In all honesty, I am tired, Bakari. Once the prophecy is fulfilled, I will have a nice long sleep. Until then, I have finally chosen a side."

"Why are you telling me this?" he asked, crossing his arms over his chest. "It would make more sense for you to keep it secret."

"No, it wouldn't. You need to know your weaknesses so you can prepare for the final battle. Losing me is a weakness. I have supplied you with many powerful concoctions and spells for quite some time."

Something burned in Bakari's chest, and he uncrossed his arms to rub the spot above his heart before realizing it was sadness. "I'm not sure what to say. Thanks for telling me, I guess. I should probably murder you but don't want to expend the energy."

Her lips formed a wistful smile. "I have been drawn to you, Bakari. To your pain and feelings of not belonging. Most see you as evil, but I see you as damaged."

"Well, you're no bed of roses either, Tatiana."

"No," she said, gaze falling to the grass before reclaiming his. "Fear and pain guide me, as they do you. I don't see happiness in either of our futures, and for that, I am quite sad."

Bakari studied her as curiosity snaked down his spine. "You have seen my death? When will it happen?"

"You know I will not answer that." Stepping closer, her expression turned serious. "But I do want to help you one last time."

"How?"

"The battle between you and the immortal army needs to happen in the field to the south of Restia, near the ether. Therein lies your only chance of fulfilling the prophecy."

"You're sure?"

"I'm sure," she said with a nod. "Draw the immortal troops there in two weeks' time and commence the final battle on the open field. Callie will be there. I have seen it."

"She will align with me?"

"Yes."

"But you still choose to side with the immortal army?"

"Yes," she said with a nod.

Frustrated, he swiped a hand over his face. If she wanted to choose the losing side, who was he to argue? Perhaps she would survive. If anyone could, it was Tatiana. She always had indiscernible motives at best, and he didn't have the will to figure out her riddles any longer.

"All right." Clearing his throat, he wondered how to say goodbye. Tatiana had been a fixture in his life for many decades, and he was embarrassed to realize he would miss her.

"You don't have to say anything, son of Markdor. I'm sorry your life has taken the path it did. You deserved better before you gave into your hate. Ultimately, that choice will be your undoing."

"My hate makes me powerful, Tatiana. I will restore balance to Etherya's realm and rule over the kingdom I was denied so long ago."

Sighing, she shook her head. "You are blinded by your pain. I hope you are freed from it someday. Until we meet again, goodbye, Bakari." With a nod, she disappeared.

"Frustrating creature," he muttered, kicking the ground before turning to face the troops. Clutching onto her assurance that Callie would align with him and fulfill the prophecy, he pushed the soldiers well into the night, ensuring they were prepared for the final battle.

Chapter 21

In the morning, Callie and Brecken rose to find warm sunlight surrounding their tent. Stretching her sore muscles, she yawned and felt him stir next to her.

"Rise and shine," she said, sitting up and swiping the hair from her forehead. "It's a great day to heal a sick kid. Let's do this."

Sitting up, he rested his forearms on his knees as he grinned. "Someone's in a good mood."

"I want heal him, Brecken, and it will cement Tatiana's alliance. If I can pull it off, this will be a pretty fucking awesome day."

"I know you'll do it," he said softly as he pushed the sleeping bag aside. "Let's get to it."

They dressed before stepping outside the tent to breathe in the fresh air. Tatiana appeared at Callie's side, and she turned to face her.

"I'm going to heal Nuka."

"I know. I have already informed Bakari I will be aligning with you."

Callie scowled. "Why would you do that? Now, we've lost the element of surprise."

Tatiana breathed a laugh. "He asked me the same thing. I have my reasons. Now, it is time to heal the boy. I must admit, I am disappointed in my failure to remedy his illness. I do not like feeling helpless. My potions and knowledge are the core of my identity."

"How long has it been since someone just saw you as *you*?" Callie asked, head tilting as she studied her.

Tatiana's eyebrows lifted. "Now, it is you who speaks in riddles."

"I'm not trying to be obtuse," she said, lifting her hands. "I just...I sense an emptiness in your words, and it makes me sad. Although you're a tough nut to crack and quite meddlesome, you deserve love like everyone else, Tatiana."

Her lips twitched, and she gazed at the ground before lifting her eyes back to Callie's. "Thank you for the kind words. I do not often receive sympathy or comfort. Your empathy is one of your greatest strengths, Callie."

Callie smiled. "I think it comes with the territory. You know, healer and all." Lifting her hands, she shook them.

Giving a nod, Tatiana gestured toward the dwelling. "I have carried on too long. Come. It is time to heal Nuka."

They followed her, waving hello to Kasa, Lonan and Adriel as they stood outside. Kasa stepped forward and pulled Callie into a firm embrace.

"Thank you," she whispered, hugging her so tightly Callie struggled to breathe. "I can never repay you for your sacrifice."

"It's not a sacrifice to heal someone in pain." Drawing back, she squeezed Kasa's shoulders. "I'll do my best."

The woman nodded, tears streaming down her face, as Tatiana urged Callie to enter Nuka's dwelling. "You all will stay out here while Callie uses her magic. Brecken and I will observe inside. It is possible the ground will shake and rocks will be displaced. Stay alert."

The family nodded, and Callie ducked slightly to enter the dim room. Nuka lay in the furs as the stench of death and illness permeated every corner of the space. Covering her mouth and nose, she closed her eyes.

"I just need a minute. The sickness is overwhelming to me. I feel it and his suffering as if it were my own."

Tatiana and Brecken stood firm, giving her the time she needed. Crouching next to Nuka, she gently touched her fingers to his burning skin.

"Hello, Nuka," she said, smiling as the boy wheezed, terror swimming in his deep brown eyes. "My name is Callie, and I have special powers." Holding up her hands, she rotated them as the boy looked on. "There is magic that seeps from my hands, and it will lock onto your sickness and pull it from your body. Do you understand?"

Short breaths exited from his lungs as he stared up at her in fear.

"*Shhh...*" she said, placing her palm on his damp forehead. "Do you feel me? I want you to try to breathe just a bit slower, okay?"

His eyes darted back and forth between hers before his chest began to rise and fall in longer breaths.

"Great job," she said, smiling as she caressed his cheek. "I've got you, sweetheart."

She stayed like that for several seconds, allowing him to feel her touch. Eventually, she pulled off the fur and pinched the fabric of his sweat-soaked T-shirt.

"I'm going to take this off, okay? I need to touch your skin with my hands. Are you okay with that?"

He gave an almost imperceptible nod, and she smiled. She tugged the fabric off his body and sat firmly on the rug, wanting to feel as grounded as possible to the earth below. Holding up her hands, she explained, "I'm going to place both hands on your body. One over your heart, and one over your belly, okay?"

He answered with labored breaths, but Callie saw the acceptance in his eyes. "When I touch you, I want you to think of your favorite thing in the whole world. It can be a toy, or the beach, or hugging your mama. Anything that makes you happy, Nuka." Lowering her hands, she placed them on his body, closing her eyes to cement the connection.

Illness swirled beneath her palms, sticky and corrosive, and she concentrated on the darkness behind her eyelids so she wouldn't become overwhelmed with nausea. Inhaling and exhaling, she used her mother's yoga breathing techniques to remain calm. Summoning her powers, she began to extract the illness from his body.

The sickness choked her, robbing air from her lungs as she struggled to maintain control. It held a power she'd never felt before, and Callie understood it was generated by someone or *something* wicked and inhuman. There would be time to analyze that later, but for now, she concentrated on dragging it from Nuka's body so she could destroy it.

Suddenly, her brain was flooded with images, and Callie's eyes snapped open to focus on Nuka. The boy stared back at her, shaking and terrified, and she longed to soothe him but was frozen by the pictures that flashed through her mind. Images from long ago of a peaceful species who inhabited a small corner of Etherya's realm. A simple species with loving families and gentle laughter that filled their pointed ears until they were all washed away in a great flood.

One of them remained and evolved into a hateful creature who would come to be known as Crimeous, King of the Deamons. But there were others who'd been washed away and survived. The destruction of their kingdom led them to the human world, where they began anew, blending in with the species and sometimes procreating with them to create hybrids. Elu, Nuka's ancestor, was one of those hybrids, and she learned the ways of witchcraft so she could cast spells to diminish the Elven genes in her descendants. She felt they would thrive in the human realm if they did not possess immortal qualities.

But the spell did not work for all of her progeny, and some retained the immortal attributes. Nuka was one of those creatures. Pressing her palms into his skin, Callie focused on the task at hand. Closing her eyes, she clenched her teeth, trying like hell to draw the sickness from his body.

"Hello, Callie," a voice called, and she turned to look at Nuka, who now stood beside her. Confused, she held up her hands, glancing at the dark dome that surrounded them.

"Hello, Nuka."

"We are in your subconscious now," he said, smiling to reveal two missing front teeth. "You are still healing me in the physical realm, but our powers allow us to speak here."

Squinting one eye, she placed her hands on her hips. "You certainly don't talk like a little boy. How old are you?"

"In the physical world, I'm five, but in the scheme of things, my soul is already wise, as Tatiana's is. It is hard to explain, but it stems from our Elven heritage. The destruction of our people was traumatic—both the Elves and our Native American ancestors—and our blood is fortified to ensure future generations survive."

Callie's eyebrows drew together. "I don't sense any special elements in your family's blood."

"No. The Elven gene lies dormant in some, and many would say they are lucky to only be human. They will never know the fear the Elven hybrids feel. The Elven council only hunts those who express the traits of our ancestors."

"I'm not familiar with the Elven council, but they sound like some pretty bad eggs."

Laughter bounded from his throat. "Your intuition is correct. They do not embrace human-Elven hybrids who exhibit Elven traits and have decreed to destroy us one by one. This is where my sickness stems from. One of the purebred Elves poisoned our stew without my knowledge. Since the Elven gene is suppressed in my mother and brother, they were not affected."

"I didn't realize there were still purebred Elves on the planet."

"It is a discovery that could only be realized once the War of the Species ended and the immortals were reunited. The Elves are an entirely different breed of immortal from Slayers and Vampyres and much more highly evolved than Deamons. There will be a reckoning in the future, where several of the species collide, but other things must happen first. There is an order to the chaos of the immortals."

"I'm guessing one of those things is that I need to fulfill the old Elven prophecy?" Callie muttered, crossing her arms over her chest.

Nuka smiled. "Yes, but you do not understand the prophecy as Tatiana and I do. You see it as evil, but I assure you, it is not. Change often arises from things we don't understand."

"Was this meant to happen? You falling ill so I would need to heal you?"

"Yes. Tatiana eventually realized this, which helped close the loop. Now, you have her alliance and can move forward."

"And you'll stay here with your family?"

He nodded. "I will experience my childhood with my family until I grow old enough to accept my position as a crusader in the human-Elven conflict. Then, I will fulfill my prophecy, as you will yours."

"You have a prophecy too?" she asked, eyebrows arching.

"We all have a prophecy, Calinda. The question is: Are we brave enough to execute it?"

Her lips twitched as she bent down, resting her palms on her thighs so she could look him in the eyes. "You're a basket of riddles, kid. I think I like it."

"Remember these words at the moment you fulfill the prophecy," he said, lifting a finger. "*May the world begin anew as the prophecy is fulfilled.*"

"May the world begin anew as the prophecy is fulfilled," she repeated. "Got it. Not really with you on the whole 'I'm going to actually fulfill the prophecy' thing, but I'll remember just in case," she said, making quotation marks with her fingers.

Stepping forward, he extended his arms, and she crouched down to give him a tight hug.

"Thank you for healing me, Calinda. The transfer is almost complete. You need to return to the physical world now."

Drawing back, she searched the darkened surroundings. "How do I do that? I have no idea how I got here."

Lifting his hand, he extended his finger. "You already know." Ever so gently, he tapped his finger between her eyes, causing her to gasp. Suddenly, her lids flew open, and she was back in the dwelling, above Nuka's body, hands melded to his skin as she drew the sickness out. Gritting her teeth, she gave a harsh groan and extricated the last of the murky energy from the boy's body.

Nuka cried out atop the furs, and Callie drew her hands away, unable to touch him any longer. They burned with the buzzing dark energy of the sickness, and she curled into a ball on the rug, gagging as she pulled her knees to her chest.

"Callie?" Brecken called, his voice so faraway as she drowned in the sticky energy.

"No!" Tatiana yelled, and Callie knew she was holding him back. "You cannot touch her. She must eradicate the sickness with her powers."

Tears flooded Callie's eyes as she gasped for air, face buried against her knees as she wept.

"I'm here, Callie," Brecken's deep voice called behind her, soothing her as she shuddered and quaked. "I'm not leaving your side no matter how long it takes. Listen to my voice. I'm here."

She nodded, unsure if the movement was visible, and clutched her sides as pain vibrated in every cell of her body. Nuka cried next to her, his weeping a song of fear and relief weaved into the high-pitched noises, and she knew he was going to live. By the goddess, she'd healed him, and he was going to be okay. The knowledge gave her strength, and she blew out huge breaths of relief before slowly lifting her head.

"Hey, buddy," she said, smiling at Nuka. "You okay?"

His shallow breaths echoed hers as his gaze latched onto hers. Giving a nod, he slowly wiped the tears from his cheeks.

"Good. I need a minute. You were pretty sick there, kid. Holy crap." Collapsing back into the fetal position, she allowed herself to relax and regulate her breathing.

Minutes later, Tatiana spoke behind her. "You can go to her now, but be gentle."

Brecken rushed to her side, tenderly cupping her arm and turning her on the ground. "Callie? Are you okay?"

Tears welled in her eyes again as she observed the concern and sentiment that laced his handsome features. Reaching for him, she clutched on tight as he drew her into his lap, cradling her as he rocked back and forth.

"That was amazing," he rasped, holding her as he kissed her temple. "I've got you."

They swayed back and forth, enveloped in each other's embrace, as Kasa rushed into the dwelling.

"Nuka? Are you okay, my love?"

"Mama?" he called softly.

Kasa rushed over, dragging him into her embrace as she wept. "My baby. Oh, god, your fever has broken. Do you feel better?" Lifting her head, she cupped his cheeks as he nodded.

"I feel better, Mama."

"My sweetheart," she whispered, kissing his forehead. Turning to Callie, she swiped the wetness from her cheeks. "Thank you."

"You're welcome," Callie said, clutching onto Brecken as he soothed her. There, between the old rock walls, they comforted each other, grateful for Nuka's recovery.

Chapter 22

Eventually, the excitement of the morning abated, and Callie and Nuka stepped outside to breathe the fresh desert air. Grasping his hand, she smiled into his eyes.

"Do you remember the conversation we had while I was healing you?"

His small features scrunched together as he contemplated. Tilting his face, he shook his head.

"That's okay. Maybe it was a dream, or maybe we're meant to reconnect in the future when you've grown big enough to remember it. I can't wait to see you again, Nuka."

He squeezed her hand, showcasing the same crooked grin he'd flashed during their cryptic interaction.

"Be good for your mom and dad, okay?"

Brown hair swished as he gave an excited nod before he ran back to join his family. Callie and Brecken trailed back to their tent, Tatiana strolling beside them.

"Thank you, Calinda," she said, facing her when they approached the tent. "I will visit Sadie and Nolan at Uteria and supply them with information on the chemicals Bakari uses in his poisons and potions. They should be able to create antidotes that will heal any Slayer affected by them, and any on the battlefield if he chooses to use them in the final skirmish."

"And you will fight alongside us during the battle?" Brecken asked.

"Yes," she said, lifting her chin. "Not only will it add a formidable ally to your regime, but it will allow me to ensure things go as planned. As I informed Calinda, there is a role in the final battle I must play. I saw it in a vision, and I take my premonitions very seriously."

"Do you want to train with us? I can set it up with Jack."

"No," she said with a soft smile. "I'll let you focus on training with the soldiers and will appear when the battle is upon us. Don't worry. I will be ready to fight when the moment arrives."

"I had an encounter with Nuka during the healing," Callie said. "Or a version of Nuka who seemed to exist in my subconscious. It didn't make a ton of sense."

"Nuka is like me," Tatiana said, gazing off in the distance. "We are remnants of mysterious creatures whose secrets have been scattered by the winds of time. He will eventually grow into the soul whom you had the encounter with. Our souls experience the world differently than others."

"He said there are still purebred Elves on the planet."

Sighing, Tatiana nodded. "Yes. That is a matter for another time. First, we must defeat Bakari. His story is tragic but necessary for all the pieces to fall into place. Now, it is time for him to leave the Earth. I look forward to our alliance and to finalizing this part of the immortals' history."

"Goodbye, Tatiana," Callie said, feeling the urge to hug her. There was a loneliness in the slight hunch of the woman's shoulders, and she took a step forward to embrace her.

"Goodbye, Calinda," she said, holding up a hand to halt her. "I must go. I will see you both in due time." Closing her eyes, she lifted her face to the sky and disappeared.

"She's so sad," Callie whispered, turning to face Brecken. "I've formed some sort of connection to her, and I can *feel* it, Brecken."

"I hope she finds happiness one day," he said, encircling her wrist and tugging her close. "For now, I just want to hold you and bask in how fucking awesome you are. Holy shit, Callie. I've never seen your powers close up like that. I'm pretty overwhelmed."

Wrinkling her nose, she shrugged. "Yeah, I'm pretty badass," she teased before giving him a wink. "I'm dying to call Mom and Dad. I can't wait to tell them everything."

"Let's pack up the tent and our bags, and we'll hike back to the car."

As they were packing, Callie thought of the days ahead. Once they returned to the immortal world, their days would be filled with preparing for the final battle. Brecken would dedicate his time toward training with the troops, and she would need to record everything that happened on their trip so she could debrief the council and arm them with as much knowledge as possible for the final battle. Of course, she was eager to help, but she wondered what it meant for her and Brecken. Would she even see him when they returned, or would they both get bogged down by real life? What would that mean for their fledgling romantic relationship?

"Brecken?" she called softly as he packed the last of the tent in the felt bag.

"Hmm?"

"I want to propose something."

Glancing up at her from his crouching position, he nodded. "Okay."

Reaching down, she offered her hand, tugging him to stand before placing her palms on his chest.

"I need one more night with you before we go home."

His lips curved as his gaze roved over her face. "I want that too, but we've got a lot of information to relay to the council."

"I know." Swallowing thickly, she felt her heartbeat thrum, most likely from fear they would lose what they'd so recently found. "But we can take one more night, right? We can go back to the hotel and rent a room. I can video chat Mom and Dad, relay the important details, and tell them we're exhausted and need to crash overnight before returning home."

Sighing, he palmed her cheek, gently rubbing his thumb over the tiny freckles that lined her skin. "Delaying one day won't push away the inevitable. We have to return to real life eventually, hon."

Callie imagined telling her family her relationship with Brecken had turned romantic. It was slightly terrifying since she'd recently been publicly betrayed and had already dragged them through that embarrassing charade. Was she ready to set herself up for that again?

"What are you thinking?"

"That I wish we could just date in secret," she said, lifting a shoulder. "Without anyone else involved. I just want it to be you and me—for a while anyway."

He dropped his hand, his expression resigned. "I don't blame you. You need time to process what happened with Zadicus and decide if you even want to be with anyone. Maybe you need to be alone for a while."

Her eyes narrowed. "You think you're some sort of consolation prize, and it's just not true, Brecken."

Lifting a hand, he showed her his palm. "I just think we need to be thoughtful as we navigate this, Callie, and you have a right to be cautious."

Sighing, she tapped her foot. "I guess so. I'm usually a person who just forges ahead. It's probably good you're making me stop and think for a bit."

Grinning, he tilted his head. "Your fortitude is one of the things I admire most about you. I think I'm just a bit more reserved. It probably balances us out."

"That makes sense considering the responsibility you inherited when your father died. You have to look out for your entire family." Stepping forward, she placed her fingers over his jaw. "For one night, I think you should choose to do something just for you. And for me, since I plan to ravish you." Biting her lip, she waited expectantly for his answer.

Chuckling, he drew her close and placed a soft kiss on her lips. "Goddess, you're adorable. I think Adriel was right. You are a little witch."

She waggled her brows. "I'll work some magic in the hotel for you."

Their laughter mingled with passionate kisses before he agreed to spend one more night in the human world. With that settled, they packed their remaining belongings and hiked back to the car. Callie clutched Brecken's hand the entire way, determined to stay in the moment and enjoy the evening before returning to the stark reality that awaited them at home.

They drove back to the hotel, securing a room before initiating the video call with Darkrip and Arderin. Callie updated them on the events of the past few days, and Brecken noticed the wonder and surprise in their reaction.

"Wow, sweetie," Arderin said, her face appearing on the screen as they chatted. "I'm so glad you were able to heal the boy. It sounds like we'll have to go back and wade through all the hidden scrolls when you get home. The fact he and Tatiana are Elven hybrids is extraordinary."

"Yes," Callie said, nodding as she sat on the hotel bed. "I'm happy to spend some time cataloging things and looking for clues that could help in the final battle. And Tatiana should be visiting Sadie and Nolan soon to turn over any additional info they need for their antidotes."

"It's interesting that she wants to be present at the final battle," Darkrip said over Arderin's shoulder. "I'm not quite sure how I feel about that."

"At this point, I think it can only help. She says there's a role she's meant to play in the final battle. I've formed a connection with her, Dad. She reminds me of us a little bit. Existing in a world where we don't have a place."

"You and your father both have a place, young lady," Arderin said, kissing Darkrip on the cheek. "I can't wait for you to come home so I can hug you."

"We'll be home tomorrow morning," Callie said, grinning at her parents' obvious affection. "Probably sometime around ten. I'm just so drained from the healing and don't want to travel through the ether tonight."

"We understand," Darkrip said. "Thanks for protecting her, Brecken. I'm glad everything worked out so you could accompany her."

"Yes, sir," he said with a nod. "I'm happy to do it."

After they said their goodbyes, the screen went dark, and Callie grinned up at him. "Well, I'm starving. Can we go find something to eat before we bang?"

Laughing, he sat beside her on the bed and tucked a curl behind her ear. "I was planning on drinking the Slayer blood in the fridge, but I don't want you to starve to death." She playfully scrunched her features before he continued. "Honestly, I'd really like to take you on a date. You deserve that, Callie. How about the Italian place?"

"Aw," she crooned, her cheeks flushing in a way that made her whole face glow. "I'd love that. Let me shower and throw on a dress so I look presentable."

"You always look gorgeous, but I could definitely use a shower too."

She showered first, and then Brecken took his turn, washing away the dirt and dust from the desert. Emerging from the bathroom with a towel wrapped around his waist, he found her dressed in a simple wrap dress that had easily fit in her small bag. She looked so pretty with her long black curls covering her shoulders, and he was honored to be her date for the evening.

They strolled to the Italian place hand in hand and had a lovely pasta dinner and bottle of red wine. On the way back to the hotel, he noticed her hiccups and teased her for being tipsy.

"I feel so good," she said, lifting her arms in the air and twirling. "Nuka is healed, I didn't croak, Tatiana's on our team, and I get to spend tonight with you. I think I'm just punch-drunk or something."

"Well, it looks good on you," he said, placing the tip of his finger in the center of her head so she could twirl beneath it on the sidewalk.

"You're getting really good at this twirling thing, soldier."

"Goddess forbid," he teased softly, taken by her beaming smile and glowing energy. When they reached the hotel, they were silent entering the room as the sexual tension began to claw at them. Kicking off his shoes, he turned to face her.

She slipped off her sandals and padded over to him in bare feet as he stood frozen by her beauty. Drawn to her, he eventually found the strength to move and slowly closed the remaining distance between them.

Her chest rose and fell with soft breaths as he lifted his hand, pressing the pad of his finger to the silken skin above the valley between her breasts. Gliding it down, he pushed the fabric aside, baring one breast and then the other as they trembled beneath the cups of her black bra.

Guiding her toward the bed, he sat, drawing her between his legs. Untying the knot at her waist, he freed the material, gliding the dress off her body until it pooled on the floor. Tracing his finger over the lace of her black panties, he hummed in approval when she clutched his shoulders.

Brecken slid his palms up her sides, reveling in the way her body trembled beneath his touch. Cupping her breasts in his hands, he ran his thumbs over her nipples, still covered in the black, silky material.

She reached behind her back, unclasping the bra and tossing it to the floor. Brecken slowly massaged her breasts as she trembled. "My greedy little sex imp," he whispered.

"Please, Brecken..." she whimpered, sending shards of pleasure through his frame when her nails speared into his shoulders.

Drawing her closer, he gazed into her eyes and rained kisses over the swell of her breast. Overcome with her tiny mewls of pleasure, he extended his tongue, licking the tight nipple as her back arched in pleasure.

"*Oh, god...*" she moaned, pressing the eager flesh farther into his mouth.

Brecken sucked her deep, flicking the bud with his tongue while he massaged her other breast. Popping her from his mouth, he trailed kisses across her chest and asked, "Do you like it when I suck your pretty breasts, hon?"

"*Yes...*" she cried, head lolling back when he sucked her other nipple into his mouth. Swirling his tongue over the sensitive bud, he reveled in her shivers as she clutched onto him for dear life.

After thoroughly flicking her nipple with the tip of his tongue, he drew back and cupped her breasts. Pushing them together, he extended his tongue, swiping it from one bud to the other as she mewled above.

"It feels so good," she said, sliding one leg onto the bed, and then the other, to straddle him. "Sorry, I was about to collapse."

"Hold on tight," he said, sliding one hand to palm her back before thrusting the other one into her thick curls. "I'm not done with these sexy nipples." Gently tugging her hair, he urged her to arch her back as he lowered his mouth to her breast again. "I need more," he rasped, flicking her nipple before sucking it between his lips. "Goddess, you taste so good."

She arched into his body, taking everything he gave her as he devoured her breasts. The points of her nipples were red and swollen, and Brecken could smell the arousal gushing between her thighs. Unable to control his desire, he slid his hand from her hair, down the side of her quaking body, and between her thighs. Pushing the slip of fabric aside, he found her slick opening and jutted two fingers inside as she writhed atop his thighs.

"*Mmm...*" she moaned, her hips gyrating as she pushed into his fingers. She pumped against him, reaching for the pleasure, as he closed his mouth over her breast. Inflamed with lust, he thrust his fingers inside her deepest place as his tongue licked and lathered her nipple.

"Brecken!" she cried, head snapping as her gaze locked with his. He nipped her breast as she pumped her hips into his hand.

"Right there," he said, hooking his fingers as her eyes closed with ecstasy. "There's the spot I remember."

"*Mm-hmm*," she whimpered, nodding as she moved above him. "Suck my nipple while your fingers are inside me."

Brecken followed her command, closing over the ruddy bud as he hooked his fingers against the tiny speck filled with nerve endings. She pressed into his body, free and open, and he knew he'd never experience anything more gratifying than making love to her. Their connection was palpable, and having his fingers inside her while sucking her into his own body consumed him.

Her spine bowed, and she cried his name as she exploded into the orgasm. Her hips jerked with wild movements as she pushed into his fingers, and Brecken stimulated the spot even more as she screamed with pleasure. His lips sucked her turgid nipple until she tugged him away, burying her face in his neck and murmuring, "Too much. Oh, god, too much."

Closing his eyes, he inhaled her scent, stroking her hair as his fingers slowed inside her body. Sighing, she shuddered against him before lifting her head and swiping the hair from her face.

"Um, hi," she said, pecking him on the lips. "You're *really* good at that. Holy shit."

Giving her a sultry grin, he withdrew his fingers, lifting them to his mouth and closing his lips over them, determined to drink every part of her essence. Staring deep into her blue-green eyes, he drank her honey from his fingers as she watched, mesmerized. Eventually, he licked himself clean, and she shook her head in wonder.

"Brecken," she whispered, sliding her hand over his jaw. "I'm so hot for you."

Chuckling, he nudged her nose. "I'm hot for you too, hon. Sometimes, when you walked with Zadicus in the garden, the sunlight would shine on you in just the right way..." Sighing, he caressed her cheek. "It made my heart splinter."

"There's my Shakespeare," she said, flashing him her half-fanged grin. "Now that we've crossed the chasm, I want to bang you all the time. Like, once an hour, every day, until I drown in orgasms."

Throwing back his head, he broke into a joyful laugh. "Wow, that's a lofty goal. Can someone actually drown in orgasms?" He rubbed his chin. "I think you might be setting me up for failure."

"I believe in you...and your cock." She waggled her eyebrows. "Speaking of, I think I need to play with him now."

Brecken's shaft jerked in his pants, affirming her statement. "I think he'd like that very much," he said, nipping her nose. He was thoroughly enjoying their banter, reminding him how much he adored her sense of humor.

Gliding off his lap, she helped him undress until they both were naked in the soft light of the bedside lamp. Urging him toward the bed, she pressed him down to lie on his back, his head resting on the pillows as she slithered atop the bed. Kneeling beside his waist, she placed both hands on his upper thighs, gliding them over the hairy skin as his cock sat proud and erect atop his abdomen.

"Is it bigger than most?" she asked, gently palming his cock with both hands.

"Never ask a man that," he gritted, drowning with desire at the sight of her clutching his cock while she sat naked upon the bed. "They'll always tell you theirs is the biggest that ever existed."

Snickering, her hands traveled up and down his shaft. "I'm just asking because it's the first one I've seen up close like this," she said, studying his dick as she slowly pumped her fists. "I mean, I saw Creigen's when I helped Mom change his diaper when he was a baby, but that doesn't really count."

"Uh, yeah, not really the same thing," Brecken teased as she giggled.

"Nope." She worked her hands over him as she gave him a curious look. "Does it feel good? Tell me what to do. I've watched porn before because I was hella curious, but I don't think that's true to life."

"Having your hands anywhere near my cock is heaven, honey," he said, reaching down to run his fingers over her arm. "But it feels better when it's wet so you can glide over the skin."

Her eyebrows drew together before she nodded. "Okay," she said softly, seeming to assess his dick. And then, she lifted him high and lowered her head, licking her lips before touching them to the tip. Staring into his eyes, she glided her mouth over his cock, from tip to base, causing Brecken to emit a loud curse.

"What?" she asked, drawing away. "Did it not feel good?"

"Goddess, Callie, it felt so good," he said, shaking his head on the pillow. "It was just intense."

Her gaze traveled from his shaft to his eyes and back to his shaft before she asked, "So, I should do it again?"

"Yes, you little tease," he rasped, clenching the covers. "Please do it again."

Smiling, she lowered her head, surrounding him with her lips and slowly sliding over every inch of his cock. Brecken clenched his jaw, unable to focus on anything but her wet mouth lathering his sensitive skin. Eventually, she picked up the pace, sucking him deep, then shallow, as he writhed with pleasure.

"Grip the base and jerk it while you suck me, honey," he commanded, possession swelling deep within when she complied. Lost in her, he realized he wanted her like this forever, bent over his cock as he gazed into her stunning eyes. Emotion swamped every cell in his body, and he had to restrain himself from blurting out words he knew it was too soon to say. Craving a deeper connection, he sat up and slid his hands under her arms.

"Hey," she cried as he lifted her across the bed, black curls splaying over the white pillowcase. "I was just getting good at that—"

Brecken sucked the words straight from her lips, devouring her in an ardent kiss as he gripped her behind the knees. Lifting her legs high, he aligned the tip of his cock with her opening, still wet with arousal. Breaking the kiss, he loomed over her as she panted.

"Tell me to fuck you," he commanded, needing her permission before he ravaged her body.

"Yes," she cried, reaching for him as he groaned. "Please, Brecken—"

He plunged inside her slick, tight channel, still wet with arousal.

She gasped below him, taking him deep as desire overrode any other thought. Releasing her legs, he balanced on his palms as he pistoned into her lithe body. "Wrap your legs around my back, honey."

Her long legs snaked around him, drawing him further inside her deepest place, and explosions of pleasure ignited in his brain. He fucked her, hard and deep, until his cock felt ready to explode. Lowering over her, he aligned their bodies, creating a more intimate angle as the sweaty skin of his chest moved over her taut nipples while his hips worked in a frenzied pace.

"Callie-lily," he breathed, locked onto her eyes as her hips rose and fell, their sweaty bodies crashing together in an intimate moment.

"*Brecken...*" She shook her head on the pillow as her nails dug into his shoulders.

"I love being inside you like this," he rasped, feeling his climax on the horizon.

She tugged his head down, drawing him into a kiss, ending all conversation as they gave into the raw desire. The slick walls of her channel choked his cock, tugging and gripping until he could take no more. He surged the head of his shaft against her inner bundle of nerves, hoping like hell it would send her over the edge with him.

Screaming her name, he began to come, shooting thick pulses of release into her deepest place as she quivered below. Her head fell back on the pillow as she broke into a blissful laugh, and Brecken knew she'd reached her peak as well. Jerking inside her body, he emptied himself, every last drop of his burning desire for his magnificent Callie. Collapsing against her, he wrapped himself around every part of her skin, craving the connection as they fell back to reality. She cinched her legs tighter around his waist, drawing him against her, and he sighed with sated joy.

"*Mmmm...*" he murmured against her neck, kissing the pulsing vein that was pumping double time due to their sexy shenanigans.

"You can still bite me, you know. I don't mind."

"Too soon," he mumbled, licking the salt from her skin, knowing he couldn't handle drinking from her yet. One taste of her blood on his tongue, and he'd never be able to let her go. Until they figured out what the hell they were doing, he would deny himself that which he craved so vehemently.

Sighing, she ran her fingers through his hair. "We'll figure this out, soldier. Mark my words."

Lifting his head, he rested his cheek on his hand, balancing on his elbow as he brushed the hair away from her eyes. Unable to resist her swollen lips, he drew her into a proper kiss as they clutched each other, sated and replete.

"Don't move yet," she said, sliding her calf over the back of his thigh. "Let's stay like this for a while."

Nodding, he lowered to draw her against his body, partially resting on his side so he didn't crush her but allowing himself to remain inside her sweet body. Nuzzling into her, he felt sleep tug at his consciousness.

Warm breaths feathered the hair across his forehead as she lazily stroked his back. Vowing to only lie there a few minutes, he was lulled by her scent and soft caresses. And then, in only a matter of minutes, slumber claimed him as he held his woman cradled in his arms.

Chapter 23

They awoke in the morning, the mood slightly somber as they dressed and packed their bags. Once they were ready, they checked out of the hotel, returned the rental car and headed back to the park where they'd crossed through the ether.

"Ready to walk through?" Brecken asked, smoothing her hair as they stood in the wooded area near the ballfield and playground.

She nodded, smiling although it didn't reach her eyes.

"Hey," he said, sliding his hand down her arm. "Don't worry, hon. We'll find some time to see each other. Now that I've kissed you, I'm kind of addicted."

"Me too." She gazed at him with those luminous eyes. "I'm fine with taking some time to digest things, but I want to date you, Brecken. I want to meet your family."

"It means so much to hear you say that," he said, rubbing her arm. "I just want to make sure you've really processed what happened with Zadicus. I also want you to really think about what being with someone like me will look like. Will you be happy in a meager home at Lynia? I'd love to tell you I'm open to moving to Takelia, but I need to be close to my family."

"Honestly, I'm ready to move out of my parents' house, and I love Lynia. Lila and Latimus live there with my cousins, and Jack's there. I think I'd really like it."

"It wouldn't be fancy. I'm a pretty simple person."

Biting her lip, she shook her head. "I'm not buying it, Shakespeare. Your letters are far from simple. There are a lot of layers I'm dying to peel away."

"I want to get to know you better too," he said, tugging one of her curls. "I want to know your fears and your dreams and learn about your powers."

Shaking his head, he marveled at how special she was. "If we do end up going for this and we figure it out, I'll do everything in my power to make you happy, Callie."

Her wistful sigh sent shivers through his frame. "God, you're so sweet. I never would've known if you hadn't written the letters. I was so pissed when I found out, but now, I'm so thankful." Lifting to her toes, she kissed him. "I already miss you."

Leaning down, he gave her one last kiss. "Ready?" he asked, gesturing her toward the ether.

Inhaling a deep breath, she closed her eyes and began walking through with Brecken close behind. The thick, murky substance was choking as he followed her, and he emerged on the other side to see her leaning over, hands on her knees, as she caught her breath. Approaching, he rubbed her shoulder as he gulped air into his lungs.

Glancing around, he noticed the four-wheeler, left where they'd parked it days ago. Smoothing his hand over her hair, he waited for her to straighten.

"I'll drive you to Takelia before heading home." His phone buzzed, and he pulled it from his bag, scowling at the screen. "It's Jack." Lifting the phone to his ear, he answered. "Hey, buddy. We just got back a few minutes ago."

"Bakari is on the move," Jack said, urgency in his tone. "He's suddenly taking the offensive and attacking outlying areas of Restia and Uteria."

Bristling, Brecken's eyes narrowed. "It's probably because he knows Tatiana aligned with us."

"Yes, Darkrip and Arderin updated the council on the information you sent back. I know you just got home, but we need you at Restia if you're able to get here, Brecken. There are several attacks happening at the moment, and we need all hands on deck. Garridan is already at the south side of the compound with Siora. She's a smart soldier, and they work well together on the field, although I'm worried they might kill each other the rest of the time."

"I'm happy to report for duty. I've got a four-wheeler, but Callie is with me, and I need to ensure she's secure before I head over."

"Darkrip should be free to transport her if you call him. I don't think the attacks are serious enough to require his help...not yet anyway."

"Okay," Brecken said, rubbing his forehead. "Let me update Callie. Give me a second." Lowering the phone, he detailed her.

"I'll call Dad to come and get me." Dialing the number, she lifted the phone to her ear. A moment later, Darkrip appeared, pulling her into his embrace as he eyed Brecken.

"Thanks for coming to get me, Dad. Brecken needs to head to Restia."

"I'm going to take the four-wheeler. You all will be okay?"

"Yes," she said, eyes brimming with concern. "Keep me updated."

"Will do." He had to squelch the urge to kiss her as her father stood at her side. "Goodbye, sir."

Darkrip's olive green eyes narrowed as he mumbled a goodbye, and Brecken had the uncomfortable feeling he knew he'd had his hands on his daughter only hours ago. Considering he was a powerful Slayer-Deamon who had once been aligned with Crimeous, concern swirled in his gut.

Realizing now wasn't the time for suspicion and doubt, Brecken hopped into the four-wheeler, ready to kick some ass and help his fellow soldiers. There would be time to assess his relationship with Callie, and he understood he needed to figure it out sooner rather than later considering her father could literally read minds. Carrying on a secret love affair with the powerful ambassador's daughter was definitely not the smartest idea. Resolved to tackle one crisis at a time, he drove under the bright sun as fast as the vehicle would carry him.

Brecken arrived at Restia, parking in the barracks behind the main castle. Spotting Commander Latimus, Brecken waved before heading into the barracks to stock up on weaponry. Once he was ready, he stalked toward Latimus and saluted.

"Ready to fight, sir. Where do you need me?"

"Jack is commanding a battalion over there," Latimus said, gesturing toward the field.

Brecken spotted his fellow soldiers and nodded. "I'll join them now. Thank you, sir."

Rushing to fill his post, he saluted Jack when he appeared. Jack tilted his head in acknowledgment before he addressed the battalion.

"This will be a test of our fortitude, soldiers," Jack's deep voice boomed. "Garridan and Siora are on the south side of the compound with the rest of the Lynian soldiers. They're holding off the Deamons, although Vadik is there. Hopefully, the new TECs work their magic."

"So, we'll flank the north side?" one of the men asked.

"Yes. Larkin spotted another cluster of Deamon soldiers in the woods outside the wall. We think it's only a matter of time before they attack. He's already there with two battalions. Commander Kenden is at Uteria, warding off an attack there. Bakari's faction is smaller there for some reason, but Kenden's troops are on it."

"Head out with your battalion, son," Latimus commanded from several feet away. "I'm staying here to wait for the last soldiers we summoned, and then I'll meet you at the north side."

"Ten-four." Turning to the troops who were now lined in formation, Jack walked over to address Brecken. "Thank you for arriving so quickly. We have no idea why he suddenly decided to attack today."

"Well," Brecken said, "let's show him he's going to fucking lose."

Jack flashed a confident grin before patting him on the shoulder. "Good to have you back, man." Placing two fingers in his mouth, he gave a loud whistle. "Load into the utility vehicles, troops, and we'll deploy to the north side of the compound."

The soldiers gave a, "Ten-four," and began loading into the vehicles. Brecken jumped in behind Jack, and his friend directed the driver toward the northern quadrant of Restia.

When they arrived, Jack jumped out, and the soldiers fell in line behind him, Brecken close at his back. Surveying the area, he double-checked the TECs on his belt and swung the rifle around his shoulder, prepared for battle.

They slowly approached the stone wall that protected the compound, and Jack lifted his walkie-talkie from his belt. "Larkin?" he asked into the device. "Do you copy?"

"I'm outside the wall." Larkin's voice crackled over the receiver. "The Deamon troops are visible in the woods. It's like they're trying to draw us toward them."

"We'll scale the wall and join your troops. Give us two minutes."

Jack directed the soldiers to climb the wall since the only opening was at Restia's main entrance miles away. They'd all completed a multitude of similar wall-climbing drills in the obstacle courses Jack ran during training sessions and were extremely capable. Grabbing onto the rock wall, Brecken began to climb, dropping to the soft grass on the other side once he breached it.

Surveying the woods, he saw the Deamon soldiers who lined the woods, their beady eyes staring back as if they were waiting for something.

"How long have they been there?" Jack asked Larkin, who approached on his right, two battalions of men falling in line behind him.

"Half an hour at least. I have no idea what they're waiting for."

They stood, alert, as the soft breeze whipped the trees. Something crunched to Brecken's left, and his head snapped toward the sound. A Deamon soldier stepped from the woods and lifted his hand high, holding a gun. He fired a shot, and chaos ensued as the Deamon soldiers yelled and began to charge.

The immortal troops rushed to meet them, rifles firing as they clashed. Several of the skirmishes became one-on-one battles, each soldier sliding the rifle behind their back to draw their swords. The immortal army was unique in that it trained its troops on modern warfare such as TECs and firearms, but also on hand-to-hand combat with swords and fists so they would be prepared for individual battles. Immortals were hard to kill, so every form of battle was taught and practiced.

Whirling, Brecken began sparring with a Deamon who rushed his side. Lifting the butt of his rifle, he whacked the creature in the face before pulling the TEC from his belt and disintegrating him into thin air. Pivoting, he clutched the TEC, ready to find another Deamon to decimate.

Feeling his eyes grow wide, Brecken froze, unable to believe the image in front of him. A huge soldier loomed several feet away, who appeared to be...Zadicus? Brecken had seen enough in his time on the planet to realize the creature before him was no longer the Vampyre who'd been his ward for several years.

The hulking soldier's skin was pale and pasty—even more so than a Vampyre's ever should be now that they walked in the sun. Blue veins showed under his skin, popping from the bulging muscles that comprised his frame. The soldier began to walk forward, his gaze cemented to Brecken's, causing him to sling his rifle around and fire at the creature.

Zadicus continued to approach, the bullets skidding off his skin as if it were made of Teflon. Eventually, he neared Brecken and thrust out his hand, surrounding Brecken's throat as he squeezed.

"What did he do to you, Zadicus?" Brecken gritted through clenched teeth as he gripped Zadicus's hands, attempting to drag them from his neck. "You don't have to fight for Bakari. We can help you."

"Zadicus is dead," the creature spoke. "You may call me Baal."

Sputtering, Brecken kicked the giant's shins, trying to break free.

"Baal is a devil in human religious mythology," a deep voice said above the sounds of swords clashing and gunfire. "I thought it a fitting name for my new weapon."

Brecken twisted to see Bakari standing several feet away, his face impassive, as if he didn't care there was a major battle ensuing around them. "My, my. What do we have here?" Bakari asked, stepping forward. Narrowing his eyes, he assessed Brecken as Baal held him by the throat. "You've been touching things that don't belong to you, haven't you, boy?"

"Release him, now!" Jack's voice boomed in the distance.

Bakari gazed at him through narrowed lids before lifting his hand. "Cease!" he yelled, and the Deamons froze. Baal released Brecken's neck, and he backed away, coughing as he neared Jack. Latimus appeared at their side, his battalion flanking them, and he called to Bakari.

"I'm sorry it has to be this way, brother. I wish you would've strived for peace, but I realize you will never choose that path."

"I have grown more powerful than you can imagine, Latimus," Bakari said, lifting his hands. "It is futile to fight the inevitable. Surrender now, and I'll spare your soldiers' lives."

"We've been at this too long for me to believe your lies, Bakari." Stepping in front of the troops, Latimus held up an eight-shooter.

"You don't have the courage to shoot me—"

The blast from the eight-shooter drowned out Bakari's words as Latimus fired. Eight silver bullets rushed forward, each directed toward one chamber of Bakari's heart. Lifting his hand, Bakari caught the bullets in one swift motion.

"Impossible," Latimus breathed, lowering the eight-shooter. "No one can stop bullets in midair."

Closing his eyes, Bakari looked toward the sky, basking in his assumed glory. "I will be more powerful than Etherya soon," he said, reclaiming Latimus's gaze before dropping the bullets to the ground. They scattered like dandelion seeds over the grass, inept and useless. "You are already doomed."

Brecken saw the confusion in the commander's eyes and for the first time wondered if they might be vulnerable to Bakari.

"The prophecy is almost ready to be fulfilled," Bakari declared. "You understand my strengths and have seen my new weapon," he said, gesturing to Baal. "I will be on the field south of Restia by the ether at sunrise in two weeks' time, ready for the final battle. Bring *all* your men. I want to eradicate them so I can easily assume the throne."

"Never going to happen—" Latimus shouted but abruptly stopped speaking when Bakari closed his eyes and began to chant. Seconds later, he disappeared...along with each and every one of his soldiers.

"What the hell?" Larkin asked from a few feet away.

"He just transported the entire army," Jack said, wonder in his voice as he gazed around the field on the immortal soldiers left behind. The walkie buzzed at his belt, and he lifted it to his ear.

"General Garridan reporting," a voice said over the device. "I'm not sure how to explain this, but the Deamon soldiers attacking the south side of Restia all just disappeared."

"Same on the north side," Jack said into the receiver. "Bakari was here, and it seems he transported them all."

Silence blanketed them before Garridan's voice crackled, "Holy shit."

Lifting his own walkie, Latimus spoke. "Get the soldiers back to the barracks. We'll regroup and strategize before sending everyone home. Looks like the final battle will take place by the ether south of Restia."

"The ether?"

"We'll explain when at the barracks, General. See you there."

Addressing the soldiers, Latimus ordered them to return to the barracks so they could debrief. Brecken followed the order, understanding time was running out and the final battle loomed large.

Arderin observed her husband stalk in their bedroom as she was adding the finishing touches to her makeup to head out to the clinic at Lynia. Alarm shot down her spine when she spied his angry expression.

"Where's Callie?"

"She hightailed it to her bedroom when we got home."

Eyes narrowing, she stood from the vanity and trailed over to him. "Okaaaaay. Want to tell me why you look like you want to murder someone?"

"No," he snapped.

Arderin bristled. "Um, excuse me. I don't know what crawled up your ass, but I don't appreciate the tone."

"I'm not using a tone," he muttered, heading to the dresser and opening the drawer, angrily shifting the clothes inside.

"Wow," she said, approaching him. "You have two point three seconds to tell me why you're being an ass, or I'm never touching you below the waist again, buddy."

Lips thinning, he glanced at her from the corner of his eye. "Sorry," he murmured, his hands stilling as he sighed.

"I think you need to do a *tad* better than that," she said, encircling his arm and turning him to face her. "Sweetheart, what's wrong? Is Callie okay?"

"She's fine."

Arderin stared at him, exasperated when he remained silent. "I'm going to need a bit more of an explanation why you're mad as a hornet." She lightly rapped her knuckles on his forehead.

Quick as lightening, he snatched her wrist and drew her hand away. Arderin frowned, and his shoulders deflated into a defeated stance. "Sorry." Kissing her inner wrist, he gave her a look so solemn she wondered what could've happened. Her husband was stoic—and a bit grumpy—but he was rarely angry at her or their children.

"Did something happen?" she asked, eyes darting between his. "Sathan texted me that Bakari and his army are attacking the Slayer compounds, although he said Latimus and Kenden have it under control."

"I told Latimus to call me if he needs me, but it's not that." Releasing her wrist, he swiped a hand through his hair before beginning to pace. Finally, he turned to her, resting a hand on his hip. "They're fucking, Arderin."

Confusion swamped her. "Who?"

"Callie and Brecken."

Arderin straightened as understanding washed over her. Tilting her head, she stared deep into his forest green eyes. "Darkrip, tell me you didn't."

"I didn't mean to," he said, lifting his hands as he paced. "But there was this weird energy between them, and before I knew it, I was reading his thoughts."

Crossing her arms, she began to tap her foot. "Darkrip, I can't believe you! You sat our children down when they were young and took an oath that none of you would read other people's thoughts."

"It was an accident," he said, halting and angrily jabbing his hand at the floor. "Do you think I *want* to see images of my daughter fucking someone? Oh, god. Kill me. Just fucking shove me in the ground and get it over with." Collapsing on the bed, he covered his face with his hands and groaned.

Arderin would've laughed at his dramatic reaction if the situation wasn't so tense. Approaching the bed, she sat beside him. "For the love of the goddess, sit up so we can talk about this."

Rising, he gave her an acerbic glare. "I have no desire to discuss this. We sent him on a mission to protect her, and he seduced her while she was weak and vulnerable after Zadicus's betrayal."

Laughter bounded from her throat as he glowered. "Callie? Weak and vulnerable? Try again, dear. Have you met our daughter?"

"Well, there's no way in hell she initiated anything."

Snickering, Arderin covered her mouth as her husband fumed beside her.

"Stop laughing," he gritted.

Facing him, she palmed his cheeks. "Darling, you're being obtuse, and it's not a good look on you."

His lips formed a pout. "Don't say it—"

"It's very possible *she* seduced *him*," Arderin interrupted, breaking into a grin. "Perhaps she sought comfort from him after Zadicus's betrayal. I mean, he's extremely hot, and they were already friends. It's not the craziest scenario I could imagine."

Sticking his fingers in his ears, he pulled away and began pacing again. "No more."

"Oh, for the goddess's sake," she said, drawing his hands from his ears. "You're being ridiculous. This hang-up you have about Callie having sex is understandable since you're her father, but it's enough already. She's a grown woman, Darkrip."

"She'll always be my little girl," he said, shaking his head. "Don't you understand she was the first thing I ever did right?"

Compassion filled her heart as she inched closer to him. "I understand. But she's her own woman, sweetheart. She's going to make mistakes and keep secrets and have sex. I'm pretty sure all of that is inevitable."

Huffing, he rubbed his forehead. "It took me a long time to get used to the idea of her with Zadicus. I had reservations, but I wanted her to be happy. I've had no time to digest this. I don't even know this guy. What if he's a jerk? What if he hurts her? I need to vet him." Standing, he began to pace again.

"You will do no such thing," she said in the firm mom tone she'd used with her children when they were young. Rising, she closed the distance between them. Grabbing his wrist, she forced him to stop pacing. "She has to make her own mistakes, Darkrip. We talked about this. She just went through a very public betrayal and canceled wedding. Can you really blame her for keeping this secret? Do I need to remind you that we kept our relationship secret from my brothers for months?"

"This is different."

Laughing, she shook her head. "No, it's not. You need to chill the fuck out and let her tell us in her own time. And once she does, you're going to apologize to both of them for reading Brecken's thoughts." Lifting a finger, she arched a brow. "Do you hear me?"

Darkrip nipped at her finger, sparking tiny flames of desire throughout her body. Biting her lip, she shook her head. "Nope. I can't bone you right now. I have to be at Lynia in thirty minutes."

Inching closer, he slid an arm around her waist, aligning their bodies and resting his forehead on hers. "I only need ten minutes."

Tossing back her head, she gave a joyful laugh. "No, Darkrip, I have to go."

Pressing his lips to hers, he spoke against them. "I'll let the situation develop with Callie, and I'll try my best not to hover. It's hard for me, Arderin. I want to protect her."

"I know," she whispered, sliding her arms around his neck. "From what I saw of Brecken in the hour we questioned him, he's a good man who has chosen to fight for our people. And he doesn't deserve to have his privacy invaded." She gave him a stern look.

"Fine." Closing his eyes, Arderin heard a *whoosh* before a rush of air covered her skin. Emitting a surprised yelp, she realized her husband had just disintegrated their clothes. Arousal surged deep within as he picked her up and carried her to the dresser. Placing her on the cool wood, he spread her legs and walked between her thighs.

"Damn it, Darkrip. I have to go—"

His fingers clenched her hair, tugging her head back as she gasped. Staring deep into her eyes, his erection rubbed against her rapidly slickening folds. And then, her husband diminished any lingering objection when he rested his forehead against hers and said softly, "I love you so much, princess. Thank you for being my partner. I'm honored to be your mate."

Sighing at the romantic words, her body relaxed as she hooked a leg around his waist. "You win," she whispered. "Make it fast—"

Her husband surged inside, capturing her lips as their bodies moved in tandem. Clutching on for dear life, Arderin reveled in the life they'd built together, thankful he cared so deeply about her and their children.

Eventually, she made it to Lynia...and was exceedingly proud of herself for only arriving five minutes late.

Chapter 24

Callie returned to real life, although the events that transpired in the desert were ever-present in her thoughts. The day after her return, she met with the council to detail the events. Miranda had asked the entire family to attend, even though some weren't officially on the council, so everyone was on the same page. Callie told them about her cryptic conversation in the dreamlike state when she was healing Nuka.

"Nuka is special, like me," Callie said as she sat at the head of the conference room table. The council members all listened thoughtfully as she relayed the information. "I mean, not exactly like me, because he's not a Deamon, but Deamons were spawned from Elves if the soothsayers' stories are true. This means they could hold powers we haven't even begun to fathom."

"Tatiana does have strange abilities we've never understood," Darkrip said, rubbing his chin. "I've always attributed them to her study of voodoo and dark magic, and the rituals she conducts that were passed from her ancestors. If she is a human-Elven hybrid, her power could be unimaginable."

"Well, I guess it's a good thing I healed Nuka and cemented her alliance," Callie said, lifting a shoulder.

"You did a great job, Callie," Miranda said from the head of the room. "And you saved a little boy, which is awesome. We're all so proud of you."

"Thank you, Aunt Miranda," she said softly, glowing from her praise.

"We'll wait for Tatiana to contact us and go from there," Miranda continued. "From what we know, she's always lurking, even if she's unseen. In the meantime, how are you, Callie? I'm sure hearing the news about Zadicus was hard."

Callie's gaze lowered as she thought about the man she'd been betrothed to. According to Jack and Latimus, he'd now been transformed into a soulless warrior named Baal and would fight by Bakari's side at the final battle.

"I'm just sad," she said, gaze dropping to her fingers as they fidgeted atop the table. "Although he was a jerk and chose the wrong side, I didn't want him to die. I feel bad for Raoul and Viessa. They loved him very much."

"It's a woeful tale and proves the lengths Bakari will go to defeat us," Latimus said. "We must prevail."

"So, the plan is for us to meet Bakari and his army in the field by the ether at sunrise in two weeks' time." Evie said. "I'm fine with that, but Darkrip and I still haven't worked out all the kinks on the forcefield we need to generate to keep Bakari from transporting so we can kill the bastard once and for all. Now that it seems like he can stop an eight-shooter with his bare hands, we need it to be perfect."

"You need more power," Rinada chimed in, causing heads to swivel toward her. Callie's cousin was reserved, with a personality more like Kenden's than Evie's, so it was a bit shocking to see her speak up in such a large meeting. "Let Callie, Creigen and me help you. I'm tired of being sidelined. We all have powers that are curses most of the time. Let's make them a blessing for once."

"You want to join all of our powers to make the forcefield stronger," Evie mused, sitting back in her chair and tapping her chin. "It could work—"

"No," Darkrip said, straightening in his chair. "It puts them at too much risk. I can't believe you're considering this, Evie."

"When did you become such a stick in the mud?" she asked, eyebrows drawing together. "Rinada has a point. If we're going to beat the bastard, we'll need all the power we can get. Great job, kid," she said, winking. "I knew there was a reason I loved you so much."

"Thanks, Mom," Rinada said, scrunching her nose. "But I'm serious. I want to help. Bakari has imperiled the kingdom my entire life. I'm over it. I want to live in a world that isn't under constant threat."

"I agree," Creigen said. "I'm in. Plus, it will make me look hella cool with the chicks."

"Not sure that's a reason to risk sudden, torturous death, but who am I to judge?" Callie murmured, giving her brother a droll glare. "I'm in too."

"Absolutely not," Darkrip said, slicing his hand through the air. "There are too many unknowns. Even if you don't die, you could be severely injured or injected with some potion like Zadicus."

"Or I could give in to the evil of Grandfather's blood and align with Bakari," Callie said, lifting her chin. "It's what everyone is thinking, so let's just say it out loud. Prophecies carry a lot of weight in this realm, and I know you all have your concerns."

"There are so many possibilities, sweetheart," Arderin chimed in. "I think that's what your dad is saying. What if Bakari somehow concocts a potion that exacerbates the evil in your blood? What if he casts some sort of spell that urges you to follow some inner calling that's lain dormant for all these years? I know it sounds crazy, but we have to at least consider every possibility surrounding the prophecy."

"This is absurd. I'm pretty pissed my own family would doubt me. You all have to see the logic of us all combining our powers."

"Let's table this for another time when we can discuss it," Miranda said, holding up her hands. "It requires a lot of consideration, and the council needs to vote on it."

"We want to help, Miranda," Callie said as her temper flared. "This is our kingdom, and we love the people too."

"I know," Miranda said with a firm nod, her tone indicating the subject was closed. "We'll discuss it at the next meeting, Callie. Thank you, and Rinada and Creigen, for offering to help." She made eye contact with each of them. "It's appreciated and noted."

Callie fumed for the rest of the meeting before heading outside to clear her head. Stalking to the River Thayne, she hiked to one of the old forts the army had used during the War of the Species. It was built into a hill and had lain dormant for decades, but the history of the forts had always called to her. They were relics of a terrible conflict and proof that peace could be secured.

Sighing, she flopped down on the grass by the fort, listening to the river gurgle. Her phone dinged, and she lifted it to her ear.

"Hey," Brecken's baritone chimed, and she closed her eyes, relishing the sound. "We have five minutes, so I snuck away to call you."

"Aw, does that mean you miss me?"

Chuckling, she could almost see the mirth that must be swimming in his brown eyes. "Always."

Plucking at the grass, she said, "I want to see you. Can we try to find a time to get together?"

"Yes. I'll talk to my mom and see when she's available. I'd love to have you over to meet her and my sisters. If you want to."

"I want to." Her lips curved into a sappy smile. "I should have you over to formally introduce you to my parents too, although I'm kind of annoyed at them at the moment."

"We can move at whatever pace you want, hon. Our situation is certainly unconventional to say the least."

Chuckling, she nodded. "It is, but I'm kind of digging it. Being with you feels good, Brecken. That's what I'm focusing on right now."

"I'm glad." A moment passed before he asked, "Why are you annoyed at your parents?"

She told him about the council meeting, frustrated when he agreed with the consensus. "I don't want to piss you off, but, selfishly, I don't want you anywhere near that field, honey."

"I'm the granddaughter of the most powerful Deamon who ever lived, Brecken. It gives me immense power—probably more than I even realize. I'm fine with that, because I don't want any part of Grandfather's evil tendencies, but it makes me extremely capable of fighting against Bakari."

"I know, hon, but I still worry. I just found you and don't want to lose you."

Melting at the sweet words, she sighed. "Okay, I forgive you for being a misogynistic ass."

His laugh traveled through the phone. "Thank you, I think? Where are you right now?"

She told him about the old forts and how they were one of her treasured spots in the immortal world. "I used to play here when I was young and we visited Miranda and Sathan. There's something peaceful and reverential about them, and they're great hiding spots when you want to get away from your little brother."

"I'd love for you to show me one day," he said. "I want to see all the places you cherish, Callie."

"Then I'll show you."

A voice boomed in the background, and he cleared his throat. "Okay, I've got to run. I'll reach out about getting together soon. I can't wait to kiss you again."

Biting her lip, she fought the urge to giggle like a teenager with a terrible crush. "Can't wait either. Bye."

Lowering the phone, Callie took some time to digest everything that had happened over the past few weeks. She thought of Zadicus, allowing herself to mourn the loss of that relationship and trying not to blame herself for being naïve. Eventually, her thoughts turned to Brecken, and she closed her eyes, thanking Etherya for her romantic, soulful soldier.

Before everything fell apart, she never would've imagined a life with Brecken. Not because he wasn't worthy or sexy—because he definitely was—but because it just hadn't occurred to her to look. Muttering to herself that she was an absolute dolt for her obliviousness, she vowed to foster their connection. After everything that had transpired in their growing courtship, Callie could easily envision a future with him. One full of laughter and love and his strong, unwavering support. Squeezing her lids together, she could almost imagine their children. Little girls with his deep brown eyes, and little boys with the cute, wayward tufts of hair that always spiked when he dislodged it with a swipe of his hand.

They would be adorable, and Callie knew a relationship with Brecken would be built on affection, loyalty and the laughter they always seemed to inspire in each other. It gave her hope after the disaster with Zadicus, and she felt the yearning deep within. Although their bond was still new, Callie could imagine it growing into something far better than she'd ever dreamed, all those years ago, as a lonely teenager in a world that didn't accept her.

Realizing her anger had abated, Callie rose, wiping the dirt off her backside and inhaling the damp, lush air. Yes, the future was bright, and she only had to seize it. She would learn from her mistakes and build something even better in the wake of adversity.

And she sure as hell wasn't going to align with Bakari. No matter what happened, and no matter what the prophecy said, she would never choose that path. Resolved, she strode back to the castle to find her family and head home.

Chapter 25

B recken threw himself into preparing for the final battle, knowing it was imperative they defeat Bakari. Seeing the power he wielded, along with the creature he'd transformed Zadicus into, left no doubt he must be vanquished. Otherwise, the kingdom would never attain the peace it ultimately sought.

Brecken agreed to help Jack with the new recruit trainings, which doubled his workload and led to exhaustion each night when he fell to sleep. It also prevented him from spending time with Callie, and he began to long for her during the lonely nights when she wasn't nestled against his side. He'd gotten used to her honeysuckle scent and brilliant smile when they'd been alone in the desert, and he missed her terribly. They texted often, and he was enamored by her gentle teasing and sexy flirting.

Finally, a week and a half after returning from the desert, Jack urged Brecken to take a day off.

"You can't keep up this pace, man," his friend said, patting his shoulder as they stood on the training field. "I need you to take a day off so you can breathe before the last push. We've got less than a week until the final battle."

Brecken mulled, wanting to make sure he did his part to help the kingdom. "Only if you're sure—"

"I'm sure," Jack said with a firm nod. "Go home and spend some time with your family. We'll be here when you get back."

With his friend's blessing, Brecken returned home that night, excited to invite Callie to spend the next day with him.

Brecken: Hey. Good news. Jack gave me tomorrow off. I already talked to my mom, and we'd like to have you over for dinner.

The text bubble appeared right away, causing Brecken to grin.

Callie: Yes, yes and yes. Do I seem too eager? You know what? I don't care. What time?

Narrowing his eyes, he pondered.

Brecken: She said to come over at three so we can chat and you can hang with everyone before dinner. Why don't you come to my house at two? That way, I can kiss you a little while before we walk over.

Callie: Perfect. Do you want me to stay over? I can tell my parents I'm hanging with Jack. I'm just not quite ready to tell them about us yet. It will lead to an intense discussion I need time to prepare for. Hope that's okay.

Scowling at the deception, he typed his reply.

Brecken: I'd love for you to stay, but I don't want to lie to your parents. Honestly, you dad scares the crap out of me. I'm terrified he's going to find out we're having sex.

Callie: I get it. We can discuss when we're together. They'll want to meet you as soon as I tell them, so you'll need to be prepared. You think my dad grilled you at the council meeting? Wait till he finds out we're banging.

Brecken: This is *not* making me feel better.

She sent him a geek face emoji, causing him to laugh.

Callie: I've got your back, soldier. We'll figure it out. Can't wait to see you.

Brecken: See you tomorrow, hon. Good night.

The next day, she arrived in a four-wheeler, gorgeous as she leaped from the vehicle in a pretty blouse, jeans and sandals. Brecken rushed down the porch steps as she ran to him, catching her when she vaulted into his arms and wrapped her legs around his waist.

"I missed you so much," she said, peppering his face with kisses as he relished being back in her arms. "Oh my god, Brecken. I don't ever want to go that long without seeing you again. It felt like forever."

Laughing, he kissed her, slow and thorough, before drawing back to gaze into her stunning ocean-colored eyes. "Forever is a bit dramatic, but I definitely missed you too, hon."

Sticking out her tongue, she swatted his shoulder. "Don't make fun of me."

"Never." Setting her on her feet, he took her hand and laced their fingers. "You didn't really get to see the property last time. Want me to give you a quick tour? It's small, so there's not a ton to show, but Jordana planted some flowers in the back, and they spruce the place up."

"Sure," she said, flashing the smile he'd craved since he last saw her.

He showed her around, a bit worried she'd think his home provincial considering her lavish upbringing, but she was extremely gracious as he showed her his back yard and the tiny creek that ran behind it.

"This reminds me of the creek behind Aunt Lila's house," she said wistfully, gazing toward it. "It's where I first discovered my power to heal animals, and I have lots of fond memories there."

They trailed around the yard as she recounted stories of working with her father to harness her powers. Eventually, they ended up inside, where he opened the refrigerator and pointed at the contents inside. "I stocked it with some food too, in case you're hungry in the morning."

Her full lips curved, warming every cell in his body. "That's so thoughtful. Thank you. What time do you have to report to the field tomorrow?"

"Eight a.m."

"Got it. I'll make sure I wake up at dawn and bang you one last time before you go so you can have something to remember me by." She chucked her brows.

Laughing, he drew her into a passionate kiss. "I'm definitely taking you up on that, hon."

After a thorough session of heavy petting, they headed to his mother's house. Brecken had prepared his sisters to be on their best behavior since they were hosting royalty, but, of course, it all flew out the window when his sisters bounded from the house, running toward them and introducing themselves to Callie.

"Okay, okay," Brecken said, holding up his hands. "One at a time. Jeez, guys. I thought we'd decided to be proper in front of Callie."

"Proper?" Callie asked, grimacing. "Gross." Facing his sisters, she lifted her chin. "Please don't ever act proper in front of me."

Rowena snickered before glancing at her sisters. "See? I told you she was cool."

"You've already met Rowena," Brecken said, giving her a good-natured glare. "This is Nala, who's fourteen and already a better warrior than I'll ever be."

"Hi," Nala said, stepping forward and extending her hand. "I've heard so much about you from Rowena. I hope to meet Queen Miranda one day, and Betsy says you can make that happen."

"Nala," Brecken said with a warning.

"Of course I can make it happen," Callie said, shaking her hand. "Aunt Miranda is hella awesome, and she'd love to meet you. And you must be Jordana," she said, releasing Nala's hand before facing her.

"Yes," she said, shaking. "Pleasure to meet you. These are my twin sisters, Ludika and Betsy."

"Lovely to meet you all," Callie said after she'd shaken everyone's hands. "Brecken has told me about you, but I want to know more. Don't hold back, okay?"

"Can you come to the back yard?" Nala said, grasping her hand. "I want to show you my training spot."

Callie grinned at Brecken. "Well?"

Wren chose that moment to appear, striding toward them with a gleam in her eye. "Hello, Callie. I'm Wren, Brecken's mother. I hope you don't mind if our girls whisk you away. It's probably easier to just get the obligatory tours of training spots and gardens over with now. Make sure you show her the calla lilies, Nala. They're blooming and are absolutely gorgeous."

"Lead the way," Callie said, sparing Brecken a grin before Nala dragged her away, the rest of his sisters following close behind.

"Well, you've finally brought a girl home," Wren said, sliding her arm around Brecken's waist and leaning her head on his shoulder. "And a kind, beautiful princess at that. How lovely."

"I'm crazy about her, Mom," he said, watching them disappear around the side of the house. "What the hell am I supposed to do? She's a wealthy princess who has extraordinary powers and is used to a royal lifestyle."

Facing him, she cupped his cheeks. "I think the answer is obvious, son. You tell her you love her, and you give me some grandbabies."

Chuckling, he shook his head. "I don't think it's that easy."

"Take it from your highly intelligent, centuries-old mother: It will always be easy if you choose love. Will you face challenges? Yes. Will there be strife? Of course. There were times I thought I might strangle your father when we were embroiled in an argument. But I loved him to the depths of my soul, and we never went to bed angry. I was his princess no matter how poor we were, and he gave me my beautiful children."

"Don't cry, Mom," he said, swiping the tear that trailed down her cheek. "I know you miss him. We all do."

"He would be so proud of you, Brecken," she said, squeezing his upper arms. "You're such a good man. Don't ever doubt that. If Callie chooses you, and you choose her, it's because of who you are, not what you possess."

"Good advice," he said, kissing her forehead. "Should we check on them? I might need to save her."

Chuckling, she patted his arm. "Yes, you do that. I'm going to finish dinner. It's exciting to cook food, and I want to make it extra special for Callie. Go on now."

Brecken trailed around the side of the house to find Callie with a sword in her hand as Nala gave her pointers on how to wield it.

"Just let me know if you need to escape!" he called, eliciting a glower from Nala.

"It's fun!" Callie replied, laughing as she swung the sword through the air. They practiced for a while, his other sisters cheering them on, before Rowena asked if she could show them her powers.

"You don't have to entertain them," Brecken said, sidling up to her. "Just say the word, and we'll tell them to scram."

"Stop it," Callie said, shooing him away. "Okay, let me see...oh, here we go. See this dying plant? I can definitely use my powers to heal it. Come on, ladies. I'll show you."

She proceeded to kneel beside the plant his mother always complained never thrived no matter how much she watered it. His sisters *"ooohhhed"* and *"aaahhhed"* as Callie showed her palms, the centers glowing red as she summoned her powers. Concentrating, with her tongue between her teeth, she cupped her hands over the plant, shooting the energy into it. The broad leaves began to turn from brown to green, stiffening and regaining their form as they reached for the afternoon sun. Eventually, the plant stood tall, and Callie fell to her butt, clutching her legs as she caught her breath.

"Are you okay?" Rowena asked, concerned.

"Yeah," Callie said, flashing a smile. "The energy transfer always zaps me for a second. With plants, it's not so bad, so I just need to breathe for a minute."

"That was so cool," Ludika breathed. "Wow."

"Thanks," Callie said, extending her hand. "Someone want to help me up?"

They collectively helped her stand and continued on, giving her a tour of their small plot of land before taking her inside and showing her the three-bedroom home. Afterward, they had a lovely dinner of Slayer blood and the food Wren prepared, Callie happily chatting along with his sisters as they got to know each other.

Finally, the night wound down, and they prepared to head home.

"Thank you so much for your lovely hospitality, Wren," Callie said, giving his mother a tight hug. "I can't wait to come over again soon. We'll need to make sure that plant keeps thriving."

"Thank you, dear," Wren said, locking eyes with Brecken over her shoulder and mouthing, *"I love her!"*

Thrilled at his mother's acceptance of the woman whom he was enamored with, Brecken gave her a hug, said goodbye to his sisters, and they set out across the field toward his home. After trailing through the brush that separated the two properties, they headed up the porch stairs. Callie pointed to her left and grinned.

"Right there."

"Right there what?"

"That's where we're going to put a swing. It will be a nice place to relax and make out."

"I can get down with that," he said, unlocking the door and gesturing her inside.

"And if things work out and we decide I should move in, we could always add on some extra rooms."

"If *we* decide?" he asked, arching a brow as she sauntered toward the bed.

"*Mm-hmm.*" Kicking off her sandals, she spread across the comforter, giving him a sultry look. "I'll pay you in sexy times for any renovations that are needed, soldier." Lifting her hand, she hooked her fingers, and Brecken toed off his shoes before rushing the bed.

Their laughter mingled as they tore away their clothes before Brecken set about kissing every inch of her silken skin. After he'd tasted every crevice of her gorgeous body, he crawled over her, overcome by her beauty as her curls spread across his pillow.

"*Brecken,*" she whispered, opening herself to him as he slowly nudged his cock inside her body. "God, I missed this."

"I missed you too, hon," he said, working his hips as he undulated inside her taut channel. "I hated washing the sheets because I missed your scent."

"Aw," she said, wrapping her leg around his waist, drawing him deeper. "I think I'm supposed to make a sexy joke about being dirty, but—" Breaking off, she gasped when he began jutting against the spot that drove her wild. "Oh, yes...no jokes now...oh, *god...*"

Breaking into joyful laughter, he surged inside her, acknowledging that she was the one. Never had he craved someone's smile...or presence...or *love* as much as he craved Callie's. In that moment, he knew he would never love another. Vowing to figure out how to make her happy, he pressed his lips to hers.

"Callie-lily," he breathed, reveling in her shiver at his sappy nickname. "I want to give you the world, honey..."

Tightening around him, she undulated her hips against his. "I only need you," she whispered, clutching him as they approached their peak. He took them both high before the inevitable crash, their bodies exploding in flames of pleasure before they collapsed against each other, sweaty and replete.

Afterward, he stared down at her flushed face and half-lidded eyes, gently running a finger over the soft skin between her breasts.

"Write me another love letter," she murmured, her lips forming a shy grin.

Glancing at his desk, he pondered. "I think the two pens I have are both out of ink."

Snickering, she shook her head on the pillow. "You're a terrible liar. Write me one here, on the fly. But just say it out loud instead of writing it down. Come on. You can do it, soldier."

Playfully rolling his eyes, Brecken admitted he was officially a lovesick sap. Denying her request was as impossible as denying himself oxygen. Sighing, he continued the lazy strokes across her skin as he began to speak, softly and tenderly.

"My beautiful Callie-lily."

"Good start," she said, adorable as she bit her lip.

Gazing down at her, he decided there was no point in holding back. Releasing every reservation and doubt, he gave her everything left to give.

"I have no idea why a gorgeous, brilliant princess ever looked my way, but when you did, my life changed for the better. Somehow, you took my impassive heart and made it beat in ways I never imagined. Many will probably say I don't deserve you, and I sometimes worry they might be right. But I'm a determined man, and I know that even if I can't give you riches, I can give you love and support and amazing orgasms."

He waggled his eyebrows as she giggled against the pillow.

"Small-minded people will always judge and fear what they don't understand. I'm sorry you had to deal with that in the years before I knew you. The fact you still thrived and developed the generous spirit you have today only proves your resilience. Those same people somehow made you feel that you didn't belong...that you were unlovable. But my sweet Callie-lily, I assure you that isn't true. There are so many out there who love you exactly for who you are, and we are all awed by you."

Tears welled in her eyes as he continued, lifting his hand to swipe away the errant drop that slid down her cheek. "You're not unlovable, Callie," he whispered, gazing deep into her eyes. "Because I love you."

A sob exited her throat, and he encircled her with his arms, aching to hold her. "*Shhh...*" he soothed against her temple. "It's okay, hon."

"Brecken..."

"I know, sweetheart," he murmured, kissing her hair.

As her sobs abated, he slid against her, repositioning their bodies so they lay on their sides. Gazing into each other as their cheeks rested on the pillow, their legs entwined as their lids grew heavy. Eventually, she fell asleep, her long, dark lashes stark against her pale cheeks. Brecken stroked her hair, inhaling the aroma of her skin as sleep tugged him closer to its wake. When they woke in the morning, they made love once more before they rose.

"I'm going to tell my parents about us," she said, slipping on her sandals.

"You don't sound thrilled," he murmured, as he laced his boots.

"I just..." Sighing, she shook her head. "It's going to be a lot to hit them with after the shit show with Zadicus. I wonder if they'll question if I'm moving too fast."

Standing, he approached her, placing supportive hands on her shoulders. "If you want to wait, that's fine, honey."

She trailed her fingers over his jaw. "I want to tell them before the final battle. Of course, I'm terrified something will happen to you...or Jack, or my uncles, or anyone I love for that matter. But I know you all are trained and ready, and I have faith you'll prevail." She absently stared at his shoulder, contemplating. "I just need to figure out the right time to discuss our relationship with my parents. Once I do, and the final battle is over and we've defeated Bakari, I'll have you over to formally meet them."

"I'd like that," he said, tucking a curl behind her ear. "Should I start preparing for your dad's interrogation now?"

"Oh, definitely, buddy," she said, chuckling.

"Honestly, it's worth it if it ensures I get to keep kissing you."

Expelling a long breath, she said softly, "My hero."

After a sizzling goodbye kiss, Brecken watched her drive away and prepared for the day ahead. It was only as he walked across the long meadow to the sparring field that he realized she hadn't repeated his words of love. Frowning at the recognition, Brecken forged ahead, telling himself not to create an issue that didn't exist. Callie had melted in his arms when he'd loved her and cried when he spoke the words. That in itself was all he needed.

Throwing himself into his work, he prepared himself for the battle ahead, pretending he didn't notice the seed of doubt that lingered deep inside from the unspoken words he longed to hear.

Callie entered her home, still glowing from her night with Brecken. After hanging up her jacket in the foyer, she turned and gasped, spotting her father in the far corner, arms crossed over his chest.

"How was your night with Jack? Did you enjoy the street fair?" Darkrip asked, his tone laced with an angry annoyance that caused her to bristle.

"It was fine," she said, lifting her chin. "I'm going to make some breakfast. Want some?" She began to breeze by him, but he stepped into her path, ire flashing in his olive green eyes, causing her to bristle. "What the hell, Dad?"

"Is this what we do now, Callie? Lie to each other? I thought your mother and I taught you better than that."

The wheels in Callie's mind began to churn as she realized he knew about her relationship with Brecken. How much did he know? *How* did he know? Eyes narrowing, she began to feel her own anger well deep inside.

"Did you read my thoughts?" she whispered.

"Of course not," he snapped.

Lowering her gaze, she mulled before emitting a soft cry. Staring deep into his eyes, she was overcome by yet another sense of betrayal. Hell, she should've been used to it at this point, after so many instances in the recent past, but betrayal by her father, whom she loved deeply, was almost too much to bear.

"You read Brecken's thoughts when we returned from the human world. Dad! I can't believe you!" She jutted her finger in his face.

Grabbing it, he furiously shook her hand. "I have every right to protect you, Callie! After everything that's happened, I'm extremely disappointed you would sneak around in secret with someone I barely know. It's dangerous and detracts from our mission to defeat Bakari."

"*You're* disappointed?" she exclaimed, yanking her finger from his grasp. "You read someone else's thoughts. Someone I care about! That's an extreme violation of his privacy."

"He should never have touched you," Darkrip muttered, crossing his arms.

"Well, I didn't give him a choice." Resting her hand on her hips, she shrugged. "I went to his house the night of my bonding ceremony and tore my clothes off until we had sex. There, you want the truth? There's the truth."

"Spare me the details," he muttered. "I can't believe you would be so reckless. People are bending over backward to protect you from your supposed role in this prophecy. Do you understand? What if Brecken is also a spy? You should've been more careful."

"Brecken loves me and would never betray my trust the way you have!" Furious tears burned her eyes before she began stomping toward her bedroom. Once there, she located her duffle bag and began stuffing clothes inside.

"What are you doing?" Darkrip asked from the doorway.

"I'm going to stay with Evie until the final battle is over. She's the only one who seems to honor promises in this family, and she supports the idea of us fighting alongside you in the final battle."

"We don't want you, Creigen or Rinada harmed, Callie," Darkrip said, slowly approaching her. "That's why the council voted to not have you fight with us."

"Well, the council can stuff it," she said, zipping her bag. "And you can stuff it too." Tossing the bag over her shoulder, she straightened, heart pounding from their terrible argument. "I should've moved out a long time ago. I love you and Mom, and it was always comfortable for me here. Safe, even. But you've ruined that by reading the mind of someone I cherish, Dad. I never thought you'd do that." Willing the tears away, she began to stride from the room.

"You kept a relationship with a man I don't know from me, putting yourself in danger," he said, grasping her arm. "That is *not* okay, Callie."

Shaking her head, she tried not to drown in the pain caused by someone she thought would never betray her. "I haven't needed your permission for a long time, Dad. I let you and Mom tether me to you because I love you, and honestly, I've had a pretty lonely life. You two were my rocks, and now you've broken that. Don't you see?" Disengaging, she gave him one last sorrowful glare. "Don't contact me. I need some time. I'll be at Evie's, and I'll be safe. Goodbye."

Pivoting, she strode through the hallway, head held high, and back into the bright sun. She trekked down the sidewalk, walking several blocks to the governor's mansion. When she reached it, she hiked up the stairs and pounded on the door.

The house manager urged her inside, and she trailed to Evie's office, finding her sitting behind her desk. Callie knocked on her open door, and Evie glanced up, smiling before her expression turned inquisitive. Rising, she slowly walked toward Callie as she struggled to keep it together.

"Well, shit," Evie said, approaching. "What did my bonehead brother do this time?"

Laughing, Callie swiped at her nose. "You're not reading my thoughts are you? Because I just had a screaming match with Dad about that very issue."

"No," she said, eyes narrowed. "I've been around long enough to know there's tension between you two, and he's been extra grumpy lately."

"He broke his promise, Evie, and I'm just so fucking pissed."

Sighing, Evie drew her into a comforting embrace. "That sucks, but I'm sure he had a good reason. He loves you, Callie."

"He didn't read my thoughts. He read Brecken's." Drawing back, she stared at Evie with wet eyes. "I'm with him, Evie. I...I'm crazy about him. It happened so fast, and I didn't want to tell my parents because I knew they would hover and question everything. Dad especially," she muttered.

"Oh, my," she said, smoothing Callie's hair. "That is big news. Well, you can stay here until the dust settles. Ken is rarely home since he's preparing for the final battle, and Rin would love to have you. You can take some time to gather your thoughts and get some much needed space from your dad. Come on. You can put your bag in the guest bedroom."

Evie led her through the hallway, and they began trekking up the expansive staircase.

"So," Evie said, grasping Callie's hand, "you finally boned someone. I don't know Brecken well, but he's very handsome." Grinning, she asked, "Did he take care of you? It was time for you to get some nookie in my opinion."

Breathing a laugh, she grinned at her aunt. "He wrote me love letters, Evie. Beautiful, heartfelt love letters. And he definitely takes care of me. He's...amazing," she finished with a sigh.

"Ah, young love," she teased, rolling her eyes. "I can't wait to hear more about it. I've got some paperwork to finish, and then we'll have lunch together. I'll ask Rinada to join us too—if you're okay with her knowing."

Entering the guest bedroom, Callie placed her bag on the bed. "I guess everyone's going to know at this point, so why not? If this relationship doesn't work out and ends in public tragedy, I'm going to throw in the towel on love, Evie."

"Well, then, we'll just have to make sure it thrives," she said with a wink. "Make yourself at home, kid. See ya at lunch." Closing the door behind her, she headed back downstairs.

Callie fell to the bed, grabbing the pillow, determined to have a good cry before letting the angst of the morning go. She hated fighting with her father, but it would probably lead to better boundaries between them, and that was definitely a positive. And this was the push she needed to announce her relationship with Brecken to the world.

After last night, there was no doubt he was the man she wanted to build a future with. When he'd looked at her with those gorgeous bronze eyes and spoken such reverent words, she'd melted into a pile of mush. And when he'd told her he loved her...

Sighing, Callie clutched the pillow, remembering the sweet moment. She hadn't said the words back for two reasons. One, she'd been a sniveling mess, almost unable to control her emotional reaction at the magnificent show of affection. But more importantly, she wanted to wait to tell Brecken she loved him until after she'd told her parents about their relationship. She didn't want to utter the words in a world where her two favorite people hadn't spent time with Brecken or given their approval.

She knew they would, of course, since he was amazing, but it hadn't felt right to speak the words until everything was out in the open. Callie felt she owed that to her parents after the disaster with Zadicus.

Of course, now, she wished she'd just said them back to Brecken since her father was a complete jerk who'd read her lover's thoughts. Frustrated at his betrayal, Callie settled into the bed, digesting the events of the morning, wishing the confrontation with Darkrip had gone differently.

Knowing she couldn't change the past, she decided she would stay with Evie until after the final battle. Once that was complete and they'd hopefully defeated Bakari, she would speak with Brecken about moving in with him. Biting her lip, Callie hoped he would be open to cohabitation. After all, he *had* said he loved her, so this was the next natural step, right?

Praying things would work out, Callie clutched onto her remaining positivity and her hope of a happy future once the final battle was over.

Chapter 26

C allie settled into Evie's home, allowing the hurt and anger at her father to slowly abate. Arderin called her to check in, and Callie relished her support.

"Your dad should've never read Brecken's thoughts, sweetie," Arderin said, "and I understand why you're upset. But I'm also really hurt you didn't tell me. I would've really liked to hear about Brecken and his courtship of you. I like him very much."

"I'm sorry, Mom," she said, picking at a wayward string on the comforter in Evie's guest bedroom. "I think I was scared it happened so fast, and I thought you all might think I was rushing into a rebound or something."

"Well, we might have, but I would've listened with an open mind. I can't speak for your father. His hang-ups about your dating life are as annoying to me as they are to you."

Laughing, she snuggled into the soft mattress. "I feel bad we argued. I love you guys so much, Mom. I'm sorry I kept my relationship with Brecken secret. I just wanted something that was mine after what happened with Zadicus."

"I understand. We'll talk after the final battle. Your dad is a wreck. He feels terrible, although he probably won't admit it."

"Good. He should. I can't believe he violated my trust that way, or Brecken's."

"You're right. As upset as you are, I hope you'll consider coming home before the final battle. I don't like the idea of your dad walking onto that battlefield while there are unspoken things between you."

Sighing, Callie pondered. "Okay. I probably will. You're very wise, Mom. Thank you for being my stable parent."

Her chuckle drifted over the phone. "Let's not tell your father that. He would probably die of exertion from the resulting eye roll."

Callie giggled. "Seriously. I love you, Mom."

"Love you too, sweetie. Text me when you decide to come home."

Callie digested the conversation, admitting she didn't want her father to enter the final battle when things weren't settled between them. Deciding she would indeed return home the next evening, she settled in for bed and texted Brecken.

Callie: I wish I could see you before the battle.

Brecken: I know, hon. I'm consumed by the training. It will be worth it once we win, but I miss you.

Callie: Miss you too. I think I'm going to go back home tomorrow night.

Brecken: Good. You need to make up with your dad before the battle. Also, I'm afraid he wants to crush my testicles. How much does he hate me?

Laughing, her thumbs darted over the keyboard.

Callie: He's going to love you once I have the chance to properly introduce you to him. I promise. Stay safe. I can't lose you, Brecken.

Brecken: I will. I have so much to fight for—the most important thing being you, honey. I want you to be free from the prophecy for good. I promise, I'll do my best to secure peace.

Callie typed back the two words that represented her strong, loving soldier.

Callie: My hero.

The next morning, Callie awoke to a call from the animal shelter at Naria. One of the puppies that was set to be adopted was sick, and the owner wondered if she could heal it. It was a welcome distraction from the drama in her life, and she immediately agreed to help. After dressing in comfortable jeans, a tank top and sandals, she stopped by the kitchen to grab an apple before heading out.

"Morning, guys," she said to Evie and Rinada, who were sitting at the large kitchen island of the Takelia governor's mansion eating breakfast. "I'm heading to Naria to heal a puppy. Do you mind if I take one of the four-wheelers?"

"No problem," Evie said, spreading butter over a muffin. "You'll have the radio with you, right? Your father and I are going to be perfecting the forcefield all day, which could interfere with any telekinetic messages you try to send us."

"I'll have the radio by my side," Callie confirmed. "Let me know how Dad's disposition is today. I think I'm going to head back home tonight."

"I think he's still stewing, but who knows with my brother?" she asked, taking a bite of the muffin. "It's kind of entertaining."

"For you, maybe," Callie muttered. "I hate that this happened right before the battle where I'm supposed to destroy the world. Yay," she finished weakly, lifting her hands and shaking them in a mock cheer.

"There's no way that will happen, Callie," Rinada said with a reassuring smile.

"Thanks," Callie said with a wink. "I hope you're right." Selecting an apple, Callie slung her bag over her shoulder. "Thanks for the apple and for letting me borrow the four-wheeler. See you guys later."

"I'll walk with you to the garage," Rinada said, rising and falling into step beside her as they trailed down the hallway.

"Creigen and I spoke yesterday, and I wanted to update you," Rinada said. "We want to help with the battle and don't want to be sidelined."

They stepped into the garage, halting on the concrete as Callie faced her. "I'm willing to help too. If Evie and Dad can't generate a forcefield strong enough to contain Bakari, the chances of victory are diminished."

"Agreed," Rinada said with a nod. "The fact Bakari can transport the entire Deamon army means his power has grown exponentially. Creigen and I have decided to meet in the forest adjacent to the field where the battle will take place before sunrise. I thought you might like to join us."

"I would," Callie said, feeling her eyebrows draw together. "We'll be violating the council's directive."

"Honestly, I don't give a damn. I'm so tired of this conflict, and it's got to end. Your brother feels the same, and Tordor does as well."

"You spoke to Tordor too?"

"Yes." She gnawed her lip. "Although he doesn't possess our powers, he agrees with our decision to defy the council's orders. He thinks it's a good idea to be present in case Latimus or my dad order us off the field. Tordor's words carry weight in the kingdom, and he's assured me he will support our efforts to join our powers with Mom and Darkrip's. As the royal heir, Latimus and Dad won't openly defy his orders, and his diplomatic skills will come in handy if he needs to explain the benefits of us being there."

"Okay," Callie said, contemplating the risks and benefits. "We'll have to make sure to keep him safe and make sure your mom and my dad don't read our thoughts."

"I don't think they would considering the pact we've all made to respect each other's privacy, but we need to remain alert."

Callie gave her a sardonic look. "My dad isn't really the best example of following that pact right now."

"True," Rinada said, arching a brow. "But Mom says he feels terrible about what happened between you two. Anyway, I agree with you about protecting Tordor. I mean, what are cousins for if not to use their powers from their evil grandfather to safeguard each other?"

Grinning, Callie cupped her arm. "It's not easy, is it? I don't want to complain, because we have so much, but it just fucking sucks to be so different sometimes."

"It does," Rinada said, shrugging. "And in my case, not only am I different, but I'm the daughter of the most beautiful woman in the kingdom. It's a lot to live up to."

Callie's gaze roved over Rinada's long, dark reddish-brown hair, the color more muted than Evie's, and her eyes, which were a deep shade of brown with dark green flecks. Tiny freckles covered her nose and cheeks, and Callie thought her exceptionally pretty.

"And now you're almost nineteen, which is a scary time in one's life. I remember not knowing what I wanted to do. Eventually, I settled on healing animals, and it's so rewarding, but it's hard to find a purpose since we don't really need jobs in the kingdom."

"Right?" Rinada said, lifting her hands. "I don't want to complain about the fact we're princesses with royal parents since that would be super-lame. But I have no idea what I'm supposed to do with my life now that I'm done with school. After I graduated earlier this year, I told my parents I needed some time to figure it out."

"That's perfectly understandable."

Excitement flashed in Rinada's eyes. "I know this sounds strange, but I find myself wondering what it would be like to go to college in the human world. Uncle Heden found a way to stream the Science and History Channels to the TV in my bedroom years ago, and I'm so enamored with the documentaries there. I'd love to train in archelogy or history even though it's the history of a different species. Is that weird?"

"Nope," Callie said with a smile. "It's actually hella cool. And you could train there and eventually bring your knowledge back to our world too. I mean, we have some insane history here that needs scientific evaluation. The Elven scrolls are a great place to start."

"Definitely. After the battle, I'm going to talk to my parents and contemplate it more. I've never lived in the human world though. Do you think I'd do okay there?"

"It's a different place, for sure, but you'd do great. You're a bit more soft-spoken than your awesome older cousin,"—Callie pointed at herself as Rinada snickered—"but I know you'd charm anyone you meet. And Rin?"

"Yeah?"

"You're really pretty, inside and out. Take it from someone with a drop-dead gorgeous mother: Comparisons will get you nowhere. Beauty is in the eye of the beholder, and when it's time, you'll find someone who adores you. I have no doubt."

"Like you found Brecken?"

"Yes," Callie said, breaking into a wide grin. "It's so strange to find someone who was there all along but who you didn't really *see*. I'm thankful for Zadicus, if only because he was the catalyst for me and Brecken."

"That's amazing. I'm so happy for you, Callie."

Arching a brow, she said, "Well, I've got a lot of shit to figure out before we get to happily ever after, but I'm determined to get there." Lifting her phone, she checked the time. "Okay, I'm a go for our plan. I'll meet you guys before the battle in the surrounding woods. Thanks for running point."

"Sure. It's time to set the realm free. I'm ready."

"Me too."

After a warm embrace, Callie located the four-wheeler she would drive to Naria and headed off toward the compound under the morning sun. Deciding to compartmentalize, she pushed away thoughts of the impending discussion with her father until after she healed the puppy. Healing the animal would bring her peace, and afterward, she could sit down and prepare what she wanted to say before heading home. Concentrating on the task at hand, she never realized she was being observed as she drove through the open fields of the kingdom.

D r. Tyson sat in the lab he'd built in the squalid Deamon cave. He'd designed it with care, and Bakari had supplied him with labor and materials to create the various chemical formulas he'd concocted over the years. Bakari had asked him to create one more batch of the super-strength formula to inject into his Deamon soldiers. It wouldn't make them as formidable as Baal, since he'd been injected with an experimental formula filled with poisonous herbs that had been perfected over several years.

After spinning the various vials in a centrifuge, he needed some fresh air and decided to head outside while the concoction congealed. Stepping through the mouth of the cave, he walked around, inhaling the warm air as he contemplated the final battle. He'd been useful to Bakari thus far, which had many advantages. It kept him alive and off the radar of the Elven council that existed undetected in the human world. Bakari had assumed Dr. Tyson was half-Slayer, half-Vampyre when they first met, but he suspected his leader now realized he was actually an Elven-Vampyre hybrid. His kind was hunted by the council, and Dr. Tyson relished the protection he received as part of Bakari's team.

But what would happen after the war was over? Bakari was no fan of hybrids no matter their makeup. Would he cast Dr. Tyson out, or worse, murder him once his mission was complete? And what if Bakari lost? Surely, the royal family wouldn't accept the scientist who'd aligned with their enemy into the realm. He would be banished back to the human world with no protection whatsoever, increasing his chances of discovery by the Elven council. Concerned for his well-being in either scenario, he pondered his future as he paced.

"You are right to fear for your safety, Quaygon," a voice called to his left. "Allegiance to Bakari no longer serves you."

Facing her, he shrugged. "I believe you are correct, Tatiana, but I have nowhere else to go."

"The threat from the Elven council will need to be addressed after Bakari and Callie fulfill the prophecy. That will be my next endeavor once I get some much needed rest." Lifting her arms, she smiled. "Even one such as I need a small respite now and then."

Studying her, he placed his hands in his pockets as the questions swirled in his mind. Eventually, he asked, "You are a human-Elven hybrid, yes?"

Dark eyebrows drew together as she gazed into the distance. Nodding, she shifted her amber eyes to his, the orbs seeming to glow in the midday sun. "Humans and immortals were never meant to procreate. This is why the Elven council wants us eradicated. Some of us are more powerful than others, and I've tried to protect the ones who are vulnerable."

"That's a big job for one woman, depending on how many hybrids there are scattered across the human world."

"It's exhausting," she said, flashing a grin, "but worth it. I care deeply for all creatures, human or immortal."

"And yet you've supplied me with enough toxins to kill many Slayers over the past two decades."

"Yes," she sighed, kicking the ground with the toe of her shoe. "It was imperative I push Bakari toward the prophecy so Callie could align with him. It is finally time, and I am glad it is almost over."

"How will the fulfillment of the prophecy help immortals or hybrids living in the human world?" he asked, lifting his hands. "I don't understand."

"You will after the prophecy is fulfilled. My advice is to return to the human world before the battle begins. Otherwise, you might perish."

Swallowing thickly, he contemplated that option. "I lived in the human world for centuries, passing as a physician and chemist. I worry for my safety now that I have aligned with Bakari as I'm sure it put me on the council's radar. They most likely want to eradicate Vampyre-Elven hybrids as much as human-Elven hybrids."

"That is correct," she confirmed. "The purebred Elves believe in an angry god who punished them for wanting more than he provided. When he washed away their world, the few Elves who remained vowed to live a simple life in the human world, secluded so they could rebuild in peace. Eventually, some of the inhabitants grew restless with that life and wanted to explore the new world they inhabited. These original dissenters are our ancestors."

"My mother told me the story many centuries ago, before she died," he said softly. "My father was an Elf who believed there was value in surveilling the immortal world to see if there was a possibility of building a new Elven colony in a place undetectable by Vampyres, Slayers or Deamons. He was captured by a Vampyre soldier and imprisoned because the Vampyre thought him a Slayer."

"The Vampyre would not have known he was an Elf," she said, compassion in her tone. "The immortals only became aware of the Elves' existence again once the War of the Species ended and they realized Crimeous's true heritage."

"Yes. They banked my father's blood along with the Slayers, although it held no nutrition for them. My mother was a laborer employed by the prison. She took him food and water, learning his story before they fell in love. Eventually, he fell ill and passed, but not before I was conceived. My mother fled to the human world, knowing she would be castigated if anyone knew of her hybrid child."

Tatiana's eyes narrowed. "It is possible your father had royal Elven blood. Otherwise, the chances of creating a hybrid are small."

"Mother never told me his name. She said it would jeopardize my safety."

"Then he must have been a powerful Elf indeed." Taking a step forward, she assessed him. "It is an interesting story, and one I would like to pursue. I hope you will take my advice and return to the human world before the prophecy is fulfilled."

"My mother passed centuries ago, and I have no idea where to go."

Tatiana closed her eyes, the pupils moving under her lids as she concentrated. "She is in the Passage," she said, lifting her lids. "How did she pass?"

"She was poisoned, most likely by the Elven council. They were probably after me, but she always tasted our food first since she was a Vampyre and had self-healing abilities. But there are poisons that can render those abilities inert if one has the knowledge. We know this all too well."

"I'm very sorry for your loss," she said with a tilt of her head. "I have also lost loved ones, and it is devastating."

Perking his ears, Dr. Tyson noted the sound in the distance. "Bakari will be returning with his troops soon, and I must head inside. Thank you, Tatiana. I will consider your words."

"You are welcome, Quaygon," she said with a gentle smile. "I hope we see each other again after the prophecy is fulfilled. Goodbye."

Closing her eyes, she dematerialized. Processing her words, Dr. Tyson headed back into the cave to finish the last formulas he would ever create for Bakari.

Chapter 27

After healing the puppy, Callie felt too restless to head straight back to Takelia. There was a small creek that ran on the outskirts of Naria, and she drove there, hoping the fresh air and gurgling water would bring her some peace as she contemplated her future. Sitting on the damp ground, she drew her knees to her chest, surrounding them with her arms as she stared at the water that sluiced over the rocks in the creek bed.

Something rustled to her right, and her heart lurched in her chest when Bakari appeared. Pushing from the ground, she eyed the four-wheeler, calculating how long it would take to sprint and grab the walkie-talkie to radio Latimus.

"There's no need to panic, Callie," he said in his deep voice. "I only want to talk. You're too important for me to harm. I'm sure you've realized that by now."

"Because I'm going to align with you and fulfill the prophecy? I don't think so." Crossing her arms, she stood firm, hoping he couldn't read how terrified she was.

Holding up his hands, he said, "I'll admit I made a lot of mistakes along the way. Once Miranda and Kenden discovered the Elven scrolls, everything suddenly made sense. I knew I'd have to find a way to secure your alliance and fulfill the prophecy once you grew into your power."

"Well, that didn't really work out for you, did it? Zadicus did a good job of seducing me, I'll give him that, but I always knew in my gut it was wrong. It was only a matter of time until I discovered his deception."

"I agree," he said, taking a step closer.

Callie bristled. "Don't come any closer, or I'm going to use some of my powers you seem so vested in."

Dropping his hand, he studied her. "I was wrong to use Zadicus as a means to gain your alliance. I realize that now. I should've just approached you directly, and this is why I am here now."

"And what makes you think I would've even contemplate listening to you?"

His lips twitched. "You're listening now, my dear. I think a part of you has always been curious about the true essence of your grandfather's blood."

"What essence?"

"The evil, Callie. Your feigned indifference doesn't fool me. I understand everything you went through as a child in this world, feeling lost and outcast. Don't tell me you never had the urge to embrace your evil and destroy those who maligned you."

"Never," she said, lifting her chin. "My parents taught me forgiveness and acceptance even for those who didn't accept me."

"Your parents taught you to deny your true heritage. Your father embraced his evil for the first two centuries of his life. He won't admit it to you, but it brought him great satisfaction."

"My father has spoken to me extensively about his past. He regrets his transgressions and is committed to embracing his Slayer heritage—to embracing his goodness. You could learn something from his transformation. I'm extremely proud of him."

"Your father knows the power of the evil in your blood because he listened to its call for centuries." Bakari took another step forward, and Callie lifted her hand, palm facing him as she prepared to freeze him in place. "Don't be scared," he said, inching closer. "I only want to show you the truth."

Quick as lightning, Bakari swung his arm, revealing a vial in his hand. Thrusting it into her arm, he emptied the contents as she struggled to push him away.

"There, there," he said, removing the needle and backing away. Placing the empty vial in his pocket, he waited as shock coursed through her body. Furious, she lifted her hand and began to choke him with her mind.

"Yes!" he gasped, clutching his throat, although his expression was delighted. "Do you feel the serum beginning to take hold? It will exacerbate the evil in your blood. Embrace it, Callie. It will make you so much more than what you are."

Callie wanted to tell him that she was already enough—that his urging would accomplish nothing. But there, by the babbling creek, something shifted inside as the serum coursed through her veins. Closing her eyes, she tried to ward off the effects, but it was too late. Lifting her lids, she tightened her invisible hold on Bakari's throat.

"You can kill me now, or you can achieve true power," he rasped, falling to his knees on the ground. "Join with me during the final battle. It is time to fulfill your destiny, Calinda."

Dark, sticky pulses jolted into every cell of her body as the potion exacerbated her grandfather's evil blood. In a few scant moments, Callie understood her father's concerns about embracing Crimeous's malevolence. It was sickening on one level, and her stomach rolled with nausea. But on another level, it was...*magnificent.*

Releasing her hold on Bakari, Callie's head tilted back, and she closed her eyes, embracing the all-encompassing feelings of supremacy and maliciousness. With this amount of power, there was nothing she couldn't accomplish. No one would cast her out or disparage her. If they did, she could disintegrate them with a snap of her fingers.

"Your parents have held you back your entire life, Callie," Bakari said, rising. "Let the evil flow. There are so many possibilities you've never even considered. You could inject your brother and Rinada with the serum, and we could all rule with dominion over the kingdom. Miranda and Sathan are false rulers who disparage Etherya. Align with me, and we will rebuild the kingdom."

Quaking with the splendor of her newfound strength, she shook her head, confusion twining in her gut. Although the evil was overwhelming due to the serum's effects, her mother's goodness and father's Slayer heritage still beckoned deep within. Callie felt the tug, and it created a dichotomy that made her want to retch.

"I don't want these powers," she cried, opening her hands and trying to expel them from her body. "I'm not evil. I want to choose the light."

"Evil is in the eye of the beholder, Calinda," Bakari said, inching forward.

"No! Don't come any closer. I can't control it."

"Good. Loss of control is a part of chaos. Align with me, Callie." He extended his hand.

"No!"

"You have felt the malevolence of your blood now. There is no turning back. Join me, and we will rule Etherya's realm and restore order."

Callie had never been able to transport like her father and Evie. Although she'd inherited the ability to read thoughts and manipulate objects with her mind, dematerialization wasn't something any of Crimeous's grandchildren had inherited. And yet, as she felt the firm ground below her feet, she knew the heightened effects of her grandfather's blood would allow her greater authority. Would she possibly be able to transport away from Bakari?

Gritting her teeth, Callie reached deep inside, combining all her fear, knowledge and confusion, and imagined transporting to the woods beside the River Thayne at Astaria. Emitting a loud cry, she fisted her hands and visualized materializing there.

"You can't escape your destiny, Callie!"

Bakari's words trailed off as she flew through time and space before crashing on a spot of soft ground. Landing with a thud, she gripped the grass, lifting her head to survey her surroundings. The banks of the River Thayne sat in the distance, surrounded by tall trees and green grass. Glancing toward the far riverbank, Callie thanked the goddess she'd transported to one of the forts she knew well. It offered her a natural shelter so she could try and figure out how to combat the serum.

Unable to gain full control of her body with the enhanced malevolence swimming through her veins, she crawled toward the fort and shuffled inside, thankful for the safe space. It offered latent comfort in a world that had suddenly turned chaotic. Curling into a ball, she lay on the soft ground, willing the serum from her body...and hoping with all her might it hadn't inexorably changed her into the person so many across the kingdom feared she would ultimately become.

B recken spent the day with the troops, performing a multitude of drills to ensure they were ready for the impending battle. Callie was ever-present in his thoughts, but he tucked them away so he could focus on the task at hand.

By the time the sun set, Brecken lifted his phone from his belt, expecting to see a text from Callie, perhaps telling him she'd returned home to speak with her father. Checking their text chain, he frowned when he realized she hadn't texted him since arriving at Naria to heal the puppy.

A small tendril of worry curled deep within since it wasn't like her to go several hours without texting him. After changing from his training gear, Brecken stepped on his porch, inhaling the warm air as he dialed her number. Lifting the phone to his ear, he scowled when it went straight to voicemail.

"Hey, Callie-lily. Just wondering if you're okay. I haven't heard from you all day. Please shoot me a text and let me know you're all right. Thanks, hon."

Clicking off the phone, Brecken stared over the horizon, unable to shake the feeling something was wrong. After an hour with no return text, he understood what he had to do. Throwing on his light jacket, he locked up the house and hightailed it to the train platform.

Entering the high-speed train car that would take him to Takelia, he was filled with a sense of foreboding. Showing up on Darkrip's doorstep wasn't his style, especially since the man knew he'd been sleeping with his daughter. But he had the nagging feeling Callie was in trouble, and her safety was more important than any wrath he would incur from her father. Arriving at Takelia, he all but jogged to her parents' home, concern growing with each moment.

When he arrived, he knocked on the door, straightening when a surprised Arderin opened it.

"Well, hello, Brecken. Nice to see you. I...uh...Callie's not here."

Brecken frowned. "I'm sorry to show up unannounced, ma'am. She hasn't texted me since this morning, and that's not like her."

Arderin's eyebrows drew together. "She's staying with her Aunt Evie. I assumed she was there."

"I'd feel better if we could confirm, ma'am."

"Right," she said, opening the door wider. "Come in. Let me grab my phone and call Evie."

She led him into the sitting room, locating her phone and selecting the speaker option. "Evie? Callie is with you, right?"

"Nope. She never came home after healing the puppy at Naria today. Figured she headed back to your place to finally talk to Darkrip."

Terror shot down Brecken's spine as fear entered Arderin's expression. "She's not here, Evie. Brecken just showed up worried because she hasn't texted him all day."

Silence stretched over the line. "Do you think Bakari got to her?"

Darkrip chose that moment to stride into the room. Focusing on Brecken, he asked, "What the hell is he doing here?"

"Darkrip just walked in. I'll call you back, Evie."

"Callie hasn't texted me all day, sir," Brecken said, lifting his hands. "I'm worried she's in danger. No one has heard from her since she healed the puppy at Naria this morning."

Darkrip scowled. "Did you try to text her?"

"I left her a voicemail and sent several texts," he said with a nod. "She's never gone radio-silent like this before."

Huffing a breath, Darkrip closed his eyes. "Let me try to locate her." His eyelids fluttered as he concentrated. Finally, he lifted his lids and shook his head. "I can't see anything. Something is blocking my powers."

"Darkrip," Arderin called, shaking her head. "What if Bakari has her? What if he hurt her? Oh, god." Lowering her head, she palmed her face and began to cry.

"Crying won't solve anything, sweetheart," Darkrip said, approaching her and pulling her into an embrace. "Shh... Let me think."

"What's going on in here?" Creigen asked, strolling into the room. "Mom? Why are you crying."

"Your sister is missing," Brecken said, observing his shocked expression. "We fear Bakari might have her."

"Well, let's go find her," he said, lifting his hands. "Dad? I'll go with you. Let's figure this out. We can look for clues at Naria and check her favorite spots, just in case she's just taking some time to think."

"We should check the forts at Astaria by the River Thayne," Brecken said. "They're a safe space for her."

"She told you that?" Darkrip asked.

"Yes, sir."

"She doesn't tell anyone about the forts," Creigen said, lifting his eyebrows. "Take it from her little brother who desperately wanted to play there with her when we were young. She always told me to get lost. Typical older sister." He lifted a sardonic brow. "I'm impressed she told you."

"So I'm assuming you know about their relationship too?" Darkrip asked, his expression acerbic.

"Rinada told me," Creigen said with a shrug. "I think it's great. Zadicus was a dick. Hopefully, you'll treat her better."

"Her happiness is my number one concern," Brecken said, pleased at his acceptance. "Callie has told me a lot of things in our short time together. I know you weren't happy about our relationship or that it formed in secret, and I'm sorry about that, sir."

"I was upset that she lied to me instead of just telling me you'd formed a bond. After what happened with Zadicus, you can understand my reservations."

"I can," Brecken said, clutching his hands over his belt. "This may not mean much to you since I'm just a common soldier from Lynia, but I love her, sir. Very much. I want to spend my life giving her everything she deserves, no matter how hard I have to work to make it happen."

Lifting her head, Arderin smiled at him through her tears. "Oh my god, that's so romantic. We just want her to be happy, Brecken, and if you're able to make her smile, that's all I really care about."

"And I don't give a damn about your heritage," Darkrip said, releasing Arderin to stalk toward one of the side tables. Yanking open the drawer, he located some flashlights. "I just care about your intentions with my daughter."

"My intention is to love her, sir. That's as honest as I can be."

Stalking over, Darkrip thrust the black object at him. Brecken eyed it before Darkrip sighed. "It's a flashlight, not a bomb," he said, shaking it until Brecken grasped it. "Unless you have X-ray vision, we'll need it to find her. I assume you want to come with us on our search?"

"Yes, sir."

"Fine," he said, rubbing his neck. "And stop calling me 'sir.' It's annoying and makes me feel like I'm a million years old."

Feeling his lips twitch, Brecken gave a nod.

"Once we find her, I want your word that you will spend some time letting me question you about your intentions."

"Darkrip!" Arderin hissed.

"I'm fine with that, sir—er, um, Ambassador. I'm happy to answer anything you want to know."

"Just call me Darkrip," he muttered before Arderin cleared her throat quite loudly. Glaring at her, he rolled his eyes. "And I'm sorry for reading your thoughts. It won't happen again."

"Thank you," Brecken said.

Darkrip's gaze held acknowledgment before he turned to speak to Arderin. "Call Evie back and ask her to help us. We can transport Creigen and Brecken around the kingdom as we look for Callie."

Lifting the phone to her ear, Arderin made the call as Brecken prepared himself for the search ahead.

Chapter 28

B recken, Darkrip, Creigen and Evie searched the entire premises of the animal shelter at Naria, finding nothing that led them to Callie. Afterward, Darkrip and Evie transported them to the River Thayne at Astaria. Darkrip faced Brecken, and his green eyes flashed in the darkness.

"Lead the way."

Brecken understood that allowing him to lead the search was Darkrip's way of showing his acceptance. Thankful Callie's father wasn't holding a grudge, they began their trek. Trailing along the riverbank, they called Callie's name, hoping to find her near one of the forts where she sought solace.

They covered several miles as Brecken struggled to control his fear she was hurt. As they neared a clearing by a bend in the river, Brecken saw something sparkle in the beam of his flashlight. Nearing the glow, he bent down and picked up the tiny stone to examine it.

"This fort has been recently disturbed," Evie said, shining her light around the inside of the embankment through the open door. "There are flattened leaves, as if someone lay down, but no one's here."

"It's an earring," Brecken said, holding up the stone.

Inching closer, Darkrip examined it. "It's is one of the opal earrings I gave her on her eighteenth birthday."

Evie and Darkrip studied the earring, silent as the gravity of the discovery set in. Callie had been here and left her earring behind, and now she was gone.

"Damn it," Darkrip said, running his hand over his face. "She loves those earrings."

"What do you want to do?" Evie asked. "We've searched extensively along the river. Should we try a new location?"

"Give me a minute," Darkrip said, backing away and holding up his hand. Closing his eyes, the ground slightly shook, and leaves rustled on the nearby trees as he attempted to track her with his mind. "She's alive," he murmured, eyes cinched tight. "I can't locate her, but I feel her presence. Something is wrong but also...*inevitable*...if that makes any sense. I don't know how else to describe it."

Evie lifted her chin. "Perhaps she is meant to fulfill the prophecy after all. As the subject of an age-old prophecy myself, I recall the trepidation and anticipation as the battle with Father grew closer. Although we all disparage Callie's role in the prophecy, it might be unavoidable."

"She won't align with him," Brecken said, firm in his belief.

"I don't believe she will either," Darkrip said. "She's too much her mother's daughter." Sighing, he hung his head. "We've searched for hours at this point. I'm willing to continue, but I think we should regroup first." Lifting his head, he eyed Brecken. "You should come to our house. I have maps of the entire realm on my laptop, and we can comb through them to theorize possible places we can look for her. It will make our efforts more efficient."

"That's an excellent idea," Evie said. "Do you want me to come over?"

Darkrip shook his head. "Go home to Rinada and Ken, and I'll let you know when we're ready to go back out. We'll search the places we come up with through mid-morning, and then you and I can take a break to practice the forcefield. I'm still not one hundred percent confident in it."

"Okay." Cupping his shoulder, she squeezed. "We all love her, Darkrip. Have faith. Summon me when you're ready." Closing her eyes, she disappeared.

"Come on," Darkrip said, gesturing to Brecken. "I'll transport us home."

Brecken held on tight before being *whooshed* to Takelia. When they arrived in the living room, Arderin rose from the couch, her expression morose.

"Anything?" she asked, cheeks ruddy under long tear streaks.

"Nothing yet, princess," Darkrip said, opening his arms so she could rush into his embrace. "Shh..." he soothed, stroking her hair. "It's going to be okay."

Brecken placed his hand on Creigen's shoulder. "We'll find her. I won't rest until I do."

"I know," he said softly, eyes so much like Callie's filled with concern. "I just hope she's okay."

"She's one of the most resilient people I've ever met," Brecken said, his heart warming at how strong she was.

"I believe that too," he said with a soft grin. "I mean, she's my older sister, and I've always looked up to her. Even when she accused me of being annoying, which was most of the time."

Brecken breathed a laugh.

"Thanks for helping us search," he said, cupping his arm. "I'm happy she's found real love this time. Don't mess it up, okay? She deserves to be happy."

"Never. She's too important to me."

Giving him a nod, Creigen walked over to hug Arderin as Brecken reminded himself to stay calm. He had faith in Callie and wouldn't rest until they found her.

After a cat nap on Darkrip's living room couch, Brecken awoke, determined to resume the search. After looking over the maps, they decided to scour the area where the Deamon caves had been destroyed after the war against Crimeous. Evie and Darkrip believed Bakari had a stronghold there, although none had ever been found. Still, with his spells and potions created by Dr. Tyson, they knew anything was possible. Perhaps he had created a cloaking spell or some other magic to shield them from the immortal army.

They looked for hours, even nearing the Purges of Methesda at one point, but came up dry. Eventually, they decided to return home. Darkrip and Evie headed to their practice session, and Brecken returned to Lynia to join the troops.

When he arrived at the sparring field, Latimus and Garridan approached, concern in their expressions as they regarded him.

"You didn't find her," Latimus said softly.

Brecken shook his head. "Darkrip swears she's alive. That he can feel her presence, but he can't track her. We're going to look again tonight, but I'll make sure to get some rest before tomorrow's battle."

"It's possible she has been kidnapped by Bakari and he will show up with her at the battle," Latimus said.

"Yes." Feeling his throat bob, Brecken fisted his hands on his hips. "I know she won't align with Bakari to fulfill the prophecy. It's not even a possibility in my mind." He tamped down the ragged emotion flooding his chest.

"I know, son," Latimus said, cupping Brecken's shoulder. "None of us believe it. Callie is too good."

"Thank you for letting me have time off to search. I guess the entire family knows about us at this point. She wanted to wait to tell everyone after what happened with Zadicus."

"Just make her happy, Brecken. That's all that matters."

"I'll try my best, sir." Gazing across the field, he noticed Siora and several of the other soldiers glancing his way, concerned. "I'm going to go do some exercises with the troops. I need the distraction."

Latimus gave a nod, and he tracked across the meadow, ready to work off some of the heavy energy that pervaded his bones. Picking up a sword from the nearby rack on the training field, he faced Siora.

"You look like you're ready for a fight, soldier," she said, marching over to pick out her own sword.

"Don't go easy on me," Brecken said, lifting his weapon as she faced him and did the same.

"Got it," she said, a challenge in her eyes along with the empathy that resided there.

Raising his sword high, he sliced it through the air, reveling in the crash of metal upon metal when it collided with Siora's weapon.

"Is that all you've got?" she asked, pivoting and setting her stance. "Come on, fancy bodyguard. I'm ready to break a sweat."

Thankful for her gentle chiding, they sparred for several minutes before the other soldiers joined in. Eventually, the entire battalion entered the fray, preparing their bodies and minds for the imminent fight yet to come. After the sun set and they'd trained long into the night, Brecken headed home and changed before Darkrip showed up to whisk him away for another search.

Hours later, Brecken returned to his cottage, despondent they hadn't located Callie. He didn't want to sleep knowing she was out there, possibly alone and afraid. But when he dragged off his clothes and showered, he fell onto the bed, murmuring her name before he crossed over to unconsciousness.

C allie huddled in the cave by the river for hours, attempting to ward off the nausea brought about by the enhanced evil coursing through her body. When she realized the serum had taken hold and she had no ability to control it, she decided to take action. Rising from the damp ground, she exited the fort and looked to the rapidly darkening sky, wondering what the hell to do.

Massaging her arm, which felt hot to the touch, Callie pondered for what seemed like hours, although it was likely only minutes. As her hand rubbed her heated skin, she realized she wasn't as afraid as she'd been when Bakari first injected her. Now that the enhanced blood had coursed through her for hours, it felt almost...normal. Lifting her arm, she studied the skin, turning it in the shafts of moonlight from the newly risen orb.

"Is this all part of the prophecy?" she muttered, studying the pale skin of her forearm. Lifting her eyes to the sky, she stared up at the stars—the same here as they were in the human world. "Was this meant to happen all along?"

Closing her eyes, Callie concentrated her energy, clenching her jaw as she attempted to transport again. Feeling her muscles contract and expand, she was suddenly conveyed through time and space. Lifting her lids, she stared down at the Purges of Methesda. It was where her grandfather's body had been disintegrated all those years ago when Evie finally fulfilled the prophecy. Staring at the swirling lava, Callie was drawn to it and extended her hand.

"Not too close, daughter of Darkrip," a voice called beside her. "It wouldn't be prudent for you to fall in."

Turning her head, she stared wide-eyed at the goddess Etherya. She'd almost become a fairy tale at this point, rarely appearing to Vampyres or Slayers after Crimeous's death. The one exception had been her appearance to Heden, which had reminded everyone of her vast power. Facing her, Arderin was awed by her ethereal form, which floated above the ground, draped in long white robes.

"I'm honored by your presence, Etherya," she said, dropping to one knee in reverence.

"Stand, my child."

Rising, she studied the goddess's long red hair, stark as it trailed over the pristine robe. "I must be in deep if you're appearing to me."

The goddess might have smiled, although Callie wasn't sure. She gazed over the Purges before focusing on Callie, her eyes dark and beady as they bore into her.

"You are now on a journey, which I knew would happen long ago. I am sad for the destruction of my world, but the Universe is fickle. It sees things I cannot, and I have learned to live with its decisions."

Tears flooded Callie's eyes as she felt the insane urge to fall to the ground and weep. "I don't want to destroy anything. I don't believe in the prophecy."

A wispy laugh escaped her throat. "That matters naught."

Staring at the ground, Callie ran her hand through her hair, realizing her earring was missing when it didn't scratch the skin of her hand. Sadness coursed through her, exacerbated by the serum in her blood.

"Do not cry, Calinda." Her airy fingers reached over to lift Callie's chin. "If I can accept the inevitable, you must as well."

"So, it's a foregone conclusion I'll align with Bakari and destroy the realm."

"Yes," she said, dropping her hand. "But destruction does not always mean death. Tatiana and her kind know this. You have always been scared for no reason, my child. Great change can only come from great destruction. You are the catalyst for this."

"I don't want to hurt anyone." Lifting her hands, she slowly rotated them. "Bakari injected me with something that enhances my grandfather's blood. Enhances my *evil*. What if I hurt someone I love?"

"Dear child, you have never been evil. Even your father, who insisted he was evil for centuries, was never truly wicked. Valktor's blood was too prevalent in his soul, as it is in yours. You will choose the light."

"I finally have something to live for," Callie said, lifting her hands. "I'm in love with Brecken, and I didn't tell him because I was waiting to tell my parents about us." Sighing, she shook her head. "Am I just destined to be an idiot when it comes to love? Good grief, I'm terrible at it."

"You are not so bad," Etherya said, tilting her head. "You and your soldier will find your way. Love is a mysterious force, but your love with Brecken is true and earnest."

"Will it go away?" Callie rubbed her forearm, the skin still warm to the touch. "The enhancement of grandfather's blood from the serum?"

"The serum has opened something inside your cells that will never truly fade. It will diminish over time, but you need the enhancement to fulfill your destiny. You've already gained the ability to transport. Embracing your newfound power will only enhance your potency."

"And that's a good thing?"

"I believe so," she said with a tilt of her head. "If you were inherently evil, I would be more concerned, but there is no need."

"So, what do I do now? Half of me is terrified to go back to the realm with my enhanced blood. It's almost like I don't trust myself. What if I somehow can't control it and align with Bakari—?"

"I will make the decision for you, Calinda," Etherya interjected, closing the distance between them and placing the tip of her wispy finger on her forehead. "You are too close to fulfilling the prophecy to detract from the mission."

Callie tried to move, but her muscles lost the ability to function as soon as Etherya touched her.

"I have placed you in a trance, my child. Dream of the prophecy and what you must do. You will wake an hour before sunset and meet your loved ones on the battlefield. Follow your intuition, and all will be well."

A cloud of deep, curling exhaustion spread through Callie's body, and she lowered onto the soft grass that lined the hill above the Purges. Closing her eyes, she felt something cover her skin and tugged it under her chin. Forcing her lids open, she realized it was a layer of Etherya's robe, placed over her by the goddess.

"You will be safe here," Etherya whispered in her ear, her breath cold against Callie's skin. "When you wake, you will be ready to fulfill your destiny. I am with you and all my beloved children, always."

Huddling under the robe, Callie felt the goddess's presence wane. Unable to fight the spell, she yielded to the visions that formed in her mind. Visions of the battle to come and what she must do to ensure Bakari's threat was halted once and for all.

Chapter 29

Brecken awoke three hours before sunrise, ready to face the most important battle of his life. Worry for Callie loomed large in his heart, and he thought of her as he dressed in his tactical gear, wondering where she was. Sending silent thoughts of love to her, he hoped she received them and knew he was waiting for her return.

Throughout the night, his belief she would appear at the battle had solidified. Still, he was confident she would never align with Bakari and was thankful he would be on the battlefield by her side.

Approaching the darkened training field at Lynia, he met up with Latimus and several battalions of soldiers. They loaded into the large tanks and headed to Restia, where they convened with Kenden's troops. Latimus and Kenden addressed the soldiers as the sky against the horizon turned from black to pale gray. After a raucous cheer from the immortal troops, they were ready to seize the day and defeat Bakari.

Latimus, Jack and their Lynian battalions would line up on the south side of the field, backed by the ether, giving them a natural fortress to launch their attack. Kenden's soldiers would wait in the nearby forest and attack from the flank once the battle had initiated. Latimus and Kenden felt this would generate an element of surprise that would allow them to employ the TECs on many unwitting Deamon soldiers, lessening the amount of Deamons Evie and Darkrip would have to destroy along with Bakari when joining their powers.

Armed with their plan, the troops departed Restia. When they arrived at the open battlefield, Brecken noticed the realm's physicians, Sadie and Nolan, had already set up medical triage tents on the east side of the meadow.

"Come over with me to check on the infirmary tents," Jack said, waving his hand at Brecken. Jumping out of the army vehicle, they strode to greet them.

"Hi, Jack," Sadie said, giving him a glowing smile. "We've set up a hundred stretchers and can nurse any soldiers who are wounded. Oh, hello, I'm Sadie," she said, extending her hand.

"Brecken," he said, shaking.

"This is the man I was telling you about, Sadie," Arderin chimed, approaching. Drawing him into a hug, she whispered, "I'm so worried."

"I know," Brecken said, squeezing her back. "I have faith in her, Arderin. I know she's going to be okay."

Arderin smiled before turning to give Jack a hug. "Me too. With you two on our side, how can we fail?"

"Hello, Jack," Nolan said, trailing over. "And hi, Brecken. Nice to see you outside of our regular army physicals."

"Hey, Nolan," he said with a nod.

"Tatiana gave us an extensive list of the chemicals and herbs she supplied to Bakari over the years," Nolan said, sidling up beside Sadie and placing his arm around her shoulders. "If the Deamon soldiers use chemical warfare or poison-tipped weapons, we'll be ready with antidotes."

"My baby's out there, and I feel helpless, so I'm going to help in every way I can." Arderin said, straightening her spine. "I don't relish the opportunity to kill my own brother, but this has got to end."

After wishes of good fortune all around, Brecken and Jack headed to the field where the troops were assembling.

"There are twenty TECs on this belt," Latimus said, handing the soldiers large leather belts strapped with the tiny weapons. Brecken fastened it over his shoulder so it hung across his torso.

"Is Arderin in the triage tent?" Latimus asked Jack, his expression sour.

"Yes. I know you're worried for her, but she wants to help."

Sighing, he placed his hands on his hips. "I don't love the idea, but I see the merits of having another medic. Miranda and Sathan are at Uteria, but I half-expected her to show up too. We've got some kick-ass female warriors in this family, huh?"

"For sure," Jack said. "Mom's with Miranda and Sathan?"

"Yes," Latimus nodded. "And the kids are there too. They'll all be safe."

The walkie-talkie at Latimus's belt emitted a low beep, and he lifted it to his lips. "Repeat?"

"Rinada and Creigen aren't here," Miranda's voice called over the device. "They were supposed to show up fifteen minutes ago. Should I be worried?"

Latimus's eyebrows drew together. "They didn't answer their phones?"

"No. And we can't find Tordor anywhere either. He usually jogs early in the morning, but I didn't expect he would *this* morning. Shit, now I'm worried. They wouldn't show up at the battle, would they?"

"The council forbade it, but has that ever stopped anyone in our family, Miranda?"

Silence crackled over the devices before she sighed. "Damn it. What can I do?"

"Keep an eye on the rest of our family and keep them safe. You and Sathan must stay far from the battle. If something happens, and goddess forbid we lose, you know where the safehouses are."

"You're not going to lose, Latimus. No fucking way. I'll keep everybody safe and calm. Now, go kick that bastard's ass. I'm ready to rule a kingdom that isn't embroiled in war for once in my damn life, you hear me?"

"Loud and clear. We're taking back our realm. I'll check in after the battle. Stay safe, Miranda."

Placing the walkie back on his belt, Latimus eyed Jack and Brecken. "Ready to kick some ass?"

"Ready," they said in unison.

Pivoting, they joined the battalion and prepared for battle.

C allie's visions throughout the night were filled with cryptic images she didn't understand. Visions of humans mingling with immortals and of purebred Elves sitting at an expansive circular table, discussing topics she couldn't quite discern. It all seemed rather confusing, and when she awoke, Etherya's spell was broken and she regained control of her body. Standing to gaze across the burning lava, she focused on the most intense vision from her reverie.

In the vision, she stood tall and unafraid, approaching Bakari as he held out his hand. He seemed sure of her alliance, although she knew deep within she had chosen the light. Slowly, she slipped her hand into his...and the sky burst into flames. Consumed in a flash of brilliant, blinding light, the entire world faded away.

And that was where the vision ended.

"Well, it's dramatic, at least," she mumbled as the molten rock simmered below.

Inhaling a deep breath, Callie embraced the moment. She was meant to appear on the battlefield today and align with Bakari. She always had been. But she no longer feared the outcome. Her role in the prophecy was embraced by Tatiana, Nuka, and Etherya. How could she be afraid when so many assured her of her destiny?

Straightening her shoulders, she accepted the enhanced blood running through her veins. It would only make her stronger, and although it was dark and murky, it gave her immense power. She knew without a doubt Bakari would perish today, which sent a jolt of sadness through her heart. Even though he'd wrought so much pain across the kingdom, he was still her blood. But he'd made his choices, and he would pay the ultimate price.

Would the rest of the world perish alongside him? Callie hoped not, considering she was only in her mid-twenties and had a lot of life left to live—hopefully with Brecken by her side. In order to make that wish come true, she needed to seize her fate.

Steeling herself, she lifted her face to the rapidly brightening sky and transported to the woods near the battlefield where she knew Rinada and Creigen would be waiting.

Brecken stood behind Latimus on the broad field as the immortal battalions loomed behind them. The first shafts of sunlight were now rising over the far-off hills, and a nervous excitement coursed through his frame.

Bakari appeared in the distance, flanked by his entire battalion of Deamon soldiers, and Brecken noted the vastness of the army. They would be formidable, but he was determined not to fail. Bakari marched closer until he was separated from them by approximately forty yards. Holding up his hand, he halted the march. Baal stood behind him, large and menacing, along with Deamon Commander Vadik and the two allies Brecken recognized as Ananda and Dr. Tyson. Ananda appeared nonplussed while the doctor seemed trepidatious, eyes wide behind the glasses he wore and hands clenching in nervous motions in front of his waist.

"Ananda and Dr. Tyson are not warriors, Bakari," Latimus called. "Although they must pay their debt to our kingdom for aligning with you, it is not fair to pit them against our immortal soldiers. Our physicians have set up a triage center to the east." He gestured toward the triage, barely visible from the battlefield. "Let us take them into custody until the battle is over. We will give them a fair trial afterward."

"They are prepared to fight!" Bakari called. "We all believe in the cause. Etherya's kingdom, rebuilt in the image she initially created."

A rustle sounded to Brecken's right, and Tatiana appeared dressed in combat gear and ready for battle. "You did not heed my words, Quaygon," she shouted, her tone angry. "It was unwise not to flee before the battle."

"I'm sorry," Dr. Tyson called, a slight waver in his voice. "I have nowhere to go."

Sighing, she closed her eyes and flicked her hand. Dr. Tyson and Ananda vanished, and Bakari cried out in frustration.

"Where did you transport them?"

"I placed a freezing spell on them and transported them to the infirmary tent." Looking toward Latimus, she asked, "Your sister will understand she needs to bind them and hold them until after the battle?"

Lifting his walkie, Latimus said, "Nolan, did you receive the two prisoners?"

"We've got them," Arderin's voice chimed over the device. "I've already slapped handcuffs on both of them, although they're frozen like a pair of rocks. We'll keep them sequestered until you give us orders."

"Ten-four." Placing the device on his belt, he looked toward Tatiana and gave a nod. Facing Bakari, he yelled, "The sun is now fully risen. It is time, brother."

Bakari held his hands high and exclaimed, "It is time to reclaim my heritage, *brother!*"

Drawing the sword from the sheath on his back, Latimus held it high and yelled, "Charge!"

The immortal troops gave a valiant cry that mingled with the yells of Bakari's army. Draped in the rays of the newly risen sun, the armies surged toward one another, determined to eradicate the other.

Chapter 30

C allie felt the soft ground of the forest beneath her and opened her eyes, searching the surroundings. Gathering her bearings, she looked for Creigen, Rinada and Tordor at the agreed-upon site.

"Whoa," her brother's voice said behind her. "When in the hell did you learn to transport?"

Turning, she smiled. "You probably could too if Bakari injected you with whatever the hell he stuck in my arm."

Tentatively approaching, he gently cupped her arms. "Are you okay? We looked for you everywhere. Dad and Evie even took us near the Purges, but we didn't see you."

"Strange," she said, eyebrows drawing together. "I was there, and Etherya appeared. Maybe she cloaked me in some invisibility shield or something. Guys, I have a lot to tell you."

Rinada rushed her, embracing her in a warm hug before Creigen and Tordor did the same.

"I don't want to be the pragmatic ruler, but there's a huge battle going on out there," Tordor said, pointing through the trees toward the field. "I want to hear everything, Callie, but we need to implement our plan."

"Agreed," she said with a nod. "Tordor, you have the earpieces, right?"

"Uncle Heden sent them by way of Tatiana, who showed up here before you all arrived," he said, handing them all the tiny earbuds. "I get the feeling he thinks it's badass we want to fight. We'll be able to communicate this way, and I'll stay in the forest as we discussed. If I sense any danger, I'll let you guys know."

"And if you need to intervene, we'll inform you," Callie said.

Tordor nodded. "Mom and Dad are at Uteria, which means I'm technically the ruling royal at this battle. Latimus and Kenden are bound by duty to follow any directives I give—well, I think they are, at least. Hopefully, they'll accept you on the field. If not, I'll order them to let you fight."

"Good," Creigen said, placing the headset in his ear. After testing them, Callie, Rinada and Creigen began trailing toward the edge of the forest. Before they entered the clearing, they turned and waved to Tordor.

"May the goddess be with you," Tordor called.

Resolved, the grandchildren of Crimeous stepped onto the battlefield.

B recken sparred with the Deamon soldiers, preferring to use his sword so he could get close enough to deploy the TECs. Every time he latched the weapon onto one of the creatures' foreheads and disintegrated them to dust, a thrill shot down his spine. Glancing around, he noticed Latimus, Garridan, Siora and the rest of the troops fighting with valor and grit. It was too early to tell if they were winning, but Brecken liked their chances.

A sudden cry erupted at his side, and Brecken turned to see Baal ripping a Slayer soldier nearly in half as the soldier screamed in pain. Dropping the man on the ground, Baal stepped forward, approaching Brecken.

"Get him to the infirmary tent," Brecken called to the soldier nearest the injured Slayer, but he already knew it was too late. Sheathing his sword in the holster on his back, he swung his rifle around and began firing at Baal.

The bullets bounced off the creature's skin as if they were made of rubber, and the metallic taste of fear flooded Brecken's tongue. But he'd felt fear before and knew it meant the stakes were high and he must not fail. Slinging the rifle behind his back as it sat strapped over his shoulder, he reached for the blades fastened to his thighs. Gripping the handles, one in each hand, he drew them, ready to fight the massive creature.

Baal closed the distance, throwing a firm punch with his thick arm that Brecken blocked before slicing his skin with the blade. It healed immediately, and they began dueling in a blade-to-hand combat Brecken knew he must win. His skill with the blades was impressive due to many years of drills and sparring sessions, and he moved with sure strokes as he fought the beast.

Suddenly, Baal lifted his arms high, emitting a roar as a sword appeared in his hands. Brecken understood Bakari had most likely materialized it in the creature's grasp from across the field, and that it was probably poison-tipped, meaning his self-healing body would succumb to its blow. Knowing he only had moments to act, Brecken threw one of his blades to the ground. Thrusting the other into Baal's exposed chest, since the creature's arms were still in descent, he twisted the weapon, opening a large wound above his heart. Grabbing a TEC from his belt, Brecken retracted the blade and shoved the device inside Baal's chest where the open wound bled.

The detonation should've blown him to bits, but Baal puffed his chest, and Brecken watched in awe as his body absorbed the weapon. *Shit.* Realizing he was out of options, Brecken tugged the knife from his boot, ready to fight the creature to the death.

"You cannot beat him, Brecken," Tatiana said, appearing at his side. Lifting her hands, her palms began to glow. "I saw this in one of my visions. It is one of the reasons I aligned with you."

Baal marched forward, knocking Brecken out of the way as he approached Tatiana. She lifted her hands and closed her eyes as she began to chant in a language Brecken had never heard.

"Witch!" Baal cried, lurching toward her before she caught his arm. Her glowing palms must've burned his skin because he began to scream as he slowly lowered to the ground.

"Dan de lum nan da lokiam..." Tatiana chanted, and Brecken swore her eyes glowed. "Your soul is not wanted here."

Baal fell onto his back, and she leaned over, placing her hand over his heart. As her chants grew louder, she clenched her teeth before plunging her hand into Baal's chest cavity. Brecken observed, shocked, as she pulled the beating organ from the creature's chest and held it high.

"May the winds of change absorb this darkened soul as the prophecy is fulfilled!" Lifting Baal's bleeding heart, she clenched her fingers together, and the organ disintegrated, scattering across the field as the warriors fought. Rushing to her side, Brecken bent down to assess her.

"Are you okay?" he asked as she heaved deep breaths, hands resting on her knees. "Holy shit, that was badass. You saved my life, Tatiana. Thank you."

Baal's body lay lifeless on the ground as she nodded. "I foresaw his preeminence and had a vision he would kill you if I did not intervene. He was a formidable creature."

A bright light burst onto the field, and Brecken whipped his head toward the commotion. Evie and Darkrip materialized several feet from the main skirmish, ready to combine their powers to defeat Bakari. Lifting their hands, they created a joint energy forcefield and surrounded an entire battalion of Deamon soldiers on the west flank. A loud boom sounded before every soldier inside the energy field was pulverized to dust.

Some of the Deamons nearby saw the destruction and began to run toward the forest. Kenden's troops emerged, fighting them valiantly and pushing them back toward the main fray. Evie and Darkrip generated the forcefield again, expanding it to surround more Deamon soldiers.

"Your powers mean nothing!" Bakari cried, thrusting his hand into the air and emitting a ball of fire from his palm. It crashed into the forcefield, disintegrating it before their eyes.

"Damn it. He's full of potions that are giving him exponential powers," Evie yelled to Darkrip. "We need more energy."

"Here," Tatiana said, transporting to Darkrip's side. "Let me try."

The three of them created a new forcefield that glowed a brighter red as Bakari began chanting one of his spells. With a flick of his wrist, he eradicated the barrier in seconds.

"We're here to help!" Rinada said, approaching Evie and Darkrip with Creigen and Callie by her side.

"Get off the field!" Darkrip yelled. "The council forbade you to fight—"

"We want to help, Dad," Callie said, lifting her arms. "Let us generate the forcefield with you."

"Calinda!" Bakari called, causing Callie to whip her head toward him. "Did you embrace your newfound powers?"

"End this now, Bakari," Callie pleaded, taking several steps toward him as the soldiers surrounding them fought. "We could still try to save you. This doesn't have to be the end. You must surrender."

"Never!"

Determined to help, Brecken grabbed his blades and began running toward the skirmish.

Bakari lifted his face to the sky, dematerializing before reappearing in Brecken's path. "I understand what I need to do to gain your alliance, Calinda."

Brecken stopped short, tossing his weapons to the ground and slinging his rifle from behind his shoulder. "These might not kill you, but they're going to hurt pretty fucking bad, Bakari." Gritting his teeth, he began emptying the magazine of bullets into Bakari.

The powerful foe held up his hand, freezing the bullets as Brecken lost control of his muscles. Locked in place, he stared into Bakari's ice-blue eyes, unable to do anything but watch as he slowly approached.

Bakari drew a strange-looking gun from his belt and discharged a small pellet into Brecken's chest. Gasping at the invasion, Brecken saw Callie appear out of the corner of his eye. She flicked her hand, and he regained control of his muscles. Stepping back, he clutched the area where the pellet now sat, directly above his heart.

"I've injected your soldier with a tranquilizer capsule containing a thousand poisons his self-healing body can't combat, Callie." Lifting a tiny vial from his pocket, he shook it. "This is the only antidote. Align with me, and I will let him live."

Callie rushed to Brecken's side as he crumpled on the ground, struggling to breathe. The tranquilizer pellet pulsed in his chest, and he clutched the skin, trying to force it out although it was impossible.

"Brecken," she said, falling to her knees and running her hands over his face, neck and chest. "I can remove the pellet with my powers."

"Do it, and he dies," Bakari said, shaking his head from several feet away. "I will destroy the antidote now if you wish."

"I know you won't align with him, Callie," Brecken rasped, his voice low so Bakari wouldn't hear. "But maybe he needs to think you will."

Tears glistened in her eyes as she gave him a warbled smile. "How did you know?" she whispered, clenching his hand as it sat over his heart. "That's exactly what I saw in my vision when Etherya approached me last night."

Brecken swallowed, tamping down the pain that pulsed through his body. "Because I love you, Callie-lily." Turning his hand beneath hers, he squeezed her fingers. "Go fulfill the prophecy...and maybe grab the antidote while you're at it."

"It is time, Calinda," Bakari called, a warning in his tone.

"I'll heal you even if he destroys the antidote," she said to Brecken in a rushed whisper. "Long story, but I'm hella powerful now. Can't wait to tell you. I have so many things to tell you, Brecken."

Lifting their joined hands, he kissed her knuckles. "When it's over," he said.

"Yes," she said, covering his lips with her fingers. "We'll say everything when I've destroyed the world." Leaning close, she placed her lips on the shell of his ear. "Destruction isn't a bad thing, according to Etherya. Let's hope she's right."

Rising, Callie faced the field and held up both hands, reaching toward the sky. Clouds rushed in to cover the bright sun, and thunder boomed over the wide meadow. Closing her eyes, she yelled, "Halt!" as bolts of lightning jolted from the rapidly darkening clouds into her outstretched hands, causing her body to emit a yellow glow. The sounds of war immediately ceased, and Bakari seemed stunned.

"Yes, Calinda," he said, extending his hand. "Your grandfather's blood runs so powerfully through your veins. Join me, and I will give you the antidote to save Brecken after we fulfill the prophecy."

She slowly walked toward him as Darkrip yelled for her to stop in the background. Clutching his chest, Brecken observed her, regal and brave as she approached Bakari. Pain sliced through his body, and he clenched his teeth, determined to hold on and watch her prevail.

D r. Tyson listened to the hurried sounds of the three physicians rushing around the infirmary tents, healing the wounded soldiers as they were brought in. Although his muscles were frozen, his mind worked furiously to find an escape as he sat against the far tent wall, hands bound behind his back. Glancing at Ananda, he noticed her stiff expression, which was generally her *usual* expression, so he couldn't credit it to Tatiana's freezing spell.

"Hey," he whispered, causing her to turn and glare at him. "We have to get out of here."

"I agree, but we seem to have lost our ability to move any muscles below our neck," was her sardonic reply.

"There has to be a way—"

Suddenly, his muscles snapped to attention, and he regained control. Realization entered Ananda's expression, and she shuffled from her sitting position to her feet—difficult since her hands were bound behind her back. Dr. Tyson eventually found his footing as well, and they listened to the sounds outside the tent.

"Callie seems to have frozen everyone on the field except Bakari, including Darkrip, Evie and Tatiana," a deep voice with a British accent said outside the tent, and Dr. Tyson knew it was the human physician the immortals employed. Armed with the new information, Dr. Tyson looked at Ananda.

"If Tatiana is under a freezing spell herself, this must be why our spells were broken. We have to make a run for it."

"Agreed," Ananda said. "I'll run to the east, and you run along the ether toward the western woods. We'll have a better chance if we split up."

Nodding, he courteously tilted his head since his hands were bound. "I wish you luck, Ananda. May you find happiness wherever you go."

"Will you still pursue Bakari's cause if he loses?"

"I no longer believe in the cause," he said, shaking his head. "I wish to live far from danger after being surrounded by it for so long."

"I will always believe in the cause, but I cannot fight it alone," she said through her thin lips. "Good luck, Quaygon."

With one last tilt of the gray bun on her head, she inhaled a deep breath and ran from the tent. Steeling himself, Dr. Tyson sent a prayer to every god he'd ever known and sprinted from the tent. He ran along the wall of ether, feeling as if his lungs might burst, noticing bright flashes of light on the far-off battlefield. Too concerned for his own safety to care, he finally reached the woods, halting beside a large tree in a dense thicket of forest to catch his breath. Leaning over, he almost didn't hear the stick crack behind him. Jolting upright with fear, he turned to find a Slayer soldier.

"Whoa," the man said, holding up a rifle with one hand and showing the palm of his free hand. "You are Bakari's doctor who makes the potions?"

"Yes," Dr. Tyson said, swallowing the lump of terror in his throat. "I no longer believe in Bakari's cause and should've defected before the battle. If you shoot me, I will bleed for days but most likely heal. I am a Vampyre hybrid."

The soldier's eyebrows lifted under his thick brown hair. "Vampyre-Slayer?"

Studying his deep brown eyes, Dr. Tyson shook his head. "Vampyre-Elf."

The Slayer considered him before slowly dropping his weapon. "What is your name?"

"Dr. Tyson."

"Your *real* name?"

Licking his lips, he softly uttered, "Quaygon."

A huge boom sounded from the battlefield, causing them both to turn their heads before their gazes locked back on each other. The Slayer's piercing eyes bore into his before he expelled a large breath.

"Go, Quaygon, before I change my mind. I don't want to see you anywhere near the immortal kingdom in the future, understood? If I do, it will be your last day in our realm. Are we clear?"

"Crystal," he said with a hurried nod. "Thank you."

"Go on," he said, jerking his head.

Quaygon turned to run, but curiosity won out. Rotating back, he asked, "What is your name?"

"Larkin," the man said, lifting his gun again. "And you have five seconds to run before I use this."

Taking the cue, Quaygon began sprinting through the forest toward the wall of ether that ran along the far side. Although he had nowhere to go in the human world and would certainly be hunted by the Elven council, it was better than death in the immortal world. Thankful for the kind Slayer soldier, he knew he would always remember Larkin, the man who spared his life.

Chapter 31

Callie walked toward Bakari's outstretched hand, veins thrumming with the gravity of the moment. Resolved to fulfill her destiny, she placed her hand in his, their touch emitting a spark as her skin glowed a soft yellow from the magnitude of her newfound power. Stepping closer, she held up her palm.

"Give me the antidote first," she said, her tone unwavering.

"It won't matter once we combine our powers and destroy the immortal army—"

"Give it to me," she interrupted, teeth clenched. "Now."

Bakari handed it to her, and she placed the vial in her back pocket. Staring deep into his ice-blue eyes, she tilted her head and slowly regarded him.

"I'm sorry it's come to this," she whispered, squeezing his hand. "You deserved better when you were born. Your later choices require retribution, but you were dealt a terrible hand. I hope you find peace wherever your soul lands."

"We will destroy the immortal army and rule the kingdom, Callie," Bakari said, although his tone lacked the confidence she'd heard in their previous interactions. "I am willing to rule with you if you pledge your allegiance to me."

Shaking her head, she felt the sting of tears. "May the goddess be with you."

Closing her eyes, she focused on the touch of his hand as she centered every speck of her power deep within her core. Bakari began chanting unintelligible words of an immortal language long since extinct, and she clutched onto the low-toned mantra as feelings of both terror and euphoria coated her skin. Sounds of thunder echoed above from the darkened sky, and the ground began to rumble.

Both armies surrounded them, still frozen by Callie's spell, and she hoped like hell her intuition was correct. If she hurt her parents, or Brecken, or any other immortal on the field, she would never forgive herself. Gripping Bakari's hand, she chanted the words Nuka had given her in the vision.

"May the world begin anew as the prophecy is fulfilled..."

She repeated the phrase over and over, her words mingling with Bakari's. Suddenly, a massive bolt of lightning blazed from the sky, reaching the ground and igniting an explosion. A red cloud of fire burst from the meadow and began to grow, enveloping the soldiers, and then the meadow, and the forest beyond. Fiery red turned to blazing white light, and all were blinded by the magnificence of the glow as one final *boom!* clapped from every possible direction.

The ground shook with the force of a thousand earthquakes, and Callie cried out, losing her grip on Bakari's hand and falling to the ground. Clutching the earth as she balanced on her knees, she struggled to inhale oxygen from the void of light that surrounded her. Lifting her head, she saw Bakari collapse, clutching his throat as he gasped. Callie's ears rang with the high-pitched sound of destruction as the blinding light faded to pitch-black darkness.

Suddenly, the ground ceased its quaking, and she lifted her head to stare into the void. Small shafts of light began to ease through the murkiness, and Callie blinked rapidly, trying to gain her bearings. Coughing, she rose and trailed over to Bakari's body. It lay still atop the ground, and she wondered if he was dead.

Surveying the surrounding meadow, she noticed immortal soldiers scattered about, sitting up and shaking off the freezing spell as they patted their extremities searching for injuries. Callie scanned as far as she could see but didn't see any Deamon soldiers.

"They have been purged," Tatiana said, appearing at her side. "All of them, including Baal and Commander Vadik. Bakari's corporeal form is all that remains." Placing her hand on the small of Callie's back, she urged her forward. "Go. Ease him into the great beyond. His tragic story deserves to end with the niece he's come to revere by his side."

Stepping forward, Callie crouched beside Bakari and took his hand. Lifting it, she held it to her cheek. "I'm so sorry," she whispered as he stared up at her with her mother's eyes. "Even I can't heal you now. Imminent death from the prophecy is too strong even with the new powers you instilled in me."

"Please," he pleaded, coughing as he sputtered the words. "My hate will make me clutch onto this world forever even though I know I've lost." Eyes darting between hers, he whispered, "Please, Calinda."

Inhaling a breath, she nodded before placing her hand over his heart. "I've only ever used my power to draw sickness from others, but I will use it to end your suffering. Close your eyes, Bakari."

Sliding his hand over hers, he cinched them together over his heart, the poignant gesture spurring a lone tear to trail down her cheek. Closing his eyes, he waited for the inevitable. Sucking in a breath, Callie centered her power into her hand, surging it into his body and stopping his heart. His large frame shook as he expelled one last slow breath before relaxing into the ground. A strong wind blew from the east, and she observed his body shrivel and turn to dust before scattering across the battlefield in one final goodbye.

After taking a moment to center herself, Callie stood and searched for Brecken. Jogging toward him, she fell onto her knees beside him.

"I need to extract the capsule," she said, tugging off his layers of weapons and helping him remove his shirt as he struggled to breathe. "If it deploys, I have the antidote and can still probably heal you, but if I extract it, that saves us the trouble. It will probably hurt."

"That's okay," he gritted, heaving labored breaths. "I trust you."

Sitting on the ground and stretching one leg over Brecken's thighs, Callie placed her hand over the entrance wound on his chest. Closing her eyes, she focused her powers, directing them toward her palm against his warm skin. Suddenly, she was flooded with a thousand heartrending images—snapshots from when Brecken had longed for her when he guarded Zadicus, and his shoulders hunched over his desk as he wrote the letters to her. Joy surged deep within, and she smiled.

"Your thoughts are coming through from the energy transfer. I can't control it."

Giving a strangled laugh, he nodded. "That's fine, hon. I think the whole world understands I'm crazy about you. I don't have anything to hide."

Smiling deep into his eyes, she concentrated, surrounding the pellet with her healing energy and slowly drawing it back through the entry wound. Removing her hand from his chest, she opened her palm, showcasing the capsule. Closing her fist, she used her powers to pulverize it before wiping away the dust on the soft grass. Releasing a breath, she drew her knees to her chest and rested her forehead against them.

"Callie is freaking tired," she mumbled into her legs, trembling as the effects of using so much of her power in such a short span began to take its toll.

Sliding behind her, Brecken encircled her with his long legs, and then his arms, burying his face against her nape as he stroked her hair. "I've got you, Callie-lily," he said, cradling her as they slowly rocked back and forth, his front bracketing her back. "I'm never letting you go."

Snuggling against him, she took comfort as she recovered. Finally, she lifted her head, her gaze landing on Tatiana, Evie and Darkrip before scanning the field. "Did I destroy the world?" she asked, staring up at Tatiana.

"You destroyed Bakari and his army. And yes, you destroyed the realm as we know it, and it exists no more," Tatiana said, quoting the prophecy.

Gently disengaging from Brecken, she craned her neck to look across the field. "It doesn't *seem* destroyed...unless this is all some really vivid dream we're sharing."

"Stand, Calinda, and observe the destruction you wrought," she said, pointing toward the ether.

Callie stood, Brecken helping her to her feet as he rose, the gash over his heart almost completely vanished due to his self-healing abilities. Turning, she gazed toward the ether and gasped.

"It's gone," she whispered.

Beyond where the ether used to exist were expansive hills lined with trees and forest as far as the eye could see. Confused, she faced Tatiana.

"Did I destroy the ether?"

"Yes," Tatiana replied, a sparkle in her amber gaze. "You obliterated the ether that separates the immortal and human worlds. It is gone forever and will now only be remembered as a relic of a long-lost realm."

Callie's eyebrows drew together as she struggled to understand.

"Your destiny all along was to destroy the ether, Calinda. Now that you have fulfilled the prophecy, you have *destroyed the realm as we know it, and it exists no more.* Now, you are one realm, coexisting with the human world, and the immortals must chart a new path to create one united kingdom upon the Earth."

"All this time, I thought 'destroying the realm' meant I'd annihilate everyone in our kingdom."

"You've finally caught up," Tatiana said with a tilt of her head. "Prophecies are murky and best not taken literally. When you've lived as long as I, you understand this."

Lifting her hands, Callie said, "I mean, you could've just told me that from the beginning, Tatiana," her tone slightly exasperated. "This prophecy hasn't been a bed of roses, you know."

Breathing a laugh, Tatiana shrugged. "I am sorry, my dear, but everything had to occur as it was meant to be. You will understand this in time. Bakari's journey upon the Earth, from the tragic events of his birth to his conflict with the immortals and his imminent demise, were all imperative to guide you to this very point. We all are products of our own destinies, whether we believe in them or not."

"We'll see about that," Callie muttered before turning to glance across the spot where the ether used to be. "What do we do now? Surely, the humans will investigate the huge hole that has opened up in the side of their world."

"Your first interaction with those on the other side will happen shortly." Taking a step back, she lifted her hands. "I will leave you to deal with those who arrive. The new era of the immortals has begun, and your history henceforward will be entwined with humans as well as other species you don't yet know or understand. Tread carefully but hopefully into the future. I will see you all again soon. Goodbye, my friends." With one last reverential gaze, she closed her eyes and disappeared.

They all stood, stunned, as she vanished under the sky, which was once again sunny and bright. Darkrip rushed toward Callie, drawing her into his arms and clutching her so tight she could barely breathe.

"I'm okay, Dad," she soothed, rubbing his back as he held her, swaying back and forth. "Everything's going to be okay."

Drawing back, he gazed into her eyes, his own brilliant green orbs glassy and filled with emotion. "I'm supposed to say that to you," he whispered, cupping her cheeks. "I was so worried. You're my heart, Callie. You know that, right? You, your mom and your brother make me who I am."

"I know," she said, unable to stop the tears streaming down her cheeks. "I love you so much. I'm sorry about everything."

"I'm sorry too," he said, kissing her forehead. "I was never supposed to be a parent. I'm fucking terrible at it. I just want to keep you from making my mistakes."

"Eh, you're not so bad," she teased, swiping her tears. "And I'm really good at making mistakes, so we're going to have to figure out how to coexist with that knowledge."

"As long as you're safe, I don't care."

"Callie!" Arderin cried, darting across the field and rushing into their shared embrace. Callie squeezed her parents tight, so thankful for them, before Creigen joined the bear hug.

"You're in big trouble for appearing on this field today, young man," Darkrip warned, ruffling Creigen's hair to soften his words. "Are you two *trying* to give your father a heart attack?"

Craning her neck to look at Arderin, Callie asked, "Has he always been this dramatic?"

"Every damn day since I met him," Arderin said, her tone filled with mirth.

Chuckles filtered over the field as the reunions continued, Rinada running into Evie's arms before Latimus and Kenden appeared. The family members embraced, so thankful to be safe and alive, and Callie tugged Tordor into her arms. "Well, I guess we didn't need you after all. Still pretty badass of you to show up. I'm proud of you, Tor."

"I'm in awe of you, Callie," he said, wonder in his expression. "Man, there's a lot to process. I can't believe the ether is eradicated. We have no separation from the human world. The prospects are daunting."

Someone loudly cleared their throat, and heads swiveled to gaze upon the woman who stood several feet away where the ether once resided. Straight blond hair fell in a short style that landed just above her shoulders, and she wore a black jacket with the initials "ITU" and black cargo pants above dark boots.

"Hi," she said, eyebrows arching as she gave a wave. "Sorry to bust up the family reunion, but we need to contain this situation, stat."

Chapter 32

T ordor disengaged from Callie's embrace and slowly approached the woman who now stood in front of where the ether used to reside. "I am Tordor, son of King Sathan and Queen Miranda, and the ranking royal on the field—"

"Yep, you can save the introductions," she said, cutting him off and giving a nod. Lifting a badge that read "ITU," she gave a cheeky, almost sardonic grin. "We've been waiting for Callie to fulfill the prophecy and eradicate the ether so we can implement our plan. Guys!" she yelled before placing her thumb and forefinger in her mouth and emitting a loud whistle. "Roll out the barrier."

A team of twenty soldiers, all dressed in black gear, rushed over the nearby hill and thrust tall rods into the ground, each about ten feet apart. Latimus and Kenden exchanged looks before Latimus jerked his head. "Go round up the troops and prepare them for more combat. I'll stay here until they're in formation."

"Ten-four," Kenden confirmed.

"Whoa, whoa," the blond woman said, placing the badge in her pocket before holding up her hands. "No one needs to prepare any troops. We're here to help."

"Help, how?" Latimus asked.

"Uh, someone's got to put up a temporary barrier to keep your realm shielded until we can approach the human leaders and explain they've got a bunch of immortal creatures joining their world. Did you think you could just hop on over and have brunch at Chili's with the humans while sharing your mango margaritas?"

"What's Chili's?" Rinada asked softly in the background.

"Human restaurant chain," Evie murmured, her arm around her daughter's shoulders. "Not nearly as good as Chipotle—"

"Enough!" Latimus called, swiping his hand through the air. "I want to know right now who you are and what your purpose is in our world."

"Wow, let's lower the temperature," the woman said, features contorting into an exaggerated grimace. "And I hate to break it to you, but it's not *your* world anymore, Latimus, son of Markdor. It's *one* world now—thanks to your magnificently powerful niece—and a proper transition needs to occur."

"I want answers now!"

"That's enough, Uncle Latimus," Tordor said, holding up his hand as Latimus glowered. Turning toward the woman, he extended his hand. "Let's start over. I'm Tordor, which you already know. And you are?"

"Nice to finally get a proper greeting," she said, slipping her hand into his and shaking. "Esmerelda, daughter of Dakath. You can call me Esme."

"Nice to meet you, Esme. Forgive me, but I don't know who Dakath is."

"Oh, yes, that would help. He's the king of the Elves, of course. Maybe you didn't see my ears." She pointed to them, noting the slightly tipped edges. "Inherited these from good ol' dad."

"Unfortunately, the history of the Elves was lost to us centuries ago," Tordor said. "My mother and uncle discovered some ancient Elven scrolls, which added to our knowledge, but we are still vastly undereducated about their species."

"You'll find out soon enough, believe me," she said flippantly, arching a brow.

"Uh, I'm not sure how to interpret that."

"We'll get around to interpretations later," she said, waving her hand. "For now, I'm here as the commanding officer of the ITU to erect a makeshift barrier so we can keep the immortals hidden from the humans for a bit longer."

"And your father sent you?"

"Good lord, no," she said, features scrunching. "My father detests me."

"Oh, I'm sorry," Tordor said, slightly taken aback. "I don't understand."

"I'm the unfortunate result of my dad's indiscretion with a human eons ago. It's a nasty little stain on his stance to only support the existence of purebred Elves. But that has nothing to do with the ITU."

"Which stands for?"

"Immortals Transition Unit. We're an underground society comprised of hybrids and humans who never quite fit in with our own kind. We make it our business to understand the history of all our ancestors, their various prophecies, and help ease the way when they are fulfilled."

"And you wish to help us transition our realm to amalgamate with the human world now that the ether is gone?"

"Yes," she said with a nod. "This will allow you to approach the humans on your own terms without them discovering you, which they will do eventually. You were already cutting it close with how much you all travel back and forth to the human world. Nice jaunt in the hotel pool, by the way, guys," she said, craning her neck to wink at Brecken.

Brecken's eyes widened as he searched for Darkrip.

"Don't say a word," Callie muttered, sidling up beside him. "Nothing to see here, guys," she said cheerfully, batting her eyelashes.

Darkrip gave a loud cough, and Callie shot him a good-natured glare.

"I like you guys together," Esme said, pointing between Callie and Brecken. "Way better than Zadicus if you ask me. Now, I'd like to get back to the issue at hand, even though I'm glad you found true love and all that jazz."

"Thank you," Callie said, grinning as she squeezed Brecken's side.

"*Anyway*," Esme continued, "humans have this propensity to declare war, use nuclear weapons and employ all sorts of nefarious methods when they're taken by surprise. Therefore, my team is erecting a temporary barrier where the ether used to be so we can approach the humans on our terms before they blow up Uteria or something." Wrinkling her nose, she said, "That would just be messy, wouldn't it? Are you catching my drift, Tordor, son of King Sathan and Queen Miranda?"

Breathing a laugh, he nodded. "Why don't you just call me Tordor? Or Tor is fine too."

"Tor it is," she said, grinning. "The barrier will take my men a few hours, and then we'd love some food and shelter at one of your fancy royal compounds if you're amenable to that."

"I don't think it's a good idea to let strangers onto our royal compounds," Latimus said.

Tordor contemplated Esme. "You must understand our concerns. We've had no time to vet you."

"I know," she said, lifting a jump drive from her pocket. "Which is why I sent an identical drive to this one to your Uncle Heden by special messenger. It should've been delivered at sunrise in Italy, and he's most likely scrutinizing it now. It has all the information he'll need to vet us, and I also sent a sample of my blood in the package so he can analyze it. It will show my immortal Elven lineage as well as my human DNA. You can have this one and study it to your heart's content."

Turning toward Latimus, Tordor asked, "What do you think?"

A muscled clenched in Latimus's jaw as he contemplated. "I'd be open to sheltering Esme and her team if Heden says it's safe. Kenden?"

"I agree," Kenden said.

"Great," Esme said, flashing a smile and depositing the jump drive in Tordor's hand. "In the meantime, I'm going to help the team erect the barrier. Nice to meet you all. Hope you're ready to charm some humans while evading my father's council of Elves intent on eradicating hybrids. Fun times all around, hey?" With a jaunty wave, she pivoted and headed toward her team.

"Wow," Callie said, staring wide-eyed at her family. "Talk about surreal."

"You're not kidding," Kenden said before approaching Latimus. "We need to regroup with the troops, assess the injured soldiers, and have a final meeting before we send everyone home for some much needed rest."

"Agreed. Let's get to it."

"I want to talk to you, but I need a huge nap first," Callie whispered to Brecken as he held her against his side.

"You can crash at my cabin if you want," he said, gently rubbing her back. "I'm going to help Jack and Latimus, and then I'll head home."

"Perfect." Facing her family, she said, "Guys, I'm going to crash at Brecken's cabin, but I promise I'll come home tomorrow after he and I have had a chance to talk. I can't wait to tell you everything."

"Sounds great, baby," Arderin said, sandwiched in between Darkrip and Creigen, her dad slightly scowling as her brother smiled. "And I'm dying to hear the story about the pool—"

"No stories about the pool," Darkrip interrupted. "Do you hear me, young lady?"

Callie playfully rolled her eyes. "Fine, Dad. I'll just tell Mom."

Darkrip muttered an annoyed, "*Bollocks*," before the family said their goodbyes. Tordor decided to remain behind and help Esme and her team, and Larkin offered to join him so he could ensure his safety. As Latimus and Kenden prepared to address the troops, Brecken turned to Callie.

"Be safe, hon. I just got you back and am terrified to let you go."

"I will be," she said, giving him a wistful smile. "I'm going to transport home, grab some clothes and then shower at your place. I'll probably be asleep when you get home," she said, placing her hands under her cheeks to mimic sleeping. "I'm freaking exhausted."

"I can't believe you can transport," he said, wonder etched across his handsome features. "I want to hear everything, Callie."

She lifted to her toes and kissed him softly on the lips. "I have an eternity to tell you everything, and I can't wait, Brecken."

"Neither can I," he whispered back.

After one last sweet kiss, Callie called upon her newfound powers and transported away from the battlefield, thankful to close the chapter of her life consumed by the prophecy, and hopeful for the next phase to begin.

B akari felt his soul reform in a void of darkness. One moment, he was gone. The next, he was conscious again. Lifting his lids, he tentatively searched his surroundings. A large fountain sat to his right, streaming long trails of water from the mouth of the statue that sat in the center. The trickling sound of the water hitting the stone was soothing, and he rose, although his body didn't feel quite solid.

"My son," a female voice whispered, and Bakari turned toward the sound. Several feet away stood a tall woman with long, curly dark hair that resembled Arderin and Callie's. Behind her stood a hulking Vampyre who looked very much like King Sathan.

"Mother?" Bakari called, his voice cracking as he stood frozen.

"Bakari," she said, seeming to float toward him across the ground that wasn't quite solid. Gently cupping his cheeks, she shook her head as tears swam in her ice-blue eyes. "How could you think I didn't want you?"

Swallowing the emotion that clogged his throat, he worked his jaw, trying to form words. "You let them take me," he rasped, angry and heartbroken all at once.

"I did not know, son," she said, running her thumbs over his face. "If I had known, I would've searched the ends of Etherya's Earth for you. Don't you understand?"

"You and Father were so powerful. Surely, you came to know of my existence at some point."

"We were slain only years after you were born, Bakari," Markdor said, approaching and gently cupping his arm. "Calla and I might have learned of your existence if we'd survived, but sadly, we did not have the chance."

"It's my fault," Slayer King Valktor said behind them, floating over to glance at Bakari with his deep green gaze. "I slayed them in an effort to save Rina, and now, my daughter is as lost to me as you were to Markdor and Calla. Our souls now reside here in the Passage as we watch over our remaining children, hoping they will correct our mistakes."

"We have forgiven you, Valktor," Calla said with a reverent nod. "And we are happy to see our kingdoms united through our children."

"But the kingdoms were meant to be separate," Bakari said, confused. "The species were never meant to procreate and form hybrids. It goes against everything Etherya originally fashioned."

"It is true that I created the species to remain separate but equal," the goddess said, floating over to address them, her long, blood-red hair stark against her white robes. "But the Universe ultimately controls all. It was a hard lesson to learn for one as powerful as me."

Regarding them, Bakari contemplated. "What was my purpose, then? I do not understand."

"It was always your destiny to be taken to the human world, discover your past, and embrace your hatred of the immortals who you believe cast you out. The Universe did not like having a hidden realm on my Earth, and now it is hidden no more. Your conflict with my species resulted in Callie destroying the ether, and the realm is now reborn anew."

As he digested the information, Bakari's skin began to tingle, and he rubbed his arm, although it felt odd in the ethereal form his body now inhabited. "I feel strange," he said as the tingles began to grow into slight points of pain, flickering over his entire body.

"You will be transported to the Land of Lost Souls now, Bakari," Calla said, her tone sad. "You have hurt too many to remain here."

Gazing at the ground, he nodded. "I knew if I lost, that would be the inevitable outcome. I was determined not to fail but will accept my fate."

"That is very brave, son of Markdor," Etherya said. "And since you were denied your birthright, I have an offer for you."

Bakari tilted his head, indicating she should continue.

"Our beloved Rina requested an audience with Darkrip centuries ago. The Universe would only allow me to grant the request if I exacted something of great value from her. She was adamant and valiantly chose to visit her son in exchange for spending eternity in the Land of Lost Souls."

"A courageous choice indeed," Bakari said.

"Yes," Etherya said, clasping her airy hands as she floated above the ground. "You will be relegated to the Land of Lost Souls instead of with us here in the Passage due to your actions upon the Earth. However, I have made a deal with the Universe that will hopefully ensure your redemption and help Rina."

"What must I do?" Bakari asked.

"Rina's mind and spirit were broken by Crimeous. She suffers greatly in the Land of Lost Souls and has fallen into a pit of darkness she cannot escape from. If you can locate her and pull her from the darkness, I will consider it an act of salvation and bring you both to the Passage, along with Marsias, who suffers there with her."

"I have taught myself to hate the Slayer and Vampyre royals for so long," he murmured, "and now, you want me to save one of them."

"That I do," Etherya said, her thin lips forming the barest hint of a smile. "And I believe you will choose to take up the mantle."

"Please, son," Calla pleaded. "Our time with you was stolen, and I would like to rectify that. I hope you will accept Etherya's mission."

Bakari stared at his parents, their expressions so genuine, and felt the tug of longing he'd suppressed so many centuries ago. Letting it reemerge, he inwardly clutched it, admitting he would like to at least try to save his soul. Straightening, he said in a clear voice, "I accept your mission, Etherya. I will do my best."

"Very well," the goddess said as his skin began to burn with the heat of a thousand suns. Closing his eyes to ward off the pain, he clenched his teeth as the visions before him began to fade. "Go now, into the Land of Lost Souls, and remember to seize the vestiges of goodness that always lingered in your heart. Your fondness for Calinda and Tatiana and your desire to know your parents. May you one day be reunited in the Passage."

"Goodbye, son," Calla's voice warbled as he fell deeper into the void. "We can't wait to see you when you return."

"Goodbye, Mother," he called, extending his hands toward the light before it dimmed into a point of nothingness. Succumbing to the void, Bakari accepted his fate as the vestiges of his spirit hurtled through space and time before entering the Land of Lost Souls.

Chapter 33

Brecken returned home just as the sun set behind the far-off hills. It had taken some time to wrangle up the troops, assure everything was in order, and send them home. Latimus and Kenden directed them to take a two-week break to spend time with their loved ones before returning to duty. The army would need to be refashioned to comport with the new circumstances of not actively being involved in conflict but living in a world that was no longer separated from humans by the ether. There would be time to reconfigure, but for now, everyone deserved a respite to rest and recharge.

Brecken cut the engine on the four-wheeler Jack had lent him and quietly entered his cottage in case Callie was sleeping. Sure enough, she lay in the center of his large bed, black curls spread across the pillow as she slept peacefully. Carefully approaching, he gently ran a finger over her cheek, overcome with the sight of her in his bed. It was as if she belonged there, and his heart swelled. She smacked her lips and muttered something unintelligible, causing him to snicker, before he left her to shower and wash away the grime from the long day.

After showering, exhaustion slammed into his bones, and he flipped off the beside lamp she'd thoughtfully left on for him. Sliding under the soft sheets, he drew her close, spooning her as she instinctively nuzzled into his body.

"Brecken," she murmured, wriggling her butt into his rapidly growing erection. Although he was beat, it was impossible to tamp down his body's response to her silken skin.

"You're naked," he murmured into her neck, sliding his arm between her breasts and drawing her close.

"Mm-hmm. I'm still so sleepy, but you can try to bang me if you want."

Chuckling, he kissed her nape. "I'm beat too, hon. We'll bang tomorrow. I liked coming home to you naked in bed though."

"I like it too," she whispered.

Inhaling her scent, he snuggled into her. "Good. We'll talk in the morning, okay?"

"Okay. Brecken?"

"Hmm..."

"I love you. I'm sorry I didn't say it back before. That was really dumb of me. I hope you can put up with someone like me who sucks at love."

Closing his eyes, Brecken relished the words. "You don't suck, honey. We're still figuring this out, that's all."

"Night," she said, yawning before nestling deeper into his body.

"Night," he whispered. "I love you so much, Callie-lily."

His thumb gently caressed the skin below her neck as he slipped into slumber, so thankful she was safe. Vowing to hold her like this every night for eternity, he succumbed to his dreams.

C allie awoke to the sound of bacon sizzling and inhaled the mouthwatering aroma. Glancing over toward the tiny kitchen, she observed Brecken standing over the stove, shirtless in gray sweatpants as he scrambled eggs with a spatula.

"*Ohmygod*, that smells good," she groaned, sitting up and pushing her hair out of her face.

Gazing over his shoulder, he grinned, and Callie's heart flip-flopped in her chest. The sight of him broad-shouldered and cooking breakfast for her was pretty much a wet dream come true. "I figured you'd be starving. I have some Slayer blood in the fridge too."

"Starving because I destroyed the world yesterday?" she teased, sliding out of bed and approaching to peer over his shoulder. "Look at my Vampyre lover cooking breakfast. It's so sweet."

After kissing her forehead, his eyes roved over her frame, filled with desire. Leaning down, he rested his lips against her ear. "I think you should put on some clothes before I abandon cooking completely."

Giggling, she nodded and trailed to the bag she'd packed. "I'm only getting dressed because I'm *starving*," she said, pulling on sweatpants before donning a tank top. "After we eat, we're totally going to have awesome, sweaty sex."

"You don't have to ask me twice," he chuckled, scooping the eggs and bacon onto a plate.

Grinning, she fell into one of the chairs by his small fireplace. He brought the plate over, and she thanked him before digging in. After pouring two decanters of Slayer blood, he trailed over and sat in the seat across from her.

"So," he said after taking a sip, "tell me everything."

Between bites, she explained the strange events that occurred. Brecken listened with rapt attention, entranced by her story. When she was finished, she sat back and took a sip of Slayer blood.

"So, there you have it," she said, lifting her shoulders. "I can still feel the enhancement of Crimeous's blood, but it's slight, like a light pulsing or something. It's hard to explain, but it's just *there*, and it's a part of me I'm not sure will ever truly diminish."

"Do you feel any urgings from it?"

"No," she said, narrowing her eyes. "It just feels like a part of me I never knew is now awake, if that makes any sense. In a way, I feel more whole. Maybe this will make me finally embrace who I really am—who I've been afraid to be sometimes with others."

"I hope so, because you're magnificent, Callie."

Reveling in his words, she stood. "Okay, let's do this right." Walking to the kitchen, she deposited her plate and cup in the sink. Brecken followed her and did the same before she took his hand and dragged him outside to stand on the soft grass.

"Wow, you look ready for some big revelations," he teased, tugging one of her curls.

"I'm so ready," she said, unable to control her wide grin.

"Me too, honey."

Inhaling deeply, she straightened her shoulders. "I know this is still new and that we need to grow into our relationship, but my feelings for you are so pure, Brecken. I assure you, this is not a rebound for me, and I know exactly what I'm asking of you. I love you, and I want to build something with you."

"I love you too," he said softly. "I fell in love with you all those months ago when I started writing the letters and convinced myself I could never have you." Closing the distance between them, he gently rubbed her arms. "And now, you're here, and I'm almost afraid to believe this is happening."

"Oh, it's happening, soldier," she said, waggling her brows. "And I don't care if you have two lira to your name. You're a good man who writes me beautiful letters and supports me in every way possible. You love your mother and sisters to distraction, which embodies such loyalty. I hope I can learn to make you half as happy as you make me, Brecken. I really want to make this work."

"Then we'll learn together," he said, slipping his hand into hers and twining their fingers. "I'm certainly no relationship expert, but I like our chances, Callie. I realized a while ago you're the only woman I'm ever going to love."

Sighing at the romantic words, she squeezed his hand. "I would love it if you would agree to take a *few* days off to travel with me sometimes," she said, lifting a finger, "and the cabin is perfect, but my Uncle Kenden loves building things. I know he would help us add on a few rooms, and it never hurts to have extra space."

Brecken glanced at the cottage, squinting as he contemplated. "I'm pretty handy and could help him. It would lower the cost significantly."

"If you don't mind doing some manual labor, I'll get Kenden to help, and maybe my dad will help too. He's not very handy, but he'll never be able to resist the one-on-one time with you so he can size you up. I'll pay for the materials as my contribution. That's the least I can do in exchange for you allowing me to move in."

His eyebrow arched as he gave her that signature smirk, almost causing her knees to buckle. Clenching her thighs together, she awaited his answer.

"Are you asking to move in with me? That's a big step."

"Um, yeah, what do you think we're doing here?" She waved her hand in front of his face. "You're stuck with me now, Shakespeare."

Chuckling, he gnawed his inner lip as he considered. "I don't like the thought of taking your money."

"*Our* money," she said, squeezing his fingers. "That's how this partner thing works, Brecken. I need you to accept that."

He smoothed a hand over her hair. "I'll try, but I want to provide for you, hon. I want to make you proud. You deserve things I'll probably never be able to give you, and I hate that."

"Give me kisses," she said, rising to her toes and pecking him on the lips. "And make me breakfast and write me love letters. That's all I need."

Breathing a laugh, he nodded. "I can do that."

"Honestly, you're getting a handful here," she said, lifting a shoulder. "If we go full steam ahead with this and eventually bond, you need to understand that having kids with me won't be easy. I have no idea what powers they'll inherit. It's a huge risk for you when you could be with someone normal."

"You're normal," he murmured.

Giving him a sardonic look, she asked, "Were you on the same battlefield as me yesterday? I'm definitely not normal, Brecken."

"Well, you're pretty perfect to me."

Grinning, she stared deep into his bronze orbs. "I'm not, but I'm so happy you see me that way. I'm happy you see me for who I am. I've never had to hold any pretenses with you. You'll never know how much that means to me."

"Well," he said, inching closer and resting his forehead against hers. "I guess we should make it formal then." Resting his palms on her cheeks, he caressed the smooth skin with his thumbs. "Calinda, daughter of Darkrip and Arderin, will you move in with me?"

"Finally! How many times does a girl have to invite herself to move in before her man gets the hint? Of course I will."

Chuckling at her teasing, he slid his arm around her waist and devoured her lips. Callie encircled his neck, squeezing him tight as her tongue roved over his, her body inflamed with love and desire as he moaned into her mouth.

"*Brecken...*" she moaned, sliding her leg around his thigh, entwining their bodies as he devoured her mouth. "I need you—"

The words were cut off as he gripped the mounds of her butt, lifting her as she squealed. Instinctively wrapping her legs around his waist, she held on tight as he carried them up the stairs, his lips continuing to steal kisses from hers as he shut the door behind them. Trailing across the room, he bypassed the bed and set her on the counter. Thrusting his fingers into her thick curls, he drew her head back and began kissing a path down her neck.

"I want to drink from you while I fuck you, Callie," he breathed in her ear, undulating his hips into hers as she writhed on the counter. "I'm dying to taste you, honey. But if you want me to wait, I will. It's a big step for both of us."

"*Oh, god, yes...*and I want to drink from you too."

Reaching for the waistband of her sweatpants, she struggled to remove them. Growling with lust, Brecken drew back, tugging them off her legs before shucking his own pants and returning to the spot between her legs. Gripping the base of his shaft, he ran the smooth head over her wet folds.

"Damn it, I should give you some foreplay, hon—"

"Screw foreplay," she groaned, gripping his hips. "Get inside me *now.*"

Emitting a strangled laugh, he slid his hand to cup her thigh. "Wrap those pretty legs around me and hold on tight."

Callie complied, opening herself to him as she clung to his broad body. Gliding his fingers into her hair, he fisted the silken tresses as he surged into her slick channel. She groaned, staring deep into his gorgeous eyes as he claimed her.

"*You feel so good,*" he growled, undulating back and forth as he fucked her in a maddening rhythm that was too fast and too slow all at once. "There's that sweet, tight little spot no one else will ever touch. It's *mine,* Callie."

"Only yours," she whispered, spearing her nails into his shoulders, causing him to groan.

"Oh, *god,* that feels amazing," he rasped, increasing the pace of his hips. "Do you how beautiful you are when we make love? Your lips get so full and red." He traced them with his finger before dipping it inside her mouth. She sucked the tip, elated when he moaned in ecstasy. "Goddess, you're so sexy."

Throwing her head back, she opened her body, wanting to feel every inch as he slammed inside her. Need curled deep in her gut as she imagined drinking from him as he claimed her.

"It will probably hurt if I bite you," she rasped, lifting her head to stare into his hooded eyes. "I only have half-fangs, so they're not as sharp as yours."

"I don't care," he gritted, palming her ass and lifting her to walk the small distance to the bed. Tossing her on top of the covers, she giggled as he crawled over her body.

"I like this rough side of you, soldier," she said in a sultry voice as he slid his hand behind her knee, lifting her leg high. Looming over her, he aligned the head of his cock with her opening and surged into her again. "Remember, I've got some enhanced blood now. It might make me even better in bed."

"You're already amazing," he whispered, drawing her into a deep, thorough kiss as his hips undulated into hers. "You ready?" he asked, breaking the kiss to stare into her eyes.

"Yes," she whispered, clutching her hands behind his neck. The smile he gave her was so adoring, his fangs white against his full lips, before he trailed a row of kisses across her jaw and over the pulsing vein at her neck. His tongue darted out to lick the soft skin, his self-healing saliva preparing it for his invasion. When the tips of his fangs scraped her, she closed her eyes in anticipation, overwhelmed with the sensation. Brecken's fingers clenched her hair, and he pierced the skin, groaning as he impaled her and began imbibing her essence.

Callie gasped at the immeasurable pleasure of having her lover inside her, both at her core and at the sensitive skin of her nape. Burying her face in his neck, she licked him, tasting his musky essence before aligning her fangs with the rapidly pulsing vein. Spearing her nails into the skin of his upper back, she thrust her fangs into his neck, joy flooding every part of her soul as his essence surged against her tongue. Pressing her lips to his sweaty skin, she drank, rocking her body against his as he loved her.

His thick cock pulsed inside her quivering core, the blunt head stimulating the tiny spot deep within that held a thousand nerve endings, and her body inflamed with the desire. Brecken's small groans vibrated through her as he drank, and she wrapped her legs around his waist, wanting to pull him inside and never let go.

"Come with me," he gritted against her neck, his hips now furiously hammering into her as beads of sweat dripped from his body, mingling with hers. "I'm so close..."

Callie surged against him, pushing the pleasure-filled spot against his shaft, causing stars to explode behind her eyelids as she crashed into a dizzying orgasm. Clutching him for dear life, she rode the wave, imbibing the metallic taste of his blood until she broke the connection, throwing her head back on the bed as his body rammed into hers.

Dragging his fangs from her neck, he pressed his face into the drenched skin, rasping her name as his body devolved into a quivering mass of jerks and spasms. Joy-filled laughter exited her throat as he shuddered against her, expelling jets of sticky release inside her deepest place. Feeling more connected to him than ever before, she welcomed the invasion, already anticipating the eternity they would spend loving each other so intimately.

Ragged breaths exited his lungs as he slowly relaxed above her, his shaft still deep inside her body as it pulsed the last bursts into her tight channel. Running her nails over the wet skin of his back, she reveled in the small tremors that still shook his frame.

"Am I crushing you?" he mumbled into her neck.

"Yeah, but I can take it."

"Tough cookie," he said, extending his tongue to lick the wounds at her neck, his self-healing saliva aiding in the healing. Callie licked his punctures, sending him into a new round of shivers.

"Goddess, that was...I don't even know how to describe it."

Chuckling, she trailed her fingers over his back. "Was it everything you'd hoped for? I know you were waiting for the right person."

Slowly lifting his head, he stared into her eyes as he gave her a slow, poignant kiss. "I was waiting for *you*."

"Brecken," she whispered, sliding her fingers over his jaw as a single tear slipped from the corner of her eye. "Thank you for loving me. I was so sure I was broken, but you never saw me that way. I'm so grateful for you."

"Loving you is the easiest thing I've ever done, Callie-lily." Resting his lips on her cheek, he sipped away the tear. "I can't wait to build our life together."

Tightening her arms around his neck, she grinned. "Once we recover, we need to go over so I can formally introduce you to my family."

Puffing out a breath, he nodded. "Your dad didn't murder me when we searched for you, so I'm seeing that as a positive."

Laughing, she shook her head, her curls bobbing against the comforter. "I'll remind him to chill and tell him to be on his best behavior. But let's lie here a little while longer. I like having you inside me, all sweaty and hot."

"I love it too, hon." Relaxing against her, he trailed soft kisses across her temple as their bodies cooled upon the bed. Free from the shackles of the prophecy and ready to exclaim her love for Brecken to the world, she held him close as their hearts beat together in one rhythm, steady and connected.

Chapter 34

Two weeks later

Miranda stood beside her husband, hating that she was suddenly an emotional wreck. Throwing her arms around her son's neck, she squeezed, causing him to laugh.

"I'll be fine, Mom," Tordor said, drawing back and smoothing her hair from her face. "I'm thrilled to join Esme's team and feel like I'm a perfect fit to represent the immortal realm as we approach the humans. I've never wanted to rule, and you two are so good at it anyway. I love diplomacy and am dedicated to ensuring a smooth transition between our worlds."

"I know," she said, swiping her nose with her arm as Sathan edged up behind her. Encircling her waist, he rested his chin on her shoulder to smile at their son. "I'm just going to miss you," she continued. "You're my baby no matter how old you are. I love you so much."

"I love you," he said, kissing her before grasping them both in one last bear hug. "I'll report back as often as I can. We'll be doing some reconnaissance, so I'll be off the grid for weeks at a time. If you don't hear from me consistently, I don't want you to worry."

"Just stay safe, son," Sathan said, his deep baritone vibrating in her ear. "We'll keep the kingdom secure for when you're ready to return."

"The kingdom is yours, guys," he said, backing toward the invisible wall Esme's team had erected the day of the battle. "It always has been. But keep our family safe, okay? I'll see you guys soon."

"Bye, super-awesome immortals," Esme called, waving as Tordor approached her in front of the wall. "Thanks for your hospitality. The team thinks you're rad."

"Bye, Esme," Miranda called. "Take care of him."

"He's a foot taller than me and has self-healing properties, but sure, whatever you say!"

Pulling a small device from her pocket, she depressed the button, opening a section of the wall. They stepped through, following the rest of her team who'd departed minutes before, and the barrier closed behind them.

Blowing a breath through her lips, it fanned the hair at Miranda's forehead as Sathan held her tight. "What if something happens to him?"

"He's resilient, little Slayer," he said, kissing her temple. "And he seems happy to have found a purpose. It's what we always wanted for him."

"Yeah," she warbled, feeling the tears form again. "But I already miss him."

Gently placing his fingers over her jaw, he tilted her head to look into her eyes. "He'll always be our son, but he's a man now, Miranda. A virtuous man who's ready to make a life for himself. We did a good job, and we must have faith in him."

"We did do a good job, didn't we?"

Chuckling, he nodded. "We sure did. And I'll save you from making some flippant comment about my inflated ego by saying I'll give you most of the credit."

She pursed her lips. "Like, eighty percent, right?"

Squinting, he contemplated. "Sixty-five."

"Whatever, blood-sucker," she teased, rolling her eyes.

Gently rocking together, they searched each other's gazes, so in tune after several decades together. Finally, he said, "It's time, Miranda."

Nodding, she slowly turned and slid her arms around his neck. "I'm ready, but it has to be a girl this time."

Arching a brow, he grinned, flashing his fangs. "And if we have a boy, what will you do then? I think we'll have to keep him."

Wrinkling her nose, she said, "Leave the jokes to me, mister. You're terrible at them."

"Arderin says I've gotten funnier in my old age." His lips formed a slight pout.

"Arderin loves you and is a very nice younger sister."

"Fine. I'll leave the jokes to Heden...and to you," he finished when she opened her mouth to argue.

Smiling, she lifted to her toes and kissed him as the gentle breeze surrounded them. "I think it's settled then. Put another baby in my belly, Vampyre. I'm ready."

"That is the least sexy thing you've ever said to me, and yet I still want you. How strange."

Throwing her head back, she broke into a joyous laugh. "I take it back. You are pretty funny. Come on—let's go home. We've got a lot of sexy shenanigans to accomplish."

Straightening, he took her hand and led her to the four-wheeler. "I can't wait, little Slayer," he said, revving the engine after he sat behind the wheel.

Miranda smiled from the passenger side and slid her hand over his thigh, the need to touch him as voracious as the day they met even after all this time. Lifting her face to the sky, she inhaled the fresh air, hair whipping in the wind as her husband drove them home.

Epilogue

Several months later

Callie watered the plants that hung next to the swing Brecken had installed for her. He'd recently renovated and expanded the home with the help of Kenden and Darkrip, although her father had griped about how terrible he was at performing the work. He certainly wasn't a master home-builder, but Callie appreciated his efforts. It allowed him to spend time with Brecken, and Callie was pretty sure they were becoming friends, which warmed her heart.

"Dad acts grumpy, but he likes our handsome soldier, doesn't he, Bertha?"

The plant's leaves blew in the breeze, and Callie took that as a "yes."

"And how are you today, Laverne?" She watered the fern as she spoke. "Oh, things are lovely here, thank you for asking. Mom called me with an update on Tordor and Esme's efforts in the human world today. Tor is doing a great job keeping the peace, but what I really wanted to know was if he's banged Esme yet." Leaning down, she whispered, "I saw how he looked at her before they left for the human world. I'm obviously no love expert, but mark my words, he wants to bone her." Snickering, she continued watering Laverne until her gaze lifted to the horizon.

Brecken appeared in the distance, walking across the meadow after a day spent helping with new recruits at Lynia's training base. Overcome with the sight of his broad shoulders and muscular body, Callie grinned and waved.

Approaching the cottage, he marched up the wooden steps and tilted his head. "Did I see your lips moving?" he asked, arching a brow. "Are you talking to the plants again?"

"Yes," she said, sticking out her tongue. "Bertha has been thriving since we started having our little talks, and Laverne's leaves are so much greener," she said, pointing to the plants. "Make fun of me all you want, but they love it."

Chuckling, he drew her close and planted a sweet kiss on her lips. "I think it's cute. I fell half in love with you when you took pity on the flower in Zadicus's garden. You tried to convince him to let it live with its friends. Remember?"

"Yep. You weren't supposed to be spying on us."

"Couldn't help it. You're too pretty."

"Aw," she said, setting down the canister and sliding her arms around his neck. "Okay, you're forgiven for teasing me about talking to Bertha and Laverne." Her eyebrows drew together. "I thought you'd be home earlier. Did the training run late?"

"No. I had an errand to do on the way home."

"Oh? Do tell."

Stepping back, he took her hand. "Come on."

Curious, Callie followed him toward the soft grass in front of the cottage. He drew them to a halt and faced her, his features so handsome under the late-afternoon sun.

"I'm in suspense here," she said, eyes widening.

Clearing his throat, she noticed his Adam's apple bob. "I stopped by Takelia to speak to your dad."

Callie's heart slammed in her chest. "You did?" she asked softly.

"Yes." Reaching into the pocket of his black pants, he pulled out a velvet box and lowered to one knee.

Emitting a sob, Callie covered her lips with her fingers. "*Ohmygod.*"

His teeth flashed, fangs resting atop his lips as he gave her a brilliant smile. "Your dad gave his blessing, thank the goddess." Opening the box, Callie gazed at the ring—a small diamond encircled by tiny blue-green stones in a silver band.

"My amazing Callie-lily," he said, love shining in his deep brown eyes. "It's not the biggest ring in the world, but I designed it myself, and it was fashioned with love. I even had Antonio help me when I was sketching it out. I wanted it to be beautiful for you."

"It's gorgeous," she whispered.

"Opals on the edges—blue and green like your eyes. And a diamond in the center to signify my love for you. It's pure and rare like this diamond, and I'm so lucky to have found it with you. I want to take every breath on this earth knowing you're my wife, Callie. Please say you'll bond with me."

Falling to her knees, she rained jubilant kisses over his face as he laughed. "I think that's a 'yes'?"

"Yes!" she cried, throwing her arms around him. "This is so romantic! Did you write me another letter too?"

"Maybe," he said, squinting one eye. "I'd like to read it to you after I shower...and once we're both naked."

"Ohhhhh," she said, waggling her brows. "I love that idea."

Taking her hand, he slid the ring on her finger, and Callie wiggled it under the rays of the sun. "It's perfect. Thank you, Brecken." Palming his cheeks, she pressed her lips to his. "And thank you for talking to Dad. You're brave."

Placing the box back in his pocket, he encircled her and lifted them both as she gave a yelp. Wrapping her legs around his waist, she clung to him as he began to slowly circle.

"What are you doing?" she asked, laughter bubbling from her throat.

"I'm twirling you, honey." Resting his forehead against hers, he twirled them over the grass as Callie's heart almost shattered from the poignant gesture.

"You hate twirling," she said, nipping his lips.

"Not anymore. I love anything that makes you smile, Callie." Cementing his lips to hers, he drew her into a deep kiss, solidifying their promise to love each other for eternity.

Desire skated through her veins when he finally drew back. Sighing, she stroked the back of his neck, feeling his body harden against her, magnifying her arousal. "My hero," she called softly.

After one last tender kiss, he carried her up the porch steps as Callie held tight.

"I think your dad kind of likes me now," Brecken said, opening the door and stepping inside.   "We've both got the stone-faced stoic thing going on."

"You're a teddy bear inside," she said as he set her on her feet in their newly added bedroom.

"You haven't told anyone besides your mom and Evie about the letters, right?" he asked, tugging off his shirt.

"Nope." She made an "X" over her heart.

Kicking off his shoes, his eyes narrowed as he shrugged off his pants. "I'm pretty sure you're lying to me, honey."

Biting her lip, she tugged off her dress. "I mean, I had to tell Lila, obviously. And Jack because he's, like, my best friend...and also *your* best friend. Oh, and Rinada. She thought it was so sweet."

Naked, he trailed toward her, hooking a finger in her panties. "Anyone else?"

She wrinkled her nose. "Maybe?"

Brecken grabbed the silk covering her mound and ripped it with both hands before tossing it to the floor. Callie's body inflamed as she giggled.

"If I admit to telling more people, will you punish me?"

Bending down, he lifted her in his arms and carried her to the bathroom. "I'm going to punish you all night long. We're going to put this fancy new tub to good use."

"Well, we *are* pretty hot when water is involved. I mean, we lit up that hotel pool."

Tossing back his head, he laughed before setting her down and turning the faucet over the tub. The water began to rush into the white marble before he faced her. "That was just the beginning, hon. Let's christen this sucker."

"I'm so ready. Do you think betrothed sex will be hotter than courting sex?" Lifting her hand, she wiggled her fingers as the ring sparkled.

"I think any sex with you is my ultimate fantasy, honey." Leaning down, he brushed her lips with his. "Now, be a good fiancée and get in the tub."

Biting her lip at the sexy command, Callie shivered with excitement before lowering into the rapidly filling warm water. Gazing at her betrothed, she watched him stroke his hardening length. Mouth watering in anticipation of their sexy times, she sighed.

Approaching, he gave her a sultry grin. "Look at you. I swear, sometimes, I feel like this is still a dream. I promise I'm going to give you everything, Callie-lily."

Extending her arms, she beamed, beckoning him toward her and toward their future together. Happiness washed over her, as encompassing as the warm water heating her skin. The lonely girl who'd written woeful tales in her diary would always be a part of her, but Callie had finally grown into herself—a woman worthy of love who'd shed the cryptic prophecy.

With Brecken by her side, she had no doubt eternity would be far brighter than she'd ever imagined. Callie couldn't wait to create their infinity together, one day at a time, in their small corner of Etherya's Earth.

Bonus Scene!

Want to find out what happened in that bathtub between Callie and Brecken? I wrote a **bonus extended epilogue scene** exclusively for my newsletter subscribers. Follow this link to sign up, and you'll be able to read it right away: **https://BookHip.com/MLFVGTC**

Well, dear readers, thank you for reading Callie and Brecken's story! I hope you enjoyed the first of many books about the next generation of immortals in Etherya's Earth. I love stories where the hero writes the heroine love letters and hope you were as enamored with sexy Brecken and sassy, kindhearted Callie as I was. As you probably expect, **Etherya's Earth, Book 7** will be about Tordor and Esme, and I assure you, Tordor is *definitely* going to lose his virginity.

In the meantime, did you enjoy meeting our awesome female warrior Siora in The Cryptic Prophecy? You can read her story in **Garridan's Mate, Etherya's Earth #6.5.** She swears she's not interested in love but sexy Vampyre General Garridan is ready to prove her wrong!

As always, thank you from the bottom of my heart for reading my books. **The End of Hatred** was the first book I ever published almost three years ago, and the characters who inhabit Etherya's Earth will always be so special to me. I'm so very glad they're special to you too, and that so many of you think of them as friends. See you in the next book, and thank you for supporting indie authors!

Acknowledgments

I am eternally thankful for you, dear readers. Thank you for continuing on this journey with me.

As always, thanks to Megan, Bryony, Anthony and Sarah for being part of my team and for making my books better!

About the Author

USA Today bestselling author Rebecca Hefner grew up in Western NC and now calls the Hudson River of NYC home. In her youth, she would sneak into her mother's bedroom and read the romance novels stashed on the bookshelf, cementing her love of HEAs. A huge Buffy and Star Wars fan, she loves an epic fantasy and a surprise twist (Luke, he IS your father).

Before becoming an author, Rebecca had a successful twelve-year medical device sales career. After launching her own indie publishing company, she is now a full-time author who loves writing strong, complex characters who find their HEAs. Rebecca can usually be found making dorky and/or embarrassing posts on TikTok and Instagram. Please join her so you can laugh along with her!